THE
GONE
AND THE
FORGOTTEN

Also by Clare Whitfield

People of Abandoned Character

THE
GONE
AND THE
FORGOTTEN

CLARE WHITFIELD

HEAD
of ZEUS

An Apollo Book

First published in the UK in 2022 by Head of Zeus Ltd,
part of Bloomsbury Publishing Plc

9 7 5 3 1 2 4 6 8

A catalogue record for this book is available from
the British Library.

ISBN (HB): 9781838932770
ISBN (XTPB): 9781838932787
ISBN (E): 9781838932763

Typeset by Divaddict Publishing Solutions

Printed and bound in Great Britain by
CPI Group (UK) Ltd, Croydon CR0 4YY

Head of Zeus Ltd
5–8 Hardwick Street
London EC1R 4RG
WWW.HEADOFZEUS.COM

Dedicated to all the bewildered, waiting
for it to make sense.

*It is no small pity, and should cause us no little shame,
that, through our own fault, we do not understand
ourselves, or know who we are.*

Saint Teresa of Avila

1

Croydon, South London, June 1993

'A lot has happened, Prue, and you've dealt with it incredibly well,' said Aunt Ruth. 'Most teenagers wouldn't have coped with what you have. You deserve a holiday.'

Prue couldn't bring herself to speak; thankfully, the crackle of a bad connection filled the telephone line.

'You're very quiet. Are you all right? Sorry, that's a stupid question, of course you're not all right,' said Ruth.

'No, I am. I'm fine,' said Prue. 'Honestly I'm... What were you saying?'

'You don't have to come and stay with us if you don't want to,' said Ruth. Which meant it was imperative that she went. 'I don't want you to feel as if you are being coerced.' Although that was exactly what it felt like. 'We are all still grieving Nana and with your mum having another one of her... episodes...' Ruth trailed off.

'I can cope,' said Prue. 'I'm older now and Mum will need me when she gets out of hospital. I'd love to come and stay with you, but I don't think a holiday right now is—'

'But Archie was so looking forward to having you here. We've been married three years now and you've never been to see where we live.' Prue very much doubted her uncle was jumping up and down in anticipation of his sixteen-year-old niece coming to stay. The man had barely acknowledged her existence the handful of times they'd met.

'And your mum won't be coming straight home after she's discharged,' said Ruth. Now this was new information.

'What? Where's she going?'

'Rehab, a rehabilitation centre,' said Ruth. 'Your mum agreed it would be a good idea to try a professional approach and she'll be admitted for three months. We're going to get her proper help this time.'

Professional help was a possibility now Nana was gone. If she were still alive, she'd never let it happen. Nana hated psychiatry, psychology and any other counselling mumbo jumbo; she was of the 'suffering is a virtue' generation.

'But what about the flat?' Prue's mind raced to all the routine chores and tasks that she took care of. 'What about making sure the rent is paid on time? What about sorting the mail? The boiler keeps going out by itself and there's a trick to getting the pilot light back on.'

'Remember my friend Anna in Clapham? She's going to come and pick up your key and deal with all of that. You're sixteen years old, Prue, this is your last summer before sixth form college and you should be enjoying yourself, not fretting about boilers. Let me worry about the flat, I promise everything will be there when you get back.'

There came another wave of crackles along the line as Prue tried to find the courage to say what she was thinking.

'Is there something else?' said Ruth.

'No,' she said. 'No, I don't think so.'

They said their goodbyes and Prue put the handset down and spun around to face Subo, who had been staring at her from where she was perched at the top of the stairs for the duration of the call.

'Well?' asked Subo. 'What did she say? Is she going to let you stay here?'

Prue shook her head. 'No, she's still trying to make me go.'

Subo visibly deflated, resting her chin on her knees. The two had ambitious social plans they had hoped to get away with now Prue's mother was otherwise occupied. It was to be their one last summer of frivolous fun before starting A levels in September.

Prue had been staying at her best friend's house ever since her mother's suicide attempt had landed her in hospital. It had been a rare upside to all the disruption that spring of 1993 had brought. Subo Sittampalam's family were messy and loud, they laughed and argued, moving from one to the other at lightning speed. Subo and her hyper little brother complained about dinner every night and their mother would shout at them to shut up unless they wanted to cook themselves and call them ungrateful brats, then grab and kiss them on the forehead as she threw full plates down in front of them. Their father, the fatigued patriarch, forever seemed to be skulking about the house, filling holes in the wall with filler or demanding possession of the remote control for the television he had paid for. Prue was fascinated by him, the way he flung down the newspaper and shouted *That's it! I've had enough!* when the chaos became too much. Despite the threats nothing ever happened, and he moved slowly from room to room, muttering about his failing eyesight, back or knees.

Prue cursed herself for not speaking up to Ruth. She could have put her foot down, she *was* sixteen, but she didn't want to upset her aunt. The perpetual need to please hard wired into her bones.

The girls stomped back upstairs to Subo's bedroom as her father shouted from where he was wedged into his favourite armchair.

'Girls! Please! Ladies are meant to be light on their feet!?'

Back in the bedroom Subo turned on Radio One and it played SL2's 'On a Ragga Tip', as Prue wedged a chair under the door handle and dragged the vintage hatstand in front of the door. Subo sat cross-legged on the carpet and took the prepared tray from under the bed which had the little pre-rolled spliffs hidden between an old copy of *NME* with The Shamen on the cover. Prue opened the sash window and sat down on the sill with a leg up.

'You're not saying much,' said Subo.

'This is the problem, isn't it? I didn't say anything, as per usual.'

'Tell her you want to stay here. We could always get my mum involved. You know she'd love to stick her nose in, and she loves having you – she thinks you're a good influence on me.' Subo pushed Prue's foot off the windowsill and sat next to her.

'I probably should go,' said Prue. 'I've never visited them up there, but—'

'But what?' said Subo, lighting the mini-spliff, inhaling and blowing the smoke out of the window.

'If only I could stay with my dad like a normal person – if I knew who he was, that is. I still can't get my head around the fact no one will even talk to me about him, and I'm meant to pretend it's normal.'

Subo shrugged. 'I don't understand why you can't ask Ruth about it, I thought you were close to her. Surely you can at least ask her *why* you don't have a relationship with your own father?'

'We're not as close as we were but we still talk on the phone, and I get on better with Ruth than I do my mum.'

'Then why didn't you ask her?'

'Because it's my family, there are things, entire subjects and people, that we aren't allowed to talk about. Number one – he who shall not be named. I bottled it, I was too scared to bring him up when I was on the spot, I'm rubbish on the phone.'

'Then write her a letter. That way you can set the agenda and she can't talk over you or make you feel guilty, so you end up not saying what you want to.'

It was an idea. Prue took the spliff from Subo.

'What would I write?'

'Er... Dear Ruth, you know how we're not allowed to acknowledge the existence of my biological father? Well, now that my grandmother is dead and we can clearly see my mum is madder than a box of frogs, do you think I can find out who he is? And by the way, I'm going to stay with Subo in London rather than come to Narnia, or wherever it is you live.'

'If only it were that easy,' said Prue.

'What is this place called anyway?'

'The isle of Noost.'

'Never heard of it,' said Subo, taking the spliff back and waving the smoke out the window with her hands.

'No one has. It's in Shetland.'

'Scotland?'

'It's not even Scotland. It's miles away, floating in the sea in between Scotland and Norway.'

'Norway?! What the fuck!'

'Barely anyone lives there.'

'Sounds boring.'

'It's not even on the main island where most people live. Noost is another smaller island all by itself – that's where Ruth lives. I'd have to get to Aberdeen, take a ferry overnight to Shetland, then get another ferry to Noost. Narnia probably has better links.'

Subo stubbed the mini-spliff out on the ledge and Prue shut the window. They would only risk smoking short little stubbies to avoid getting caught. They moved the chair away from the door, put the hatstand back and flopped down on the double bed they shared.

'You can't go there,' said Subo after a long pause that both had spent contemplating summer without the other. 'What will I do without my wingman?'

'You mean your pet nerd.'

'You make me seem like I have hidden depths.'

'I help you with your homework.'

'It's not all one-way. When I met you, you were still wearing virgin socks. Do you remember those god-awful white knee-highs with patterns made of holes?'

'God, I know. Tragic.'

'I practically saved you from years of bullying.'

'What would I do without you?'

There was a knock at the bedroom door and they both leapt off the bed. Prue kicked the tray back under the bed as Subo span around trying to find the deodorant.

'I can smell it, you know,' Subo's mother hissed through the door. 'If your father catches you, he'll skin you alive. Prudence – I expected more from you.'

Subo doubled over laughing in silence as Prue winced. She couldn't stand disappointing people's mothers and she hated being told off, full stop.

Later that evening they spent several hours drafting various letters to send to Ruth. It was past midnight when they eventually agreed on the final version.

Dear Ruth,

I thought it best to write as I feel more able to express my feelings on paper than I can on the phone. I hope you understand that this is a difficult subject for me to bring up with you so please try not to be angry with me. I only ask because for years now I have been aware that my father must be out there somewhere, but I have never been allowed to talk about him as it would have upset Nana and Mum. But I am sixteen now, technically an adult, and I realise that this might be difficult, and I have also considered that the man who is my father may not want to talk to me, but I have to know who he is, even if it turns out he doesn't want to know me. I think it might be best if I stay in London this summer at Subo's house and see if I can find out who he is. If you know anything or have a name or an old address, or any information that could help me find him, then I would be really grateful if you would tell me. You must know something.

Yours,
Prue

PS: Please try not to be angry with me.

Prue started sweating as she sealed the envelope and still couldn't believe she was really going to send it. The next morning, as she was having doubts, Subo marched her to the red letterbox at the end of the road and, without warning, snatched the letter from her clammy hands and posted it. As soon as it dropped Prue felt sick, but perhaps this was what had to happen for things to change.

2

The letter reached its target faster than anticipated. Ruth must have torn open the envelope the second she received it and the next thing Prue knew the phone in the Sittampalam hallway was ringing. Prue felt such furious urgency in the shrill tone, somehow she knew it was Ruth calling.

'Impossible. That's quite impossible, Prue... out of the question. You must come and stay with us.'

Prue could feel rousing anger finally beginning to stir.

'Look, darling, I know you're sixteen, I do. I know you're not a child any more. I'm not telling you, but I am asking you, please come and stay. Things will be different, and we'll talk, I promise.'

Subo stared at her from the stairs again and Prue shot her a look that said she was losing and turned away. She could feel her bottom lip tremble and her fleeting resolve disappear.

'All right. I'll come but we have to talk about things...

I can't keep pretending as if everything is normal. There's things I have a right to know.'

'I know, my darling, I know.'

The conversation swiftly turned towards lightweight territory: the weather, how she would get there and when did she want to come. Ruth spoke with excitement at the adventures Prue would have and Prue played along out of manners or respect, or perhaps past affection for her aunt, but felt like a spineless coward. Ruth would book her tickets and had offered to pay for any mode of transport. The plane? Train? But Prue opted for the coach all the way from Victoria to Aberdeen, then she would need another for the ferry from Aberdeen to Lerwick which only travelled overnight. Ruth would meet her at the port in Lerwick in the morning and travel the rest of the way with her by car. When Prue told Subo about the journey, she said she was crazy.

'Why would anyone choose to go on the National Express when someone offers to buy them a plane ticket? It's so council,' she said. 'How long is that going to take?'

Prue shrugged. 'Around twelve hours.'

'For someone so intelligent, Prue, that's a really dumb idea.'

But Prue had never been anywhere on her own in her entire life. She was petrified of getting the train, what with all the platforms, announcements, and changes that could go horribly wrong. She spent most of her time at school or at home or traipsing after her mother. Making sure she turned the iron off, opened the mail and dealt with bills on time. That or emptying bins, opening and closing curtains to mark the passing of day and night, a chore her mother could never discipline herself to do. Often, they would go to her grandmother's house – when she was still alive. A few years before, when they had finally moved out of Nana's house into their own flat, Nana had repeatedly told her mother, *You won't cope, you know*. Prue had thought it an odd thing to say at the time, despite being only twelve, but she put it down to her Nana wanting them to stay with her. Now when she recalled it, it made perfect sense.

'Cope with what!?' her mother had shouted back eventually, after days of ignoring the comment.

'Life,' Nana had said.

Maybe what Prue was really frightened of was life, and she wouldn't be able to cope with it. Some big, invisible, unidentified monster was going to get her, and if she didn't know what form it took, or what it looked like, how would she know when to run away?

Prue made the long journey in the third week of June, a week after the last phone call from Ruth. There was a heatwave in London, and it was baking hot with no escape. The coach was sweaty and boring, and after a few hours the whole coach had a funky stench. When Prue boarded the ferry in Aberdeen, she expected a responsible adult to stop and ask why she was travelling on her own, but no one paid her a blind bit of attention. She followed the herd up to the open deck to look out to sea and observed an eclectic bunch. Children like small specks waved from the port as they sailed out of the terminal and gangs of noisy gulls fell in behind, weaving in out and of each other over churning sea foam. A man leaned with a foot on the rail and held onto his cowboy hat, a guitar case at his feet and carrying a tape deck. But mostly it was a herd of pensioners with shiny bald heads and grey brushed-out perms dressed as if they were off to Antarctica. Prue found herself a wind-battered space at the railings beside a family that had the ruddy cheeks and cagoules of the shamelessly self-proclaimed outdoorsy.

The mother barked instructions at the father as if he was one of the children, ordering him to fetch something from one of their multiple rucksacks while trying to stop her children fighting. The father moved like a sloth, finally producing a sandwich in tinfoil that was snatched by the mother and stuffed into a small boy's mouth, a ploy to distract him from being an annoying little shit for all of two minutes at best. The father had the ghostly expression of someone who wished he was somewhere else, golfing, out with the boys, at work, anywhere actually. At the mother's bark they marched down below deck in a line with the father dragging his heels at the back, carrying three rucksacks.

Prue's mother's past litany of boyfriends had made Prue wary of men. It was strange that men wanted to seek out women at all since they appeared to feel so restricted by them. Her mother tended to attract men as childlike as herself, which never made for longevity. What Prue had learned about men, through her tenure as a reluctant witness to her mother's tragic dating, was to avoid artistic types at all costs. They make for charismatic people, that is, when they are playing whatever instrument they play, acting, or singing, but aside from that, they're lazy, self-absorbed and practically useless at everything else, like paying bills or being reliable. Prue was even more wary of their opposite number, though, the alpha male, but had made some distant observations – male dominance seemed to be indicated by leg girth. From the patterns she had seen, which was of a very small number, the thicker the thigh the more emotionally constipated a man will permit himself to be. The thinner – the more likely he is to be a needy crier. Her mother had always been drawn to the latter.

If Prue ever married, she wanted someone organised and dependable, an accountant or an IT consultant. They would go to dinner and split the bill. Go on long-haul holidays and he would have a cool hobby, like photography or rock-climbing, and she vowed never to date a person with bongos in their living room. First, she would have to find a way of getting over her extreme awkwardness in front of men. Prue wanted to be normal. A normal *girl* – the kind people described as 'bubbly'. One who loved chatting on the phone, a people person, but that would never be her, if only for the fact she'd met a fair few people throughout her sixteen years and an alarming number of them had been awful.

An announcement over the tannoy said that the restaurant was open. Ruth had paid for a two-course dinner on her ticket but there was no way Prue was going to stand in a queue and try to find a seat with her tray among all the families, pensioners and lonesome crusties, so she starved. She spotted the cowboy again; this time he was annoying everyone by playing loud American folk music from his tape deck.

All around the kitchen
cock-a-doodle-doodle do.
All around the kitchen
cock-a-doodle-doodle do.

It was all harmonicas and banjos. She was desperate to know if he was a real cowboy – he *was* wearing spurs. He caught her staring and winked, then went back to bobbing his head along to his awful music as everyone else huffed and puffed. There was a red-nosed man with a giant recorder he had taken out to clean. How odd an adult would choose to play the recorder? She had assumed it was an instrument purely invented to torture parents. She returned to her single-berth windowless cabin and got ready for bed. The sea was calm, and she drifted off to sleep, wondering about the man who might be her father. What was Ruth going to tell her? What if he wore spurs? What if he played an instrument as pointless as the recorder, or danced around the kitchen... *Cock-a-doodle-doodle doo.*

The ferry pulled into the port in Lerwick, the biggest island in Shetland, at half past seven in the morning and the cowboy's song was still playing in Prue's head when she opened her eyes. She brushed her teeth in the tiny cupboard bathroom as the man called various passengers to disembark. The fluorescent strip lighting made her complexion green, which was a shame as she had caught a tan over the last month, which for someone as pale as her meant she had developed more freckles. Now it looked as if any colour had been sucked away overnight. She stuffed her belongings into her rucksack and left the cabin to see what kind of place she had been exiled to.

The first thing that hit her was how quiet it was despite the passengers ambling out. There was an eerie stillness and lack of ambient noise, no engines running, cars overheating, the vibrating buzz of the city. People disappeared into the lanes on the left or walked along the main road to the right. The car park had a handful of cars and gangs of birds circling, swooping for scraps. Old stone houses sat beside industrial buildings and pebble-dashed monstrosities. It was an odd mix, old and new, historic and functional. It was a shame Nana had never visited before she died. It was like a quaint market town in the home counties crossed with a Nordic fishing village, with a few awful industrial bits Nana would say ruined it.

A bright red shawl billowed in the wind straight ahead and there was her Aunt Ruth; she looked like a mountain shaman with her white-blonde hair shaved up the back and long on top, blowing about. Prue galloped up to meet her and was gripped in Ruth's skinny arms. She could feel her bony chest and smell her, washing that hadn't dried mixing with a strange floral scent.

'I am so glad you are here, my darling Prue, thank you for coming,' she said. 'Let's get you to the car.'

Prue's mother had often bitched how Ruth had married her way into money at whirlwind speed while off travelling, but the ancient beige Ford they stopped at didn't exactly fit the narrative.

'I know, it's a shit-heap,' said Ruth, 'but it's all I need. Archie hates it too. It's the colour, isn't it?' She took Prue's rucksack and stuffed it into the boot, slamming it shut.

'I wasn't thinking anything,' Prue lied, and got into the car. The gear stick was long and waggled, like a stick in a bucket. Ruth turned the engine on and somehow shifted the waggly stick into gear and pulled away. The engine sounded like a hairdryer about to explode.

'We are so excited you're here,' said Ruth.

Prue very much doubted her uncle shared this excitement. How could he? They barely knew each other. It was a relationship based on Ruth and her own mother signing their respective names on their behalf at the bottom of Christmas cards once a year, and little else.

She managed to snatch a brief glance at the street as they passed what was Lerwick with its shops, cafés and historic grey stone buildings. Brightly coloured bunting flapping in the wind linked the buildings overhead. They came to a roundabout and saw more houses and buildings, but beyond them as far as the eye could see were sloping hills of greenery. They never really left the sea and it was as if the water followed them everywhere. People always made such a big fuss about the sea, but it had never raised much of a pulse in Prue. Nana had taken her to Brighton to play the slot machines on the pier as a child and she remembered the windy pebbled beach and how dirty it was.

Ruth slammed a slender foot onto the tiny metal pedal, not that it made much difference, and rolled down the window.

'You don't mind if I smoke, do you?' she shouted over the wind.

'No,' said Prue, but Ruth already had a cigarette between her lips and was lighting it with both hands sheltering the flame while balancing the steering wheel between her knees. The wind blasted through the window and the smoke blew back into Prue's face and she shrank down into her seat. There really was no point having the window down. The road turned into a dual carriageway and ahead was an endless grass horizon that only stopped when it hit the sky. Ruth smoked as if it was her last cigarette on Earth and then flicked it out of the window and wound it back up, but the smoke clung to the car.

Prue wanted to ask Ruth what she had meant on the phone when she promised things would be different. *How?* Was she meant to wait until the subject was broached or bring it up herself? She turned to the window and realised she'd never been able to see so far without buildings, like concrete blinkers, always in the way. Maybe things *would* be different. Maybe she would find out who her father was, and it would be one of those funny stories where they'd lived within a mile of each other all these years. She'd go to his house at Christmas and drink snowballs, and no one would slit their wrists or spend the evening crying, smoking rollups under the extractor.

'I didn't realise quite how low your mum was,' said Ruth, wrenching Prue away from her dolly daydream of a responsible father in a Christmas jumper. 'I shouldn't have pushed her, shouting at her like that. It was out of order and I'm sorry.'

'It's not your fault. No one made her do it. Besides, it's not like it's the first time, is it?'

'Still, I should have controlled myself.'

'Don't worry about it.'

'I never had the chance to talk to you alone, because I wanted to ask about what happened the day Nana had the heart attack.'

'You know what happened.'

'Did she seem ill in the weeks leading up to it?'

'The news was on, and Joan Gardner was on it. Well, not *her* obviously, but they talked about the case. That's what caused it, the shock, I think.'

Ruth stiffened and her hands gripped the steering wheel until her knuckles were white and she wound the window down and lit another cigarette. There were tendons at the front of her neck that had risen as if something had pulled on the ends.

'You know who I mean, don't you?' Prue tried again.

'Of course I know who she is, Prue, it's not something you forget.'

'The news came on and a woman said she was campaigning for vulnerable convicts and that she was going to try and get the Gardner case looked at because her conviction wasn't safe. Mum and Nana started fighting and then Nana had the heart attack.'

'Oh, Prue,' said Ruth, 'I swear the police are meant to inform you of things like this.' Prue could only shrug in response. No one had ever involved her in such conversations, although she doubted very much that they went on at all.

'Surely they can't let her out if she confessed to murder?' asked Prue.

'She was never convicted of murder.'

'But she confessed!'

'She confessed and then changed her story several times. In the end they decided it was best if she was detained in a secure hospital, so they convicted her of child abduction. She wasn't right in the head; she had learning difficulties or was disabled in some way – I'm not sure. They put her in a secure hospital. They promised us it was as good as convicting her of murder and that she'd never get out. Right, this is the Mainland but we are going to our island over the water – Noost. We have to take the car ferry, which runs every day, several times a day, and it doesn't take long – honestly, you'd never know it was another island really. It takes no time at all, no need to feel isolated.'

The ferry terminal was nothing more than a hard edge to the land covered in tarmac. A corrugated building, a standalone block of toilets and an old red telephone box with the glass smashed in and graffitied over. Across the water was Noost but the sky was grey and cloudy and the island looked as if it had a mist hovering over it. They sat with the engine idling as Ruth lit her third cigarette with the end of the last one.

'Is Archie going to be home?' asked Prue.

Ruth rolled her eyes, flicked the old cigarette out of the window.

'No, he won't be back until late tonight, or tomorrow morning, I forget exactly. He's on a fishing trip.'

'Oh.'

There was a loud rap at the window on Prue's side that startled her. Peering through the glass was a man in a yellow hi-vis with the hood up obscuring his face, and Ruth smiled and waved back and pulled forward onto the ferry. It had started to rain, and the sky grew darker with burgeoning purple streaks like varicose veins.

'That's the mullet man,' whispered Ruth out of the side of her mouth in case he could lip read.

'Who?' said Prue.

'That man who sold me this car. I don't know his name; I only know him as the mullet man.'

Several cars had turned up to travel over the short stretch of water. Once parked up, Ruth insisted they go to the viewing deck. What for? To look at more grey skies and get thrashed about the face by the wind? Prue bit her lip, forced a smile, and followed her aunt. Under the sound of the wind the engine drummed, somewhere between a drone and a chug, vibrating every bone. Again, noisy gulls chased the white foam whipped up by the ferry. What was this perpetual obsession people had with the sea? Prue told Ruth she was going to get a hairband from the car and went back to the parking bays. She had got her rucksack from the boot and was sitting in the car when she stuck her hand into a pocket and, instead of a hairband, found a forgotten ten-pound note Nana had given her months ago. Prue gripped the tatty old note in her hand. It stank of Nana's house – menthol cigarettes. She missed Nana. Overbearing, rigid and casually bigoted opinions, and all.

Nana had always told her she was a special girl. So special she wasn't even born like other children and didn't need a daddy. Nana told her a fantastical story of how one day her grandfather had been digging over the borders in the garden and found a baby girl in the mud. He saw a naked foot in the earth and pulled her out, and that's how Prudence Mary MacArthur came to be. Years later, Prue would work out that he couldn't possibly have dug a hole in the first place because the man died before she was even born – not that timing was the only thing wrong with the story. At sixteen she'd have a whole host of other problems if she thought babies came from the ground, but her grandmother liked to make things up. Like when she told Prue she got her freckles when God sneezed over the cinnamon as he was making her, like a biscuit. Her grandmother was also the magnet that kept all the other pieces – Prue, her mother and Aunt Ruth – from flying out of orbit. She was such a strong immovable force, the family didn't know how to do anything but rotate around her. This was the woman who called Greenpeace terrorists, said environmentalists were stinky hippies and that crying was self-pity. A&E was only for compound fractures and even then she'd make you take the bus – no one called for ambulances on her watch. While the world worried about the rainforest, Nana thought they were fools who should wash their net curtains. She watched the same TV shows every day but never had the sound up enough to hear because of her ornaments on top. If the sound was up, the glazed gentlewoman with the lurcher at her knee vibrated until she fell onto the carpet as if she was throwing herself off a cliff.

It had been a boring, dull afternoon when the news cut to an interview with a young woman campaigning for vulnerable people convicted of crimes. She stood on the steps of a magistrate's court with the sun shining in her eyes. People behind her waved placards and chanted. Some mad, homeless person had been acquitted of something because of her group, Hope 4 Freedom, and it turned out she was Hope. Hope was barely twenty-one years old, being interviewed on TV and running her own not-for-profit for a selfless cause, and there was Prue, sixteen and sat round her Nana's house, listening to her grandmother's damp coughing and her mum slurping hot tea. The spark, the little flint that set off the chain of events that mushroomed into Hiroshima proportions, was when the journalist asked what was next for Hope. She dared to say one of the banned names – Joan Gardner. That was the A-bomb and Nana even turned up the volume, and the glazed woman began to vibrate.

A jolt of electricity ran through Prue when she heard that name. Nana knocked her ashtray off the arm of the sofa and had a coughing fit. Her mum spilled her tea on her own legs and leapt up, pulling her leggings away from her thighs, swearing and hopping. Hope squinted and explained why she was helping Joan.

'Joan was, in our opinion, wrongfully convicted of child abduction back in 1984. No one doubts this is a tragic case – an innocent child died – but Joan was kept without legal counsel and has a mental age of an eight- to ten-year-old child. She was convicted on the flimsiest of circumstantial evidence and has been detained ever since. It was a witch hunt and the police hunted and found their witch: a vulnerable woman with special needs...' Prue didn't hear the rest because Nana and her mother started arguing.

'Caroline! Did you know about this?' said Nana. She stood up and stepped straight onto the ash she had spilled on the carpet. Her mum didn't take her eyes off the TV.

'Caroline, have you checked?'

'Checked what? I didn't know.'

'Caroline, you've got to do something. Caroline! What are you going to do? You have to make a statement, or something, phone up the papers,' said Nana.

'What do you mean *make a statement*? To who?'

'You should call someone. You should *do* something!'

screamed Nana. She stood up and started coughing. The woman had lungs like maracas and she started to shuffle over to Prue's mother who was transfixed by the TV despite the fact the news had finished and the weather was on.

'I... I don't know what to do,' said her mum.

Nana was still coughing but her face had turned purple, as if she couldn't catch her breath.

'Nana, have a drink of water.' Prue stood up to get her grandmother a drink, but Nana was inching over the carpet towards her in slippers. Gasping, sweating, then she collapsed.

'Mum!' Prue's mother dropped to Nana's side. She was hysterical, grabbing at Nana's hands that were twisted around her chest as if she was having a fit. Prue watched, paralysed, until she switched into gear and ran to the phone and called for an ambulance.

One minute her grandmother was being loaded into an ambulance with a suspected heart attack, the next they stumbled into stage four lung cancer. It was the start of a heatwave and there were electric fans all over the hospital ward which only pushed hot air around. Both daughters, zero husbands, and Prue, were crushed together in a tiny space around a bed with only a thin curtain to separate them from three other patients in the Critical Dependency Unit. They were stuck in between breathing machines and beeping equipment as Prue's almighty Nana made repeated attempts to either get up or die. Occasionally, the nurses stopped chatting and laughing at the reception desk and came in and pumped more morphine into her. They realised she was dead when she stopped writhing and lay completely still with the machine still inflating her lungs.

Moments later Nana's skin had turned bright yellow and when they took the mask off her face her mouth was stuck in a wide-open scream from where the machine had forced air into her lungs for so long. Prue wished she hadn't seen that.

The subject of Prue's mystery father wasn't the only thing that was never discussed. They were not permitted to mention the name Joan Gardner or anything about what happened, but Hope hadn't been briefed on the MacArthur family policy of stoic silence on all unpleasant matters when she had gone blurting it out on TV.

Prue found a hairband, left the ten-pound note in the rucksack pocket and went back to Ruth who had her face into the wind. She pulled Prue in close and now she could smell funky washing, that strange scent, and cigarettes.

'Look! Prue!' Ruth said, pointing across the water. 'It's our island! I know you're going to love it.'

Prue smiled but the bowling ball in her stomach told her not to be so sure.

3

On Noost and back in the beige tin can, they hurtled down the road as fast as the car would carry them. It had taken only twenty minutes to reach the little island from the Mainland, but they may as well have travelled through time. A brutal landscape in every direction, one that couldn't help assaulting the senses with its eerie silence. The grass was even different, less green and fine, more straw-like; yellow and rough.

The handful of cars that had accompanied them sped off, leaving Ruth's little beige car rattling behind. The absence of buildings and people for Prue's eyes to wrap themselves around filled her with a hollow dread; it jangled the nerves. She hadn't realised places as barren as this still existed. The car felt vulnerable, like a deer in an open meadow. They drove past fields of the strange grass as the wind tore through and thrashed at the wildflowers. Occasionally, they would come upon a single-storey pebble-dashed house and then more unending openness; the only living things were grazing sheep. The sheep would stroll near the wire fencing and be startled by the car; they would scurry away from the roadside causing a flurry of panic in their flock. There weren't any pavements, and the only evidence of human occupation came in the form of moss- and lichen-covered stone walls that looked to have only gravity holding them together. Strange flowers like cotton wool on stalks wobbled in the wind and broken-down pallets and other debris had been dumped on the side of the road and left to rot. They passed a loch with a rocky beach covered in bright green kelp and seaweed. This island came with a ghostly sense of abandonment.

'Those flowers, Ruth, what are they – the white blobs?'

'Bog cotton, I think. Although doubtless the islanders will have their own name for it. Beautiful, isn't it?'

'Oh,' said Prue. Beautiful wasn't the word that had sprung to mind.

The sky continued to darken and fill with clouds bulging with rain. The two MacArthur women drove in silence. Ruth sat pitched forward, her skinny fingers clenching the wheel and her hands set at ten to two. A rowing boat had been discarded, no logical explanation as to how it could have got there, but it had a huge hole in the underside as if headbutted by a shark.

'It's quiet, isn't it?' said Prue, anything to break the stillness.

'You'll get used to it. It can be strange at first.'

'How many people live here?'

'On Noost? Not sure… can't be more than a couple of hundred, maybe three.'

Three hundred? There were two thousand pupils at Prue's school. Three hundred was nothing, not even a year group.

'Most people live on the Mainland,' said Ruth. 'You can't blame them. There's no jobs over here, especially if you don't work in fishing or oil.'

They came to a side road and then turned left onto a smaller winding country road with even more sheep and stone walls. Turning off again they bumbled down an uneven dirt track lined with bushes and skinny bent trees. Prue realised they were the first trees she had seen. Ruth's car slowed to a crawl when they came to an old wooden gate on the left leaning against a wall that didn't look as if it would survive being shut. *Dynrost House* was etched into a wooden plank on the gate. Ruth turned into it and they were swallowed into a driveway with dense trees and bushes.

'Here we are, home sweet home,' said Ruth, as she pulled on the noisy handbrake.

Dynrost House wasn't what Prue had expected at all. She wasn't sure what she'd expected but it certainly wasn't this. Her mother's stories of old money and family wealth had given her the impression Ruth lived in a mansion, and this was a big pebble-dashed house, which seemed to be the local uniform. It had no obvious shape, a higgledy-piggledy house, a misshapen potato. The windows were all different sizes, some portholes and others square. It had two storeys and a peaked roof, unlike the infrequent single storeys they had passed along the way, but it had black spots creeping over the surface as if it suffered from a disease. Attached to the left of the house was a squat block that looked much older than the rest, medieval even, and was made of sandy-coloured stone with high narrow-arched windows. Somewhere a cockerel crowed.

'Was this a church at some point?' Prue asked, shutting the car door behind her.

'Something like that,' said Ruth. 'Best to ask Ronnie.'

'Who is Ronnie?' Prue spun round so fast she almost cricked her neck. Ruth hadn't mentioned anyone else being here, and certainly not a Ronnie. Her stomach tightened. What other new and intolerable man was she going to have to live with aside from Ruth's husband? Ruth opened the boot and looped her hands through bags of shopping.

'I stock up whenever I go to the Mainland,' she said by way of explanation for the great mass of plastic bags. 'Will you give me a hand?' Prue put her rucksack on both shoulders and scooped up as many as she could. This was something she could do expertly from years of living in the flat above a shop.

'Ronnie is Archie's grandmother,' said Ruth. 'She lives with us.'

'Grandmother? But you never mentioned her.'

'Didn't I?'

'I would have remembered.'

'I thought I had, sorry. Don't worry – she's quite harmless. Ronnie's husband – Archie's grandfather – is dead and so is their son, Archie's father. They both died years ago so she's on her own. She told me once that the men in the family often have a genetic flaw – weak hearts, or something or other.'

'What about Archie's mother?'

'Oh, yes, she's dead as well.'

'Jesus, has anyone tested the water?'

'Prue, she's a little old lady, it's completely logical that she'd know a lot of dead people.'

'I suppose...'

Prue followed Ruth up to the imposing timber front door laden down with bags. 'How is living with your husband's grandmother? Does that make her a super-mother-in-law?'

'Ronnie's not like that. Honestly, you wouldn't know she was in her seventies. I swear that woman will outlive us all.'

'Is there a graveyard out the back where all these people are buried?'

'No,' Ruth tutted. 'There are no dead bodies in the garden if that's what you're worried about.'

'I'm only asking.'

The door opened and they stepped into an old square hall filled to the rafters with plants, like a botanist's greenhouse. There were plants along every wall, in every corner and dangling from hooks along the beams overhead. Leaves and flowers became a reception of faces and fingers as she stepped further inside. All over a side table, a glass cabinet, and even trailing up on each step of the staircase were more potted plants. Creepers hung down and wrapped themselves around the banisters like snakes. Prue sneezed but couldn't cover her nose because of the bags she was carrying, and the power of her sneeze sent dust particles flying around in circles. Everywhere she walked she came within a hair's breadth of being tripped up, tangled, tickled or poked. Above the hall was a landing that ran along the back adjacent to the stairs to the right. Several doors led off the landing and underneath was a dusty old fireplace with a mantelpiece as high as Prue's shoulders. Old yellow glass uplighters tried to light up the gloomy room with flickering bulbs from behind smothering foliage. Giant palm trees lined the stairs.

'Leave the bags there!' Ruth shouted, and her voice echoed as she disappeared through an ivy-covered doorway in the far corner.

Why hadn't Ruth thought to mention this leap away from what anyone would perceive as normal? Prue unknowingly drifted under dangling tendrils and when they tickled her neck she squealed as if a wasp had stung her.

'I am lucky,' she closed her eyes and whispered out loud. She had her arms and legs, and she should be grateful. She could have leprosy or had her legs blown off by a landmine. 'I am lucky,' she whispered again.

It was as if a sudden tug from a giant elastic band had dragged her back to the woods by the old cottage. She saw her seven-year-old legs in the white socks with the holes in but they were muddy and wet, and she was stood over the stream of dark green mossy water.

'Well, there you are!'

Prue spun around, eyes open, to see a tiny old lady sweeping towards her at such a pace, she didn't think she would stop. She grabbed both of Prue's hands (hers were freezing) and pulled Prue towards her with strength she wouldn't have guessed the old woman had. She pulled Prue down so she could kiss her on both cheeks. She wore waxy red lipstick which Prue was sure was now smeared across her face.

'Prue, it's so wonderful to meet you. My name is Veronique Charlotte Lewthwaite MacNair but then I married and became Mrs Anderson. Please call me Ronnie. Veronique is such a mouthful that ends with that clicking sound at the back of the throat and it reminds me of my dearly departed husband training his gundogs. I have heard so much about you.' She stared at Prue as if she was a marvel. 'Oh, my, how fabulous you are. Do you feel that?'

'Feel what?'

'The universe drawing us to where we must be.'

'Is it?'

The woman stood so close that Prue stopped breathing because, if she exhaled, she could have blown the chalky powder from her wrinkles. Ronnie was all of five feet tall, rail thin, with silver hair in a shoulder-length bob poking out from beneath a black silk turban with tassels hanging from each side like earrings. She had grey cat-like eyes lined with thick mascara and wore a kaftan that wafted around as she waved her arms. She was only missing a cigarette in a filter and an accent, and she could have been Greta Garbo.

'When Ruth said you were coming, I was overcome with a rush of energy and I said to myself, Ronnie, this will change everything, and at that very moment I looked at the clock and the time was exactly 11.11, and now you are here – isn't that something?'

'It is?' She still had hold of Prue's hands. The ice from her fingers travelled up Prue's arms and she struggled not to shudder. She wanted very much to take them back and kept looking towards the door in the corner willing Ruth to return.

'Please accept my condolences for the loss of your grandmother and my sympathies regarding your mother. Ruth tells me she struggles with depression – such a cruel beast... My daughter-in-law was similarly afflicted.'

'Thank you,' said Prue, but Ronnie still had her hands.

Was she meant to pull them free or wait for her to release them? 'What is 11.11?'

'11.11 is a message of reassurance from the other side and it means you are manifesting. Be careful of your thoughts, my dear girl.' Prue wasn't sure what she meant when she referred to the other side, but assumed she wasn't talking about the Mainland.

'It's a good thing you're here, my dear girl, the spirits want it to happen,' Ronnie explained.

'Ah.' This was up there with being dug from a hole or sneezed on by God. Ronnie spoke in aristocratic tones; in fact, she sounded very much like the woman on the telephone if you don't dial fast enough who tells you to *please replace the handset and try again.* That funny old clipped English that sounded like a recorded news bulletin from the war.

'Do you know that numbers are the universal language given by the deity to us on Earth as confirmation of the truth?' Ronnie gripped Prue's hands and stared hard into her eyes. Prue wanted to blink and felt as though she couldn't.

'Ahh! Fantastic! You've met Ronnie.' Ruth swooped in to scoop up the remaining bags.

'Let me help.' Prue pulled her hands free of Ronnie's icy paws.

'She's stunning, Ruthie, you never said,' said Ronnie, stepping back to hang on the wooden acorn on the banister poking up from under leaves.

'That's not true,' said Ruth.

'You certainly underplayed it, my dear. Mind out for those hunters, my little Pru-Pru. I think you'll find yourself the last pretty caribou on this deserted island. Watch out, my girl, or you'll find yourself brought down by those long legs of yours—'

'Ronnie, stop teasing!' said Ruth. 'Why don't you help Prue get settled.'

'Of course. Let me show you to your bedroom – you will be staying in what used to be the nursery. Follow me, young Prue,' said Ronnie, and for the second time she had hold of Prue's hand.

'You don't sound Scottish,' said Prue.

Ronnie stopped abruptly and held Prue in a shocked stare, then burst out laughing. 'I'll forgive you this once, my little ignoramus, but the MacNairs can be traced back to the 1500s, my girl. I'm as Scottish as they come. The Lewthwaites were a very prominent family in Glasgow, and my own aunt ran with the Glasgow Girls.'

'The Glasgow Girls?'

'The artists?' She huffed and shook her head. 'Never mind.' Ronnie let go of Prue's hand and stepped in front to lead her up the stairs, weaving between the plants.

'By the way, it's probably worth mentioning this isn't Scotland. I'd get that into your head quick smart. For the record I grew up in Glasgow about a hundred years ago. I'm joking, of course, I'm seventy-seven, not a hundred, but I am from Glasgow – don't I look good for my age?'

'Amazing, but how come you live here?' Prue did her best not to catch the ivy or trip on any of the pots under her feet.

'I followed a boy,' she sighed and flashed a wicked grin over a shoulder. 'I married into the Andersons. My husband was educated in Edinburgh, naturally, but the Andersons have been landowners here for many generations. My brother-in-law married into the Bolts – now there's a family you can't escape in Shetland. Bolt is a Norwegian name which means short and powerfully built, and if you ever had the bad fortune to meet my sister-in-law, you'd find it freakishly accurate. How did I end up here? You'll find this place has a habit of getting under the skin – like bot flies or scabies. Now come, let's get you settled. You've migrated a long way, my pretty caribou.'

Prue had been assigned a big bedroom in the back corner of the house with large windows that overlooked the garden. It had a double bed with a synthetic bedcover in pistachio green, which can't ever have been in fashion and looked highly flammable. The curtains had mould. It did, however, have its own bathroom with a roll-top bath and a shower that sat above the tap like an old telephone. More bizarrely, the bedroom and the bathroom were stuffed with plants along with dried upside-down flowers hanging over her bed and a bowl of potpourri on the bedside table that stank to high heaven. Prue touched the ghostly pale leaves of a plant with spidery red veins running through them.

'That's a caladium, my dear,' said Ronnie. 'Be careful what you touch here, sometimes the sap can irritate sensitive ones.'

A woven basket hung from the curtain pole containing a plant with curly pale green fingers covered in fur that gave Prue the creeps. On the chest of drawers was a big jar of bright yellow roses with hints of pink. All the scents were fighting against each other, and she had the beginnings of a headache.

As soon as Ronnie left, Prue locked herself in the bathroom, sat on the toilet with the lid down and cried. It was a brief and sudden attack and she wasn't even sure why she was crying. It must be the weariness from travelling, and so much had changed in such a short relentless burst after years of being exactly, torturously the same. Prue had begged for change to come but now she knew that change doesn't tap you on the shoulder and give you polite notice – it hits you in the face with a closed fist and laughs as you bleed.

The intense Ronnie had made such an embarrassing fuss about how pretty she was, but Prue knew this to be false. She had frizzy reddish-brown hair and wore glasses. Her legs were too long for her body, and she had shoulders like a man, which the boys at school had told her on a regular basis. Prue left the bathroom and reminded herself again how lucky she was. She unpacked by emptying her clothes into a heap inside the wonky wooden wardrobe with doors that didn't quite close. The cockerel crowed outside again. How the hell was she going to last the summer?

She stripped away her grimy clothes and lay down on the bed with the intention of resting her eyes for a few minutes and then fell asleep for hours, star shaped, on the shiny, potentially flammable bed.

She dreamed she was watching her seven-year-old self from above, like a bird, and she was running in the woods by the cottage again. She skipped and hopped under the shadow of the trees towards the stream with her white socks on the boardwalk. Then she was in the kitchen pulling at her mother's wet skirt and trying to hug her legs. Prue tripped, jolting herself awake and sat up. The weather had worsened, and rain and wind beat against the single-pane windows, making them rattle. She pulled back the mouldy curtains to see outside but it was too gloomy and wet. The garden was enclosed inside a stone wall running either side and beyond was a dark mass of trees. The house was sat in a trough between hills that climbed up behind the trees, and up ahead on the brow of the hill was a big white building with yellow blinking lights. Ruth banged on the door and opened it without waiting for an answer and Prue was standing in her underwear.

'Oh, sorry,' Ruth said, covering her eyes and pulling the door back on herself so she could talk through the gap. 'Just to let you know dinner will be in half an hour.'

'Thanks, I'll be down in a bit.'

Ruth closed the door. Prue thought it was only her mum who never waited for an answer before barging in. It must be a MacArthur thing.

When she went down to the kitchen for dinner there was water running from both taps into the sink and steam rising from the hob of a bottle-green AGA. There was a round wooden table and timber beams on the low ceiling. Nautical lamps hung from the walls and there were more terrible flowery curtains at the windows. It was the least plant-infested room but had herbs lining the windowsill and along the countertops.

'Ronnie is the cook, thank God, saving us all from my culinary torture,' said Ruth. 'She asked me what you ate.' Ruth presented her with a plate and set her own down while Ronnie followed with hers in a small bowl. 'You're all right with spaghetti bolognese, aren't you?'

Prue hadn't eaten meat in three years, and for a second,

she thought she might cry again; how stupid and unlike her. She never cried. In fact, she disliked criers because they reminded her of her mother who cried at adverts with babies or even nappies. Prue stared at the plate and resigned herself to eating it. She was being fussy and oversensitive, that was all. She had been told many times how she tended to dwell on things, would give silly points too much importance and find a way to make them hurt her. She took flippant comments and lazy sentences, filed them to a point, found the fleshiest part of herself and jammed them in like a harpoon. But she could have sworn she had spoken to Ruth about being a vegetarian. How could she not remember?

'I love Bolognese,' said Prue, and pushed her glasses up her nose. They needed tightening.

'Who wants to try one of my new wines?' Ronnie disappeared into a little pantry, returning with two bottles of a dark liquid, almost brown in colour. 'I have a couple of recipes I've been refining. I am grateful for all feedback, however harsh.'

Ruth slapped the table and made Prue jump. 'Ronnie is right, we should be celebrating. We have our own little tribe, even if only for a few weeks. Cheers, and welcome, Prue!'

The wine didn't taste normal. It was flowery and had a funny smell, but alcohol wasn't something Prue could easily get hold of. Her mother drank after Prue went to bed – she knew because she'd seen the bottles in the outside bin – but Nana had been teetotal. Nana could be funny about certain things and had got drunk at her wedding reception and never touched a drop again, she said. She also wouldn't let Prue buy *More!* magazine because she saw *position of the fortnight* once and said it was teaching girls to be whores.

Soon the wine fug hit Prue and her cheeks were rosy. She was putting away piles of pasta and trying to explain the English exam system to Ronnie. Ruth started to talk about the island, and Prue got the distinct feeling she was being sold to.

'When we first moved back here,' she said, 'I hated it. I thought it was too still and quiet, but what I found was it wasn't emptiness but the complete absence of demands and, all of a sudden, there wasn't any pressure, I was free simply to exist. It felt so strange. And so, at the age of forty, after losing my first career and my first husband, I found my second self. I can finally call myself an artist – it's what I always wanted, but it took my old life to be smashed to smithereens for my new life to be created. Up here so far away from everything else – all the things that made me feel so busy and important before really are quite worthless.'

Her mother had been fifteen when Prue was born and her older sister, Ruth, twenty-four. There was a nine-year age gap between the two sisters, and they were poles apart in personality. Nana had mentioned there had been failed attempts to have a baby in between.

Prue was putting away the strong flowery wine and eating red meat had made her thirsty.

'Will you show me your studio tomorrow?' she asked.

'Tell her about your course and that exhibition,' said Ronnie, fidgeting like an excited sprite.

Ruth waved away the attention with a little embarrassment and explained, 'I took an art class a few months ago on the Mainland, then there was an art exhibition at the museum organised by the teacher and she invited two of us to showcase our work. I sold two pieces!'

'That's amazing. Congratulations.' That should have sounded more enthusiastic, but Prue noticed she felt hot and woozy.

'It was only £50, but that's not the point. I've been invited to take part in a bigger exhibition in Glasgow so it's all very exciting!' Ruth continued. 'You have to be prepared to put in the work for very little return to be an artist. Archie has a waiting list for his paintings and they're always of the same thing... Still... one day. I'm not sure you'll be interested, to be honest.'

'Brace yourself, young Prue,' said Ronnie. 'Some of it is quite disturbing. Ruthie is... what would you call yourself? A gothic surrealist? Give me a bowl of fruit or a landscape any day.'

'I'd still like to see,' said Prue.

'We'll see,' said Ruth. 'This island is full of magical energy, Prue. The wildlife, the landscapes, the sea. I want you to get outdoors and inhale and enjoy it. It's why I've always been so keen on you coming to stay, and your mum. I had this silly idea it might help.'

'We could certainly do with some magic,' said Prue. 'First Nana, then Mum... they say bad things happen in threes and I wonder what's next.'

'Nothing, bad things happen but it doesn't mean there's going to be anything else,' said Ruth.

'What if the Joan Gardner case is the third thing?' said Prue.

'Who is Joan Gardner? What case?' said Ronnie, looking between them as if she was watching ping pong.

'The woman... who stole the baby,' Prue said.

'What baby?' asked Ronnie, her hands flat on the table, neck stretched. This part of the family history had clearly been left out.

Prue looked at Ruth in desperation, hoping she would leap in to pick up the explanation, but she was staring at the table, ashen faced. Prue would have to explain.

'Holly, the baby's name was Holly. She was my little sister and... Joan Gardner took her.' Prue swallowed, her heart rate up. Even hearing the words leave her body was unnerving. It was as if she'd done something wrong.

'Good Lord! Ruth, you never told me this! What happened to the baby?'

'She drowned her. Holly drowned. Then before Nana had the heart attack, on the TV they said that she might not even be guilty—'

'Let's not ruin a pleasant evening with this, Prue,' Ruth snapped and stood up, nearly knocking her chair over, and started snatching up the plates while Ronnie and Prue leaned back in their chairs. It would seem dinner was now over. When Ruth had stacked up the plates she turned to Prue and remembered to winch up a smile. 'We won't let anything bad happen to you, will we, Ronnie?'

'Relax,' said Ronnie. 'All things considered, if the grim reaper comes calling, statistically it'll be for me.'

'Ronnie!' said Ruth.

'What?' said Ronnie. 'I'm merely stating fact!'

Prue's stomach was bloated; she stifled a sick-flavoured burp, took her glasses off and set them down on the table.

'Ronnie, you said you followed a boy, but why stay somewhere so far away from everywhere else?' asked Prue.

'There's too much history here – makes it difficult for one to leave. The plants aren't the only things with roots. Besides, I could never live in a city again. People exist like ants. Up here, a woman can be her own Queen. Rules, laws, schedules, urgh. My dear girl – it's like government taxes, they're only for the little people.' She winked. Ronnie must have been very beautiful once. She still had the delicate features, small chin and high cheekbones and those slanting eyes of a cat-like fairy queen, like Titania from *A Midsummer Night's Dream*.

'Shall we call it a night?' said Ruth. It was a rhetorical question. The plates already stacked up on the side and the glasses snatched away. 'Leave what's left,' said Ruth. 'It's a tomorrow problem.'

As she was putting her chair under the table, Prue noticed the big thick timber door behind her.

'Where does that lead to?' she asked. 'It looks like a door to a dungeon.'

'The cellar,' said Ruth.

'The cellarium,' Ronnie corrected.

'What's a cellarium?' asked Prue.

'Basically, much like a cellar,' said Ronnie, and Ruth rolled her eyes.

'You won't ever need to go down there,' said Ruth. 'Only Archie does, when the electrics play up.'

'It's part of the original priory,' said Ronnie. 'Hundreds of years ago this was a safe place for travelling monks who stopped on the way to Iceland or Greenland before the Reformation.'

'What's the Reformation?' asked Prue, and they both looked horrified.

'The Reformation,' said an incredulous Ronnie. 'When the Church broke away from Rome? The religious rebellion that challenged Rome's power all across Europe. Honestly, what are they teaching children these days?'

Ruth shook her head as she blew out the last candle.

4

Prue couldn't sleep. Her stomach felt as if it was trying to process a rhino through a grinder the size of a golf ball. All she could do was lie on her back groaning and listening to a constant dripping noise coming from somewhere. Drip, drip, hesitant pause, two quick drips, and then it started over. She kicked off the covers and checked the taps in the bathroom. One of the plants by the sink had thin thread-like foliage that kept trailing into the sink and catching on her hands, and on the other side was some kind of shrub. Who put plants in a bathroom? Weird. She took both and pushed them up against the wall in the corner. She checked the taps again but the leak wasn't coming from them. Then she realised she must have left her glasses downstairs but there was no way she was going down by herself in the dark, not in this creaky old house. As she got into bed, she accidentally caught the bowl of potpourri with the blanket, spilling dried red and purple petals all over the floor. She scooped them up in her hands and their strong musty aroma travelled fast up to her brain and tweaked a nerve behind an eye. Prue was lightheaded, had a dull headache, a dry mouth and could not sleep. Her mind raced. How tense Ruth had seemed in the car and then at dinner. She must still be grieving the loss of Nana too, or perhaps she was upset about her little sister trying to kill herself. Maybe it was both.

Archie was actually Ruth's second husband. Prue had really liked her first, Will. Nana had called them 'the yuppies' because they spent their money on clothes, city breaks to Europe, drank red wine and had strange cheeses in the fridge. Before then Prue thought the only cheese was cheddar. Will had an affair and left Ruth for a younger woman, and then a few months later, Ruth's marketing agency made her redundant and she went a bit 'round the bend'. We all have it in us, you only need to find the right combination of buttons to push, and Ruth's was her sense of purpose. Ruth had to move back in with Nana, and consequently, Prue and her mother. Prue was only eleven; it was before they moved out into the flat and Ruth would take Prue to the park to escape Nana's nagging about her drinking and going out every night. They would sit on the park bench with Ruth hungover in sunglasses, a strung-out Marlene Dietrich, and laugh at all the mummies steering their children away in pushchairs as she chain-smoked next to the playground, blowing smoke in the children's faces. She always admired Ruth for her honesty. The way she didn't make things out to be special when they weren't. She was brave enough to call Nana out on the silly little rules she lived by that didn't make sense. She was a doer. With Prue's mother it had always been *if I feel up to it,*

or *we might, oh, it's too late, we should stay home now.*
Ruth grabbed you by the hand and ran – you were lucky if
you got to bring your coat. It was Ruth who had put Prue
completely off the idea of having children because she told
her which hole babies came out of and what it did to you,
and that's why Nana couldn't go on trampolines any more.

Ruth took her divorce settlement, her redundancy pay
and disappeared travelling around Asia and then came back
married to Archie. The man had stolen her beloved aunt
and lobotomised her. He'd turned her into what he needed,
whatever that was.

The pillows of the bed were too soft and no matter how
much she plumped them up they just deflated again. Her
stomach churned. Her tongue was like a pumice stone and
she hadn't brought a drink upstairs so had to get up and
slurp from the cold tap in the bathroom every so often. She
stared at the stippled ceiling glowing pale in the moonlight
that wasn't blocked by the thin curtains whatsoever. She
was sure it was that stuff that had asbestos in it – she'd seen
a documentary about it.

Prue must have drifted off, but woke up from her
dry-mouthed broken slumber and vomited a bellyful of
Bolognese onto her lap. She could have sworn she'd left
the bathroom light on, but it was pitch black. She got up,
cradling the hot mass from her stomach inside the duvet
and hobbled to the bathroom, trying not to retch at the
smell. She pulled the light on and flipped the contents of her
guts into the toilet bowl. When she pulled the chain it was
as if a brass band played behind the walls, and when she
tried to turn the taps on to wash the duvet off in the bath,
the pipes clanged from behind the walls and water came

out in thunderous gushes. Minutes later Ruth rushed in, all wafting nightie, skinny legs and mole eyes.

'Oh, Christ,' she said, 'don't tell me you're ill.'

Ruth took the wet duvet, disappeared, and returned with a clean blanket, an empty bucket and a pint of water.

'I'm sorry I woke you.'

'It wasn't you, it was Archie,' said Ruth. 'He's back. He said he could hear you throwing up from the landing. Don't worry, you can't help being ill.'

'The pipes are really loud.'

'It's an old house, it creaks and groans. I'm used to it now.'

Ruth remade the bed and tucked Prue in like a child after a nightmare. As Ruth went to turn the bathroom light off, Prue asked for it to be left on. Ruth flashed a look, as if she should have grown out of that by now, then blew her a kiss and closed the door.

Prue kept picking up the same surreal dream in between bouts of waking. A blur of running room to room looking for Joan Gardner but she was forever a second behind, and as Prue entered a room and caught a glimpse of her baby blue coat with the hood up, she disappeared out of view and Prue had to chase her into the next. She ran into her bedroom at Ruth's, the nursery with the mouldy curtains, and saw two bright yellow hands appear from the chimney. The fingers outstretched and the nails cupped like talons, they tapped on the stone as they reached the hearth. A head emerged and as it looked up, she saw it was Nana with her mouth stuck open in the ventilator scream. Prue jolted herself awake. The sheets were damp, and she worried she might be sick again and her rabbit heart raced. The bathroom light was off again, but this time she *knew* it had been left on.

It was still raining and blowing a gale outside. Prue was hot, and still nauseous. She got up and stood between the window and the curtain with her burning forehead against the cold glass. It was an old house, she told herself, that's why the lights went out.

Outside was a smeared dirge of petrol blue and tar black; without her glasses she couldn't see properly – an indistinguishable mass creeping with movement. An empty plastic pot was rolling about the patio when she saw what she thought was the flash of a bare white-skinned leg. It was there and then gone. She rubbed her eyes, looked again but nothing was there so she stepped away. It *could* have just been plastic or loose tarpaulin flying around. Prue worried she should at least tell Ruth – what if someone got inside the house, murdered them all and it turned out she'd done nothing about it? Don't be silly. It *was* plastic. It couldn't be anything else.

When she turned around, both wardrobe doors were wide open. Prue froze with fear, then pulled herself together and jammed them shut with both hands, hard. A loud crack came from the bathroom, and she held her breath and peered through the gap in the door, and of course there was no one there. Maybe it was the pipes contracting back into place. The wardrobe was as old as the rest of the house, it couldn't have been shut properly. There was no way she was going to go into her aunt's bedroom and talk about plastic loose in the garden and wardrobe doors popping open – she saw the look Ruth had given her when she asked for the light to be left on. Prue dismissed the crack as one of the creaks and groans of the house. Then in front of her the wardrobe doors slowly opened themselves, and the bathroom light switched itself off. This time she screamed.

'Archie's gone to look at the fuse box.' Ruth ran in carrying a giant monstrosity of a lamp. 'They're all set up under different things. The plugs in the wall should be OK, he said, it's on a different thing.'

Ruth set down a sculpture of a woman in Roman-style robes by the potpourri on the bedside table. It had a drugged-out blissful expression painted on an eggshell-pink face. One hand was on top of her heart with blobby red nails, the other reaching out. A baby lamb nestled against her legs on a wooden plinth but whoever had painted the face had done such a bad job it looked demented.

'Is that meant to be the Virgin Mary?' asked Prue.

'I gave her a Vegas-style makeover. What do you think?'

Of all the lamps in the world, she had to bring Mary the actual mother of God with unblinking eyes to stare down at her. Prue stifled a shudder and smiled with the same expression as the lamb. Ruth's modifications had included a halo of small bulbs around her head.

'Does it work?'

Ruth plugged it into the wall and Mary lit up like the Vegas strip. It can't have been a look she would have endorsed herself.

'Ta-dah!' Ruth pronounced, chirpy for someone who had been woken up twice. 'There we go – knew she'd come in useful.' She stood back, pleased with her work, and then the main lights came back on.

'Ah, see? Archie's fixed the thing.' Prue was sat up in bed and Ruth sat down next to her legs and squeezed both

Prue's knees under the duvet. 'Told you, it was the lights. It's an old house, it's noisy. Things break, you'll get used to it.'

'I'm really sorry.'

'Don't be. I'll leave Mary, in case it happens again, then you won't be plunged into darkness. I never knew you were so scared of the dark,' said Ruth.

'You must think I'm a nightmare.'

'No, not at all. Look, Prue, you've been through a lot. We all have. You more than anyone absorb it all so quietly. You always have. It makes people think you are mature but that's not fair, you shouldn't have to be.'

'I don't understand. What do you mean?'

'Nothing... I'm waffling. I am sorry me and your mother have never really got on. I always put it down to the big age gap but it's more than that. It's not *all* her fault, it's mine too, but she brings out the worst in me. Anyway, try and get some sleep.'

'Wait... so... what do we do?'

'Do?' Ruth looked perplexed by what Prue thought was an obvious question; they couldn't go back to normal after everything, surely there had to be some kind of plan.

'Nana's gone... and now all this stuff about *her*—'

Ruth interrupted. 'It's not a conversation for now—'

'But you did say we would talk?'

'Yes, and we will, but not now. Patience, my darling.'

5

Prue was woken up the next morning by birds squawking outside her bedroom window. Exhausted as soon as she opened her eyes, she rolled down to the kitchen like a zombie in search of her glasses, but they weren't on the table where she'd left them. They weren't in the kitchen at all. Last night's mess had been cleared away so someone must have moved them. She was a bit short-sighted – enough to make the writing on the whiteboard blur at school, but she felt naked without them.

Prue knocked on the door to Ruth's studio, which was the room next door to hers, but as she knocked it slowly opened a few inches and she peered through. Inside she saw a table covered in artistic clutter, lidless tubes, brushes, jars of dirty water, scissors. Paintings were on the wall opposite alongside a collection of antique crucifixes. To the right she could see an old rubber gas mask for a horse. She was about to step in when the door was opened from inside.

'Morning, how are you feeling?' Ruth blocked the

entrance with her body. The horse mask and its googly eyes loomed behind. Prue already had a foot over the threshold but felt as if she should take it back.

'I'm feeling a lot better, thank you,' she said. 'Can I come in?' Ruth hesitated then stood back.

'I'm sure you won't be interested,' she said. 'It will be awfully boring for you, and you must promise not to laugh – art is so subjective, isn't it?' Ruth threw her head back laughing, but it was nervous laughter and she twiddled with the shortest hair at the back of her neck.

'I'd never laugh,' said Prue. 'What's wrong with your arm?' She pointed at the back of Ruth's forearm where there was a red rash. Ruth glanced and dismissed it as nothing.

'I don't know, it suddenly appeared. Something must have irritated it, paint, turps, God knows. Could be anything.'

The room was a chaotic mess of half-finished canvases and sculptures arrested in mid-development, like the pottery room at school, but it was bright and airy unlike most of the house. Prue found her eyes drawn to a huge oil painting.

'What's this?'

'It's called *St Lucy*,' said Ruth, perching on her desk in front of the horse mask.

'Who was St Lucy?'

'Patron saint of the blind.'

'It's beautiful.' Technically it was very good, if you could get past the fact St Lucy carried her own eyes on a golden plate in front of her, and her sockets were two black holes. On the tray along with her eyeballs were sugar cubes and a distinctive patterned teapot in orange and brown.

'That's Nana's old teapot!' Prue squealed.

'Is it?'

'Yes! It must be. It's exactly like it, you must remember that hideous thing she refused to throw away?'

Prue walked to a picture all in black and white. It wasn't a painting, but pieces of white material had been cut and stuck onto a black base like a roll of negative film. It was of a wooded area and the trees had been created by the contrast with strips of white. At the centre on the ground was the shape of a woman on her knees, hunched over, her hair in front of her face as she leaned forward.

'That's a little experiment I did using contrast and shapes,' explained Ruth. 'An early piece – my teacher liked that one.' Prue saw the title in the corner.

'*The Grieving Mother*,' said Prue. 'What mother?'

'Oh, you know,' Ruth giggled, 'I was trying to be dramatic.'

Prue's eyes raced and fell upon a bizarre painting in blocks of bold colour of three women swung around a maypole by their extended lizard-like tongues, their feet off the ground and a burning sky behind them. This was called *The Three Witches*.

'I like this one,' said Prue. 'It's good. Odd but good.'

'Thank you.'

'Nana used to call us the three witches, didn't she?' asked Prue, turning to Ruth.

'Did she?'

'Yes, of course she did.'

'I don't remember.'

'How can you not remember? She used to tell us we were just like the three witches from *Macbeth*. You must remember.'

'Sorry, I don't...' Ruth laughed. Prue found herself growing annoyed.

'But you must...'

Ruth shrugged. 'I needed a title and I guess it must have popped into my head from somewhere.'

'Why are they swinging by their tongues?'

'It's just art.' Ruth shrugged again. 'Anyway, I should crack on—'

An eruption of high-pitched squeals and whoops of laughter intruded from outside and they both went to the window.

'Oh, I forgot,' said Ruth, deflated and stepping away, leaving Prue to watch. 'Archie has a photoshoot. A magazine is writing a piece on him, and those girls are some of his models.'

'Models? What does he need models for?'

'His portraits.'

'Oh, I didn't know he was famous.'

'Don't be silly, he's not famous, but the art world is a small incestuous industry.'

On the patio beneath the window were a group of four older teenage girls. It was a spectacle of coloured hair, purple, black, pink, blue and lots of skin. Some had thighs like corned beef from the cold, and all had piercings and tattoos. It seemed a strange scene in such a quiet rural setting. A man crouched taking photographs as Archie stood in the middle with girls draped either side of him, laughing, arms folded. Ruth acted as if the whole thing wasn't happening.

The first time Prue had met Archie was at Christmas at Nana's house the year he and Ruth were married, which was a shock in itself. He'd worn a tatty old pair of jeans with paint splatters and a long-sleeved T-shirt with the sleeves rolled up. Prue had found herself obsessed by the scrawled tattoos on both forearms, faded and half obscured by wiry man hair bleached from the sun. They reminded her of pre-cooked roast chicken – tanned and sinewy, as if he'd recently come back from living at sea for weeks and had every intention of going back as soon as possible. He had deep-set eyes under a heavy brow and eyebrows close together, a small mouth with lips locked in a straight line and hair a faded blondish brown. It was scraped back into a ponytail that was always unravelling. Broad and muscular, he had thick legs and big shoulders; everything about him was man-size and intimidating. A proper *bloke*. An Alpha. One of those weird creatures Prue had observed from a distance. The ones that backslapped each other, called each other legend, mate, geezer, fella in rounds of ritualistic mutual petting and enjoyed throwing their weight around pretending they had no idea how much space they were taking up. Or that's how Prue saw him. He always stood with his legs needlessly wide apart with his thumbs in his pockets, and for some reason this particularly irked Prue. Will had been friendly, polite, approachable and well groomed; Archie was not. They were not the pairing Prue would have made. They didn't match – not in her mind anyway.

'Where do the girls come from?'

'The Mainland. They're strange creatures, students, you know, tortured types. They'll be gone soon.'

Ruth opened a drawer in her desk and Prue heard foil being broken and turned to see empty blister packs of pills in her aunt's drawer spilling out. Ruth pushed the mess back in the drawer and closed it.

'I keep getting headaches,' she said. 'It's eye strain.' Prue turned back to watch the girls and Archie on the patio.

The photographer said something, and they all burst out laughing but she couldn't hear what had been said. Then Archie led them further into the garden where she lost sight of them behind the bushes. Like the Pied Piper of Hamelin, the long-limbed colourful creatures trailing in a line behind him. Prue was so transfixed that she didn't see the girl left behind looking up at her. She only noticed when the girl jumped and waved, and Prue nearly died of embarrassment at being caught. This exotic bird with black hair in pigtails and bright pink ends had dark lipstick on the fattest and most beautiful mouth. She winked at Prue and waved again with the tips of her fingers and bit into her bottom lip. Prue brought a feeble hand up to wave back but her eyes went blurry. She had to close and rub them, and when she looked again, the girl was racing to catch up with the others. Her eyesight must be worse than she thought.

'You haven't seen my glasses, have you? I left them on the table at dinner, and they're not there now,' she said.

'No, but they must be around somewhere.'

Hours later, Ronnie, Ruth and Prue were in the kitchen when the troop of girls paraded past the window, still shrieking, on the way to their minivan which had been parked out front all day. They heard the wheels screech down the driveway as they left. God only knew what the mullet man would make of them. When Archie came back, he looked into the kitchen as Prue glanced up and they caught each other's eyes. Prue froze in a panic; she couldn't even bring herself to smile. Paralysed like a deer in headlights, she went bright red as Archie looked at her as if he'd never even seen her before. Then he winked, like the cowboy on the ferry, and carried on past the window. When she turned back Ruth had seen the exchange and wore a strange expression – Prue didn't know what it meant but her mother often wore the same face.

For the second night her sleep was broken again, littered with wild dreams and waking moments of creaks and groans of the house. Sometimes when she woke she found herself freezing cold, then the next boiling and sweat drenched. When morning came she was happy to see the sky had cleared to baby blue; it was sunny but not hot. Prue went downstairs through the creeping plants and towards the music playing loudly somewhere. It was old-fashioned big band music and she traced it to a record player in a large bright room with open French doors onto the patio. The song finished and after the crackling it started into the next; she knew it was 'Don't Sit Under the Apple Tree' because Nana used to hum it when she was in a good mood. Sheer white voiles to the open doors floated towards her on the cool breeze and she stepped outside, but couldn't see Ronnie. In front was a huge bush that blocked the view of the garden and when she walked around it, she found that this was where the garden really began.

The ground was a carpet of overgrown grass. There was a wooden table on which were hand-size terracotta pots of shrubs and seedlings and an open notebook with handwritten notes, observations, plant names and dates. A bleached wooden outbuilding with lines along the grain had horseshoes nailed on the outside. A gravel path with grass sprouting up led to the door and either side was bulging with bushes, weeds and purple and white flowers. An old Belfast sink was on a stand surrounded by glazed blue pots.

Prue walked in bare feet with her baggy bed T-shirt barely covering her bottom and found herself wandering down endless winding pathways as the strains of the Glenn Miller Orchestra faded behind her. Around every corner was another section of new flowers and plants as big as her Nana's garden back home. Soon she wasn't sure where she was – at the end or beginning – or how to find her way back. It would be too humiliating for words if she had to be rescued from the garden. She fell upon another shed and here the grass was shorter, plants and bushes arranged in circles bordered with log rolls. Purple, pink, white, scarlet, orange. Bluebells that were small and violet, not blue. Flat roses in scarlet and alabaster. What looked like coral pink daffodils and plum-coloured orchids the size of her thumb. The spectacle was endless, and when she found the pond, it was completely by accident. She saw the steps hidden by long grass and climbed up them to find a vast expanse of duckweed-covered water. When she turned to come down, the grass around her was twitching like little electric shocks taking place in random spots on the ground. She bent down and saw a baby frog, no bigger than a pinhead, and realised she was in the middle of hundreds of leaping baby frogs. She caught one in her hands and sat down on a step. It was so little it still had part of its tadpole tail.

'Good morning, my dear.' Ronnie appeared, her hair wrapped under an elegant scarf and topped off with a wide-brimmed hat. A long blue shirt with the sleeves rolled up flowed past her knees. 'In case you were curious, Ruth is over on the Mainland with her art friends; she'll be back later.'

'You haven't seen my glasses, have you? I haven't seen them since the first night we arrived.'

'How blind are you?'

'I'm a bit short-sighted, everything far away is blurry.'

'Well, in that case, take a step back and I'll look even more fabulous.'

'You already look amazing, I wouldn't worry.'

The noisy birds started up and Prue looked up to see five or six black birds fly overhead.

'Do the crows always squawk so much? They woke me up this morning.'

'They're not crows, my dear, they're ravens and ravens don't squawk, they cronk. They nest on top of the trees. So, what do you think of my garden?'

'It's not really a garden, is it? It's more like Kew Gardens – I feel as if I should have to pay an entry fee. How do you do it all?'

'With increasing difficulty, my dear, and a lot of dedication. There are thousands of species now. Why, around us there's Bulley's primrose, red campion, bugle, columbine, London pride, marsh orchid, creeping velvet grass, flame azalea, bleeding heart...' She sighed and put her hands on her narrow hips. 'Come along,' she said. 'Why don't I show you around the house properly – you might stumble across those beastly glasses.'

'Be careful of the baby frogs,' said Prue.

Ronnie trudged over the twitching grass without a

second thought as Prue crept on her tiptoes trying to avoid crushing any.

The house was a rabbit warren of hallways and windowless rooms with no symmetry or rhythm. It was all wonky walls and tilting steps, covered in trailing leaves and flowers as if they were furniture. Prue's eyes began to sting and water; she sneezed more than once.

'You'll get used to it,' said Ronnie.

'Why keep so many plants in the house?' Ronnie stopped walking and Prue almost bumped into her.

'Homes are sentient beings; plants are living things and everything that is and ever was alive carries an essence, capable of bleeding one into the next. My plants are my children, and they've kept me company over the years and they're part of me, and I'm part of them. The purest beings: they only know to love and grow. Like a child, they might need a little care, but unlike human offspring, they give hope and beauty back to their mother. Human children are greedy little monsters who grow up to be greedy big monsters. I have so many children to care for now – I'll never be alone.'

'Uh-huh,' said Prue. Not knowing what to say to a woman who thought her children were plants. Was it dementia?

The kitchen had a rickety old door to a mud room, as Ronnie called it, but Prue would have called it a porch. All the doors were left unlocked, so the house was open for anyone to walk in. The room with the French doors was called the Morning Room and had a drinks cabinet that spanned a whole wall, packed full of alcohol as well as handwritten, labelled bottles, homemade wines and cordials. There was a table on wheels for making cocktails, but the chairs didn't match and came in hideous floral fabrics. It was like an old hotel bar in the Peak District whose glory days were far behind. The Morning Room was also crammed with plants like the hall and stairs.

'I married Archie's grandfather, Alastair, in 1934 when I was eighteen,' said Ronnie. 'Two years older than you are now, isn't that madness? A mere child. Robert was born the year after, and we lived here during the war. When the war was over and Alastair came back, we all lived together. Those were the best years, they really were.' The record player was still playing big band music and Ronnie sat on the arm of a sofa going misty eyed. 'It really is a vocation to keep a house like this at its best. My mother-in-law, Maud, designed the gardens, oversaw the renovations, but I've had to sell a lot of things over the years. Perhaps the plants have taken over a little, but it stops the shell looking bare. We may own land, my girl, but that doesn't translate to money the way it did years ago. I'm afraid everything's changed.'

'Why? What happened?'

'They call it progress but it's not progress to me. From the late seventies the Mainland was flooded with awful factory ships, full of Europeans, and you couldn't walk on the Mainland without hearing all these foreign languages. People would find these foreigners going through their bins, like raggedy old cats. It was the collapse of Communism, you see, and all these poor people came rushing over, as if we didn't have enough poor people of our own! Heavens! The Mainland was ruined in my opinion. Before then, things were orderly, the system worked, and people had respect. We had servants back then, but we can't afford them any more. No offence, my dear, but young people are lazy and allergic to hard work these days and they all want to be famous, don't they? We can't all be famous, no more than all of us can be rich. There will always be a hierarchy, my dear girl. These do-gooders cause chaos telling everyone we can all have what we want; life doesn't work like that. It's such a shame, we're losing our way.' Ronnie drifted off and stared out of the doors then snapped back into life again and startled Prue.

'It really was wonderful when Archie and Ruth married and came back. I wanted Archie and Ruth to have the house, legally, before I become compost, so I signed the deeds over to them; also because I refuse to pay death taxes, bloody Marxists.' Ronnie wasn't so very different from Nana after all.

The dining room had walls like marble but on inspection Prue could see they were painted with swirls and little grey rosettes to look like marble. There were big sash windows with cream drapes to the ceiling, discoloured from mould and dust. Ronnie saw Prue studying the fake marble walls.

'Do you know how much it would cost to drag real marble up here, to this island? Maud had an artist stay for months. Took the poor man hostage, but he was French and he hated it – far too cold and damp for him.'

Ronnie had such affection for the house, she saw something different when she looked at those fake walls. A misty filter of former glory, elegant parties and good manners – the best snippets of a time that likely never really was. Prue saw faded colours, like an old seaside resort with dive-bombing seagulls and broken lights on a run-down promenade with newspaper flying about. Prue felt a little sorry for Ronnie, how she'd filled the empty house with her plants, called them her children and nurtured them until they dominated everything.

Ronnie's bedroom, the white room, was the grandest, with a four-poster bed that almost touched the ceiling. There was a table of old photographs, one of a man in uniform, a dirge of browns except for the palér sepia of his face. His black hair swept into a sharp side parting like the Lego men Prue used to play with.

'That is my husband, Alastair, wasn't he a dish? What is it young girls call handsome men these days?' Prue shrugged. 'He was thirty-four when the Second World War broke out. He had all these silly romantic notions that he'd find glory in the war but there wasn't any. Men can be so stupid, don't you think?'

'I wouldn't know,' said Prue. 'Ruth must have mentioned that I don't know who my father is. My mother refuses to tell me anything about him.'

'All I know is that your mother has depression, my dear.'

'And who's this? She's beautiful, like a movie star!' Prue scooped up a photograph of a young woman, impossible to age in the way that old photographs make people look young and old at the same time. She was sat dressed in a black off the shoulder dress looking back over her shoulder towards the corner, not engaging with the camera. Her dark hair piled in curls around her head and she wore a sparkling necklace. She had a round mouth so softly curled in the most subtle smile, and an air of confidence and deliciously upturned eyes fringed with black lashes. Such a delicate beauty with her elfin chin and pert little nose, but with the haughtiest of expressions that screamed handful.

'That, my dear, is Veronique Lewthwaite MacNair in her

heyday. It's me! Wasn't I something? I had no idea at the time. Why, I must have been all of twenty in this, it was taken after we married. I had several copies made because I wanted Alastair to have one when he went away. You know, he still had it when he came back, a little worse for wear, of course. I look at this and it makes me think of what could have been if only I'd known how beautiful I was. Take it from me, Prue, by the time you realise your own worth, your stock has already plummeted.'

The empty rooms upstairs were dreary, cold and neglected and the plants hadn't made their way into them yet. Prue didn't have the same memories Ronnie held onto to infuse them with a rose-tinted filter. On the route they took in Prue's bedroom, the nursery.

'I can't think where my glasses could be unless I didn't have them at our first dinner, and put them somewhere else, but I thought I did,' said Prue.

'I'm sure they'll turn up,' said Ronnie. 'Sometimes if you look too hard for something you end up chasing it away. How are you finding the nursery?'

'I keep having the strangest dreams, really vivid. I even had a nightmare Nana crawled down the fireplace.' Prue shuddered at the thought.

'You're unsettled, and in a new place you must give yourself time. Oh, the fireplace! Remember how I said the cellarium is the oldest part of the house? Well, there are hiding holes hidden all over, and Maud tried to keep them during the renovations and there's one in this room. Allow me to educate you, my girl, witness a little bit of history.'

Ronnie got down on her knees and pulled open the chimney and had Prue look up. Inside there was a hole fifty centimetres or so up, big enough for a child to squeeze through.

'A person would crawl up and scuttle along a channel and I think it used to lead to the old roof.'

'I thought this was the new building?'

'Maud kept as much as she could. Walls. Fireplaces. Little holes. The cellarium was the most intact but the rest of the building was derelict, she tried to build around it. This was the old central wall, I believe. It's really a mongrel house, bit of this and that. Healthiest way to be, so they say! Rooms added and walls built around.' Ronnie knocked on the fireplace wall as if to reassure herself of its sturdiness.

Prue took another look up into the dark and damp cavity and wondered what kind of hell it must have been for a person to crawl into such a space. Then she heard the dripping louder than ever, the one that was tormenting her at night.

'Do you hear that?' Prue asked Ronnie. 'That dripping? There must be a leak.'

Ronnie sighed. 'Something else to add to the list, my dear. We'll block it back up and pretend we didn't notice. I'll let Archie know. I'll wait until he's in a good mood; that in itself is a rarer thing each day.'

On their way back downstairs Ronnie stopped on the landing and opened one of the wooden panels framed by wainscotting on the wall. Behind was an open void, a hollowed-out shell of cold air and dusty stone walls big enough for four or five people.

'There's stories of people starving to death in these places,' said Ronnie.

'And this adds to the charm, you say?'

Ronnie shrugged. 'It's history. It's quite desperate when you think of it, waiting in the darkest of holes. Heavens! I nearly forgot to show you the study, and that's the very last room.'

They took a loop back on themselves into a narrow hall from the kitchen to the dining room. The hall was wood panelled and painted white and there was a door on the left easily missed. Inside was a windowless study; the floor was covered with overlapping threadbare rugs with a big indent where a desk must have stood for years. Along one wall were shelves stuffed full of books and, in front of the books, vases, mason jars and jam jars all full of flowers, plants and dried grasses. Crammed among the clutter was a stuffed duck in a glass case, a model of a sailing ship in a bottle and a pile of old children's books, puffy and yellowing. A wooden tennis racket, an old Polaroid camera and a particularly lethal-looking pair of old ice skates were on the bottom. Prue picked up a bright red book, *Fifty Favourite Songs Everybody Loves to Hear!*, and scanned the list of songs it promised she and many others would appreciate. 'Mr Bojangles', 'Puff the Magic Dragon' and 'Hava Nagila'.

'Whose is this?' she asked, holding it up.

'Archie's. I bought him a guitar one birthday and he would sit in here and teach himself songs.'

'Really?' Prue screwed up her nose. This did not align with the impression of Archie she had. She assumed he'd been born thirty-five with a five o'clock shadow and a Swiss army knife.

'Archie was a very sweet boy, very quiet and shy. His father, Robert, thought him soft so to toughen him up he would wake him in the middle of the night and take him out to the woods and make him find his own way back to the house.'

'Wow, I thought my Nana was mean for threatening to hit me with a spoon.'

'I would give Archie things to sneak out there, a sleeping bag, a torch, a coat, so when the time came for his father to play his tricks again, Archie would be prepared. The next time it happened, Archie didn't come back, and Robert sat up all night waiting. In the early hours he began to really panic. He and his wife Dotty were soon out screaming for him, but Archie had already snuck inside the house – it was our little secret. His father never did it again.' Ronnie burst into hysterical laughter as Prue smiled along, but it sounded like a cruel thing to do to a little boy and these days social services wouldn't be impressed.

'Why didn't his mother stop his father from doing it?' For all her faults, her own mother would never have treated Prue like that.

'Dotty was pathetic; a twittering gerbil of a girl and certainly no match for Robert.'

Prue put the red book back. 'Why is there a bed in here?'

'Didn't I say, this used to be Archie's room. You must pay attention,' she said.

'But you said he was in the nursery.'

'At first, but his mother, Dotty, used to make such a racket with her night terrors. Up and down. Up and down. All hours. We ended up having Archie down here so he could be near me since my bedroom is also on the ground floor. Dotty was locked in the nursery at night to stop her wandering and hurting herself, or others. I used to tell Robert, *Dotty by name, Dotty by nature.*' Prue wasn't sure how to respond so turned and absent-mindedly reached out to touch a flower on the shelf.

'Don't touch that!' Ronnie flew forward and snatched the flower away and set it back on the shelf. Prue leapt out of her skin and felt her cheeks burn. 'Silly girl, you have to be careful. You must learn to be gentle with my babies.'

'I'm sorry, I didn't mean...'

'Only their mother knows how to care for them.' Ronnie smiled. 'But perhaps... perhaps it'll be you I teach one day, the way Maud taught me.' Prue fidgeted, she didn't want to learn about flowers and certainly didn't want to be shouted at.

'Where is the TV?' Prue hadn't seen it yet.

'We don't have one,' said Ronnie.

'What? How can you not have a TV!? How is that even possible?' This was by far the most bizarre discovery.

'Oh, you won't need one. Besides, they never work and there's never anything on. We haven't had one for years. You shan't miss it.'

'Er... I think I will. What am I going to do? How am I... What...' Ronnie cupped Prue's face with one of her icy cold hands.

'You will survive, my sweet.' But Prue didn't want to survive without one.

In shock at how the house managed without TV or, as had been increasingly important to her, MTV, Prue followed Ronnie back to the garden, still in her T-shirt and bare feet. Ronnie showed her where she was planning to grow pumpkins, marrows and kale and had woven baskets full of soil and seedlings ready to make hanging baskets to be hung up at the back of the house.

'No point out the front, the air is too harsh,' she explained. 'Maud taught me what to grow – Peruvian lilies, wandering sailors, Australian daisies... It's not what can grow in the summer but what can survive an island winter.'

'What's in the greenhouse?' Prue had seen the high point of a big greenhouse at the back of the garden.

'Maud travelled – Africa, India, Central America. She brought back seeds and specimens. I'm sure it's illegal but the law never bothered a pioneer. Now, you see the trees?' she said, pointing ahead. 'It's the only densely wooded area on the island. People think the lack of trees is because of the weather but that's not true. There were plenty of trees and shrubs, but settlers cleared them for agriculture, firewood and sheep. Philistines. The walls around the garden are to stop the sheep because they'll eat everything, but the walls don't keep everything out.'

'Birds?'

'Yes, birds, and there's a dog that's been digging its way in under the gate at the back. It digs holes, steals my bulbs, takes a huge shit wherever it fancies. If I see the bastard, I'll shoot it.' Prue had to assume she was joking. 'Prue, you can be my little helper. Lord knows I could do with someone with cartilage in their knees – I'm seventy-eight this year.'

'I know, and yes, you look amazing.'

'I make my own toiletries, you know, none of that toxic, processed mass-produced rubbish.'

'You make it all yourself?'

'Absolutely – do you think I'd have skin like this using Oil of Ulay? It's taken me years to get everything working. It's one of life's cruel tricks that just when you feel like you're getting on top of things, your body starts to crumble.

I might not have my beauty but at least I have my garden. You can get all the salt- and wind-proof plants you like but the soil here is peat bog, not sand, and I've killed a lot of lavender over the years. I've improved the drainage and soil with sand and seaweed, and I use lime for the hellebores. You hang around, my girl – I'll put those knees to use.'

'What about the trees? Am I allowed out there?'

Ronnie laughed again. 'What a funny question! Of course you are. This is Anderson land and we own most of this island, my dear.'

'Ruth said there was a shop in the village centre. I thought I might go and find it, you know, look around a bit.'

'Then take a straight path through the trees,' she said. 'There's not much there, my dear, I don't want you to think there's a thriving metropolis waiting to be discovered.'

'I need to start finding my own way around if I'm going to be here all summer, and I want to start running again.'

'That explains the legs. If you don't want to go through the trees, you could always follow the shoreline, but I'm afraid they are both uphill. If you do go through the trees, when you come to the dying American larch take a right and follow that path. You'll find a metal gate at the end of the garden in the stone wall. You can't get lost, but it can be a little disorienting,' she smiled. 'Pick a direction and see it through. The worst thing you can do is come down with self-doubt – *that's* how you get lost.'

6

Prue made her way to the back of the garden, keeping to the pathway lined by the big buttercups as instructed. She reached the metal gate but not before she passed the large greenhouse, ornate and painted white, like a grand old Victorian conservatory.

At the metal gate she saw the trench the dog had dug to get into the garden and on the other side were the woods, a step further into the wild. Little purple bluebells gave the ground a violet haze, and Prue continued until the trees began to thicken and it became quite dark. The path then forked, but Prue had no idea if the fallen tree in front of her was a larch, but assumed it was and went right.

She followed the path up to the stone wall and found a stile and climbed over; on the other side was an open field. The sky was full of clouds moving fast, in the same direction she had yet to walk. Prue couldn't wait to be able to drive – a moped if necessary. She had tried to talk to her mother a few months ago and she'd scoffed at the idea, naming the cost as the barrier but wouldn't let Prue get a job. She said it was too dangerous to work in the evening and come home in the dark, and most Saturday jobs in retail wanted shifts on a Sunday and Thursday night. It wasn't fair; Prue wasn't asking for handouts, only the opportunity to make the money herself but she was being held back and couldn't understand why. For years it had been only the three of them, Nana, her mother and Prue. Suffocatingly close, but never affectionate. They never hugged or kissed. The MacArthurs didn't do that sort of thing. They may bicker with passion and find affection in heated debates, but they never, ever touched. It wasn't until Prue was twelve that they moved out of Nana's into the flat above the shop.

Something growled behind her as she was climbing over the stile. She could see the top of its ears through the trees and could make out a giant head. It had to be the dog Ronnie had talked about. It growled again, and her knees started to shake, then it sprinted off, and Prue exhaled like a burst balloon. Ronnie had told her the dog was a demon, but hadn't mentioned it was the size of a wolf.

At the top of the hill, she saw the big white building with the blinking yellow lights she'd seen the first night from the window. Prue made her way up onto the road with thighs on fire and in every direction was a wide expanse of desolate openness. There was something so unnerving about all this silence, like being stuck in a perennial calm before the storm. Prue followed the road and met a white donkey. It approached and rested its chin on the fence, expecting food, but it would have to make do with a wary stroke on the nose accompanied by some squealing. Prue had never met a donkey before and was scared it might bite.

The village centre, if it could be called the centre of anything, was a ghost town of dreary pebble-dashed buildings and corrugated steel sheds by the water. It had a sloping edge where boats could be taken in and out of the water and concrete steps covered in slimy green moss. The pier was littered with discarded crabs' legs and up ahead in the distance there was a cluster of buildings on another hill a good hike away. There was no pastel bunting here, only the wind whistling through carrying an ache, as if it was yearning for something to wrap itself around.

The only village shop was a wooden building, painted white, with big red gas canisters stacked outside. Prue paced up and down and then back again for a good ten minutes, building up the courage to go inside. She was determined to make full use of this freedom and do things for herself. She had made it to Scotland, and then Shetland and then Noost; she could bloody well walk into a shop. She pushed open the door but one of those god-awful bells rang, *ting-a-ling*, and she sank down inside her jumper for fear of everyone looking at her, but the shop seemed to be nearly empty. There were only two people inside and it appeared as if they were arguing.

'I'm only wanting the wan,' said a woman in a long green coat with straggly grey hair. She had skinny white legs and wore sandals. For a second, Prue thought of the white-skinned leg from the other night. Her mind, and her eyes, were playing tricks on her. She needed to find her glasses.

'I'm no selling to you. I've been telt not to. I'm no being

the wan to give it to you.' The cashier was having none of the woman's bargaining.

'Wha telt you?! Please, I'm having a bad day o it. I need wan drink and den I'll be off it again. I'm better than I was. Just give me one of the peerie ones.'

'I'm sorry, Gladys. No.' Their accents were different to the Scottish Prue had encountered before, but as Ronnie had told her, this wasn't Scotland.

Prue tried her best to browse and went to push her glasses up her nose out of habit but poked herself in the eye. She thought she could hear someone else behind the shelves she was browsing, but she couldn't see. She wanted to leave but felt compelled to purchase something so grabbed a packet of tampons and made strides towards the till, hoping they'd stop bickering to serve her.

'Gladys, I hae a customer,' said the cashier, ushering Prue forward. As soon as she put the tampons on the counter, she wished she had picked something else.

The cashier had a crispy fringe and kept looking at Prue and handled everything at a glacial pace.

'I dunna recognise you, you visiting someone?'

'Erm, yes. I'm staying with my aunt and uncle.'

'Oh, lovely. Wha's your aunt?'

'Er... Ruth.'

'Ruth?' The cashier stopped handling the easiest transaction in the world and put all her resources into thinking who this Ruth could be. The old woman who wanted a bottle stared at Prue; she could feel her eyes burning the skin of her cheek but she dared not look.

'Ruth Anderson. Their house is Dynrost, the one by the woods.'

The cashier's mouth opened and she stared bug-eyed at Prue and then nervously glanced towards the woman by the side of the counter. It was as if she had dropped a curse into the conversation.

'I dunna ken your aunt,' said the cashier. 'But welcome to Noost!' she added, bursting into a forced veneer of customer service. Prue paid and had one hand on the tampons.

'Aren't you a peerie bit young?' The woman in the green coat stepped towards her with an elbow on the counter. 'To be one of his lasses, dat is?'

Prue could smell her, unwashed. She didn't know what she was referring to then remembered the models.

'Oh, I'm not a model. I'm staying with my aunt.'

'Well, I hope you have a lovely stay with your aunt Ruth,' said the cashier, who snatched the tampons out of Prue's grasp and put them in a striped plastic bag that she didn't ask for or want or need.

As she handed them over, the smelly woman took a step closer, until she was inches from Prue's face.

'And your folk don't mind you being at dat hoose with him?'

'My mum is in hospital – I have to.'

'I'm sorry aboot dat,' said the woman. 'I hope she gets better. My peerie girl never came home.'

Prue wanted to ask what she meant but she didn't dare. She took the striped bag and walked strides towards the door.

'Do da corbies still gather?' said the woman. Prue stopped and turned back.

'I'm sorry, the what?'

'Gladys, please, leave da lass alone, she might no ken,'

whispered the cashier. What did that mean? Most of the words were the same but the odd one was different; Prue wasn't sure she understood what was going on.

'I said,' the strange woman said louder, 'do da corbies still hang aboot the hoose?' Then she pushed off the counter with an elbow and limped towards Prue with a long wooden stick. She kept walking until Prue stumbled backwards into the door and dropped the striped bag.

'Gladys! Stop!' the cashier shouted.

'What's going on? Cheryl!?' a man shouted from somewhere in the shop.

Prue was pinned against the door as the woman pointed a finger in her face. 'You tell da bastard, corbies ken da truth.'

Prue fumbled for the door and squeezed herself out, leaving the woman in the doorway.

'Go you!' the woman shouted. 'Be careful! I'm betting you're his type!'

Prue ran and didn't stop and wouldn't have done, even if she had heard the man behind calling out for her to stop.

7

Shaken by whatever had happened the first time she left the house in this alien place, Prue rushed up to Ruth's studio and banged on the door. There was no answer, so she opened it.

'Ruth?' Still no answer. Prue felt as if she might not be allowed inside although no one had told her she couldn't, so she slipped through the door.

The horse's gas mask with its googly eyes stared her down. How edgy Ruth had seemed when Prue had been looking at her paintings and how she had fidgeted, but that wasn't the only thing that struck her as odd. It was the paintings themselves that bothered her. The blackened woods called *The Grieving Mother*. Well, *which* grieving mother inspired it? The women swung around by their tongues, *The Three Witches*, Nana had called them that, and *St Lucy* holding the tray with her own eyes with Nana's teapot and sugar cubes. Nana always insisted on sugar cubes. They used to laugh about it. How could Ruth not remember? But why lie?

Prue came to a painting of a man stood over a square hole and below this was another man looking down through the same square hole. This image repeated until the one at the bottom was a little stick man. It was called *The Square*. The next was *To the Host*, and was of a woman's face staring straight ahead but her eyes were dragged downwards, as if someone had put a finger in the bottom eyelids and pulled. Her belly had been scooped out and inside was a pile of bones. But it was the next painting that startled Prue because she distinctly remembered the scene when it had happened. It was of a little girl in front of a tank of exotic fish with the shadow of a man the other side of the tank staring at her.

Her mother had taken her to the aquarium at London Zoo once. It was a stark memory because she had wandered off in the dark and lost her mother. It was too specific not to be a reference to that. Ruth had somehow heard and remembered the aquarium but not Nana's infamously hideous teapot. Prue snuck back out, but as she closed the door, Ronnie was standing behind it.

'Jesus!' Prue clutched her heart.

'He won't answer.'

'Pardon?'

'Jesus, he has a habit of not returning calls. Anyway, I saw you come back. You seemed a little flustered – did something happen?' Ronnie studied her, seemingly looking around the edges of her ears for something that might appear.

'No, I'm fine, I was looking for Ruth.'

'Hmmm. Why don't you let me fix you a drink? To steady the nerves or soften the edges, whatever works for you.'

'Isn't it a bit early, what time is it?'

'It's well past midday, if that's what you're worried about.'

'I'm sixteen, I don't worry about drinking at all.'

'Perhaps that's where we're going wrong, my dear.' Ronnie adopted a pout belonging to a sullen child. 'Ronnie is lonely, won't you come and play?'

'All right, but only if you promise never to speak about yourself in the third person again. It's as if your evil twin might appear.'

'Who said she's the evil one? You young people do get awfully worked up about the most trivial of matters. Very well, come along, to the Morning Room! Follow me. It's like an adventure through the eyes of alcohol. It's going to be marvellous.' With that, Ronnie took Prue's arm in hers and led her downstairs.

Prue sat on a sofa in the Morning Room, as Ronnie mixed up one of her special cocktails.

'If it were up to me, day drinking would be mandatory; it can make even the dullest people bearable,' said Ronnie. 'Most people are at their best when slightly lubricated. Not drunk, drunks are hideously vulgar, but when the world takes on that orange glow and you can sense the angels coming.'

On the coffee table was a collection of birds' nests with unhatched eggs. Nana once told her she had a great-aunt who lost her mind during the war and started making things out of her own hair and twigs, and she wondered if collecting dead birds' eggs was the same sort of thing. Ronnie chopped frozen coriander with a herb knife and sprinkled it in her drink. Prue hated coriander.

'It really is rather wonderful having you here, Pru-Pru. I love to cook and create new recipes and cocktails, and what with Archie rarely around and Ruth being a fussy eater of late, it's really rather good timing. You can be my little guinea pig. I for one am rather excited. Now here, bottoms up.' Ronnie handed Prue her drink and she tentatively sipped it.

'I didn't know Ruth was a fussy eater.'

'She's been a little under the weather. Does tend to put herself under an awful lot of pressure that one.'

'I'm not sure I'm the best person for your recipes.'

'Oh, but why not?'

'I'm actually a vegetarian – well, I was.'

Ronnie's head tilted. 'But what about dinner the first night? Ruth had me cook a peasant's dish – spaghetti Bolognese – and you ate it.'

'I know, and I threw up. I hadn't eaten meat in years. I guess my stomach didn't like it.'

'Good heavens, girl! Why didn't you say? You MacArthurs are a funny breed, aren't you? I disagree: vegetarianism could be quite exciting, a new string to my bow. I have the garden for it and you should see my greenhouse. Vegetarianism it is!' said Ronnie, and she held her drink up until Prue clinked glasses.

Prue sipped out of good manners but it tasted foul and she had to spit the coriander leaves back into the glass when Ronnie wasn't looking, and the taste made her gag.

'You don't like coriander, do you?' Ronnie soon asked.

'Not really, no.'

'Well, why didn't you say? You silly girl. Here, give me that, let me get you another.'

'Oh, no, it's fine,' Prue insisted.

'You know that's a genetic trait, don't you?'

'No, I didn't. My mum likes it so does that mean I inherited it from my dad?'

'Possibly,' said Ronnie, who pushed the coriander reassuringly to one side and poured Prue another drink.

It seemed completely irrelevant but this could be the first real fact she'd learned about the man.

'What's in this?' asked Prue as she sipped her new drink.

'Wildflowers, tormentil and lousewort and a whole lot of gin. Prettier than they sound. Tormentil tea can be boiled up and used for toothaches and headaches. Children used to suck on the stems of lousewort and call them honey-sookies.'

Prue felt herself loosen after a few sips. A relief after feeling so tightly wound. She even told Ronnie about the smelly woman in the shop but stopped short of repeating what the woman said, the *bastard* surely only being Archie.

'You probably think I'm being oversensitive,' said Prue.

'Never let someone call you oversensitive. When people say that it means they're trying to make you feel less than they are. The truth is, whatever is important to you simply isn't important to them.'

'I never thought about it like that.'

'Well, you should. Do you think you might be an empath, my dear?'

'I think I know what empathy is but—'

'No, an empath, it's different. Being an empath is the ability to absorb what others are feeling; it can be overwhelming. Sometimes all those feelings can overwhelm a person and drown out their own, but if you harness it properly it could be a real gift.'

'Oh, I don't know about that.'

'I myself am a floral empath. I can sense what plants need and communicate with my children on an intimate level. There are different empaths. Some are connected to animals; some absorb feelings from objects or belongings; and some can even touch the earth and sense a disaster coming. Anyway, the islanders – ignore them! They are idiots – uneducated people. Trust me, you won't find any empaths there! All they have is local gossip and empty lives full of gutting fish and complaining about how many jobs they have.'

Prue giggled. 'Ronnie, I can't help but think of you here all alone for so many years – how did you do it?'

'I was never alone, my dear, I have my children, although I suppose it has got a little out of hand. I can't ever leave this house, Prue. I'll never sell, and I'll never go willingly. The only way I'm going out of here is in a box. It can't fall into the hands of strangers, or *silver-tongued capitalists who sell the rope that communists would use to hang them*.'

'Someone famous said that, didn't they?'

'Lenin.'

'Who is he?'

'Good Lord! Did you go to school at all?'

'Yes! I'm top of my year in most subjects.'

'Then as a nation we are doomed. Look, don't let the islanders bother you, they're superstitious and have never liked us because we are private people. They simply don't understand the kind of quiet dignity we value. It's a cultural difference, that's all.'

There were more family photographs on the mantelpiece,

but Prue noted she hadn't seen a picture of one particular person.

'Is there a picture of Dotty here?'

'Oh, *her*... I didn't keep any.' That struck Prue as odd, not even one picture of Archie's mother, if only for him.

'Can I ask what happened to her?'

'Of course, my dear, she threw herself out of a window,' said Ronnie as if she was casually mentioning it was raining. 'Cracked her head open on the patio.' Ronnie waved towards the steps outside the French doors.

'Her bedroom window... The nursery? But that's the room I'm sleeping in.'

'Ah, so it is, but don't go telling Ruth I told you.' As if by cue the door opened and Ruth's head appeared.

'Did I hear my name?'

'No, my dear,' said Ronnie. She winked and Prue stifled a smile, then found her eyes drawn back to the steps where she imagined a head smashed open like a watermelon, and the smile left.

Ruth entered brandishing a striped plastic bag. 'I believe you left these behind, Prue? Dropped off by a very polite young man. His mother runs the hotel.'

'Hotel!' scoffed Ronnie. 'Is that what they're calling it now?'

'All right, it's a pub with some rooms – a B&B.'

'That no one stays at,' said Ronnie.

'Anyway,' said Ruth. 'This young man was charming and about your age, maybe a little older.'

'God, how embarrassing,' Prue cringed.

'He was in the village shop when you dropped your bag, said you'd told the girl at the till where you were staying and so he offered to drop it off. He was at the door for ages, bless him. He was charming, not like most young men who won't make eye contact, and he's only just left. We had a lovely conversation – you should go and thank him. I thought it was very sweet for him to bring your... things over. Chivalrous even.' Ruth shook the bag and threw it at her.

'It's mortifying,' said Prue, catching the bag. 'He *must* have looked inside,' she huffed. 'I'll go tomorrow, when the pain is less raw.'

That night Prue went to bed anxious about sleeping. She tried to tell herself she was overthinking the very concept of sleep, and if she could only switch off her racing mind, then it would come. It didn't work; she could only focus on the wind howling and rattling the windows loose in their frames as her mind whirred with the word *bastard*. And what were corbies? She also couldn't shake off the weird feelings she'd had about Ruth's paintings. At every noise she sat up to check the fireplace, imagined some poor soul shivering inside the cavity or her grandmother's cupped nails tapping on the hearth. Then there was Dotty. What on earth could have made Archie's mother throw herself out of a window? The infernal drip on the inside of the walls reminded her of the hours passing and she was awake for every single one of them. She finally drifted off but the creak of floorboards woke her again. Someone was on the landing, most likely Ruth, as it was too light-footed to be Archie. Prue rolled over and went back to sleep.

The bathroom light had been left on, but it was a near certainty it would turn itself off, so when she woke up in the dark, she didn't think much of it. The wardrobe doors had popped open but that didn't scare her either. However, this time she was unnerved by her bedroom door being wide open. She got out of bed to close it and rattled it to make sure the latch had caught and slammed the wardrobe doors shut. Poor old Dotty was likely driven insane by the dripping, doors popping open and bad electrics and simply had enough one day. At this rate Prue didn't blame her, but when she climbed back into bed, she caught a whiff of something, unclean, fuggy, like unwashed clothes. The moonlight from behind the curtains shone into the room and there was a new silhouette in front of them. Her heart began to thump, setting off alarms along her nerves. The shape was where the square back of the chair should be. She reached out to touch it, but her hand touched rough material covering something hard. Then came the stale smell again and the woman from the shop leaned forward, bringing her face into a slither of light.

'Shush!' she said, with a finger over her lips.

Prue tried to scream but had no voice. She fell out of the bed, onto the floor, scrambled up and ran for the door, hands like jelly fumbling for the handle. She tore it open, finding her voice and, screaming, ran towards Ruth's bedroom along the landing. As Ruth opened the door Prue fell into her, almost knocking her over.

'What's the matter!?' said Ruth, pulling her upright. Prue pointed back towards her room, her whole arm shaking.

'There's a woman... a woman!' Archie flew out from behind Ruth and ran to Prue's bedroom. Ruth pulled Prue inside and slammed the door and they sat huddled together on the bed. Ruth was quiet and still as Prue trembled in her arms.

'Why aren't you calling the police?' Prue whispered.

'There aren't any police on the island. Archie will handle it.'

After what seemed like hours Ronnie opened the door with a perfect hostess smile, wearing her silk turban and her dressing gown.

'Good evening,' she said. 'Guests will be relieved to learn that normal service has been resumed. Perhaps a drink to settle the nerves?'

They sat in the kitchen with Prue trying to force down brandy to dampen the adrenaline surging through her.

'I'm sorry you had such a fright,' said Ruth. 'I'm afraid that woman... She's done this sort of thing before, hasn't she, Ronnie? Although she's never actually wandered into the house.'

'Oh yes, she has,' said Ronnie. 'Years and years ago, but most of the time she loiters in the trees, although we have found her in the garden before. She's harmless, bloody annoying but harmless – she's a drinker,' she said by way of explanation, which Prue thought ironic considering how much everyone in the house seemed to drink.

'I saw her today, in the village,' she confessed.

'You never said,' said Ruth.

'It didn't seem relevant.'

'What did she say?' asked Ruth, snappy and upright, like she was in the car ride when Prue had mentioned Joan Gardner.

'I don't know,' she lied. 'I couldn't understand her.' There were two pairs of eyes on her now and she felt as if she was the one accused of something. 'She's mad, like you said.'

'Madness is a terrible curse,' said Ronnie, shaking her head.

'I thought she was an alcoholic?' said Prue.

'They're not mutually exclusive,' snapped Ruth. 'Are you sure she didn't say anything that you remember?'

'No, nothing.'

'Come on, drink up.' Prue stared down at the brown liquid. She knocked it back in one, even though it was disgusting. She hated that bedroom, even if it did have a roll-top bath.

8

Ruth described the boy from the hotel as tall and slim with reddish brown hair. The next day when she dragged herself over to the hotel and saw the lanky octopus with pint glasses for fingers, she knew it was him – and he was ginger. He wore a white shirt and blue jeans. The white jarred with the paleness of his complexion and made him look ill. Only tanned people should wear white, or anyone other than people as pale as her, and, it would seem, this boy. He smirked as soon as he saw her so he must have looked inside the bag. She wanted to die – she could have picked up anything. Literally anything.

'Hi,' he said. 'Your aunt said she would have you come over, but honestly, you didn't have to.'

'Well, I'm here now, so thanks.' She felt herself going red for no reason. All she'd done was speak a few words and her skin was on fire. Her hands were claws on the inside of her sleeves and her shoulders up by her ears. 'I'm Prue, by the way,' she said, and waved at him. He was standing a metre away and she waved. God, she hated herself.

'I'm James,' he said, not waving, like a normal person. He dumped the dirty pint glasses on the bar, wiped his hands on his jeans and held out a hand for her to shake. She looked at it as if it was a poisonous viper, but shook it because good manners dictated she must. It was sticky, as she feared it would be. 'Nice to meet you, Prue. Would you like a drink? On the house, of course. I can offer you soda or a lime cordial if it's the taste of excitement you're after?'

'Lime cordial, please.' Prue didn't want a drink, but she had already played out the awkward scenario of trying to refuse one and him insisting over and over until she gave in. She took the short cut to the same result, and a seat at the bar, and wondered how long she had to stay before leaving.

The bar was dingy with low timber-beamed ceilings, open brickwork and a roaring fire that made Prue sleepy simply by looking at it. A dog lay on its side and two old men had pinned themselves to separate corners with their backs to the wall. One coughed phlegm into a handkerchief and both slurped cloudy ales. The carpet had dark swirls and the air was thick with several life cycles of smoke and sticky beer. James set a tepid green drink down on the bar in front of Prue. An old lady either blind or transfixed by the swirly carpet was the only other person in the bar.

As she reached out for her glass the sound of a scuffle broke out. Prue followed James around the corner into a room under an archway with a pool table and dartboard. A man with blond dreads was trying to fend off the barmaid who was swinging at him with arms like raw sausages. It was a messy scrabble until one of her powerful arms connected with the man's face and made a terrific slap. This drew intakes of breath from the two old men, clearly familiar with the sting of a woman's hand.

'Stupid bitch!' The man leapt back with a hand to his cheek.

'Fuck off!' The barmaid swung for him again, but he bent out of reach. The barmaid stomped off leaving the man behind. He inhaled hard with his eyes closed, exhaled and then puffed his chest up and turned to face the measly audience with open arms. It was as if he was about to perform a Shakespearean monologue.

'I guess I'll be fucking off then,' he said, and took a theatrical bow. That seemed to be the cue for the bar to return to staring at the carpet, including Prue and James who slunk back to the spot marked by the green drink.

'Welcome to Noost,' James leaned over the bar and whispered. 'As you can see, we have a wide range of biodiversity on the island.' Prue smiled and played with the straw in her drink. When she had drunk a third of it, she would leave. She kept one eye on the man because he seemed volatile, like someone who should always have an eye on them, especially around unattended handbags.

He was dishevelled; baggy jeans, grungy clothes and dark stubble on an unshaven face with the, unacceptable at any time, blond dreads. He was mid-twenties with a pretty boy face and was clearly bad news. This meant it was impossible for Prue not to find him intriguing, even if she knew this to be unwise. She tried to be discreet as she checked him out but when he slammed his empty pint glass down on the bar, they locked eyes and she cursed herself. She was forever getting caught staring at people like a pervert. He flashed an impish, slightly wonky grin, which only made him seem more attractive somehow, and walked by Prue far too close to not be on purpose and took a very unsubtle look at her tits. Prue even looked down at them herself, trying to understand what he could have seen since there was barely anything there.

'Sorry about that, sweetheart, I'm actually a really nice guy,' he said. He backed out of the door giving Prue the wink and the gun and made a clicking noise with his mouth and said, 'Don't go changing.' Prue didn't know where to look.

James rolled his eyes. 'You know those older kids you look up to – the cool kids?'

She nodded.

'Well, that's Charlie O'Hara,' he said with a tilt of the head at the now empty doorway. 'He's at least twenty-six now, bit of a record, delivers animal feed for a living, among other things. Him and his cousin come in to pester the barmaids. My mum used to bring us to Noost to see my grandparents every summer and I feel as if I've personally witnessed Charlie's decline each passing year. It's sad really, he's a lesson to us all – don't peak too early.'

'Peaking at all would be good,' said Prue.

'Do you fancy a walk?' he said, and her heart sank; there would be no quick exit now. She'd forced down nearly a third of the drink and would no doubt need a wee during the walk and be too awkward to mention this and hang on and be forced to pee behind a tree on her way home.

'That'd be great,' she said.

They took a walk downhill to the village centre Prue had discovered the day before and walked along the shoreline past the war memorial with the wind tearing at them, throwing water like grit at their faces. They ambled like two pensioners resolved to enjoy a walk outside despite the weather making it deeply unpleasant.

'Thanks for bringing me my er... things,' she said.

'You're welcome,' James laughed. 'I wouldn't want you being caught short. I feel like I should be apologising on behalf of old Gladys. I can't imagine what you were thinking. I felt bad for not getting involved but I didn't think it would get hostile like that. Everyone is really friendly here, very welcoming. You got the wrong impression, really you did.'

Prue looked around. Who was everyone? There was barely anyone there.

'Where are you from?' he asked.

'Croydon, it's outside London. Basically, still London but shitter.'

'I'm from Aberdeen – sounds a bit like Croydon in places but it's pretty in some. I'm going to give you a few pointers. This place doesn't run to the same time we're both from. It's not 1993 here, it's somewhere else.'

'You're going to have to explain.'

'My mum is an islander, and when my parents divorced she decided to come back and bought the B&B. She has this crazy idea of turning it into a hotel and bringing tourists over, and she's opened a camping bod.'

'What's a camping bod?'

'It's a place where hikers and campers can rent a bed for the night. Do you know where the old ruins are?'

'No, I don't know anywhere. Yesterday at the shop was the first time I'd ventured out of the house.'

'I'll show you. No one has rented a bed yet, but she's determined it will come. I'm only helping for the summer before I go to university in Aberdeen. The islanders really are welcoming people, but the older generation can be wary. They love their culture and heritage and feel like people are always trying to bring too much change. They want people to come and move here, they do, but they want folk who appreciate Noost for what it is, instead of soothmoothers trying to tarmac it over, and charging people to use it.'

'What's a soothmoother?'

'People who come in on the ferry in Lerwick. We're soothmoothers, neither of us come from the islands. Most young people born on Noost move to the Mainland because there's not much work. All that's left behind are the old, the poor or the bewildered, and if my mother has her way, the odd camper and travelling crusty.'

'So that woman, which is she? Old, poor or bewildered?'

'Poor Gladys is all three.'

They stumbled into a group of loose sheep, heads down, grazing. As they got closer each one stopped and stared and until that moment Prue hadn't realised she was frightened of sheep and found herself clinging onto James's sleeve.

'Why are they staring at us?'

'Because they're nervous, they're *sheep*.'

'They won't charge at us?'

He burst out laughing. 'Not comfortable with the whole outdoors thing, are you?'

'Er... no, no, I'm not,' Prue said, shuffling behind, using James as a human shield.

She pushed them both past the sheep and then let go of his sleeve. They walked to the edge of the concrete pier with its metal fence and double yellow lines, waddling along kicking bits of dead crab into the water.

'Gladys is harmless but there's history there,' James said.

'Last night, Gladys walked into our house and I woke up to find her at the end of my bed,' replied Prue.

James stopped kicking. 'No way! Shit! That must have been terrifying. She's scary enough to look at during daylight.'

'You think? They said she's done it before but not for years. Yesterday, she was saying things. So... if you were there – did you hear her and do you know what she was talking about?'

James stared at the ground and kicked another crab's leg into the water. 'Corbies are another name for ravens. There's an old myth that ravens gather where dead bodies are hidden – it's an old wives' tale.'

'Never heard that one.'

'Ravens are scavengers, like vultures, so they'll hang about where they think there's something worth picking off, so there is logic to it, but it's only a myth.'

'I take it you are a birdwatcher?'

'Not really,' he said. 'I like birds, but I like all animals, Prue from Croydon. I'm guessing Prue is short for...?'

'Prudence,' she said, rolling her eyes. She hated her name and cringed whenever she had to say it. 'My grandmother named me after her grandmother.'

'School was pleasant?'

'It didn't help. She said it was a family tradition, although if she thinks I'm ever calling a baby Sybil...'

'If it makes you feel better, I spent two years wearing an orthopaedic shoe at a boys' school – good times. How come you're here anyway? Unless *you* like birds?'

Prue wanted to explain but worried about oversharing. She never knew where the appropriate lines should be drawn, and this was why Nana had always told her to say nothing.

'My mother is in hospital,' she said, staring at the ground, looking to find more dead things to kick.

'Oh, sorry.'

'No, it's fine, she's not sick or anything. Not like that. She has depression and she tried to kill herself but she's OK, and she's tried before. My grandmother died a few months ago and they were really close, and I don't know my dad so I can't stay with him. So, that's why I'm on Noost, staying with my aunt and uncle,' she shrugged.

They stood on the concrete, not moving even though it had started to spit and threatened to rain. Prue didn't know what to say and, going by his expression, neither did he. She should have kept her mouth shut.

'Don't I feel like the arsehole for asking.'

'No, honestly, it's fine! I was worried I'd said too much, and you would think I was weird.'

'No, I don't think you're weird. What were we talking about?'

The panicked little voices began to crawl back down the holes from where they came, and Prue felt a wave of relief.

'The woman,' said Prue. 'Ravens, corbies and the history, and you were going to tell me about it.'

'Ah, was I?' James bit his lip and squinted at the horizon. 'So, how close are you to your uncle?'

'I barely know the man. I've met him three times in my whole life, and then my aunt drags me up here to stay. I've been here days and I've seen him through a window, once.'

'If I tell you, you have to swear not to tell anyone it was me. Especially your uncle.'

'I promise.' She crossed her heart for some reason, not that she was religious, but it seemed the right thing to do.

'Also,' he sighed, 'I can't help but feel personally responsible for you having at least some fun on the island, so you have to let me show you around a bit. It can be beautiful, but you have to know where to look.'

'You don't think I'm crazy after what I told you?'

'I'm studying Psychology at university so you'll make a good case study – nah, I'm kidding, but I am extremely bored.'

'Oh, I get it, you're a funny boy.'

'Come on, Prudence, I have to compensate for being ginger, although it doesn't look as if you escaped the gene yourself. You're darker, I'll give you that, but definitely a carrier.'

'Fine. You can... show me the island and force me to have fun.' They shook hands.

'Great. Let's go back inside. I have no idea why we're trying to walk through this weather when there is a perfectly good bar my mother owns that way,' and he strode off with his long loping legs.

'Hang on! This was your idea!' she shouted.

They took a table at the back near one of the old men whose head kept falling forwards as he nodded off; he jolted himself awake every time and startled the ancient collie at his feet.

'Do you want to ask, or shall I tell?' said James.

'Tell and I'll interrupt and ask questions.'

'Oh-kay, because that doesn't sound annoying at all.'

'Go on.'

'There was a girl called Evelyn O'Hara who was only seventeen at the time, and your uncle was the same age. They were together, dating, you know, boyfriend and girlfriend. That was a bit weird in itself because the Andersons... they're not known to fraternise with us mere mortals. One day Evie tells her mother she's off to see her boyfriend, Archie Anderson. She leaves and disappears, and has been missing ever since.'

'That's it? And so what? People think my uncle did something?'

'There's rumours, that's all I'm saying. That woman you bumped into yesterday, that was Gladys O'Hara, Evie's mother.'

'Oh! So that's why it went weird when I said I was staying at Dynrost? But surely anyone could have done it. Why is she so sure it was him?'

'The police investigated but the Andersons said Evie never made it to the house. Your uncle was never charged with anything, no one was.'

'Gladys thinks he killed her, and the ravens still gather at the house... so she thinks Evie's body is there?'

'Shhhh,' said James, looking around and leaning in. 'It didn't help much that not long after she disappeared Archie joined the army and the police let him go, despite Evie not being found. People thought it was the old Andersons getting away with everything as usual. Money talks – that sort of thing. All these years pass and then out of the blue your uncle comes back, married. Some people took it as a kick in the slabs, especially Gladys.'

'Why hasn't Ruth told me any of this?'

'I can't answer that, I'm afraid. Maybe she didn't want to lend it any credibility or freak you out. Maybe she didn't want you worrying your uncle might be a murderer.'

'All they told me was she was an alcoholic and that she wandered into the house and loitered in the garden. He *can't* be guilty.'

'He's not: innocent until proven guilty, and the police didn't find anything – the poor girl quite literally disappeared. Still, a lot of islanders believe the rumours and I guess Gladys wants to keep them alive. Oh, also, Charlie, the guy from earlier who peaked too soon? That's Evie O'Hara's younger brother.'

'You're kidding! Is anyone not related to this girl?'

'Pretty sure I'm not.'

Prue sat open-mouthed trying to process it all when a beaming middle-aged woman with sequins on her jumper approached the table, and slapped James hard on the shoulder.

'James, aren't you going to introduce me to your new pal?'

'This is Prue, Prue, this is Mrs Sparkle – my mother, or as she's locally known, the Tyrant.'

'Welcome, and lovely to meet you, Prue, I'm Sharon.'

'Mum,' said James, 'Prue had a bit of a run-in with Gladys yesterday, and Charlie was here earlier – I was explaining about Evie O'Hara.'

'So awful,' said Sharon, tutting and shaking her head; she had one hand on her hip and the other still on James's shoulder as if he was keeping her upright. 'Dat poor wife, Evie going missing broke her but the whole island was devastated, and the Andersons... they didn't help matters...' Prue could feel James cringing as his mother carried on with more tutting and head shaking.

'Surely there were other suspects?' asked Prue.

Sharon gawped at Prue and even the two old men and old lady looked at her now, eavesdropping on the conversation.

'No,' said Sharon. 'No islander would do such a thing.'

Prue made a mental note never to propose such a possibility in front of people ever again. 'But what about a stranger? Or someone travelling through...'

'No one travels through here, no back den,' said Sharon.

'Not now either,' said James.

'Wheesht!' Sharon slapped James around the head as he took a sip of his drink. He put his glass down and glared as if his mother was already grinding his gears. Sharon pulled a chair up and sat down.

'The thing is, Evie wasn't the first to go missing fae dat hoose.'

'Oh, here we go,' said James. 'I hope you like folklore, Prue. Mum, I should probably explain who—'

'There's always been rumours about Dynrost. Number one – the Andersons never mix, and see themselves as better than wis, you ken, typical laird, born to rule types.'

'What's dat you said?' The old man who had been dribbling into his pint chimed in. 'Andersons? It was the last woman, she started it. Da last one, no this one, da wan who shot at da sheep.' Prue recalled that Ronnie told her

98

how Maud would shoot at sheep to keep them out of the garden before the wall was up.

'Is that right?' said James. 'Anyway, as I was about to say—'

But the old man went on, 'Back in the late 1800s, my grandfaither telt me a story aboot how it took three years for da wark to be done in dat hoose.' The man held up three fingers. The two other islanders grumbled along and bobbed heads in agreement. 'They had twelve men go in but three years later only ten came out. Twa went missing.'

The old woman joined in. 'My midder telt me a spirit of a woman could be heard laughing in the room upstairs, but no woman would ever be found. Da laughing was coming fae behind da walls, she used to tell us this to scare wis!'

'There was a Danish servant lass, I think it was the twenties or thirties,' said Sharon. 'There's a story she was changing da beds when she heard a baby crying. There was no baby in da hoose, so she runs fae da hoose screaming her head aff and never went back. Years later when they were repairing a lum in da big nursery, workmen found a bundle wrapped in sheepskin and inside were the bones of a peerie baby, too young to be born, they said.'

'What's a lum?' asked Prue.

'A chimney,' whispered James.

The smattering of glum souls in the bar collectively shivered and Prue had another reason to hate that bedroom.

'Did you tell aboot da Dutchman, da big, tall man? Come to the island telling the Andersons owed him money. He went missing too,' said the other old man.

'When was that?' asked Sharon.

'Must have been '63 or '64.'

'People have gone missing fae dat place over the years. Always foreign, Dutch, Danish, Norwegian, never an islander, not until our Evie,' said Sharon.

'The Anderson boy did it,' the first old man shouted to more nods and groans.

'Gladys swears she's in those trees, buried, and then there's his paintings,' said Sharon. By this time James had his fist in his mouth.

'Mother! If I may... this is Prue – otherwise known as Archie Anderson's niece,' announced James, loud so they could all hear.

'Ah,' said Sharon, and all the nodders and groaners shrank back to their pints. The wet coughing returned, the old lady went back to staring at the carpet and a stony silence enveloped the bar.

'By marriage,' Prue offered. 'I barely know him and to be honest I think he's a bit of a knob.' As if that might ease everyone's discomfort. James was trying his best not to laugh.

'We're having a quiz night at the youth centre on Tuesday,' said Sharon, cheeks with a rosy flush. 'You'll be welcome to come.' James finally burst out laughing, which earned him another slap about the head, less playful this time.

'Ow! I didn't say anything!'

'I'm your mother – I can tell what you're thinking.'

James walked Prue back down the hill to the edge of the trees. 'Are you sure you're all right going through them trees on your own?' he asked, jokingly.

'I'll take my chances, thanks. What did your mum mean by Archie's paintings?'

'Have you not seen them?'

Prue shook her head and James smirked and started to back away with his hands palms up. 'Well, when you do, let me know what you think. Think of this place as a very small cage with no curtains, Prue. Everyone is looking in and there's nowhere to hide – except for those trees, of course.'

She walked back home more confused than ever but desperate to find out more about this missing girl.

9

That night more noises stopped Prue from sleeping but it wasn't the creaks of the house or a wandering madwoman, but her aunt and uncle having sex from across the landing. Old houses were meant to have thick walls, but these must be hollow. The screws of their bed were squeaking, and the headboard knocked against the wall, not to mention the stomach-churning groaning like a grunting opera. Prue lay with her head sandwiched between flat pillows trying to block out the intrusive horrors of her uncle attacking Ruth like a rutting pig. An insatiable beast. *That bastard*. Killing one woman and devouring another – her own aunt, no less, the one he'd stolen and lobotomised. Prue was angry that no one had seen fit to tell her about the missing girl, even if they did dismiss it as bitter suspicion. *We'll talk. Things will be different*, Ruth had said. It was all lies.

Prue was seven years old and wearing those white socks with the holes and her mother was calling her to come inside. She had to find the black wolf-dog because Ronnie was going to kill it and she ran, looking for the dog, but she tripped and woke herself up. Her heart raced and her skin was wet. She kicked off the clammy sheets and let the cold air hit her wet skin. At least they had finished what they were doing across the landing.

She hadn't had a decent night's sleep since being in the house. It was this room, with its bad vibes and secret holes and awful history – perhaps it carried bad energy, as Ronnie would say. She stared at the ceiling. Nana had the same kind at her house and there had always been a strange square on the ceiling in the hallway. The lines reminded her of the scars her mother hid on her stomach and thighs, and in her head she had referred to it as the ceiling scar. When she was no more than nine or ten, she had made the mistake of asking about it. Nana was at the sink with a cigarette in her mouth, and when Prue asked, she had frozen until the ash on her cigarette started to tilt.

'Nana. Your ash,' Prue said.

Nana let the cigarette fall into the dirty dishwater and then balled up her fists and shook them in Prue's face.

'Don't you dare talk about that! Ever! Do you hear me!' she screamed and her cheeks went purple. A colander was on the draining board full of washed cabbage and Nana swung at it and sent it flying across the kitchen where it hit the wall and covered Prue and the kitchen in wet cabbage leaves. Prue ran to her room, jumped on the bed and stayed there, terrified, having no idea what she'd done. She heard her mother and grandmother fight and shriek until they both cried, but she didn't come out of her room. Prue knew she was never to ask about marks on a person but hadn't realised this extended to ceilings.

She fell asleep tossing and turning, her legs dragging the damp sheets with her as she rolled over and over, but when she heard a hard thud as something hit the floor, she sat up again and it was pitch black. She tried to switch the lamp on, but Mary wasn't working. When she heard a baby cry, she opened her mouth to shout for Ruth but only the sound of ravens cronking came out.

Prue sat upright; the ravens were outside being noisy and it was already morning. The Mary lamp was buzzing as she'd been left on, frying all night, so Prue switched her off. Her legs ached, her head felt thick and heavy, as if she was coming down with a cold. She was brushing her teeth in the bathroom when she heard Ruth talking on the landing. She put down her toothbrush, wiped her mouth and opened the door, but Ruth wasn't there. Still not feeling right, she knew Ruth had paracetamol in her drawer so knocked on the studio door to ask if she could have some, but it was locked. How odd. The doors were never locked.

Prue heard something squeak and turned to see one of the potted plants hanging above the banister swinging on its own. The thick wooden banisters were barricaded by potted plants, palms and ferns and the handrails were covered. Hanging baskets and pots hung from hooks in the ceiling but only one was swinging. In front of her, it swung and dropped to the carpet, spilling earth everywhere. The local gossip of missing servants and laughing women whirled around her head. *Don't be stupid, Prue. It's the sort of thing Mum would freak out about.* She bent down to scoop up what earth she could with her hands and put it back into the pot and then stood up to hang it back on its hook, but she couldn't quite reach it. She carried the chair from her bedroom to stand on, admitting as she did so that it was an irresponsible thing to do but she would be careful. She stood on the chair and hung the plant on the hook, easy. She was about to step down when she felt faint, and everything went black. Prue fell forwards, opening her eyes as she fell and grabbing at the plant she'd just hung up, tearing it off the hook, screaming.

She saw the flagstone floor rush up to meet her as she flipped over the banister. Swinging on one arm and sending plants crashing to the floor, she hung from the handrail but it was too thick to hold onto. With her free hand she grabbed the balustrade in front of her and then grabbed it with both hands. She wasn't going to be able to hang on for long. She saw herself like Dotty, with her smashed watermelon head on the flagstone floor beneath her. How long would the blood take to scrub off this time?

Archie came running into the hall, saw her dangling and burst out laughing.

'What are you doing!?'

'Quick! I can't hold on.'

'Let go, I'll catch you,' he said.

'No! Get a ladder.'

'Are you shitting me? Shall I put the kettle on? You fancy a tea? Come on! Let go. It's not as high as you think. I'm going to catch you. Let go.' He kicked the smashed pieces of pot from underneath.

'I can't!'

'Do it!'

Prue didn't have to let go; she simply couldn't hold on

any longer. When she fell, Archie did catch her – of sorts. It was the worst of situations. She landed on him with her bottom on his chest, and her T-shirt around her waist. He wrapped his huge arms around her and rolled them both onto the floor. Prue was shaking. Archie, however, thought the whole thing hilarious.

'Whoa! Come on, up you get.' He pushed her off him and stood up, dragging Prue up like a rag doll. She couldn't find her feet to stand steady and had pins and needles behind her eyes.

'You hit your head?' he asked.

'Something's wrong.' The sweat poured down Prue's face and Archie looked very far away. His hands were like tractor buckets as he came towards her and gripped her shoulders.

'You need to breathe.' His eyes fixed on her arm. 'What happened here?' With his huge hand he lifted her arm up and there were angry red welts.

'Oh God,' she said, and fainted.

When she came round, she was back on the floor again. She'd never fainted before and wanted to die. This was without doubt the most humiliating thing that had ever happened and the longest time she'd ever spent in the company of her uncle, apparently a suspected murderer, and he'd seen her knickers. She even cried and she never cried. She kept saying, *I'm so sorry, I'm so sorry,* over and over but it was unintelligible because she was crying so hard. Archie sat next to her on the bottom step of the stairs with his chin in his hand not having much clue what to do. Prue had her face buried into her knees and her T-shirt pulled over them as Archie tried to make out it really wasn't that bad. He kept talking about a man called Alan who'd had diarrhoea in front of him on a camping trip, and told her he himself had been violently ill both ends over the side of a boat in Botswana.

'I've seen far worse,' he kept saying.

'Please don't tell Ruth about this.'

'We'll see.' He sighed. 'You know when I first saw you through the window, I didn't recognise you. You're like, tall.'

'I grew.'

'You certainly did.'

'At least you noticed. If you could let Ruth and my mother in on the whole growing up thing, that would be great.'

'Go and… sort yourself out,' he said.

Prue had one foot on the landing. Her face was blotchy; red and white – she was not a pretty crier.

'Prue,' said Archie. 'You're not pregnant, are you?'

Her whole body went rigid. 'No!'

Archie was as embarrassed as she was. 'I don't know. What with the fainting and I don't know… I'm out of my depth here, OK. Are you sure? You don't need a test or anything?'

'Stop! Please! I can guarantee it.' Prue, as rigid as an ironing board, turned and scurried along the landing, not a shred of dignity left. She had nearly made it to her bedroom door when she stopped and shouted over the banister, 'Thanks for not being mean.'

He laughed, he had a wicked grin.

'What can I say? I'm a sucker for a girl in tears.'

You tell that bastard… He didn't seem much like a murderer. He seemed quite considerate, but then Prue had read somewhere even Hitler liked dogs. When she came back, Archie wanted to know how she ended up hanging from the banister.

'A plant fell down and I went to hang it back up and stood on a chair and I... I know, I lost my balance, I guess – stupid, right?'

'The plants are too much,' he said. 'It's really got out of control. I'm going to have to bring it up with Ronnie, it's dangerous.'

'Please don't mention this to Ruth or Ronnie, and please don't talk to her about her plants, she loves them.'

He stewed on the request for a few moments, looking down at her. 'Fine,' he said eventually, 'this time, but for God's sake be careful, and maybe consider wearing bottoms.'

That evening, Archie joined them for dinner. Ruth spotted the red marks on Prue's arm as she reached to take some bread and grabbed her arm.

'Let me see,' said Ruth.

Prue caught Archie's eye and she raised her eyebrows in a *told-you-so* way, and he rolled his.

'There's nothing to see,' said Prue and she snatched her arm away from Ruth.

'Why won't you let me see?'

'Why don't you like me looking at your paintings?'

'What? Why are you being so dramatic?' asked Ruth.

'You're the one being dramatic.'

'Sorry for caring, Prue.'

'I'm not a child, Ruth, please, you don't have to worry about every scratch and scrape.'

'I never said you were a child.'

'Ruth, leave it alone, the girl's fine,' said Archie.

'Oh, I see.' Ruth looked between the pair of them with narrow eyes. 'I see you've formed a little gang. She's been under our supervision for five minutes and she's broken out in impetigo or eczema.'

'Don't be daft,' said Archie. 'It could be worse – she could be pregnant.'

'Archie!' squealed Ruth.

Archie sniggered at his own joke. Ronnie's eyes narrowed as if she knew she'd missed out on something and didn't like it.

'How did you get those marks?' asked Ronnie.

'No idea. I woke up, they were there.'

'How strange,' Ronnie said. 'How is your mother getting along in the asylum?'

'It's not an asylum, it's a rehabilitation centre,' snapped Ruth.

'I don't know,' said Prue, feeling guilty; she'd barely even thought about her mother since she'd been there.

'It's good to have a break,' said Ruth. 'I'm sure she's fine.'

Prue knocked her fork off the table and it clattered to the tiled floor, but when she bent down to pick it up, she saw Archie's hand in between Ruth's legs. Prue bumped her head on the underside of the table on the way up, flushed with embarrassment.

'Oops,' she said, not able to look either of them in the eye. It was worse than hearing them at it at night and now she'd lost her appetite.

'Me and my big mouth,' said Ronnie. 'I'm sure Ruth is

right and your mother is having a whale of a time, healing or drawing pictures of her feelings, or whatever it is they do in those places. Funny, isn't it, those marks appearing from nowhere; at least she's not self-harming, Ruth, because I read somewhere that's what teenage girls do these days. Self-harm, it's a growing phenomenon. Then we'd all be worrying she'd inherited "the gene".'

'What gene?' asked Prue.

'The suicide gene,' said Ronnie.

'Ronnie—' said Ruth.

'What suicide gene?'

'That's what they think these days, isn't it? That suicide is passed down like brown eyes or curly hair – or hating coriander. What with your grandfather and then your mother's attempts—'

'What a macabre conversation—' said Ruth, but Prue wasn't letting it go.

'What do you mean about my grandfather?'

'Oh, am I mistaken? I was under the impression that he'd hanged himself,' said Ronnie.

'What?' That wasn't true; Prue had been told he'd died in an accident before she was born.

The lights tripped and they were plunged into the violet-tinged blue of an early evening.

'For God's sake. Not again!' said Ruth, relieved something had stopped the conversation.

'It's the fuse box,' said Archie. 'Ruth, light the candle.' Archie stumbled about in the kitchen drawers, opening and slamming them in frustration. 'Fuck! Where's the fucking torch?'

The familiar scratch of metal of a lighter flicked until a

flame burst into being. Ruth lit the candle and Archie found the torch.

'Where's the torch for the cellar, Ruth?' asked Archie.

'On the hook, where it always is,' she replied.

'It's not,' he said.

'I haven't touched it.'

They bickered and engaged in the operatic farce as Ronnie and Prue sat in candlelight as if at a séance. So her grandfather had hung himself. Yet another secret. Another lie. Something stirred in Prue, as if a switch had been flicked somewhere and it wasn't the fuse box, but a white hot flame burning deep inside.

'Found it!' said Archie, the sound of his boots thudding on the wooden staircase. Within seconds the lights were back on.

Prue caught Archie's eye and she could have sworn she saw pity and it hurt. She looked away, bit her lip and tried not to cry. But this time, these were tears of anger and frustration.

Ruth exhaled. 'Well, that was a bit of comedy drama, wasn't it?'

It had been three whole days since the bombshell about her grandfather's suicide had dropped when Ruth asked Prue to go with her to the Mainland. Ruth hadn't mentioned it and Prue was waiting to see if she would. But not a word, not even an acknowledgement of the lie she'd helped to sustain for sixteen years. Nothing had changed at all. It was a bright and sunny day but Prue didn't notice. Fast growing tired of being everyone's good little pet, obedient and patient, waiting for Ruth to initiate these discussions she had promised they would have. If they'd lied about her grandfather, what else were they lying about?

Lerwick had a high street of grey and mauve stone buildings with little shops, cafés and lanes that led straight onto the water or uphill to the old fort. It was small and quiet, a perennial Sunday with terraced houses with courtyard gardens and painted doors in green, pink, red. They stopped in The Peerie Shop and she picked a card to send to her mother.

'Come on, what do you need? New trainers?' said Ruth, trying to muster up good energy between them. 'There's a sports shop and you like to run. I'll buy whatever you want, I want you to have fun.'

'Doesn't everybody,' Prue muttered, remembering how James told her he wanted her to have fun, but he'd not made contact since. Why did people say things they didn't mean?

'Consider it a gift from Archie.'

'I can't, that makes it worse.'

'He's paying for your mum's treatment too. Look, I wasn't going to tell you and I realise now that's partly the issue, isn't it? Me not involving you in things. He did it for me, because I felt so guilty about your mother trying to kill herself that night after we argued. There, I've told you, now can we go for lunch?'

In a café Prue took out the card and a pen with fluff on the tip from the bowels of Ruth's handbag. She hesitated over the blank page; the words saying *Get Well Soon* somehow seemed sarcastic.

'What should I say?' she asked Ruth.

'Christ. Erm... hope you are feeling better? You were right, Ruth's a complete cow, can't wait to come home.'

'You're not a cow, not *all* of the time.'

'Well, thanks, I appreciate it,' she said, sipping a glass of white wine.

'Do you ever miss home, I mean London? Or your old life?'

Ruth looked confused. 'Oh gosh. Sometimes, perhaps a little. But it wasn't working out for me. I had some awful jobs, relegated to processing invoices and taking minutes for smug boys in sports jackets.'

'You had an amazing career.'

'I did, and then what happened? I was binned off. There are four distinct stages to a woman's career, Prue, but you will only learn this once you've been churned through each level like mincemeat. Stage one is the whipper snapper. You've got thighs smooth as tinned hotdogs, the wide-eyed stare of Bambi, you unfortunately still believe in the good guys and unwittingly make yourself available for date-rapes and minor sexual assaults. Stage two is the ingenue, a bit older and wiser and knows who gets handsy after a few. You earn more than your boyfriend and still do all the housework. Stage three: feisty totty, you're now smart and experienced, but struggle to get recognition because when you do win, it can only ever be *low hanging fruit*. You get hired by the creepy dads on the board as one for the spank bank. Stage four: you are at peak earning capacity, weighed down with HR hand grenades and kamikaze projects no man will go near. Developing visible signs of wear and tear. Gaining weight. Adrenal fatigue. You open the fridge door for wine before you take your coat off. Your old lazy boyfriend is now your lazy husband and, guess what, now he earns more than you. Everyone finds you a hostile threat – even other women – because when you're a minority in the corporate world it's like *Highlander* – that film with Sean Connery where he plays a Spaniard with a Scottish accent – there can be only one.'

They laughed together, Prue happy to see the glimmers of the old Ruth, and then she finished writing the card and sealed the envelope.

'Why didn't you tell me?' Prue couldn't let the face to face go to waste. *We'll talk. It'll be different.*

'Tell you what?'

'About Grandad. Why didn't anyone feel the need to tell me that he killed himself?'

Ruth squirmed. 'Ronnie has such a big clumsy mouth, I could kill her sometimes.'

'That's not the point. He hung himself – why?'

Ruth looked out of the window. 'He was very depressed and he had lost his job not long before. He'd got himself into a terrible hole and couldn't dig himself out.' The comparison reminded Prue of the story about her birth, how she was dug from a hole in the earth by her grandfather. What tripe. Then she had a sudden thought.

'The ceiling scar, in Nana's hallway.'

'The what?'

'The square in Nana's house on the ceiling. That has something to do with it? It does, doesn't it?'

Ruth nodded. 'He cut out a part of the ceiling and hung himself from the banisters, to give himself enough of a drop.' Ruth struggled to swallow on the last word.

'Oh my God,' said Prue. She thought of the painting in Ruth's studio. *The Square*. The man looking down through a hole with the image repeating itself over and over like a torture that would never end.

'*The Square*. Your painting. That's about him, isn't it?' Ruth fidgeted, looked about for a distraction. 'You said we would talk and things would be different. You promised me. I'm here, I kept my end of the bargain, so when are you going to keep yours?'

'Honestly! I'm not—'

'There's more, isn't there? I know it. Who is my father? Do you know his name?'

'No,' said Ruth, bringing herself to meet Prue's fierce eyes. 'Me and your mother were never close. I'm the last person she's going to confide in. You have to remember I was nine years old when she was born.'

'Maybe I should ask Ronnie.' Prue sat back in her seat.

'OK, I should have told you about your grandad and I would have, but it's not like the subject came up naturally since, well, there's been a lot going on, hasn't there. I'm sorry.'

'Why create the lie in the first place? I don't understand.'

'Nana didn't want you to think badly of him, that's all. There was no conspiracy. Now, remind me to stop at the off licence before we get on the ferry, we're running low on wine. There's always the shop, but I only go there when desperate.'

That'll be because everyone thinks your husband is a murderer. Prue tried to bite her tongue. She'd pushed things far enough already. She really should be quiet and try again in a few days. It would be the mature thing to do.

'Is that because of the rumours about the missing girl?' she said. Whoops. She couldn't help it. It slipped out.

'I beg your pardon?' Ruth's face, already pale, had a red flush run through it all the way to her neck. 'Who told you about that?'

'The woman, the mad alcoholic, she's called Gladys O'Hara and she's the missing girl's mother. Archie was her boyfriend, and everyone thinks he had something to do with her going missing. Again, that's another thing you should have told me and yet you didn't,' Prue said, feeling triumphant at her newfound bravery and then slurping on her drink through a straw.

'Did that boy tell you?'

'No. An old lady asked me where I was staying, then she told me about the missing girl. It's a small island...' Prue shrugged, and hoped Ruth bought it.

'Do you really think I would marry a murderer, Prue? For twenty years Gladys has convinced herself that Archie killed her daughter and there's never been a shred of evidence. It's a tragic story and I do have sympathy but... she's turned us into victims too. I didn't want you to be bothered by any of that. I wanted you to—'

'I know... to have fun.'

Ruth knocked back the rest of her wine. 'The problem is when you get people like that,' she carried on, 'they shout very loudly and anyone who maintains a dignified silence appears aloof. Cue the villagers with pitchforks. Oh, look how windy it is, Prue, we should make a move.' As she was looking out of the window studying the weather, a drop of blood ran from Ruth's nose.

'Your nose, it's bleeding,' said Prue.

'Is it?' Ruth touched her nose and looked at the red droplets on her fingers. 'How odd, I wonder what's brought that on.' They scrabbled around for tissues, but it was only a trickle and stopped almost immediately. 'Oh, we must stop for wine, you didn't remind me.'

'That's because it's only been two minutes.'

Back at the house, via the off licence, Ronnie ushered them into the kitchen where she had set a huge bunch of flowers in the middle of the table.

'I trimmed and put them in water for you,' she said. 'The boy from the hotel dropped them off while you were out.' Ronnie nudged her in the ribs. 'Someone has an admirer. Those are wild daisies, there's soft lady's mantle, dotted loosestrife, coppery monkeyflower, red campion, some bog cotton, and that is a marsh orchid. Oh, here, he left a note.' Ronnie handed her a scrappy piece of folded paper; inside was a handwritten message.

See? Beautiful. You only need to know where to look, James.

Ronnie tried peeking over her shoulder, but Prue screwed up the note.

'What does that mean?' asked Ronnie.

'Nothing.'

'How charming,' said Ruth. 'What beautiful flowers.'

'Please, Ruth, a woman must be conquered. At least teach the girl to play a little hard to get,' said Ronnie. 'So, he tore wildflowers from the side of the road, it's hardly ground-breaking. Honestly, a woman needs someone who can throw her around the room – in a good way. I saw that boy, he struggled tearing those poor babies out of the ground.'

'Ronnie – you are a very difficult woman to please,' said Ruth.

'I prefer the term *perennially disappointed*, my dear,' she said.

10

Croydon, South London, April 1993

The instructions Nana left in her will were crystal clear. The house was to be sold and any remaining monies were to be split equally between the two daughters, but Prue's mother had another idea. What she would inherit from the sale of the house would be enough for a deposit, but she would never be able to get a mortgage on her salary, even for a studio flat in London. If Ruth would agree to Prue and her mum moving back into Nana's house for an agreed term to save on rent, they could save a lot more money. If her mum was able to take some training or find a better job, then at some point in the far off, can't quite see it, distant future, the house could be sold and split. It did sound reasonable, until you considered the fact that Prue's mother was thirty-one, hardly a girl any more, and had lived rent free with Nana for years and still hadn't found any determinable profession or saved any money. So it was fair to see why Ruth wanted to know what was going to be different now. Why was she going to be able to discover life's true calling – what had stopped her before? Prue heard her mother thrashing out the proposal with Ruth over the phone one night and that's when the bickering started.

'Don't you think I'd have a mortgage if I could? Or a career? I haven't been able to focus on myself – I've always had Prue.' That hurt. All Prue heard was that she was the root cause of her mother's failure to launch.

A few days after Nana's funeral they arranged to start clearing the house out. Prue's mother's mood was already dark, she was barely speaking that morning; being trapped with her in the car was like being stuck next to a black hole that sucked everything towards it. The more her need for comfort, for something, Prue didn't even know what, the more people around them, even acquaintances, withdrew, but Prue had no sanctuary. Without Nana they were aimless and drifting and it was as if there was no order in the world any more. They had to walk back into the house that Nana was missing from, and Prue found an open jar of mouldy piccalilli in the fridge and when she looked inside it was as if Nana had recently stuck a knife in it. Ruth caught her staring into the jar.

'Chuck it in the bin, will you? No one is going to want that,' she said.

But when Prue threw it away it felt as if she was throwing Nana away with it. There was still a stain in the carpet from where she had trodden in the ash when she collapsed. It was very much as if, any second, she would walk back into the house and start shouting about the mess. It was baking hot that day and it didn't matter how many windows or doors were propped open, there was no breeze. Occasionally a door would slam shut as if to prove them wrong and everyone was complaining about how hot they were. Ruth was like a coiled snake and Prue could only try to mediate between the two sisters. She found an old shoe box full of photographs upstairs and a photograph of them all in the garden with Prue as a baby. She ran downstairs to show them, thinking it might spark some fuzzy memories and the tension might loosen. Prue – fat and ginger and much like a bullfrog – was on Nana's lap while her mother, Caroline, looked impossibly young and had a curly perm, and spindly Ruth a spiky crew cut.

'Oh dear,' said Ruth. 'I see why people used to call me anorexic.'

'You were taking a lot of drugs,' said Caroline. 'Just look at Prue's frizzy hair.'

'I know! Now look at her! Prue, you could be a model. How tall are you? Five-nine? Who would have thought a fat little ginger would turn into such a fox?' said Ruth. 'I'm still waiting for my swan moment.'

Ruth and Prue hovered over the photo as her mother slipped away and withdrew from the nostalgia, but she could feel her watching them. It was so hot, and her mother had worn black leggings and a big black billowy dress over the top and must have been roasting under all that fabric. Prue wore shorts and Ruth had a silk kimono that kept slipping off her razor-thin shoulders. Prue disappeared back upstairs to find more photographs and heard her mother speak as soon as she thought Prue was out of earshot.

'I wish you wouldn't keep calling her pretty, she's cocky enough.'

'Don't be ridiculous,' snapped Ruth. 'All girls should be told they're beautiful.'

'You tell yours then,' said her mother. Prue was halfway up the stairs but stopped to wince.

'You do realise she doesn't actually belong to you, don't you? She's not your own personal teddy bear,' said Ruth. 'If I think she's beautiful, I'll bloody well tell her.'

Prue spent as long as she could finding more boxes. When she came back down she and Ruth were distracted by all the photographs again and didn't realise her mother had disappeared until she came flying back in a frenzy.

'Where is Mum's jewellery? I can't find any of it!'

'I have it,' said Ruth. 'She didn't want it left in the house. Mum decided who should have what in hospital and asked me to take it for safekeeping.'

Sounded logical enough, but her mother shot Ruth a look of concentrated venom. Ruth looked mystified and then stood up and stamped her way to the kitchen and started tearing out utensils from drawers and throwing them onto the worktop. Her mother marched over to the window and lit a cigarette.

'Please put that out, Caroline!' shouted Ruth. 'We're supposed to be selling this house. If you really must smoke, go outside.' Prue slunk into the hallway and braced herself under a door frame, as you are meant to in anticipation of an earthquake.

'I'm the youngest, so no doubt I'll get all the shit you don't want! As fucking usual! What about Mum's wedding ring, how do we decide who gets that?!' screamed her mother.

Ruth slammed a kitchen drawer and marched up to her younger sister and squared up. Ruth had this artsy kimono and it billowed behind her, making her look like one of those lizards that puffs up to scare its enemies. Prue thought for a second that Ruth might punch her mother and she could only watch, feeble and passive, her hands together like a racoon caught in the bin.

'Caroline, call it a perk of death, but Mum gets to choose who has what, like she gets to tell us to split the house, and I certainly don't think it's appropriate for you to have her wedding ring, do you?' said Ruth.

'What's that meant to mean?' said Prue's mother.

'It means whatever you think it means.' Ruth threw her arms up and walked away, silk kimono billowing, then changed her mind and stormed back. 'I'm sick of it! You're a grown woman for fuck's sake, and you're still whining like a little cunt!'

If there had been a panic room, Prue would have locked herself in it. The sisters started screaming over each other and the ash on her mum's cigarette was about to drop on the carpet.

'Ash,' Prue whispered. She ran and grabbed a saucer and put it under her mother's cigarette.

'I guess you'd be a lot happier if I killed myself, then I wouldn't be so much of a burden!' her mother shrieked.

'For fuck's sake, Caroline, stop going on about it! If you are going to kill yourself, do it properly this time. Do it lengthways, like you mean it,' said Ruth.

Her mother stormed out into the street, screaming, as neighbours twitched their curtains. Ruth slammed the front door, but Prue was still inside along with her mother's car keys. There was a horribly awkward part where the sisters had to pass keys and Prue – like a hostage swap. Then everyone sloped out to their respective cars. They all ended up sat in a queue at the same red light, trying to not catch eyes in the rear-view mirror. Hiding behind sunglasses. Prue watched the heat rise off the bonnet, but it could have been her mother's rage. Her mother kept turning the knobs to the air con, complaining that it wasn't getting cold, and Prue didn't have the courage to tell her it hadn't worked since the year before.

Her mother spent the night drinking cheap wine from the corner shop and smoking rollups under the extractor fan with her legs up on the hob, crying. Prue stayed over at Subo's because she didn't have it in her to comfort her. Prue was empty. Or tired. When Subo's mum asked her how everything was she said, *Fine*. Subo managed to persuade her mum to let them finish an open bottle of red wine. They shared it in her bedroom and watched a French film, *La Femme Nikita*. Subo's parents would, on occasion, turn a blind eye to their lame attempts at underage drinking and watching inappropriate movies if they stayed indoors where her mother said she didn't have to worry about Subo *being fingered at the skatepark*. Subo said she would rather stay in self-imposed isolation than ever hear her mother say that sentence again. That night there was a thunderstorm and after a huge flash of lightning they looked out of the bedroom window to count the seconds until the thunder. The break in the weather would clear the air and dampen down any raging tempers. It was the heat. Things would simmer down in the morning.

It was boiling again the next day when Prue walked home; the sun beat down on her head as she trudged along rows of shallow-fronted terraced houses, gardens with dried-out grass, dodging the stinking bins. Girls with their bellies out licked ice cream and dropped wrappers on the pavement. Boys swaggered like scaffolders with their feet turned outwards, shirts tucked into back pockets. The rain may as well have never happened; if anything, it was hotter and the air shook with frustration. Something was wrong. When she got home, Prue found her in the bathroom in a bath of tepid water. Her wrists open; *lengthways*. There was so much blood in the water it didn't seem as if there could be any left in her. She was grey, the colour of an uncooked prawn. Her grandmother's skin had turned yellow and her mother's grey. Death is much more colourful than they tell you. It comes in a kaleidoscope of colours.

Prue didn't remember picking up the knife from the floor. Only that when she looked down, one of the steak knives from Nana's house was in her hands. Her mum always did bang on about having a proper set of steak knives. She dropped it into the sink where it bounced and clattered. She dragged her mother onto the floor and her skin slapped the lino, which is a very undignified sound. She put her mother's head on a folded towel and felt for a pulse but couldn't find anything. Time slowed down. She watched everything play out as if it was standing next to herself. Then she felt a tiny, faint little flicker of something against the flesh of her fingers and time started moving again – she was still alive.

At the hospital where she had been a few weeks before to see her grandmother die, Prue was again visiting because her mother had made a valiant attempt to join her. There was an inappropriately jolly nurse munching her way through a packet of biscuits who told Prue that cutting your wrists lengthways was the proper way to do it, that horizontal cutters tend to be a cry for help. She asked her without blinking or taking a breath if Prue had ever thought of self-harming, which she hadn't.

'Good for you,' she said. 'It seems to be all the rage in girls these days. In my day, it was eating disorders, everyone was anorexic 'cos of Karen Carpenter and Lena Zavaroni.'

The nurse's chatter saved Prue from having to engage in small talk with her mother. The times before when she'd done these things, Prue had worried about her endlessly and aspired to learn and know what could help or fix her. What could she do? She would have been willing to scoop out her own insides to make her mother happy again, but this time, she didn't feel like that at all. Prue was numb. Her mother had a glazed look, as if her sorrow was drowning her from the inside and the water had reached her corneas and she kept speaking in a fragile whisper. When anyone came in and asked, *How are you today, Caroline?*, which Prue understood to be a simple greeting and, most of the time, a rhetorical question, she would reply, 'Yes, a little better, I'm getting there…' in that stupid whisper, which, for reasons Prue could not explain, made her want to smother her with a pillow. When she did eventually speak it was something that didn't have any relevance to the situation, unless it was purely designed to hurt Prue.

'I always hated the name Prudence,' said her mother. 'I wanted to call you Zoe, but I wasn't allowed.'

Well, Prue hated her name too, but no one wanted to hear their mother say that. She put it down to the medication. Thankfully, the nurse with boundary issues kept them from re-engaging in their fractious relationship.

'Do you want another Hobnob?' said the nurse. 'Please say yes, or I'll end up eating the whole packet.'

11

In the first week of July the island would start to see its longest days. The sun was up before four in the morning and there was every good chance it would be bright and sunny, but it was far too breezy to ever get hot. At night, the sun would go down around ten and the birds would sing until late. Prue knew them by sound, if not by name, with shrill calls, peeps, yelps and cackles. The island was a confusing place: one minute the sky would be miserable grey, and it was nothing more than an abandoned old bog. Then the sun would burst out to scream how freakishly beautiful it was, the wildflowers would bob, and seals, or selkies as they called them, would lounge in clusters on the sandy bays like fat Brits on a Benidorm beach. The sky would be baby blue in the morning, then the wind would come up and it would become a dark oppressive presence with purple clouds like swollen blood vessels, threatening to burst open. On peaceful evenings the clouds would amble across in ice cream colours – peach, strawberry and vanilla. Nothing had a firm grasp of itself and could change like a chameleon into whatever it needed to be in the moment. Prue had only been on the island a short while and already the days had started to bleed into one another with no routine to chase.

One afternoon the shrill bell of the telephone rang in the hall by the big front door. Ronnie answered and tried several times to repeat the caller's name but kept mispronouncing it; at one point Prue heard her say *Booboo*. Prue knew exactly who it was and flew down the stairs.

'It's for me,' she shouted, rushing and trying not to become tangled in the living trip hazard that were the plants.

'It's a girl with a funny name. I think she's a *foreigner*?' Ronnie mouthed the last part.

'She was born in Tooting, she's hardly foreign,' said Prue and took the phone. Ronnie rolled her eyes and walked off, waving away Prue's disdain.

Subo lurched straight in. 'Hey, how's it going? I am literally dying to hear. Have you and Ruth had the big talk yet?'

Prue looked around to make sure the coast was clear and that Ronnie really had gone back to the garden.

'No, and I don't think she has any intention of talking either. Ronnie, the woman who answered the phone, is Ruth's grandmother-in-law, and the other night she blurted out that my grandfather hung himself – he didn't die in an accident like I was told.'

'Wow! No way! Shit.'

'Ruth told Ronnie the truth but carried on with the lie to me, for sixteen years! If she's lying about that, what else is she lying about?'

'Jesus, talk about family skeletons. Erm, are you OK about your grandfather?'

'Absolutely fine, I never met the man. I'm not sentimental, just angry. Ruth has no intention of telling me anything unless she's forced to.'

'So you're no closer to finding anything out?'

'Actually, you know how I hate coriander? Well, Ronnie told me I could have inherited that from my father – apparently it's genetic.'

'Fantastic, what a breakthrough! Now all you have to do is get a list of all the men between sixteen and seventy who were in Croydon in 1976 who hate coriander and you'll be halfway there. Are you taking the piss?'

'OK, I get it. It's hopeless unless Ruth talks, but it's not been a complete disaster.'

'You're easily pleased.'

'No, there's a boy. He's eighteen and he gave me a massive bunch of flowers, which is a bit weird and old person-like, but to be honest, there's not much else here to give. Anyway, he's up here on holiday too and he's from Aberdeen. I think he might like me, but I can't be sure.'

'Oh! This is progress! You should definitely do him.'

'God, I'm not even sure I like him.'

'Irrelevant. What did you say to me? Allow me to remind you: you said, under no circumstances could you go to college a virgin and that it was my job to help. Then when we finally had a window of freedom, you got summoned to doom island and I'm guessing you don't have a lot of options. Think about it, this is actually better because this way you get the deed done and never have to see the guy again and no one from home will know him. It's going to be shit and underwhelming, Prue, deal with it. Get it over and done with, then you can start living life with that embarrassing milestone gone.'

Prue went quiet. It *did* make sense. It had been a perpetual worry that she would end up having to go to college full of highly sexed nymphs and be lagging behind as usual. Under her own steam she'd be a virgin forever. It was never going to happen; she didn't like anyone at all. Ever. Subo was right.

'Are you still there?'

'Yes, I know it was my idea. But I'm… I'm a bit worried about it. The thought makes me feel a bit ill…'

'Drink your way through it, it's what everyone else does. What's it like up there?'

'Erm… kind of like a village that's suffered a massive nuclear fallout and been deemed uninhabitable. Try and imagine a medieval Chernobyl. There's a lot of sheep and grass and it's very windy. The Mainland is busier but that's a ferry ride away.'

'Sounds fucking shit. I do miss you. You made me look cool and now I have to work at it.'

'Twat… There is something else. Actually, it's right up your street.'

'What's this?'

'Well, James, the boy, told me that years ago a girl went missing from the woods behind Ruth's house. Disappeared, no body, nothing.'

'James, is it? At least it's a good name, not dorky like Gary or Kevin. I mean, who calls a baby Kevin?' Subo barely reacted to the missing girl, but then coming from London, missing girls were two a penny.

'Listen! The missing girl was my uncle's girlfriend at the time and… the islanders think he killed her and buried her in the woods. Can you believe it? I always thought he was a bit weird. Subo – my uncle could be a real-life murderer!'

'Did that actually happen or is this James guy winding you up?'

'Oh, it happened all right. I asked Ruth about it and she went all defensive. The girl's mother is a crazy alcoholic. I bumped into her in the shop, which is basically an old person's front room except even more depressing, and then that night I woke up and found her in my bedroom – she'd walked into the house because no one locks their doors here!'

'That's insane! No wonder people go missing. What's wrong with these people? How can you even sleep?'

'I'm not! Honestly, going to sleep at night is awful. The house is creaky and it's old and noisy, and Archie's mum killed herself in the room I'm sleeping in, and I've been having awful dreams.'

'Oh my God, sleep somewhere else! It's probably haunted, Prue, get out of that bedroom. Don't you remember when we watched *The Omen*? We had to go to the toilet together at night the whole week. I wish I could come up there. I'm lonely… and bored. We could stalk your uncle and see if he led us to the body.'

'Trust me, I would rather be back with you, but I can't come home without finding out something about my father. The more I think about it, the more I'm convinced Ruth knows more than she's letting on. I have to get her to talk.'

'Get you, this *is* progress. You go girl. Do it.'

'I saw her studio and her paintings and, I can't explain, but I'm sure she knows more.'

'Such as?'

'I swear her paintings are about our family, memories and things that happened. She doesn't like me being in there.'

'And this James boy, what's your game plan?'

'I'm going to do it. It's what I wanted, so I'm going to make it work.'

'Wow. Who are you? Good work, soldier. I'm here if you need me, and stay away from your creepy uncle.'

'Trust me, he's got zero interest in me. Besides, I don't think he did it. It was probably some random pervert like it always is.'

The front doorbell rang. It never rang. Clutching the phone Prue stretched the telephone line so she could open the door, and there was James.

'Subo? I've got to go. I'll call you later.' Prue hung up on her best friend before she could say goodbye.

'Hey,' said James. 'Wondered if you wanted to come out to play?'

'Thank you for the flowers,' she said.

'No problem. I thought, well, I don't know what I thought but... I hope you didn't think it was lame.'

'No! Honestly, they're really, erm... they're nice,' she said. Oh God, what a terrible adjective – biscuits are nice.

Then came the long and awkward pause and Prue froze, gripped by fear of an expectation to do and say something spectacular, but when she tried to scramble for something, all she could see was a fuzzy blank space. The air fell flat, and she knew she had dropped the ball and now they both stared at the ground as if something tangible really had fallen there.

'Do you want to come and see the old ruins?' James said, perking up. 'The ones I told you about the other day?'

'Yeah, cool,' she said, nodding. Urgh, who says that? She was sure her back was sweating. 'Hang on a minute, I'll get my jumper.' Yeah, to hide any visible damp patches.

It was best this way, thought Prue. The element of spontaneity didn't give her a chance to overanalyse meeting James again.

They went on a long breezy walk to the former gatehouse. This was now the camping bod his mother had opened and was at the bottom of a hill. Looking up, they could see the old ruins, a lumpen opaque shape against a silvery sky. The gatehouse was a single-storey brick house with a wooden gate and a laminated piece of A4 stuck on the window with phone numbers for booking. Prue opened the gate and looked inside: there were bunk beds and a wooden chair – but not much else.

'This is part of my mum's vision,' said James. 'Apparently, tourism on Noost is the next big thing. It has the wildlife and the geology and she thinks if the community gets organised, they can build something for young people for the future, and then more will want to stay.'

'It is a good idea,' said Prue. 'And at least your mum has ambition.' Although she wasn't sure the Costa del Sol brigade would be giving up their three-star half board to come to Noost anytime soon.

'Do you scare easy, Prue?' asked James as she closed the gate behind her. What an odd question to ask a girl you supposedly liked, or maybe he didn't. Maybe she was a raging narcissist and actually he was simply a friendly guy. They didn't exist.

'No,' she said in a surly tone, 'I'm from South London.'

This, of course, was a lie that would crumble under the lightest of pressures, which is what motivated her to add the cringe-inducing South London part. A comment she immediately regretted.

'Good, follow me.'

They marched up the hill on a stony path with small trenches and wire fences either side. Sheep grazed both sides and dogs barked in the distance. At the very top were the old ruins, a wide stone building half collapsed and taken over by brush and nettles that had at one point been quite grand.

'It's haunted, so they say. It's built on an old Celtic burial site.'

'Isn't this the plot to *Poltergeist*?' asked Prue, breathless from trudging uphill. James, however, seemed fine.

'It's true! A couple of years ago some people on an archaeological dig found two skeletons from the fourteenth century. Someone had bought it, Americans apparently, but when they had the surveys completed, they found the bones and then the archaeologists came in and found more bones, and nothing has happened since. No one has lived here since the early 1900s but my mum said the old man who did was a hermit who lived in one room and the rest of the house was taken over by cats.'

'God, imagine the smell.'

The building itself was fenced off with barbed wire at hip height. James pushed down the wire and slung a lanky leg over.

'Won't we get into trouble?' Prue asked. James looked at her, a little surprised.

'Come on, London girl.'

Prue dithered, trying to find a part low enough. It reminded her of the hurdles at school where she never once managed not to kick it on the underside and inflict terrible bruises to her leg in front of the whole class. She put her hand inside her sleeve and pushed the fence down and tried to get her leg over the barbed wire, but James ended up holding it down for her, amused by her lack of physical prowess. She climbed over and followed him up to the house. There was an old crest carved over the front door and two chimneys at each end. A huge part of the roof was missing and the front door was long gone but there were remnants of a grand wooden staircase left behind, now falling apart. The ground was covered in rubble and broken roof tiles. It was overgrown with nettles and covered in bird poo. They stepped into a room with little recesses high up in the walls. Eerily, the recesses had been stuffed with sticks, plastic, rope and sheep's wool.

'Who could have done that?' pointed Prue, suspecting witchcraft.

'We should go,' said James.

'Why?' Prue was on edge. 'Why should we go?'

'Can you hear that? There are baby starlings in the wall. The parents won't come back until we leave. It's not fair, come on.'

Prue exhaled. 'I thought you were going to say it was devil worship.'

'There's something behind you!' James suddenly grabbed her by the shoulders and shook her.

Prue screamed, smacked his hands away and spun around, and of course, there was nothing there. She turned and thumped James with her hands inside her sleeves as he shielded the blows, laughing.

'You arsehole! You said this would be fun. Urgh!'

'It was fun for me,' he said, still laughing as Prue tried to escape the house.

That same week, James took Prue for a picnic. Prue hated picnics, she couldn't even stand the word: *pic-nic*. What a ridiculous word. She had an issue with eating in front of people she wasn't comfortable with and, given her plans for James, this meant nothing was digestible. She could only nibble around the edges of a sausage roll as her stomach turned over with hunger. James didn't say a word, but he certainly noticed, and she felt compelled to dominate and direct the conversation by pointing out all of the flowers she'd learned from Ronnie.

'That one there is tormentil, then there's lousewort but they call them honey-sookies, and sea pink, which is thrift, and marsh marigolds, which they call blugga, and my favourite, the little puff balls you find on the bog, called Luckie-Minnie's Oo. Doesn't that sound rude?' she asked.

He leaned over and picked a dandelion head of pure white fluff from the ground and held it in front of her so close she went cross-eyed. The dandelion disappeared and there she was with her seven-year-old legs again in those white socks, dirty and wet. The windows to the cottage had been left wide open, anyone could walk inside. Why did this keep popping into her head at the most random moments?

'Do you want to blow, Prue?' said James. She was unnerved, unsure if he was trying to be funny or flirting.

'If you're referring to the dandelion, the answer is no.'

He grabbed her round the neck and kissed her on the lips. 'You have a dirty mind, Prudence MacArthur,' he said, then he blew the dandelion head himself as Prue blushed, watching the fluffy white seeds drift away. This must be flirting.

Thankfully they gave up on the stupid picnic and retreated to his bedroom above the bar. James spent the afternoon watching TV on his bed as Prue became engrossed in his Game Boy, which he found amusing until she beat his scores on Tetris and Super Mario Land. His mother came up every so often to make sure his bedroom door was open the required six inches. She would peek through the gap and wave at Prue, and ask if she needed anything, if she was hungry or thirsty, too hot or too cold. This was every forty minutes or so, James growing more and more irritated each time.

On the way home he took her past a croft where he knew there would be lambs.

'No one can be scared of sheep, this is part of your therapy – I'm going to fix you, Prue, on the sheep thing anyway. Pretty sure you're fucked on the rest of your problems.'

'Ha-ha, very funny. Why does one of the lambs have its tail painted blue?'

'It's to stop his mother chewing on his tail.' Prue looked sufficiently horrified. 'Over-vigorous cleaning. Once the tail bleeds, the mother will only clean it more. She sees the blood and can't help herself; she doesn't know she's doing more harm than good.'

* * *

Later that week they went to a food and music festival on the Mainland by the arts centre and drank pints from plastic cups listening to folk music and walked around the food stalls. She didn't recognise many of the names: *fleuk, hoe, lempit, skeetik, troot, yoag,* but there were some she did: cod, crab, lobster, and there was a competition for something called *krappin.*

'It's made of chopped fish livers,' said James, 'flour and oatmeal and stuffed in the head of a fish that's then boiled and served in a kale bled – which is a cabbage leaf. You want to try some?'

'I'm good, thanks.'

James laughed. 'My grandparents used to hang up *reestit* legs on the wall over the fireplace to dry. *Reestit* is mutton.'

'My Nana used to hang dreamcatchers over the fireplace and I thought that was weird – we're not Native American.'

When they walked through the small crowd watching fiddle music James tried to hold her hand, but Prue pulled it away and pretended her nose was itchy. On the ferry the wind blew her hair in her face. James reached out to brush it away and Prue flinched as if he was about to hit her. This wasn't going to plan and it was Prue messing it up. What was wrong with her? Why couldn't she be normal like all the other girls who went on about the boys they fancied and had sex all the time? It seemed the whole world was at it like rabbits except for her. They all went on about how they loved it and couldn't get enough and did all sorts, but Subo had told her sex can be really boring. Most boys haven't a clue where the clitoris is and you might have to show them or else they'll go at you like they're sanding down driftwood, but either way, she wanted to fit in.

After the failed attempts at seduction that saw Prue recoil like an abuse victim, there was a lull in James's efforts. Prue had hours to herself and spent most of them sighing and following Ronnie around waiting for menial tasks that might give her sweet relief from thinking about her never-burgeoning sexuality. She had made such a good assistant, she was promoted to helping in the greenhouse. Tidying, sweeping, watering and heaving bags of compost, but this was a step up – Ronnie didn't like other people being in her greenhouse.

'Spit it out, I cannot bear the brooding,' said Ronnie after Prue sighed again.

'What?'

'Oh, please! You really must put up more of an effort if you're going to lie. Is it that boy? That piece of string with the flowers? Has he done you wrong? Tell me and we can plot our revenge.' Ronnie smiled, her head wrapped in an orange silk scarf.

'It's not him, it's me.'

'Oh God! Here we go – what *about* you?'

'I dunno,' shrugged Prue. 'If I were shorter or more tanned then things might be different. I always wanted to be Spanish or Italian, but no, I'm as exotic as white bread. It's hard to feel attractive when boys spat half-chewed crisps at me through most of high school and my hair looks like I come from a family of clowns. I'm too tall and I'm too pale. I don't have any boobs, my feet are too big for my body and I have manly hands, look.' She held up her perfectly ordinary hands to show Ronnie.

'Can you even begin to imagine what I look like naked, Prudence? At this age? It's like looking into a bucket of melted cheese. I wish you could appreciate what you have now because I didn't and now look. You've nothing to fear, dear, you are stunning.'

Prue sighed again. 'I know you're trying to be kind, but it doesn't help because it's not true.'

Ronnie threw down her trowel and took off her gloves and threw those down too.

'Right, come with me,' she said, and, taking hold of Prue's hand, she marched her back into the house and only let go of her once they reached her bedroom. For an old woman, she moved fast.

'There! Sit! Sit! Sit!' She sat Prue at her dressing table and sat next to her, forcing her to budge up as she opened all her vanity cases and drawers, searching out particular pieces of makeup, small bottles of oils and pots of cream.

'You made all these?'

'I only use pure ingredients. No processing or bulking agents or toxins. What you need is not cosmetic help, you need a little magic, a sprinkling of fairy dust – something to give you a… nudge on your way to perfection.'

'Perfection?'

Ronnie stood up behind her and held her head in her hands and forced her face towards the mirror. Then she took a bottle of orange oil and poured a coin-sized drop into the palm of her hands and smoothed the oil through Prue's tangled hair and massaged it into her temples. It smelled of citrus, oranges and vanilla perhaps, fruit with woody undertones.

'What is this?' Prue felt ridiculous but didn't have the heart to stop it.

'It will smooth down your hair, but if you inhale the scent from your pulse it will help you be more... hmmm... how should I put it, confident! The rituals we imbue with importance help us move towards positive vibrations. We have to imagine ourselves doing things before we achieve them. You have to control and nurture what's going on in here.' Ronnie pointed at her head.

'How do I do that?' Prue hoped this wasn't going to get any weirder, but she was willing to give anything a try.

'My dear, I swear, if you master your mind then you won't be controlled by your emotions or other people's definitions of what you can be. Have I mentioned alchemy?'

Ronnie sat back down and picked out a little glass bottle of oil. 'People think that alchemy is about turning metals into gold but it's not – it's the belief that everything naturally moves toward perfection – even sixteen-year-old girls with big feet. But perfection is a state of mind and nothing more. A dream or a vision. Do not lose yourself to a boy... men are mere distractions for us to toy with.' Ronnie pushed Prue's hair behind her ear and Prue stiffened; she felt very much like a pet cat. 'They're weak,' Ronnie whispered. 'They're animals. It's women who have all the power. It's why they are so afraid of us.'

'Men? Frightened of women? In what world is this?'

'Why do you think they burned educated women at the stake? They can't bear to let us be free because they're frightened of us, so they shackle us, cover us up, legislate our bodies, beat us, exploit us, sell us, rape us, deny who we really are. They lie to us and our culture tries to manipulate us to live under the shadow of unachievable virtue. It's smoke and mirrors, my darling. Trust me – they're all little boys behind closed doors. Have your fun with them by all means but remember who *you* are, Prudence. Here, take these.' Ronnie handed her a few pots and bottles. 'Have a bath, spoil yourself, and for God's sake moisturise – sometimes when I look at your knees, I think of elephant's feet.'

When James called again and asked if she wanted to see the cliffs she leapt at the chance for redemption. It was already mid-July and hard to believe she had been there three weeks already.

On the walk they passed a man in bright yellow wellies cutting slabs of peat out of the ground, stacked up on the banks like giant pieces of dark chocolate. They trudged uphill, huffing and puffing into high wind, until the land plateaued and suddenly there was a sheer drop down to the sea as if a god had fallen into it with a chainsaw, cutting the land in a ragged shape. The ground at the cliff edges was covered in sea pink and silverweed like little yellow stars.

On the highest point there was a small building. Someone had attempted to cheer up the dour communist block with a layer of green paint, but it gave it a sinister undertone, like a clown that stinks of alcohol. Inside, the walls were putrid green, and it had a steep metal staircase in the middle which led up to a big window in the shape of an oversized letterbox, with two metal army bunks on either side. Prue looked out the window to a raging sea and straight down where the waves crashed like glass shattering against the rocks, spewing up white foam metres high.

'Shame about the weather being dreich,' said James. 'The window is for pointing guns out – this used to be a gun tower.'

'To shoot at what?'

'Nazis.'

'Nazis were birdwatchers?'

'Sometimes, Prue, you're really clever and other times… In case they tried to occupy the island, dummy? As a base to invade Scotland.'

'Oh.' Prue ran back down the metal stairs. It was like a caretaker's shed with boxes and junk. Old paint cans and dried-up brushes, what looked like a boiler. James sat on a crusty old sofa, while she squatted on an upturned bucket.

'My grandad built this place.'

'Did he have to keep watch?'

'Knowing him, he volunteered, anything to get away from Grannie. Me and my brother used to camp out here. We made fires and pretended we lived in the wild. We had this whole story we made up where our parents died in a plane crash, and we had to live off the land – bit morbid really. My parents would open the door of my grandparents' house, tell us to watch out for the cliffs and be home for dinner. It's a wonder we survived. My grandparents retired to the Mainland and they're in Sandwick now. What's it like where you're from?'

'Croydon is OK if you like shopping centres,' she said.

Earlier she had used the oils and creams Ronnie had

given her and moisturised her whole body, including her elephant knees, and borrowed some of Ronnie's less crazy lipstick and mascara which she was sure was older than she was. The perfume was weirdly addictive; she could smell peonies or suede or wood, and all sorts of other things. She had applied it on her pulse points and kept sniffing her own wrists when James wasn't looking. He searched through an old box and took out a half-empty bottle of something yellow.

'What is that?'

'Limoncello,' said James. 'I knew this was still here! Try it.'

Prue sipped some and it tasted of toilet cleaner. Disgusting. She wiped her mouth with the back of her hand, and when she opened her eyes, James was smirking.

'It's disgusting, isn't it? Me and my brother snuck it out here last time we were here. We used to play games and burn shit and smoke cigarettes.'

'I don't smoke and I'm not really into arson. So, let's play a game.'

'OK... Truth or Dare?'

'Truth.'

'OK, erm... tell me the worst thing you've ever done.'

'Let me think,' said Prue. She hadn't really ever done anything bad or naughty. She struggled to think of anything. She had a detention once but that was a whole class detention and she had been told off for cheeking the teacher, but there was only one thing that might possibly qualify as *really* bad.

'OK, there's a possibility, I think, perhaps that I might have put an innocent woman in prison, and if that turns out to be true then that would definitely be the worst thing I've ever done.' It wasn't that bad; it felt good to say it out loud.

'What?' James was about to take a swig from the bottle but missed his mouth. 'When was this?'

'When I was seven. I was the eyewitness that placed a woman at the scene of the crime but there was other evidence too, and she confessed, but then she denied it later.'

'What did she do?'

'She stole a baby. She took her from her Moses basket and drowned her.'

'Fuck! I was expecting a weird childhood crush on a teacher or breaking a neighbour's window. This is not what I expected.'

'There's people who think the woman, her name is Joan Gardner, she might not be responsible for taking the baby after all and the police bullied her into confessing. What if it's true? Can you imagine being locked up all these years and being innocent?'

'What does your aunt say?'

'Nothing, she doesn't like me bringing it up. What if she didn't do it? It was me who put her there.'

'First of all, the police put the case together – not you – and second, you were a kid, and thirdly, what was her defence doing?'

'I don't know. I honestly can't remember much about it, isn't that strange? I don't even remember what she looks like, yet it was me who identified her. It's as if the entire thing never happened at all. We'd moved out of Nana's house with my mum's boyfriend but only for a year because this happened, and we had to move back with Nana. But if Joan Gardner didn't do it, who did? Are the police even looking? You know, I can accept bad things happen but what I really struggle with is that someone can walk around living a normal life knowing something and keeping it to themselves. It's like the missing girl the islanders think Archie murdered. People don't vanish. Someone knows something. It's enough to drive you insane if you start thinking about it. I try not to, but I can't help it.' She took the bottle from James and took a gulp and shuddered.

'It's unfortunate but it's not your fault,' he said. 'For what it's worth, don't go blaming yourself.'

James was on the sofa with his feet up on the arm. Prue was feeling good. This perfume was working, she felt lighter and free as she got up. The scent really had gone to her head. She pushed his feet off the end of the sofa and sat down and could feel her own blood pumping. The colours were vibrant, and it was as if her senses had been turned up to maximum; she could feel everything. Her eyes were wider.

'Let's take a walk. I want to show you the cliffs,' said James.

The wind was fierce by the edge of the rocks and they could see all the way down to the sea. They came to a narrow inlet with a steep drop down the side of the cliff, with stacks of rocks where the waves broke against them, making huge sprays. The cliffs were packed with noisy fulmars. A prehistoric landscape that didn't seem real. Further along, a gradual slope led down to rocks and at the bottom was a series of azure rock pools, sheltered from the violence of the sea by a horseshoe shape of stacks and skerries.

'Can we go down to the rock pools?' asked Prue.

'If you like, yeah,' said James. 'You were scared of sheep last week, what's going on?'

'I guess I developed a sense of adventure,' she said.

They climbed down the steep grassy slope and over the rocks covered with seaweed and barnacles as sharp as broken glass. Prue never knew places like this existed; her life had been a blur of buses, school and dinners of chips and beans.

'I'm going in,' she said.

'Are you serious?'

She took her trainers off, then her jumper and her jeans, and piled up her clothes on the rocks. James watched with his mouth agog and Prue saw herself through another lens, stood beside herself, like the time she found her mother in the bath. But this time it felt good.

'Come on, don't be a pussy, I dare you,' she shouted at James, who looked bewildered.

'You're really doing this?' he asked.

'Yeah.'

She lowered herself in over the slippery rocks and into the water and gasped. It was pure and clear, but fucking freezing.

'Come on!' she shouted, her voice quivering as much as her jaw.

James shook his head in disbelief and then stripped off and climbed in after her, shaking and shouting at the arctic temperatures. They hopped about, squealing and laughing and shuddering.

Subo had told her that boys will fuck anything and not to take it as a compliment. The only difference is whether they brag about it to their friends or not. It was a question of supply and demand and back home there were millions of girls. She was a boring, plain daisy in a field of dog poo and empty crisp packets in South London, but here, she was an island daisy – *da kokkiluri* – bold and pretty. She was alive and beautiful and surrounded by a million different shades of blue and green. This wasn't even Earth. It may as well be the moon, or another dimension.

She stood up where the water came up to her belly button, took her bra off and threw it at the rocks where her clothes lay. James stood up and pulled at his wet boxer shorts.

'What are you doing?' he said.

'Do you want to have sex?'

There was a second of stillness where the world's lens shrank in on her then James burst out laughing, hard. Choking, even. Suddenly there was only one blue and green and she wasn't on the moon. She was here, very much on Earth, and she was stupid, idiotic Prue. Sad, weird, boring and disappointing Prudence Mary MacArthur. She crossed her arms over her chest feeling utterly stupid.

'Can you at least tell me why it's so funny?'

'No,' he said, putting his hands up. 'I'm not laughing at you. I'm shocked. You shocked me. I really wasn't expecting that.'

Prue strode out of the water and climbed over the rocks to her clothes.

'Hey! Hang on! I want to make it clear I'm not saying no.' James leapt out and skipped across the rocks to reach Prue. 'I just... er... Can we see what happens?'

'But if you see what happens, nothing happens – you have to make things happen.'

Prue moved away and James grabbed her arm. She

looked at where his fingers dug into her flesh, and he let go. 'Sorry. It may be worth mentioning that my penis has retracted into my body, and I think I'm perilously close to being hypothermic.'

They ran back to the gun tower carrying their clothes and wriggled out of their wet underwear and threw them down where they made a splat like vomit hitting concrete. They sat side by side on the crusty sofa as if waiting for a bus, shivering, and trying to get warm. James moved over and the sofa sank to the floor on one side.

'What are you doing?' she asked.

'Making things happen,' he said. He kissed her and she let him. This time she remembered not to flinch.

Prue crept back into the house with wet hair. She was within inches of her bedroom when Ruth came out of her studio.

'Where've you been? And why is your hair wet?' she asked.

Prue's head was a spinning wheel of unfeasible excuses – something about water fights and rogue waves. As she took her hands out of her pockets somehow her wet knickers got caught and flopped onto the carpet where they both stared at them.

'And why are your knickers in your pocket?' Ruth asked, folding her arms, leaning against the doorway.

'We had a water fight.' It sounded terrible and was lacking in conviction.

'And was his penis involved?' Ruth asked, without missing a beat.

Prue stood with her mouth hanging open, unable to think of a single word that would help.

'Hmmm,' said Ruth, as she scooped up the offending knickers from the floor on her index finger and handed them to Prue.

'Thank you,' she said, and took them and ran back to her bedroom. She put her forehead to the back of the door and let out a groan of pure humiliation, as if it would ease the pain of what she had put herself through that day.

12

The day after the embarrassing knicker incident, Prue woke up foggy headed after another bad night, slithered out of bed around eleven and went to help Ronnie in the greenhouse.

'I'm finished in here, help me collect poppy seeds.' Ronnie held each of the wilted poppies and when she shook them there was a faint rattle inside.

'Hear that? Those are the seeds. You're going to hold the little paper bags as I empty the pods.'

'Why do they have to be paper?'

'So they don't get fungus.'

'Are these heroin poppies?'

'No, opium poppies are pinker and purple, less red. The leaves are a bluish green and they have fat green seedpods. When you score the seedpod with a knife, out comes the sap – like a milk – and that's where opium comes from.'

'How do you know all this?'

'I'm old – when you get old you know things.'

That wasn't necessarily true: Nana had been very old and

was wrong about practically everything, except how to get most stains out. Ronnie seemed years younger than Nana but was actually a good five or so years older. She took care of herself, did her hair and makeup, and had passion. Nana had been rigid, inflexible, a *she knew what she knew* kind of person. Not that Ronnie was immune to crazy theories. As well as the plants, birds, eggs and an obsession with alchemy, she told Prue that to get what she wanted out of life she would one day have to choose what she would sacrifice. She also told her that if she ever wanted to learn to play the blues, she should sit in a graveyard at night and the ghosts would come and teach her – so she wasn't in the spirit of taking much seriously.

'Robert Johnson was a legendary blues guitarist,' said Ronnie. 'Only he wasn't having much luck until the day he met the devil at a crossroads.'

'Is this supposed to be a true story?' asked Prue. Ronnie shot her the look that said she should be quiet and carried on.

'The devil took the guitar, tuned it for him, gave it back and from that moment on Robert Johnson was a star. The world wanted a piece of Robert Johnson and he became one of the greatest blues guitarists that ever lived. Unfortunately, he died at the age of twenty-seven, because all deals with the devil come at a price.'

'So... you're saying I need to hang out on street corners until I meet the devil? I'm not sure that's sound advice, Ronnie, it kind of goes against the stranger danger message.'

'It's not really about the devil, stupid girl!' Ronnie snapped. 'The crossroads is a metaphor for a place or a time where you must offer something in return for a gift. It could be success, money, power, fame, opportunity, loyalty, even complicity. It's about what you're willing to do to gain control in a world of corruption and chaos, my girl, and the price you're willing to pay, and it starts, here.' Ronnie poked her finger hard in the soft part in between Prue's ribs.

'In my solar plexus?'

'No, in your gut! We are taught to be thinkers; we spend too much time in our heads, but it's the thoughts we must control – it's the gut we must listen to. It's your instinct. Most of what we think comes from what other people have told us. We're so far away from our instincts we can't hear them any more, the faintest of whispers drowned out by that television you insist on sitting in front of all the time.'

'If only we had a TV, I could prove you right.'

But where was her little voice? If she were to find herself at a crossroads and the devil appeared and asked her what she wanted, what would she say? It had to be the truth about everything – her father, Joan Gardner, and whatever else there was to know.

There was one little voice she had been ignoring, the one telling her how much she hated sleeping in the nursery, so after dinner she stuffed her belongings into her rucksack, unplugged Vegas Mary lamp, and marched downstairs, trying not to fall while carrying the giant statue or trip over any plants. She would not sleep in that room another night. It was hexed, with its wandering visitors, strange drips and noises and creepy hiding holes. She stopped in the kitchen to let the others know that, from now on, she was sleeping in the study, Archie's old bedroom with the metal bed. At her announcement, Ronnie leapt to her feet looking between Archie and Ruth. Ruth danced in front of Prue as she struggled to make her way back out of the kitchen and down the corridor to the study, as if she was marking her in netball.

'You can't!' said Ruth. 'It doesn't make sense. The nursery is the best bedroom. What if you need the bathroom at night?'

'I'll take a torch. Didn't Archie used to sleep in that room?' said Prue. 'I don't see what the big deal is.'

'Archie?' said Ronnie, and she and Ruth both glared at him, willing him into the situation.

Archie glanced up from his paper and shrugged. 'What? It'll be fine, just don't break anything.'

That seemed to seal the deal and Prue carried on triumphantly to the study, curious how Archie seemed to have the final say. She guessed this was why people put so much on being a Daddy's girl – not that she would know.

Ronnie entered the study as she was pulling out her crumpled clothes and went about reminiscing over every picture, toy or book, recalling how it came to be in the house. Prue was on her front under the old squeaky bed searching for a socket for the lamp. Ronnie sat her tiny doll frame down on the bed and it made a sound like a child playing the violin and nearly crushed Prue underneath.

'You must promise me you won't touch these books, Prue. Some of them are very old and the pages will fall apart. Literally, they'll disintegrate. Do you promise you'll leave them alone?'

Still trying to find the socket, she said, 'They'll be quite safe from me.' She found the plug and crawled back out.

Ronnie nodded at the books again. 'Remember not to touch the plants, won't you, my dear?'

'Yes, yes, I know, the sap and sensitive skin,' she said. Ronnie hung at the door, and then left.

What was the big deal about this room? Prue looked at the books and wasn't remotely interested in any of them. Never much of a reader, she didn't even like stories. Preferred fact. Truth. Real life. She saw a book on Shetland's wildflowers and, ignoring her recent promise, carefully moved the plants and took it off the shelf to look through the pages. As she was flicking through, two pieces of paper flew out and floated to the floor at her feet. She put the book down and picked them both up. One was the shape of a swan, folded up origami-style, and the other was a paper fortune teller. A game she had played herself in primary school where paper is folded into triangles with messages on the inside, usually about a crush. She sat on the squeaky bed and wondered who could have left it there. It was the same paper game – pick a colour, pick a number – and she unwrapped it to read the messages:

You will meet a witch
Kiss Evie's lips
You'll fall under her unbreakable spell
Kiss Evie behind the ear
You'll fall hopelessly in love
Kiss Evie's neck
You will worship her!
Kiss Evie... wherever she commands

No, it wasn't remotely like the version she had played at primary school. It couldn't possibly be *that* Evie, could it? The missing girl? Her name was Evie. How could a little paper game find its way inside the pages of a book of wildflowers and stay hidden all this time, and who put it there? *Kiss Evie... wherever she commands.* Good God. That meant the messages were for her uncle. Urgh. Gross. She closed the game back up. She could hear the banging headboard from the other night. She put the paper game back inside the book. James had said Evie had been seventeen when she disappeared, practically the same age as her. Was this how to be *sexy*? She put the book back on the shelf. This was a revelation. No wonder James had laughed at her.

James's mother had offered Prue cash in hand for a few shifts cleaning at the bar since she'd lost a barmaid. Her duties involved laughing with James, elbows up on the bar, running the same bacteria-infused damp rag over the sticky tables every so often.

She was on her way back from one of these shifts walking through the trees as the heavens opened. It grew dark, worse under the leaves, and Prue thought of Evie and her handwriting inside the paper game. Before, the missing girl had only been a name and she'd seen the names of a lot of dead or missing girls in the news or on TV. But after touching the paper, Prue could imagine her giggling as she wrote the messages. What if she was murdered where she was walking now? Anyone could have been following her, waiting until she was in the darkest part where no one else could see. Her body could be anywhere in those trees hidden in a shallow grave. She could even be walking over her right now.

Prue spooked herself enough to break into a run and didn't stop until she made it into the garden. Ronnie had made her fill in the trench the demon-dog had dug, and she was disappointed to see her handywork intact, although going by the size of its head it could have easily leapt the wall.

As she passed Archie's studio in the garden, she saw the door was wide open and slowed down to a treacle-like crawl to peer inside. She had a foot over the threshold, but no one was in there and the lights weren't on. Her eyes struggled and all she could see was a dark room.

'You can come in if you like.' Archie appeared behind her and blocked the doorway, forcing Prue further inside. She leapt out of her skin and span around as he stepped in, pulled the light cord and shut the door behind him. She could hear her pulse pounding and the buzz of the bulb overhead. Then she heard the groaning he'd made the night she'd heard him with her aunt, and the words from the paper game flittered past her eyes... *Kiss Evie...* What would she do if his spade-like hands were to reach for her neck and start to squeeze? Would it hurt very much?

'Sorry,' she said.

'What for?' He folded his hairy tattooed arms across his chest, looking down at her. He was built like a rugby player, intimidating, and he also knew it. She wouldn't have had a chance if he wanted to hurt her.

'You're here now, why not take a look?' he said, and gestured she should turn around rather than continue her awkward gawping. 'I promise I won't bite – not on your first visit,' and he laughed, amused by her discomfort. She pulled her hood down and folded her arms across her body and turned around.

Opposite was a bare-brick wall with rows of Polaroid photographs. It was hard to figure out what the photos were of at first, only rows and rows in lines. Then she realised every picture was a girl, or part of a girl's body or face – a mugshot gallery of flesh. Close-ups of open mouths, heavy-lidded eyes, tilted necks, there were thighs, feet and hands. Each one had writing in black marker underneath, names and dates. They had been lined up with precision and must have covered a space as big as her bedroom floor back home. It was a photographic catalogue of every female who had passed through his studio disassembled in parts. A study of the flesh without a person.

Archie sat on a wheeled stool with a seat like a saddle and watched as she looked around the room, painfully self-conscious. There were paint-splattered work benches, canvases stacked against the walls, or doubled up on easels, some half-finished, some blank – but all of women. The room stank of oils and turps and there was a sofa covered with a paint-encrusted dust sheet and material screwed up on the seat. An old metal storage chest acted as a coffee table and was covered in lumps of paint and stains. Archie picked up and threw down various tubes of oil paints, muttering and swearing, searching for something specific among the mess.

On the bare-brick wall next to a mirror were framed newspaper and magazine articles. Prue went to look at them as Archie carried on searching for something, but at least he wasn't staring at her any more. There were double-page spreads and clipped-out columns and photographs all about Archie the artist. Prue scanned through an article, and it mentioned how Archie had been wrongly accused of murder in his youth, almost to add to the dark allure about his art, but it didn't mention who the victim was. The photograph alongside it was of him with a girl leaning against him with her head resting on his shoulder. She was naked from the waist up with a white fur shrug covering her breasts and she wore a crown of antlers which Prue noticed were hanging up on the wall. When she looked back at the paintings, she realised they were all of girls posed or painted, tattooed, and wearing animal heads, crowns or antlers like in the article on the wall. Some had their hands bound; in the more disturbing ones the girls were crying. One girl dangled by her wrists from a beam with a crown of thorns on her head and she stared straight ahead, bug-eyed, glazed over. Prue recognised her as the girl with the black and pink pigtails and beautiful fat mouth who had waved at her. If Archie *had* murdered Evie, he was very much prepared to rub the islanders' faces in it. If he *hadn't*, this was a strange fixation for a man to foster if he wanted people to think he was innocent. She hadn't realised Archie had stopped searching and was sat watching her as she studied the paintings with her mouth open.

'Ronnie doesn't like my paintings either,' he said, jolting her back to the room in real time.

'I didn't say I didn't like them.' She tried to sound assertive, but it came out snappy. 'They're not what I expected.'

'Oh, what did you expect?'

'I'm not really sure. I knew you were an artist, so I guess I expected watercolours of landscapes or portraits of royalty, I dunno, animals.'

He laughed and turned back to his canvas, his legs wide apart. His arms looked as if they had fat serpents curled around the bone beneath the skin. He had big hands, but his fingernails were bitten down to stubs. Something made him bite them.

'Maybe you should pose for me?' he said.

'I'm sorry?' Horrified, Prue span around, unsure if she'd heard her uncle correctly. 'Pose? Like these girls? No! No, I couldn't.' *Kiss Evie…* She squeezed her eyes shut so it might block out the thoughts.

He laughed, and the guttural sound filled the room. He shook his head. 'No, not like those girls. I don't think that would be on, do you? I assume you don't have tattoos. I need reference photographs of unblemished skin.' He pointed down at Prue's bare legs in her shorts.

'Oh…' She began blushing. God, as gormless as a goldfish. It was made much worse by the fact he'd seen her faint in her knickers and she'd cried in front of him. Why would anyone want her to pose like those girls, what an idiot.

'I didn't mean to embarrass you.'

'I'm not embarrassed,' she insisted.

'You're blushing,' he said.

'No, I'm not,' she said, and turned away to hide her burning cheeks. Then she heard a lighter striking behind her, and she smelt it – he was smoking weed. She turned around again, shocked.

'Does my aunt know you smoke that?' she said, sounding like a hall monitor.

He laughed again, not so hard this time but enough to deepen the lines around his eyes. He drew breath to answer but the door flew open and there was Ruth in the doorway in the pouring rain.

'Prue? What are you doing in here? Archie! Are you smoking in front of...? What the fuck, Archie!'

Ruth's eyes dropped to Prue's bare legs and then back to her face. Her mouth opened and shut a little too tight and she stiffened in the doorway, wrapping herself up in her baggy cardigan.

'Prue, go back to the house,' she said, and held the door as Prue ducked out underneath her arm and then slammed it shut, locking herself inside with her husband. Prue could hear Ruth shouting at him as she ran up to the house.

13

A couple of days later Ruth went to Glasgow for a few days for meetings to prepare for her all-important upcoming exhibition and Archie disappeared on another fishing trip. Prue and Ronnie were alone in the house.

It started to rain and didn't seem as if it would ever stop, and James called to say not to worry about coming for a shift as a big storm was on its way. Subo had told her on the phone that there was still a heatwave in London and Prue tried her best not to be bitter as she stared out the window with rain coming down in great fat droplets, propelled by a terror of a wind that forced it sideways. If you dared go out, it hit you straight in the eyes like needles and the fog was so bad that you could barely see more than a few metres in front of your face. In such terrible weather, the weaknesses of the house were exposed, and it seemed older and ached and groaned under the wind that whistled through it, rattling the windows and doors in their latches. It was cold and damp and condensation was on every window.

Draughts lifted the leaves and creeping tendrils appeared alive and the hanging pots swung like hammocks on a ship.

Prue thought this the perfect opportunity to get into Ruth's studio again but when she tried the studio door it was locked again, ridiculous. The front door left open for any person to walk in, but inside doors – locked. Why would Ruth do that if she wasn't hiding something?

Out of desperation she scanned the bookshelves in the study looking for something to read – *Maritime Law, Ship Brokering, Naval Architecture, Cargo*. Nothing was appealing but then she had a thought: what if there were more paper games inside the pages? She manoeuvred vases out of the way and found the first book that had nothing to do with water, *The Rise and Fall of the British Empire*, and when she flicked through, the book fell open to a page with a wad of twenty-pound notes jammed inside. Prue snapped the book shut and returned it, moving the vases and plants back in place. She was not meant to find that. Was that why Ronnie was so nervous about her being in the study? It must be her money. Enough nosing for now; curiosity killed the cat, as her Nana used to say.

Prue picked up her clothes from the piles she'd left on the floor and hung them on the mantelpiece with coat hangers from upstairs; she even briefly considered dusting. Then she phoned Subo, who wasn't in, and went straight back to the study and started to check the books. She stood on the end of the bed on the footrail and started at the top left corner, working her way along methodically, from left to right, top to bottom, a shelf at a time. She didn't find anything until she came to a spiky blue flower in the shape of little helmets and took the book behind it. Inside she found more money.

Stepping back, she noticed most of the plants were flowerless, but the two books she had found with money had flowers in front. To test her theory, Prue went straight to the next book behind a white flower in a mason jar and in two places found more cash. When she backtracked to check the others – no money. That was the simple system Ronnie was using to hide money in the books. It must be one of those bizarre habits old people have. Her Nana used to hide toilet paper under dollies with woollen dresses and insisted stomach ulcers were caused by stress and spicy food. She wouldn't accept it was bacteria even though Prue had learned that two doctors from Australia won a Nobel Prize for working out the truth. Stephen Hawking could have come over and told her and she would have argued to his face he was wrong. Nana had done her banking at the post office and Ronnie didn't even leave the house, let alone the island. There was no bank, and the banking van only came to the village for half a day, once a week.

It wasn't money Prue was hoping to find, though, and she felt disappointed, then fell on another book: *Edgar Allan Poe*. It wouldn't do any harm to try one more, she thought, and as she flicked the pages, they fell open to a piece of paper folded in half. Flush with excitement, she was about to take it out when the door opened, and Ronnie walked in. Prue leapt on the bed and pretended to be reading.

'It's only little old me, brightening up as usual, my dear.' But when Ronnie saw her with a book she froze in horror and the new flowers almost fell off her tray.

'What are you doing?' she said. 'You told me you didn't read.'

'I *can* read, the state school system isn't that bad.' Prue tried to make a joke of it, although Ronnie's face said she was in no mood to be amused. She looked as if she'd seen a ghost.

Ronnie composed herself enough to focus on her purpose and began taking down the dying flowers and replacing them with fresh ones but there was a palpable tension radiating from her. Prue had had enough practice anticipating her mother's moods to know when someone was off kilter. She had become so attuned that she could tell what kind of evening was in store by the way her mother turned the key in the front door. Prue must have read the same page four or five times. When it came to leaving, Ronnie stopped at the door.

'Prudence, remember to be careful of my books. Some are worth a lot of money, so if you want to read one, ask me and I'll get it for you.'

'OK, will do. Sorry.' Prue looked back down at the page, but Ronnie didn't move. She put the tray on a side table and sat down next to Prue on the bed. Prue looked up and Ronnie was gazing at her, then reached up and pushed her hair back behind her ear like a pet again.

'I have to be sure you won't damage things. You don't want that, do you?'

'No, of course not. I'm sorry.'

'It's all right,' said Ronnie. 'But don't do it again. There's a lot of things about this house you don't understand.' Ronnie finished with her most serene smile. The moment was so hideous, Prue thought she might develop an ulcer from the stress and prove her Nana right after all.

When Ronnie finally left, she let out a huge sigh and felt her shoulders collapse, but the exchange only made her more curious. Being an old house most of the doors still had keys in them, so she locked the door and sat back down and found the page with the paper inside. She had butterflies as she took out the yellowing paper and opened it. It had jagged edges along one side as if it had been torn and was handwritten in blue ink. In the top right-hand corner was a printed date – Monday, 20th August 1973 – so it *had* been torn from a diary.

My dandelion boy, I love you so it hurts. I'm not joking! My bones ache. The reason we fell for each other so hard is (I think) we both know what it's like to have a hole left by our lost mothers. We found better in each other. The black sheep. The outsiders. They can call us stuck up, rude, unfeeling for all I care but it's us who were wronged. I'm so happy we found each other.

I'm worried we should tell Ronnie. I'm bursting to tell someone and she adores you. Please think about it. And stop your worrying about me, I'll be fine. It's our adventure! Like you said – we will build an empire! Like the Romans! Except we won't mess it up because we are soul mates and meant to be. Get a lot of sleep because when you come back, you won't be getting any.

Things will be all right. I have faith in you. There's a whole world out there and it's going to be all ours. I think I want to do something in psychiatry or psychology, I'm not sure which but I'll figure it out.

PS: If you look at another girl I will KILL YOU!!!!

Evie (the future Mrs Anderson – doesn't Evie Anderson
sound good? Like I should be famous!? Maybe one day
I will be Dr Anderson!)
Ha Ha! love you.

Prue read it over and over. What was a scrawled note
from a missing girl doing in the pages of a random book?
Who put it there? Dandelion boy?! That couldn't be Archie?
For the first time Prue felt sorry for Evie. Poor missing Evie
who never got to build her empire and was so in love.

When she tried to find the same place in the book to put
the note back, she spotted something: jammed against the
spine inside the back cover was a Polaroid photo. It was
blurry with terrible contrast, a picture of a boy and a girl,
lying side by side. The boy, who she had to suspect was
a very young and skinny Archie, had taken the picture at
arm's length. The girl had to be Evie. Her hair spread across
a pillow. Young Archie with his smooth skin and golden
hair strained to look at the camera while kissing Evie on the
cheek as she laughed with blissful eyes. Neither seemed to
be wearing any clothes, but the photo only showed the top
part of their shoulders. It was a moment of pure happiness
with messy hair and lean, tangled bodies and no space
between them.

She couldn't stop staring at them both and read the note
over and over, and in her mind, she could hear Evie's voice.
Poor tragic Evie had vanished and never had the chance
to tell anyone about this secret or decide whether to be a
psychiatrist or a psychologist. It wasn't fair. But there was
something else, a little envy perhaps, because what she saw
in the picture was what she desperately wanted for herself,

and she couldn't imagine it ever happening to her. She could barely fathom what it would be like.

What it would have been like to know the Archie in the picture, and not the one who kept a gallery on his wall of crying or bleeding girls. How did he become *that bastard* when he had been Evie's own dandelion boy? On the back was a date, 23rd July 1973, in the same writing; it was twenty years ago. How odd that these slips of paper had remained hidden away for almost exactly twenty years and her curiosity had found them. Now she was powerless in the face of temptation. Be it a distant voyeurism or macabre stalking, she was going to have to go through every book and find what was hidden inside.

For three whole days the torrential rain carried on, like a never-ending wet play session, where Ronnie tried to teach Prue poker in the Morning Room as the windows steamed up. The lights were on because it was so gloomy, and rain lashed at the windows without pausing for breath. Prue couldn't stop daydreaming about Evie.

'Ronnie, can I ask you a question?'

'If it's not about plants or poker, I'm no expert, but go ahead,' said Ronnie, laying down another card.

'It's about Gladys O'Hara.'

Ronnie focused on the cards and raised an eyebrow. 'I told Ruth you'd find out. Rumours are like water and this island is no submarine. Have you spoken to Ruth?'

'I tried,' she said. 'It made her angry. I seem to be good at that these days.'

'Well, my dear girl, it's understandable. Some of us have

had longer to grow a thicker skin about the whole debacle,' she said, and looked out of the steamy window. 'You know, I think it's time to start drinking?'

Ronnie fixed the drinks and put a crackly old record on the record player. Her music was awful, even worse than Nana's; at least Nana had liked a bit of Queen, even if she had refused to accept Freddie Mercury was bisexual.

'Who is this?'

'Doris Day and the Mellomen, it's called "Again". I love this song. Alastair and I used to dance to this in the dining room. How did you find out who Gladys was?'

'I overheard people talking about it at the bar in the hotel.'

'You'd have thought they'd have found something else to gossip about after twenty years,' Ronnie huffed.

'All I know is a girl went missing and that some people, including that woman, think Archie had something to do with it.'

'Allow me to translate island nonsense for you, my girl – Gladys O'Hara is insane and a drunk!' Ronnie used an ice pick to crack a block of ice and Prue thought she would stab her own hand. 'She's deranged!' Ronnie carried on. 'Someone should do something about her. It should be a criminal offence what she has done to us.' Ronnie waggled the ice pick in her direction to prove her point. 'That woman has kept rumours alive all these years. She's obsessed. They never found a shred of evidence; did you know that? No! They won't tell you that part. The police searched this whole house, tore it inside out, searched the trees. We were violated! They never found a bloody thing and you know why? Because Archie is innocent. There was nothing to find! He was a sweet but stupid boy who got himself wrapped up with the wrong girl.'

'Why was she the wrong girl?'

'Evelyn O'Hara was never his *girlfriend*,' spat Ronnie. 'They all said that, but it wasn't true. They were running around together, yes, but she was never a girlfriend. It wasn't serious,' Ronnie bristled. Maybe her skin wasn't as thick as she thought. 'Evelyn left quite an impression on people – when I say people, I mean men. Archie was only young, your age. Evelyn was a few months older. He'd been thrown out of school and Robert, his father, wasn't easy on him and then Evelyn swept in, all wide eyes and thighs; she was a welcome distraction.' Ronnie finished pouring the cocktails and handed Prue her drink before sitting down.

'I thought you said that you didn't mix with the locals – how did they meet, then?'

'There was an event at the war memorial and, being a naval family, Robert had us march down there like the Von Trapps. Evelyn turned up in shorts and all the men were trying not to get caught drooling but it was hilarious to watch all the eyes continually gravitate to her thighs. I mean, how inappropriate? The event was to honour the war dead and the girl turns up in hotpants! Still, I thought it amusing – that was, until I saw who she was looking at. Archie was a handsome boy, he stuck out against the local boys, who all looked as if they had rickets or only one good lung. I remember thinking, now there is a girl who knows what she wants.'

'And what did she want?'

'A way out,' said Ronnie.

'Of what?'

'Her situation, her family. Even we had heard the O'Hara brood were known to be... unpredictable. They weren't islanders; I believe they came over from Liverpool in the fifties, or somewhere else grim and depressing. They're all dead or long gone now, except for Gladys and her reprobate of a son. One minute laughing, the next swinging punches – you know the type. Spent most of their time feeling sorry for themselves and wailing how life wasn't fair.'

'What was Evie like? From what you say she must have been pretty?'

'No, pretty girls are like lollipops – two a penny. Evelyn O'Hara was stunning, and by God, she knew it. Archie told me her father was a Norwegian sailor, which doesn't narrow it down, but Lord knows how she came out the way she did because you'd never guess by looking at her mother. Gladys was a raggedy thing even back in the seventies.'

'What do you think happened to her?'

'Who knows! Her mother told the police she was on her way here to see Archie, but she never arrived.'

'I heard they thought she went missing in the woods.'

'They say that, but... We've only her mother's word for that. No one saw her. One is forced to speculate and ask yourself this, why would the mother shout so about the trees? What if it is to take the focus away from herself? We only have her word Evelyn left her house in the first place – what if it's all an elaborate ruse to cover up what really happened?'

'You think Gladys killed her own daughter?'

'I don't know, Prue, perhaps. Then again, perhaps she went to the Mainland. There were lots of ships from Europe even then, she could have got on any one of them and gone anywhere. A sailor could have killed her or abducted her. They didn't listen when I told the police that; they dismissed me as a silly woman. They never explored any other suspects, only Archie; wasted their meagre resources and found nothing.'

'Don't the rumours drive you mad? Surely you want people to know the truth?'

Ronnie smiled. 'Oh my dear Prue, you should know there is something deeply troubling about most people, and that is they will believe what suits them and most of the time the truth doesn't matter. Truth is such a pure concept and the execution so mired in confusion, it's why God invented lawyers. What do you think of the orange gin?' But before Prue could answer there was a loud crack outside.

'What was that?' said Prue.

They both sat upright. Then a dull thump hit the glass of the French doors and fell to the ground, leaving a red smear dripping down the windows. Prue ran to the doors.

'Be careful!' Ronnie followed.

Prue opened the door and on the step outside was a heap of black feathers. She knelt as Ronnie bent over, looking out at the garden to see who could have thrown it, but there was no one there. It was one of the ravens, dead – all twisted and bloody.

'The poor thing,' said Ronnie.

'It can't have fallen like this,' said Prue.

'It didn't. That was a gunshot. Someone shot it and threw it at our window. Someone is trying to scare us. We will not be intimidated by philistines!' Ronnie shouted, then to Prue she said, 'Come along, close the door.'

Together they prepared to go out to see if anything else

had been interfered with in the garden. Prue armed herself with a broom and Ronnie the metal bin lid from the mud room. It wasn't a very convincing armoury.

'I'll be only a moment.' Ronnie disappeared into her bedroom and reappeared minutes later with an old gun.

'Ronnie! What's that!?'

'It's my husband's old handgun.'

'But... It doesn't work, does it?'

'Perhaps we'll find out.'

They braced the weather blowing a hoolie, and went into the maze that was the garden, looking for evidence of intruders or anything someone may have left behind. The weather was awful and the search fruitless so they abandoned it after checking behind the greenhouse and making sure the sheds were empty. Later, when the wind had died down enough, they buried the dead bird in one of the borders. Prue dug the hole as Ronnie watched, directing and holding an umbrella. When she was finished, Prue leaned on the shovel, sweating in the rain and drenched; Ronnie was bone dry.

'What do we tell Ruth and Archie?'

'Nothing. Archie will get angry, Ruth will worry. Best we keep this to ourselves.'

'Who do you think did it?'

'Could be any one of them. I wouldn't be frightened – more like some idiot's idea of fun than a threat.'

'Can we at least lock the doors tonight?'

'Very well, but only until Archie and Ruth are back. I refuse to be a captive in my own home.' Prue didn't see how locking the doors from the inside made you a captive but it wasn't worth arguing.

The house was an echo of droplets. There were two leaks in the ceiling in the rooms upstairs and Ronnie had Prue keep checking the buckets. After endless rounds of cards, they decided to get drunk and Ronnie made every cocktail she could think of. Soon Prue was rolling around on the sofa and everything was hilarious. Being drunk was so much fun. She forgot she was ugly or stupid or hated herself and didn't care what she might have done to Joan Gardner or why she hadn't had a boyfriend at the ripe old age of sixteen. Soon Prue lost track of time and everything went hazy.

'Did you know that the word *occult* actually means *hidden*?' asked Ronnie. Prue remembered this part. 'And I bet you didn't know that Jesus's real name was Yeshua bin Maryam, and that for hundreds of years after his death, the Romans regarded him as a magician.'

Prue found this hysterically funny. She could only think of Jesus in a long white robe and a top hat in front of a red curtain. She was laughing on her back and felt so light, as if she was floating around the room, her nose skimming the ceiling.

'What was Jesus's real name again?' Prue asked. 'And what does he have to do with soldiers?' Prue laughed so much she cried, and soon she was a beetle on its back, laughing at what, she didn't know.

At some point they moved to Ronnie's bedroom, and she was lying on the big white bed and the bath was running. Then she was in the bath, naked, with Ronnie telling her she was going to expel the spirits of guilt and the feelings she had infused with importance. It wasn't real, she told her. Nothing was. Ronnie's face blurred in a kaleidoscope of colours and shapes and there were things in the water, honey, lemons and petals. Ronnie was dropping coloured petals over her and then her face faded away and she felt as if she were sinking into the bath and through it. She remembered thinking she might drown but didn't mind at the time, it was so good to feel free, as if she was floating.

Prue heard her mother's voice. When she opened her eyes, they were sitting underneath the old lacy tablecloth with their legs crossed in Nana's garden. The sun beamed through the holes in the cloth like spotlights.

'Do you remember the game, Prue?' her mother asked. 'You can magic all the bad things away and always be free.'

But I don't want to forget. Why can't I remember?

'Shush, make a wish, Prue,' said her mother, and she held a fluffy white dandelion head up for her. 'Look, close your eyes and make a wish, and all the little fairies will carry it away for you.'

When Prue woke up, it was morning, and she was in her bed in the study in her bed T-shirt. She felt odd and paranoid; her hair was stiff in places as if it had something in it and it had dried. She had vague memories of what happened the night before, but after the bath, even in the bath, she had no idea if any of that had really happened or if she had dreamed it, but she felt unsettled and scared.

14

Four days after she left, Ruth returned to the house without Archie but brought back better weather. It was as sunny and warm as it was ever going to get in the last week of July and Prue ran straight back to pick up with James.

Subo told her during one of their phone calls to think of sex the same as brushing your teeth and making sure you drink water. A habit we learn. She simply wasn't trying hard enough to make a habit of anything sexual with James. They were more like friends, or a good brother and sister; they had fun but there wasn't any lust. Subo said passion was bullshit anyway.

'You get on with it and once you've done it a few times – it doesn't seem like such a big deal,' she'd said.

But to Prue it did seem like a big deal. A huge mountain. Not so much in the physical sense but within her. She'd never really been attracted to any one person. She'd never felt burning desire but knew from the girls on MTV that hot girls were highly sexed and wielding their sexuality like a swinging axe. She'd once had a crush on a girl in Year Nine and spent a whole year thinking she might be gay, but it wore off as the girl turned out to be horrible. Then there was the time she kissed Subo; it was actually her first real kiss, and it had been with a girl. This was before they were best friends and because of a dare.

All the boys had been perving over Subo but she'd said she'd rather kiss Prue, who happened to be behind her walking home from school as Subo was being hustled by a group. They called her bluff and Subo dared Prue right then and there and so they kissed in the middle of a group of boys whooping and laughing down the alley to the playing fields. Prue had obsessed about what this meant for weeks but Subo didn't give it a second thought. That's how they became friends. Prue was basically adopted by Subo whether she liked it or not. But she liked it; she'd been lonely before and never really able to connect to anyone.

She'd never had crushes on the boys at school or been able to join in the conversations girls had about how hot some boy was or how fit another was. How could she when they were all idiots? Maybe desire came after the act and the body would know how to respond and she should stop overthinking it, the way she overthought everything.

Subo might not be around but someone else had given her some clues about how to be sexy, so the next time she was in James's bedroom she closed the door and jumped on his bed cross-legged.

'Face me,' she told him, then she took out the paper fortune teller she had made, exactly like the one Evie made for Archie, except this only had *Kiss me* inside. Prue didn't have the resolve for any other messages. Baby steps.

'Haven't seen one of these for years!' said James, then he picked a number and colour, and inevitably got the message. 'All right, close your eyes.'

Prue waited with her eyes shut and James pulled her towards him. She thought of brushing her teeth or drinking water. They both lay down and James leaned on top of her, and his hands travelled between the covers and her clothes, his fingers like worms trying to navigate. His mouth found the skin of her neck, and she could hear the sound of his kisses against her skin. She turned to face him so that his tongue could find her mouth and they kissed as James's hands made their way under the waistband of her shorts. Stick to the plan. This is what she wanted but what should she be doing?

'What do you like?' he asked her as his hands crept under her knickers and between her legs. She couldn't answer and she dared not move. All she could do was take his hand and show him, because she'd done it to herself often enough.

'Is that door SHUT?' shouted his mother up the stairs. James jumped off and Prue scrabbled up to sitting. He thumped over to the door and wrenched it open the dictated six inches.

'For fuck's sake! No, Mother. It's not!'

'Do you think I'm a glaikit eejit? It's ma hoose... and under my roof—' James slammed his bedroom door, muffling her ranting.

He huffed and leaned against the door. 'We need more privacy,' he said. 'We may have to retreat to the gun tower. Bring the game.'

★★★

As they walked to the gun tower, Prue started to feel the pressure, and now whatever carefree nymph act she was attempting to fake was impossible. She didn't feel sexual, it was too bright, it was during the day, she felt bloated, it was a bit cold. At the gun tower the paper game seemed irrelevant, despite the fact she had stuffed it into her pocket. Prue wasn't sure what she expected, only that she would definitely need to do something to James this time. This was what she wanted, and she had put herself in this position, yet she wasn't really sure what to do or how to do it and that made her feel sick. It felt as if she was playing a part, an actress in a role, a bad one. She had to be coquettish and seductive, but she hadn't been on a training course and didn't know what she was doing. She really, really wished she'd asked Subo for more practical guidance.

James had his tongue in her mouth as soon as they were inside the gun tower, and she threw herself into her role with the gusto you would expect from a red-blooded South London girl. But the acting was gossamer thin, like that veil she was born under. The caul – the piece of the amniotic sac that was still over her face when she came out that her Nana told her was good luck. Urgh! Now Nana was in her head. Go away!

James's hands were all over her and inside her top. Prue thought of the movies and music videos with teenage girls throwing themselves around on top of cars or in front of singers, and tried to banish Nana and her maraca lungs, although she kept trying to poke her nose in. Her white socks were wet. She saw the knife clatter around the sink and her mother was in the bath again, then she heard the indicators of the police car, *tick-tick-tick*. She pulled away.

'What is it?' asked James. His lips had swollen from all the kissing and his eyes danced about her face; he looked stupid.

'Nothing,' she said, and she tried again, kissing him with all her force, almost smashing teeth in the hope the energy she invested would trigger some prehistoric urge and push out everything else swimming around her head.

He started to kiss her neck and pull her top off her shoulders and put his wet kisses all over her shoulder. Prue stared at the ceiling, her neck bent at an awkward angle, and she wondered if there was any limoncello left. He pulled her bra down and his mouth found her nipple. She thought about asking him about the limoncello then he unbuckled his trousers and oh my God – this was really going to happen – but this was the plan. He grabbed one of her hands and tried to put it inside his boxers but there was no way she could do that. Prue snatched her hand back.

'What's the matter now?' he asked.

'... I don't feel well.'

'What? How? Like, how unwell?'

'I'm sorry,' she said, and ran out of the gun tower, pulling her top up and leaving James utterly confused with his flies undone and his mouth open.

By the time she made it to the trees she was crying. She was an imbecile, a clown and a joke. She'd really blown it. Stupid, stupid Prue. She relived the moment over and over like a form of medieval torture and cried all over again. She sat snivelling to herself by the dying American larch until her eyes dried and she looked, she hoped, less blotchy.

Ronnie was in the greenhouse and waved at her when

she walked past. This was the last thing she needed: the woman was impossible to hide anything from. She dragged herself over and Ronnie met her at the door, unlocked it and beckoned her inside.

'I could do with some help if you aren't busy?' Prue nodded and went inside.

There was a wooden table with pear-shaped glassware filled with bubbling liquid over a naked flame. All around were bowls and dishes filled with mashed petals, bark and leaves.

'What is all this?'

'Alchemy, my dear girl. Do you know, between the two world wars there was a rather thriving scene in Germany? Of course you didn't. Based on some of the techniques pioneered during the era, I am making herbal medicine involving distillation, fermentation and the extraction of minerals from various species. I'm extracting pure magic from nature and will use it for tea for ingestion or an oil infusion, maybe both. It's for Ruth. She's been having stomach aches, not to mention that rash on her arm. Talking of hanging around, I could feel that black cloud of yours enter before you did. Has something happened?'

'No, I'm fine.'

'Pants on fire, Prue.'

Her eyes were nailed down, feigning interest in Ronnie's experiments. Ronnie whipped off her gardening glove and put a finger under Prue's chin and lifted her face, so she had no choice but to make eye contact.

'Hmmm, puffy eyes, you might be able to lie to yourself but not to me. It's not about that boy, is it? I thought I'd imparted my wisdom on that subject.'

'No, it's not. It's me. It's always me. I think there's something wrong with me. I feel... odd, like I don't fit in.'

'What do you want to fit in with exactly?'

'Anything, anyone,' shrugged Prue. 'It sounds stupid, but I feel as if something is missing.'

'Oh dear,' said Ronnie. 'We have stumbled down the melancholic well today, haven't we? What's the point of fitting in? I can't think of anyone who has achieved much or stood for anything worthwhile who has. My girl, give it a few years, the tables will turn. When those peers of yours are pushing prams around and going home to cook pie and mash for the first boy who proposed to them, they'll wish to God they'd had a little something odd about them. Most people prefer not to think, Prue, and even if they had free will, they wouldn't use it. Why not start questioning what it is that's expected of you to fit in? The world needs pioneers, Prudence, not more sheep. We have plenty of those already.'

Later that evening when Ruth knocked on the study door and told her James was on the phone, she was shocked; she was sure she'd never hear from him again.

'Hey,' he said, 'I wanted to check in and see how you were feeling. Any better?'

'Yes, I'm a lot better, thank you.'

'So what was wrong?'

'I don't know. I... came over really sick all of a sudden.'

'Oh, right, well. OK. I mean, it wasn't me, was it?'

'You?'

'I was worried it was something I did, or I scared you off...'

Prue laughed; she heard herself laughing like a maniacal witch and in turn hated herself even more. It sounded so awfully false, a forced cackle. If she had one of Ronnie's pointed trowels, she would have stabbed herself with it.

'Don't be silly, of course not,' she said. 'I felt sick, so I ran home.' No, she wasn't a sad little virgin who, when pressed in the moment with the expectation of handling someone's penis, didn't know whether to butter it or stick it in her ear. 'I'm sorry for running out on you. I guess it must have been something I ate.'

'Right,' said James, although she wasn't sure he was buying it. 'Do you want to go over to the Mainland tomorrow? There's a couple of books I've ordered, and they should have come in, so I thought, if you weren't still ill, and the sight of me didn't make you feel physically sick, we could go for a few drinks.'

'That sounds fun,' said Prue.

This was another chance. Maybe there was a God. The plan was still the plan, she could save this. She didn't quite understand how, but James was still interested.

They met at the point where their paths would cross if they were both to walk to the ferry. Prue tried her best to smile and be effervescent and James responded by politely ignoring whatever it was that had happened in the gun tower the day before.

The books turned out to be texts for his Psychology degree. After collecting them they wandered around the streets of Lerwick, made their way up to the old fort with views out to sea and an ancient cannon. They stopped for ice cream and when it was already gone four in the afternoon they tried the small dingy bar along the front of the road by the ferry terminal because James said they never asked for ID. It wasn't very busy inside the dark and windowless bar, which was almost like a converted house. They found a spot in the corner and James put the thick textbooks on the table.

'A bit of light reading,' said Prue, nodding at the heavy books.

'I don't know who I'm kidding, I probably won't look at them until I start.'

'So why Psychology?'

James shrugged. 'I like to understand people. My dad always used to tease me for being a big girl's blouse but Mum told me he always was an insensitive prick. She said when I was small I would notice little things other people didn't. I would feel sorry for runts, get involved in lost causes and try and rescue things, and animals. Like when my mum and dad argued after we'd gone to bed. I couldn't lie upstairs listening to the screaming and shouting. It would upset my brother and could go on for hours. Once I went downstairs and demanded they stop because we had school in the morning and told them they should be ashamed of themselves.'

Prue laughed. 'How old were you?'

'About ten; what a nerdy little knob.'

'I think it sounds brave, noble.'

'That's a word you don't hear often, noble, I like it. I wasn't that brave – my dad shouted at me and I cried and ran upstairs. The same thing carried on for years; they only divorced when I was sixteen.'

'I think it sounds cute,' said Prue, and she meant it. It was hard not to feel for a tightly wound little boy marching downstairs in his dressing gown to tell his own parents to pull their socks up.

'I know I'm punching above my weight with you, Prue. I'm not stupid.'

'What!?' Prue baulked. Where was this coming from? She was the one out of her depth; she hadn't imagined James might be feeling insecure.

'You're tall and gorgeous, you only noticed me because we're on a barely inhabited island. Back home I'd have no chance. Guess I must be a masochist.'

'You're talking daft.'

'I don't mind working hard, Prue. I think that's what I'm trying to say, if I think someone is worth it.'

Prue squirmed. The way his eyes bored into her as if her insecurities might ooze out of her pores, she couldn't look at him. She'd finished her pint quicker than he had and as it was her round, she gave him the money to go to the bar since she was technically underage. He came back with two more pints of the cheapest draught lager and she started to neck hers. They carried on talking rubbish, laughing, and ploughing their way through weak lager and tearing the beermats into pieces.

'When I was about eight,' said James, 'we were given duck eggs to incubate. My mum has a habit of taking on projects – you may have noticed.'

'Duck eggs?'

'Yes, one of the baby ducks hatched with splayed legs, they were pointing the wrong way in his hips and I wanted to try and help it but my dad told me you can't interfere with nature. I've been painting my dad in a bad light in these stories, haven't I?'

'He does seem to do a lot of shouting.'

'He was never that patient with us as kids. Anyway, I digress. The baby duck – my dad wanted to kill it.'

'Kill it? That's awful.'

'Put it out of its misery, so to speak. But I begged him to let me try and save it, so I built, and this is true – you can ask my mum – I built a cradle out of Lego, with wheels. I strapped this little guy into the cradle which forced his legs the right way and left him in it overnight and it worked.'

'No way! Really? This isn't a joke, right, because I'll be devastated if this isn't true.'

'I fixed him – the duckling's legs were fine the next day.'

'That is adorable,' she said, and it *was* adorable and for a brief moment she thought how awful she was for using James and how that might be a little manipulative. She had never considered his feelings; he was a boy, they didn't have any, right?

'I've been doing all the soul bearing here,' he said. 'You talk.'

'God, like what?'

'Why don't you tell me about your exes?'

'Oh, wow! OK.' Prue panicked; obviously there were none. Subo. Now *she* had exes. 'Well, my last ex was a guy called Manny.'

'Manny?'

'It's short for Emmanuel. He was sweet and everything but...'

'But what?'

'He was too short, and he rode a bike. It made me feel like

I was at primary school.' This was true, sort of. Manny had gone out with Subo and he had ridden a bike but he also sold weed, and that had been the basis of their relationship. After a few strung-out weeks Subo had dumped him.

'Then before that there was Rob. He was really into computers and made his own music,' said Prue, marching her way mentally through Subo's back catalogue. 'And he was eighteen.'

'Wow, now he sounds like a cool guy.'

'There's no need to be sarcastic. He was all right but...'

'... he had a tiny penis?'

'No! He expected me to hang out in his bedroom watching him play on his computer.' Subo had only gone out with Rob because he was tall, worked out and was at college, but she said that wore off as soon as she realised how boring he was. 'Before that there was—'

'You know what, I've heard enough.'

'What about your exes?'

'Mine?'

'Yeah, your girlfriends, tell me about them.'

'I've only really had one what I would call proper girlfriend, Sabine. She was a French exchange student and had blonde hair and brown eyes, which is an intoxicating combination. She also had a mole on her cheek about here.' He pointed at the area above his lip and to the side of his nose. 'Like Cindy Crawford. My parents had divorced and I was living with my dad who gave not a single fuck if I had girls in my bedroom or who slept over. Which I confirm was great. She was the first girlfriend I had who could sleep in my bed and she was hot, and French, and had a mole...'

'... OK, she was hot, I get it.' There was no way she

was going to stack up against a hot French girl with a strategically aesthetic mole.

'Not as pretty as you, mind.'

'Yeah, right.'

'Seriously, between me and you, she was a little on the heavy side and in the sunlight she had a moustache. Not that I minded, it's all good.'

'Christ, do I have a moustache in the sunlight?'

James squinted and pretended to study her top lip. 'No, you're good; besides, there's creams you can get for that – my mum uses them. You really have no idea how pretty you are, which is rare because most girls who are pretty know it, and they're mean—'

'If I don't have facial hair, why did you mention the cream?' She covered her upper lip area with a hand.

'You try and make everything funny, as if you can't stand to leave things on a bad note, you try and finish it with a joke. You're complicated – I guess I am a masochist.'

'Great,' she said, still blushing, taking her hands away. 'Thanks for the overview.'

'Why do you do that?'

'What?' Prue shrugged.

'Try and make a joke out of everything, no matter what.'

'I didn't know I did. I'm only trying to help, I want everything to be good.'

'Ah ha – I see.'

Prue rolled her eyes and knocked back another gulp of lager. She was almost lapping James on drinks and must have been three pints in nearly. 'Buy me another drink and abandon your amateur psychology today, Dr James – at least start the course first.'

'Fine! Probably best, I don't want you to unravel before I'm qualified, but you need to stop drinking so fast – I'm only halfway through mine.'

James stood up to check his pockets, but when he looked at Prue, he did a double take and leaned over.

'Your pupils – they're really dilated.'

'What?'

'Your pupils are huge, like saucers.'

'Are they?'

'Well, if it isn't ma fellow islanders?' Charlie O'Hara appeared from nowhere and dragged a chair over and plonked himself down in it at their table. James sat down again. 'You dunna mind if I take a seat? What are we speakin aboot? Da price of petrol? How quickly tatties get eyes?'

Prue looked for comfort in the bottom of her pint glass while James shot her a look that said they should escape. Charlie leaned on the table with his elbows, grinning at them both, determined to enjoy their discomfort.

'How are you, Charlie? Business quiet at the moment?' said James. An admirable attempt at defiance.

'Oh you ken, Jimmie-boy, I fancied a day oot,' said Charlie, 'a girl has to let her hair doon, don't you agree?' he asked Prue, and nudged her arm with his knuckles. She didn't answer and stared at the table, so he asked again, 'Do you like letting your hair doon? How's young love? You two bumping uglies?' Charlie punched James on the arm, too hard to be playful then turned to Prue. 'Does he make you come all right?'

'Fucking hell, Charlie, really?' said James, and Prue looked at him in disgust and turned away.

Philistine. Ronnie was right. He could have shot the

raven, he was the type to kill an animal for amusement. Thick as mince. She turned away and nearly knocked over her empty glass when she saw Archie approaching.

'Oh, hi,' said Prue. Her face must have lit up. Charlie, on the other hand, shrunk in his chair.

'Hello, Charles, fancy bumping into you,' said Archie, who was the one grinning now. He knew exactly what he was doing when he stood with his thighs pressed against the edge of the table with his crotch in their faces.

There was an odd dynamic between Archie and Charlie. Prue wasn't sure what the chemistry between them should have been, all things considered, but it wasn't Charlie acting like a submitting dog.

James looked emasculated but surely Archie turning up was a good thing. 'Ruth said you were on a trip?'

'I just got back.'

'Prue,' said James, 'your nose is bleeding.'

She touched her nose and sure enough when she looked at her fingers there were bright drops of blood, the same as Ruth had when they'd had lunch. The woman at the next table handed James a tissue.

'Let me look,' said Archie, and he tipped up her head and peered up her nose. Lord knows what he expected to see. 'I was going to have a sneaky half but I won't bother. Why don't I take you both home? I'll give you a lift now, come on.'

They left Charlie with his leg bouncing under the table, looking around the bar as if Archie wasn't there. James wouldn't look Prue in the eye as they followed Archie out of the pub. She poked him in the ribs with an elbow but he ignored it.

'Yeah, you bairns best get on home,' shouted Charlie. 'Night!'

It was a quiet drive back with the battle between testosterone levels in the car. James had the hump and Prue wasn't sure what she'd done wrong. They dropped James outside the hotel like he'd been over for a playdate. The wind blew out his jacket and he had to lean into it. He looked like a scarecrow striding across the grass.

'Jesus Christ, what the hell happened between you two?' asked Archie. Prue jumped in the front seat. She had relegated herself to the back to soften the damage to James's ego.

'Nothing.'

'Are you sleeping with him?' asked Archie.

'I'm not actually.' She regretted answering but he caught her off guard. Adults talk about sex and if Subo asked her – she'd answer.

'That'll be why then.'

'No, it isn't.'

'Why was Charles O'Hara with you?'

'He wasn't, he was being a knob.'

'How do you know him?'

'Seen him at the hotel, that's all. I know who he is. I guess he knows who I am.'

'Stay away from him.'

'Er... OK.'

Prue's head fixed towards the window as Archie put the pickup into gear and pulled away. Back at the house he parked on the drive and the crunch of the gravel under the tyres was deafening; this side of the water seemed so still and isolated.

'You want to come to the studio?' asked Archie, but Prue hesitated. She wanted to but she didn't want to get in trouble with Ruth again.

'If you help me carry my stuff, it would be doing me a favour.'

'I can do that,' she nodded; that seemed a good enough reason.

He loaded her up with bags and Prue trudged behind like a milkmaid. She felt a little pang of sympathy for Ruth, as they had snuck in without even saying hello. Prue was tipsier than she thought and she found herself putting on a cringeworthy performance of confidence out of some perverse desperation for Archie to think she was cool. There was a half-smoked spliff in an ashtray and Prue picked it up and attempted to light it. Archie glanced over with a raised eyebrow as she flopped down on the sofa and put her feet on the metal storage unit. Subo told her you can do one or the other, or both at the same time, but never get drunk and then smoke weed because it's a fast track to chucking a whitie – throwing up and embarrassing yourself.

Archie sat on his saddle stool, pushed off with his feet and flew over to Prue. He knocked her feet off the metal unit and held out a hand to confiscate the spliff.

'Are you trying to get me into trouble?'

She passed it back and Archie put it between his lips and pushed off again.

'It's not as if I've never smoked weed before,' said a petulant Prue. She had, but maybe not as much as she was making out.

He turned on the radio while Prue bunched up a couple of cushions and lay on her side. All the mugshots of Archie's girls were lined up in their neat little rows on the wall, no doubt lamenting her performance.

'I lived in London for a couple of years – at a house in Balham,' said Archie. He had the spliff balanced between his lips as he moved the rucksack and sports bag she'd carried to a huge metal cupboard and locked them inside. 'It was a squat.'

'Sounds grim.'

'Oh, it was awful, a compete shithole, but a lot of London was a shithole then. There were about twelve of us living there. I met your aunt in that squat.'

'I thought you met in Nepal?'

'I met her *again* in Nepal and by complete chance – how weird is that? The first time was in the squat. This mad girl walks in, towering over everyone. She was throwing her weight around, smoking cigarettes with a filter, this big platinum blonde calling everything patriarchal because she'd read Andrea Dworkin. Six-foot with an undercut and she had these maroon Doc Martens and legs up to her armpits. She kicked in the back door of a nightclub with those legs, and we had to run from the bouncers. She nearly got us both arrested that night. I didn't see her again until we bumped into each other in Nepal. We convinced ourselves it was meant to be and got married three weeks later. Now she worries if we're eating enough vegetables or the gutters need cleaning.'

'I remember those Doc Martens.'

'She still has them.'

'The vegetables might be my fault.'

'Oh?'

'I'm a vegetarian, or at least I was. I told Ronnie and she's been trying her best to cook everything possible without meat, although I think I'm going to tell her to give up. I don't think I can handle any more chickpeas.'

'The sudden influx makes sense now. Are you going to let me take those pictures?' Archie picked up the Polaroid camera. Prue's mind leapt to the blurry image of Evie's sweet dandelion boy, the photo with their naked, happy bodies squished together.

'Maybe. Not right now.'

'Are you a tease, Prue, is that what you're doing with poor little gingersnap?'

'No.'

Everywhere there were half-naked women with glazed eyes, lips and limbs, in poses closing in. From the corner of her eye she could have sworn their smiles were broader, their eyes blinked, toes twitched. She shouldn't have come in. Archie wheeled over again. Prue was paralysed.

'Do I make you nervous?' he asked, and he smiled. His eyes with the deep lines around them, flecks of wickedness. He had a scar on his nose she'd not noticed before and she wanted to know how it got there.

'No.' A lie in a voice like air slipping from a balloon. He brandished a freshly rolled spliff and held it in front of her.

'Liar,' he laughed, and gave it to her. 'Why don't you light it since you're a confirmed toker.' She tried to take it without her hands shaking. 'I'm only teasing about the picture. You don't have to do it if you don't feel comfortable.' But she wanted to be comfortable. She was such a hopeless little prude.

He stood up and walked towards her, then lifted her legs and sat down next to her and lowered them back down so they were over his. She could feel his body temperature through his thighs and hoped he couldn't feel how tense she was.

'I take it you heard I murdered my girlfriend? You know it's horseshit, right?' He surely must be able to hear her rapid-fire rabbit heart.

'If I let you take my photo, would you put me up on the wall?'

'I think I could sneak you up there.'

'But Ruth might not like it.'

'It can be our secret,' he said. He sounded like Ronnie. 'Have you heard anything from your mother, how she's getting along?'

'No, Ruth said it's best to leave her until she's ready. It's not like we get on; Ruth isn't the only one who argues with her. I can't stop fighting with her either.'

'What about?'

'It's like she's scared of something happening to me, which I suppose is normal but it's on steroids. I want to learn to drive but she said we can't afford lessons, but then she won't let me get a job in case I have to come home after dark. She wants me at home all the time, but she exists in her head, so I'm on my own. It's like being in solitary confinement. I really hope this rehab works. Ruth said you paid for it so I should thank you.'

'You're welcome.' He reached out for the spliff. 'If you want, I can teach you how to drive.'

'Yeah, right.'

'Seriously,' he shrugged. 'I won't be going away for a while. I need to finish a few paintings so I'll be around most of August and you don't go home until September so I can teach you how to drive before then. You'd still need lessons but it'll save some money.'

'Why would you do that?'

'Why wouldn't I? Call it a trade. I'll tell you what, you let me take a few pictures and I'll teach you to drive. I'm all about life skills. Come on,' he said, throwing her legs off and standing up. 'We should go inside.'

They walked from the garden to the back door into the house and Prue practically had to stop herself skipping. She glanced up and saw the curtains to Ruth's studio twitch. A strand of light appeared and disappeared in a moment. She was sure Ruth had seen them.

15

On the first day of August the demon-dog made a big comeback. He had enjoyed a wild night, digging up borders and beds, dragging plants out with roots and all, leaving huge holes, and finishing off with a large shit.

'That bastard!' Ronnie flew in through the back door in tears, waving her hands in front of her eyes. 'Someone needs to shoot it before I do.' She did a circuit of the kitchen flapping her arms. 'Prue! You must come and pick up its mess,' she said, and stomped back out.

Prue was picking at leftover chicken straight from the fridge. Her principles of vegetarianism had gone out of the window as everyone kept complaining about dinner and the effect lentils and beans were having on them.

'That gun she has, does it work?' she whispered to Archie.

He shook his head. 'It's my granddad's old Enfield .38, but there's no bullets.'

'Prue, I wish you'd get a plate and not pick at the carcass straight from the fridge,' said Ruth.

Prue slammed the fridge shut and went to help Ronnie. She was right, it was an almighty mess. There was earth and plants everywhere.

'Do you want me to help with the beds?' she asked Ronnie.

'No, dear,' Ronnie said, dragging a heavy spade along the ground and clearly struggling with the weight. 'Get rid of the dog mess. Do that.'

On the ground ahead lay the rotting carcass of the dead raven they had buried. The dog must have dug it out of its shallow grave, rotting entrails and all. Ronnie must have wanted it covered over before Archie or Ruth saw it, but as she ran to help, Ronnie screamed at her.

'Did you not hear me!? Get away from here! Do as you're told!'

It was like the time she ended up covered in wet cabbage after asking Nana about the ceiling scare. Prue stopped and was stunned, hurt, and left her to it. She grabbed the dog shit with a plastic carrier bag and lobbed it in the bin with tears in her eyes. There she was, being oversensitive again.

She retreated to the study to get changed for a run, but after being screamed at, she didn't feel any obligation to remain obedient. As she took off her T-shirt her eyes locked on the book that had the letter inside and, in her bra and shorts, she picked out the next book and swore to herself she'd only check one or two. She found more money, but it took a whole shelf before she stumbled across what she was really looking for inside a book about Genoa. Her stomach turned at the sight of a piece of paper. Again, the lined page had been torn and had the same printed font of the date in the top right-hand corner. It must have been ripped from the same diary as the one before. Prue took a deep breath, and opened it with goosebumps running along her arms.

Tuesday, 3rd July 1973

My lover, my lover, my lover. I am addicted to saying that. I've never had a lover before. I am obsessed by you, Mr Anderson. You are my new hobby, passion, vocation and I hope whatever spell you've put me under never ever wears off. You have me, I'm yours, and I'm trapped in a daydream and practically useless at anything else. I'm supposed to be finishing my college applications but I can't get through a sentence without thinking about you. This is hopeless. I am thinking of you at EVERY SECOND OF EVERY DAY. I can't stop.

I want to travel the world. Where do you want to go? I've always wanted to go to Petra, and the Amazon, Machu Picchu and Australia. I want to live in the jungle in a treehouse in Costa Rica and look after sloths.

Does it make me a bad person if there is part of me that wants you to be miserable when I'm not there with you? I want it to hurt you the same way it hurts me. I'm not sure if that makes me a bad person or not, and I've never thought of myself as jealous. I have this funny idea we are old souls and we've both been lovers on Earth before and have somehow found each other again.

I LOVE YOU.

Ev

Prue had a rush of all the emotions flooding through her as if she was Evie and she could feel flutters in her stomach as she read it over and over. Evie was head over heels and so was Prue, vicariously. The more Prue read the letter, the less she thought Archie could have hurt her. How could someone be in love with their own murderer?

But the more she learned of Evie's experience, the more she felt that whatever her mother had been involved in wasn't like this. If her mother had been in love with someone and felt this much, even fleetingly, she would have talked about it, wouldn't she?

Prue finished getting changed and stepped out of her room but could hear Ruth and Ronnie in the kitchen. Now was a chance to sneak into Ruth's studio. She crept upstairs and let herself in but left the door open slightly so she could hear if anyone approached, and she had every intention of being quick.

She found the painting of her as a child at the aquarium. It was a strong memory for Prue, but she didn't remember ever telling Ruth, so it had to have been her mother. Then there was the painting called *The Three Witches*, with the women swung by their tongues. Nana had called them – her mother, Ruth and Prue – her three witches. But why would Ruth paint them being swung around by the tongue – did it mean something? Or was it just art? She moved along to the next, and this one she hadn't seen before; it was called *Motherly Love*. It was like a Salvador Dalí painting, where solid objects were liquid, and nothing made sense. It was of a woman holding a cocktail shaker as another poured what looked like rubbish into a child's open head. The child staggered about in a blindfold, playing blind man's bluff, while another figure – dark and in shadow – blew a pipe and the smoke drifted into the child's ear.

'What are you doing?' Ruth snapped in the doorway. Prue hadn't heard her approach or notice the door creep open.

'I only wanted to look. Sorry, do I need permission?' Prue surprised herself by her own response; normally she would leap to apologies, but there was something alive now in Prue that made her defiant. She didn't know where it had come from, but the change caught Ruth off guard.

'I... I only asked why you snuck in here,' Ruth said.

'I didn't sneak, the door was open.'

Ruth was beyond her usual pale with dark circles under her eyes, and when she drew breath a drop of blood ran from her nose. She reached up to touch it and then looked at the red blood on her fingertips.

'Oh.' She walked over to her desk to get a tissue. 'Why does this keep happening?'

'You should go to the doctor, Ruth, something could be wrong,' said Prue, rushing up to the desk. 'Perhaps you're allergic to something in the paint.'

'No, I'm all right,' Ruth laughed. 'It's probably the menopause!' She wasn't the only MacArthur who leapt to humour to manage the situation.

'It could be a reaction to stress, what are you worried about?'

'The exhibition,' said Ruth. 'I've got a lot to do.'

'If it keeps happening, promise me you will go to the doctor,' said Prue.

'Look at you,' said Ruth, holding a tissue to her nose. 'All grown up and looking after me now. I hope you feel the same when I'm incontinent and you're pushing me about in a wheelchair.'

'I'll try to avoid the cliffs,' said Prue and they both laughed. There, James was right. Rather than talk honestly about the subjects that crucified them they hid behind humour. It wasn't the exhibition bothering Ruth, they both knew that. Like the three witches in the painting, they were strung up by the tongue. Swinging around in the only game they knew how to play.

16

Prue went for a run, but not before she snuck back into the kitchen and smuggled some of the chicken from the fridge into a tissue and into the pocket of her hoodie. She shouted goodbye to whoever might hear and made her way out of the front of the house to avoid Ronnie. Running was good for thinking, and she wanted to think. There were things to work out and everything was connected, she was sure of it.

At the beginning of the last year of school, Prue had been invited to join the long-distance running team. Prue took the letter home and was told that her mother would need to make an appointment to see the PE teacher because it was a commitment. It meant practice on weekends and travelling to events out of school hours. After the meeting, her mother told Prue that they still had to make a final decision between a few girls, and they were going to call her to confirm if Prue won the place. This didn't fit with her take on it; she'd thought she was being invited, not part of a selection process. When her mother told her she didn't get in, she was gutted. She'd never been picked for anything, and certainly never been on a team in sports. It was the only thing in PE she was good at. Then right before they broke up for exams her PE teacher asked how her asthma was.

'What asthma?' she asked. The PE teacher seemed confused and said she must have got herself mixed up. A few days later, she pulled Prue aside in the corridor.

'Look, Prue,' she said. 'Your mother definitely told me you had chronic asthma when she came in. When I said that exercise might help, she told me the doctors advised against it. That you were hospitalised at one point.'

'Thanks for telling me.' Prue didn't need to tell her that it wasn't true – the teacher could see by her face, but neither pushed it.

Insane with rage, she confronted her mother as soon as she got home. She dumped her bag on the floor and stomped to the kitchen where she found her mum.

'I guess you must be relieved my asthma cured itself.'

'What are you talking about?'

'That's what *I* said. My PE teacher asked me how my asthma was. Why did you do that? Why did you say I had asthma when I don't?'

'I don't know what you mean, you're not making sense.'

'*I'm* not making sense?'

'I'm not going to continue this conversation if you're going to be rude.'

'You made up that I had asthma so I couldn't join the running team! Didn't you? Why would you do that? Why would anyone do that? You told me I didn't make the team, that I wasn't good enough, but I *was* good enough. Why would you let me think that? Why are you obsessed with keeping me indoors and stopping me from doing anything?' Her mother was squeezing a teabag against the side of a cup with a teaspoon with a bemused face that only made Prue angrier.

'I don't know what's got into you but I want you to sort your attitude out right now,' she said. 'I don't remember anything about any running club. You've got yourself mixed up. You've never been good at sport.'

'But I can run. I'm not any good at anything else but I *am* good at running.'

'OK, if you say so,' and she laughed. She tried to shrug it off as if it was nothing. Maybe it was to her, but to Prue it was something. An opportunity. She might have made friends. She might have met other people who were like her. She might have made the Olympics. OK, that was a stretch but who knew? She was stupidly upset, way more than even she thought she should have been about some crappy running club.

'If it's up to you, I'm never going to be allowed to do anything, ever! I shouldn't take Science. I shouldn't run. I can't hang out with kids my own age. I have to stay here with you under lock and key, forever! Why? What's wrong with me?'

Her mother didn't answer. She wouldn't even look at her. She was still squeezing out the same teabag and then left the bag on the side of the counter and pushed past her. The bin was a metre away. Could she not even put the teabag in the bin? She always left them on the side and made a little mountain of dried-up cold teabags that left brown stains all over the worktop. Prue picked it up between her thumb and forefinger and threw it in the bin. Then stood in the kitchen and screamed. Her mother shut the living room door and turned the TV up louder.

Prue could feel her anger growing inside her as she ran, and she pushed herself until her lungs burned and her legs were almost too heavy to pick up. She slowed down and went off the path, through overgrowth, forging her own tracks. She heard something scuffling in the brush behind her and stopped, and saw it through the trees, its ears pointing straight up and alert – the demon-dog. The black beast had his chest puffed up like a majestic stag. Short-haired with upright ears, he had a big square head that could break walls. He sat down, scratched an ear with a back paw and yawned, flashing a bright pink tongue, and then, not remotely perturbed by Prue, sauntered off.

'No! Come back!' Prue shouted, and disturbed a colony of birds hidden among the branches overhead. She flinched as a chorus of wings rattled like thunder as they took off. The dog reappeared and skipped ahead of her, through the silverweed. It wasn't such a demon; he hopped over the brush like a deer and led her through the densest part until they spilled out to a natural clearing with a fallen tree, but this was not the dying larch and she wasn't sure where she was. The dog rushed around the clearing in circles in excitement, spinning. Prue took out the chicken in her pocket and threw it on the ground. The dog stopped, tilted his head from side to side, sniffing the air, then gingerly approached the meat. She took a few steps back; someone must have tried to catch him or hurt him to make him so wary, but he ate the chicken and Prue crouched down. He cowered when she sat on the ground but didn't stop eating, only kept an eye on her. The poor thing, perhaps there was somewhere he could be taken; she would ask James.

There was a rush behind of rustling, and Prue and the dog looked up. The dog had a stiff tail and stared in one direction, but Prue couldn't see anything. The dog growled and Prue grew nervous. The breeze nudged the branches making the leaves rattle and the sunlight was blinking in her eyes.

'Hello!' Prue stood up and shouted. She cleared her throat and tried again. 'I know you're there!'

A buzzard sitting at the top of a dead tree opened its giant wings above them and flew off. It startled both of them, and the dog barked. He ran off and now she was by herself in this strange clearing. There was no sound at all and she was all alone, except for whatever or whoever had made the noise.

Evie. What if Evie walked here? She shuddered. Then the rustling happened again, and she spun around because she was sure she knew which direction it came from.

'Who is it?' Now might be a good time to run, a little voice said.

But she stood waiting for her legs to pick up the message. Her eyes trying to absorb as much as they could in every direction. Start running now. Another rustle. This time it was closer, and she turned in time to see a slither of a white face disappear behind a tree. That was a face. It had *eyes*.

'Leave me alone!'

The wind fell and the leaves had stopped shaking. There was nothing but the anticipation of what would happen and who would move first. Finally, her legs responded and she ran leaping over branches, tore her hoodie on a branch, scratched her hands and legs on thorns and nearly tripped over the ivy covering the ground like tangled up wires. She glanced over her shoulder and saw a figure but it was the stick that gave it away. The stick could only belong to Gladys O'Hara. The madwoman on the prowl, wandering in the woods searching for her lost daughter like a cursed spirit.

Prue made it to the stile, threw her legs over and powered up the hill. It was hard not to feel for the woman. She'd lost Evie and continued to be tortured by the endless combinations of 'what if' and 'how', and Prue thought of her own mother. How she and Gladys O'Hara wore the same lead coat, an iron aura.

Ronnie told her that there was no such thing as coincidence and that everything happens for a reason. Whatever takes hold of your brain will creep like an unstoppable moss until it chokes out everything else and you can't help but be pulled towards it. When she made it up to the roadside she stopped, nearly puking, hunched over, hands on knees, and tried to catch her breath.

'Are you all right?' A maroon car trundled to a stop beside her and there was Charlie O'Hara with that impish smile.

'I was running,' said Prue, between gasps.

'Fae what?'

'Running… as in… exercise…'

'Oh. Want a lift?'

'No, it's fine.' She tried to wave him on.

'You look like you need a lift.'

'I don't need—'

'I'm not a rapist.'

'Oh, well, that's settled then,' she laughed, but Charlie O'Hara didn't. He looked confused.

'So… you're Archie's niece?'

'Is that a problem?' Prue said, straightening up, bracing herself.

'Not with me. Get in.'

He opened the passenger door and scooped crap off the front seat and threw it into the back. There wasn't much point in a lift. The house wasn't far and Archie's words rung in Prue's ears, telling her to stay away, but she didn't want to seem rude so she got in. There she was, getting a lift home from the younger brother of the missing girl the islanders thought her uncle had murdered. Which was a unique and especially complex situation she'd managed to attract with her thoughts – whatever they were. They drove in silence for a few awkward minutes as he kept looking over but she just stared straight ahead.

'I'm Charlie,' he said eventually, and he stuck out a hand.

'I know. I'm Prue.' She shook it. He had dirty fingernails. That upset her.

'I want to apologise.'

'What for?'

'For being a dick both times we've met. You have the wrong impression of me, sorry.' He was looking out of the window and over his shoulder, rubbing his face and blinking as if he might have a tic.

'Are you looking for something?'

'Not something, someone,' he said. 'My mam's gone walk aboot again. Thought I'd go for a drive and see if I could find her.'

Torn between keeping her mouth shut or mentioning what she had seen, Prue thought it would be cruel not to come clean.

'I think I might have seen her... possibly,' she said.

'Where?' His neck near snapped off.

'I'm not completely sure it was her, but when I was running I thought I saw someone with a walking stick in the trees – near the end of the hill.'

'Fucking great,' he said, and smacked the steering wheel. 'Fantastic. Honestly, she is a fucking nightmare. I'll drop you off and go find her, thanks,' he said.

'Drop me here, there's no point you taking me all the way to the house.'

'I'll drop you and then find her. It's not like she'd be going anywhere fast, is it?'

They turned into the driveway through the ageing wooden gate and rolled towards the house. Prue hoped she could hop out without anyone seeing them together. The gravel had never seemed so loud; all they needed now was the cockerel to start up.

'My mum's a nightmare too,' she said. 'She has issues, that's why I'm here. My point is, I get it. Drop me here and I'll jump out.'

He didn't stop and rolled up to the door. Prue went to get out as he grabbed her arm.

'Please dunna tell Archie you saw her. I'll find her and take her home. No harm done, yeah?' Prue nodded in agreement.

'Why are you scared of him?' she asked, remembering how submissive he had been in the pub on the Mainland.

He raised both eyebrows. 'I'm not scared of the big man, I just dunna want any aggro. Your uncle and I have an understanding,' he said.

'What does that mean?' asked Prue, unable to fathom

how there could be an understanding between them, when so much hostility was palpable.

'Maybe you should ask him,' said Charlie, smirking; he was enjoying the opportunity to be cryptic.

'Thanks for the lift,' she said, as she got out and shut the door.

She ran up the steps thinking she'd got away with it, but as she reached for the door handle Archie opened it and her stomach fell through the floor.

'See you aboot, Prue,' Charlie shouted through his open window.

Prue tried to slip past Archie but he grabbed her by the upper arm and pulled her towards him. She lost her balance and stumbled into him but he held her up.

'Don't you go far,' he growled, then let her go.

She lingered by the stairs and rubbed the grip of his fingers from her arm. He sauntered painfully slowly towards the car, making Charlie wait, and leaned into the passenger window. Prue couldn't hear the conversation but it looked functional as opposed to hostile and she didn't understand how that could be. Charlie wouldn't look at Archie and they spoke for no more than two minutes, then Charlie wheel-spun away.

Prue waited as she was told. She expected a ticking off. A lecture perhaps. Some strain on the guilt strings. Something about a reiteration of the ground rules and definitely something about respect. But Archie slammed the front door and marched towards her at such a speed she thought he might hit her. She was as far back to the wall as she could go without tripping over plants when he grabbed her by the shoulders and shook her.

'One thing, Prue,' he said, and he pointed a finger in her face, and she went cross-eyed looking at it. 'I am not asking you. I am telling you – stay the fuck away from the O'Hara boy. Is that clear?'

Prue nodded and he released his grip on her and walked away. His shoulders were hunched together as if held up by invisible hooks. The fingernails bitten to the quick. She had never been told off like that, not by a man; it was different, and she had to admit – a thrill. Her blood was pumping but she had his attention to herself, and it felt good. Where was dandelion boy? Or was this the intensity that she lusted after at her own cost? Prue was trembling at the bottom of the stairs when he came back, she thought, for another ticking off.

'Get changed,' he said.

'What? Why?'

'We're going out.'

17

They drove in silence. The steam rose from Archie in the same way it had radiated from her mother that day of the argument with Ruth. They ran into traffic in the village, the traffic being one Metro too slow for Archie's liking. He was near growling when he overtook and Prue suggested he might struggle with the traffic in Croydon; he finally cracked a smile.

'I'd probably have an extensive criminal record too for losing my shit and smashing people's faces into their steering wheels,' he said. They both laughed, then Prue wondered if it was a casual turn of phrase or an admission of a violent temper. The photograph of him kissing Evie flashed in front of her and she blinked to banish it. There was a comfortable silence now that the tension had been broken and Prue felt privileged to have his attention. This was the Archie who barely took notice of his own wife, who painted scores of girls in compromised positions, took photographs of intimate parts of them and plastered them all over his wall. The one who had loved Evie O'Hara and promised her things, enough for her to adore him, and call him her dandelion boy, and then she disappeared.

If someone murdered a person, was it inevitable they would be tempted to kill again or could they live a mundane and ordinary life? Prue found herself examining Archie's hands. She had butterflies being so near him but wasn't sure if it was excitement or fear. Perhaps both. She liked the thrill of being in potential danger. After years of being smothered and being the responsible one, being cavalier was an adventure.

They drove to a wide open patch of bumpy grass near an old unused watermill. Seabirds squawked overhead but there was a distinct absence of other human beings. Archie put the handbrake on and left the engine running.

'Where are we?' she asked.

He got out of the car into what seemed like a hurricane. His hair was blowing about as he bent down, attempting to hold his hair back and shouting above the wind.

'Get out.'

'What?' They were in a wide-open big empty space with no one else around. Her stomach lurched and all the hairs on her arms stood to attention. Maybe it wasn't such a novelty. Surely he wasn't so angry she'd spoken to Charlie that he was going to do something. It couldn't be that simple. Ruth would notice. Her mother would notice. People would miss her. Shit.

'Jesus,' he said, tapping on the window, 'stop looking so scared.'

'Why are we here?'

'My dad taught me how to drive here. He made driving

seem as disorienting as trench warfare and I'm going to recreate that magic for you.'

She exhaled and realised how ridiculous she had been to think he might hurt her; then that was immediately replaced by the fear of driving.

'But I don't know how.'

'I'll tell you what to do. Get out and sit in the driver's seat.'

'I might crash.'

'But you might not,' he winked.

She undid the seat belt, unconvinced she was about to do something so reckless. Her mother would be having kittens.

'OK,' she said. Idiots drove every day and managed not to kill anyone. Archie rapped his knuckles on the window again, *come on.*

Prue had to adjust the seat so she could almost rest her chin on the steering wheel and kept checking the pedals. She adjusted the mirror and the wing mirrors, put the seat belt on, and repeated this at least four times before Archie lost his patience and told her to hurry up.

'Now what?'

He ran through the pedals and the gears. He told her to listen to the engine and get used to the noises it made when she needed to change gear.

'What about the indicators?'

'Who are you going to indicate to?'

'Don't I need to know that?'

'Let's focus on stopping and starting without stalling, blowing up the engine or lurching forward.'

'Right.' Prue tried to pull away and stalled the car immediately, and several more times before she managed to hop along ten metres. Then she made it to second gear, which may as well have been motorway speed.

'You might want to think about turning,' said Archie, after she'd been pootling along in second gear over the bumpy grass in a straight line.

'What?'

'If you keep going forwards, we'll be going for a swim, via some rocks.'

'What?! Why bring me to a cliff?'

'Prue, we're going ten miles per hour. If we go over, we deserve to be removed from the food chain.'

'OK, I can do this.'

'Yes – you can.'

Prue did manage to turn the wheel and then after making it to third and then fourth gear was practically a Formula One driver in her head. They spent hours driving around in circles.

'Can we go the other way now, because I'm starting to feel sick,' he said. But Prue was too busy smiling, a grin fixed to her face.

'This is amazing! I'm like a proper adult! I'm a whole grown person!' she shrieked. Turning them both dizzy with her endless circling. Archie laughing. He had a hazy, glassy-eyed pleasure from her exhilaration. She saw the Archie from the photo and for a moment she felt herself flush with affection. There he was, a small glimpse.

'You know what this means, don't you?'

'You don't have to shout, I'm right here,' he said. 'What does it mean?'

'I'm free! I can do things. I can do anything I want. That's what it means,' she said.

'Yes. You can do whatever you want. Don't let anyone tell you otherwise.'

He taught her to reverse and she practised shifting through the gears, turning the engine on and off and putting the handbrake on. That was lesson one. When Prue had tried to talk about learning to drive with her family, her grandmother had cringed and told her it was very expensive and her mother made it seem as if she'd asked to climb Everest next weekend. Driving was something impossible for Prue. It was another thing to be scared of and a huge mountain that must be overcome, but after only a few hours with Archie, Prue had seen she could choose for herself, free of other people's fears and unhindered by the ceiling they wanted over themselves. Faint little flickers of choices she was free to make – and they had nothing to do with anyone. That morning driving a car had seemed insurmountable, and a few hours later she drove them back home, albeit like an old lady.

When she pulled into the driveway, she indicated.

'Stop dicking about, there's no one to indicate to,' he tutted.

She was on such a high, she continued to skip behind him like a puppy back into his studio and couldn't stop talking. He let her smoke as he primed a new canvas and sketched out the outline in burnt umber, then blocked in the darks.

'You still owe me,' he said.

The last time Archie had mentioned taking photographs she could have broken out in hives, but now she didn't feel scared at all. It was another part of the adventure, of pushing boundaries and being free.

'Fine, I'll do it,' she said, feeling bold.

Archie dragged a wooden platform made for models to pose on into the centre of the room. He pulled cushions from the sofa and threw them on top.

'Get comfortable, I need you to be still for some time so find a good position. Legs and arms uncovered. Here, wrap yourself up in this. I won't look.'

He threw a jumper at her. Prue wasn't sure if she was meant to put it on and ended up wrapping it around herself and tying the arms around her waist, as she peeled off her jeans and kicked them onto the floor. She took her socks off and bundled them up. It wasn't a big deal. It was the same as getting changed under your clothes at the beach. Besides, Archie had half-naked girls in his studio all the time. The walls were literally papered with them. He stood waiting with the camera.

'How do you want me to be?' she asked. Now she was nervous, she could feel something in her stomach.

'Relax, you're doing fine. If you could turn slightly towards the wall, put your leg out and point your foot so your leg is extended. I need as much skin as possible. I'm going to take a few pictures.'

'OK.' Her voice sounded small.

Archie picked up on her nerves and brought over the ashtray and told her to smoke and relax, then he started to take pictures.

'You have amazing skin. It's like you've been painted in one colour, there's no undertones. Honestly, if I paint you like that, no one will believe it's real.'

'I have freckles,' she protested.

'They're adorable. Can I try something?'

'What?'

He put the camera down and took the antlers off the wall.

'Here,' said Archie, 'put these on.' He lowered them onto her head. They weighed a ton and Prue could barely move her neck for fear of them falling and her breaking them.

'Oh God, they're heavy. Are they real?'

'Yeah, they are. Caribou, reindeer, whatever you call them. I get caribou from Ronnie. Did you know that caribou are the only deer where females have antlers too? Fact of the day for you.' *Caribou. Hunters.* Ronnie had told her on the first day, Watch out, my girl, or you'll find yourself brought down by those long legs of yours.

'How did you get them?'

'My dad got them on a hunting trip. Now you look regal.'

'Poor reindeer.'

'Yeah, he was an arsehole. One of my models came up with the idea of making them into a headdress. Can you roll your vest up, so I can get your stomach?'

'Erm... OK.'

She lifted up her vest and pulled it up and over. She and Subo had done the same thing at school in the summer with their PE tops and the teachers shouted at them for being indecent. Everyone did it. It was fine. Archie put the camera down and crouched in front of her. He moved her into position and extended her leg. He touched her foot and Prue got goosebumps and held her breath and prayed he didn't notice. He turned her shoulders one way and put his hand under her chin and tipped it up. He unwrapped the jumper she still had around her waist and threw it away. Now she was sat in her knickers, a vest as a makeshift bra. She didn't say a word.

He pinned the Polaroids on the side of a canvas. He told Prue she was stunning. That the arch on her foot was beautiful. Apparently, the way her legs curved made them amazing to paint. She heard the flattery for what it was, but it still had an intoxicating effect. She let herself be poisoned by words because it felt too good. She wanted to know what it was like to be adored and she very much wanted him to like her. This is a weakness, she told herself, but it was filling a hole she hadn't realised was there.

'I'm done,' he said. He helped her remove the antlers. Prue got off the box and put her jeans back on.

After she dressed, they were back smoking weed on the sofa side by side. The conversation veered to the subject of her father.

'Does it really matter who he is?' he said.

'It's about the truth. Basic facts I have a right to that are kept from me – do you have any idea what that does to a person's head?'

'Aren't you setting yourself up to be like your mother? Allowing something you have no control over to define you? Do you really think if you'll find out a name, two words, everything will fall into place? Trust me, it won't. Be angry and frustrated but use it – channel the energy into something useful. Get something you want instead of being a victim.'

'Can I ask you a personal question?'

'Go ahead.'

'How come you and Ruth never had kids?'

Archie baulked and Prue thought she'd overstepped. He took a long toke of the spliff and passed it to Prue. She was crouched up on the sofa hugging her knees and facing him. He slouched with his legs wide apart, like always.

'I didn't want them.'

'Why?'

'I didn't want to be tied down and Ruth wouldn't want to do everything herself, so why would we have kids when it would make both of us unhappy?'

'Oh,' she said; it sounded practical.

'I've got friends who have had kids and the worry they seem to go through looks awful. I'm not up for that. A friend told me it's like having your heart walk around on the outside of your body. Why would anyone choose to exist like that? Worrying, scared something might happen. Nah, not for me.'

That wasn't the answer she expected, and she couldn't help but think it had something to do with what had happened to Evie. *It's like having your heart walk around on the outside of your body.*

'I know you're desperate to find out who your father is, Prue, but family isn't everything. Figure out what it is you want and focus on that. Don't waste your life analysing the past, it's a cowardly way to live.'

'I'm scared of going back home,' she said. 'I'm scared of being trapped with my mother. I know it sounds stupid, but I feel like the more I'm around her, the more I'll get used to it and then I'll never leave.' Archie didn't tell her to be quiet, or shut up, or not now, but nodded like he was really listening.

'There was a time when my mother was being locked in my old bedroom, the nursery, at night because she had really bad nightmares and would sleepwalk,' he said. 'Somehow one day she got hold of a pair of scissors and cut off all her long blonde hair, down to the scalp. I was on the patio with Ronnie and my dad when she started throwing her hair out of the window, laughing, and shouting, *She can't get me now – not now I have no hair*. It was terrible and I felt so much for her, desperately wanted her to be happy, but I was a kid, and my mother was hallucinating and paranoid, especially about Ronnie. People who don't understand what it's like to see someone they love with serious mental health issues every day say all sorts of rubbish, even the doctors. *It's not contagious, it shouldn't be a stigma*, but it *is* contagious. Nothing makes people back away faster than mental illness and, like my mother, if they do succeed in killing themselves, you have to put up with the chorus of the empty *if only they'd asked for help*. Anyone who kills themselves tried reaching out plenty of times and everyone looked the other way.

'Look, having a dad or two parents, or money or whatever, isn't going to make you happy; you've got to work out what that is for yourself. Based on you, not your mother, or father, or ginger boy and certainly not the bum that is Charlie O'Hara. Don't waste time digging in the wrong holes, Prue, you don't know what horrors you'll find. I promise, life will get better and one day you'll only have to drag yourself to see your mother at Easter and Christmas.'

They carried on smoking. It was easy and comfortable, and she didn't even find herself trying to make a joke; she could really talk to him, no subject was off limits. It was a revelation – he was a revelation.

'There's a painting in Ruth's studio,' she said. 'I swear it's of me at the aquarium. My mum took me to the aquarium when I was small. I think I was only five or so, and it was dark. I was looking at all the glowing fish and I heard her calling me, but I was standing next to this man. He had these glasses that reflected the light from the tanks so it looked like the fish were swimming in them. He looked exactly how I thought a dad should look. Like he would hold me upside down but not drop me. Make me eat vegetables and clean my teeth but not get hysterical if I got muddy. I got so carried away I put my hand inside his. God knows what I was thinking. Anyway, it was awful. He leapt two feet in the air and started talking German and he had this horrified face, as if I'd bitten him. Then my mum found me and they both laughed. I mean, really laughed, and I was so embarrassed I cried and Mum told me off for being silly. I hate that word. She uses it all the time with me. As if I'm still a little girl and it's so condescending. Well, I think trying to kill yourself is *silly.*'

Archie smiled and held out his hand and it took Prue a minute to realise he was holding it out for her. She put her tiny hand in his huge shovel. 'Here, I promise I won't act like you bit me. Now close your eyes and enjoy the fucking fish,' he said. They sat side by side on the sofa, smoking weed with their eyes closed, listening to the tinny radio and describing imaginary fish to each other.

The paint-encrusted dust sheet over Prue was whipped away and she was shaken awake. Ruth looked down at her, her blonde quiff limp, and she wasn't happy.

'What are you doing in my husband's studio?' Prue sat up and looked to see if the ashtray was still around but it was gone. Archie was gone. The easel and photos of her were gone too. Thank God.

'You can't sleep in here.' Ruth had her arms folded and her words stuck to Prue as if she'd been tarred and feathered, *my husband's studio*. Why was she referring to Archie as her husband? Prue knew who he was.

'I didn't mean to. I must have fallen asleep.'

'Stop pestering Archie. He's working.'

'I'm not pestering him. Where do you want me to be?'

'If you're bored, you can come sit with me in the studio or help Ronnie. Now get back to the house.'

Prue didn't move. She couldn't. A lump of something heavy as concrete sat inside her. Ruth's eyes demanded she jump to attention, beg for forgiveness and scurry back to the house like a child caught raiding the biscuit tin. Prue had to fight the feeling that she had done something wrong, and when she remembered the photographs, she felt sick. Prue got up and walked out with Ruth watching her every move; she was damned if she was going to give her the satisfaction of hurrying.

What Ruth wouldn't know was that Archie and Prue continued with the secret driving lessons. It was like an addiction and consumed Prue's waking thoughts. It was like a magnetic pull towards him she couldn't control and succumbing to it made her feel happy. He was as good as God.

18

Ronnie had made herself a production line and was breaking up blue pellets and pressing the pieces into balls of raw mince.

'Morning, my dear, you're up early.' She spun around to see a bedraggled Prue enter through the back door to the kitchen. 'Or maybe you haven't been to bed – did you sleep in the garden?'

'What are you making?'

'I'm going to fix that dog once and for all. Have you ever heard of Dr Cream?'

'No.'

'Dr Cream was a nineteenth-century murderer. He used strychnine – rat poison. Now, the interesting part is that strychnine comes from the seeds of a fifty-foot tree, also called the vomit nut.'

'You're going to poison the dog, aren't you?'

'I'm going to leave raw meatballs out tonight and if it

eats them, it will die. I'm not forcing it, the beast has free will.'

'Seriously? Isn't there someone we can call to come and catch it? Why don't you give me a day or two and I'll find out? I'll ask at the hotel – Sharon, James's mum, I'm sure she'll know.'

'Getting quite close to the islanders, aren't we, dear? No, I've waited long enough for Archie to pay attention, it seems I must solve this myself.'

Prue locked herself away in the study. She kept thinking about Archie and the photographs of her the night before and tried to convince herself there was nothing wrong in what they'd done. So why did she feel so uncomfortable about it? She saw Ruth's face over her as she tore the sheet off and felt sick. Guilty. Awful. If Ruth found out about the photographs, she'd go through the roof, but did that make it wrong? What would Subo think? Subo would be fine with it, Archie was an artist after all. Everything new felt weird at first: driving, James, even being here felt odd. It was because it was a new experience, that's all, and it was her relatives that were the odd ones. They were small-minded, rigid, overprotective and suffocating. Happy to cut off anything for Prue that was outside their own limited aspirations. They'd even given her the name Prudence for fuck's sake. Who on earth calls their child, quite literally, a prude?

She picked up the last book she'd checked. She had searched a whole shelf and found nothing and was deflated, but she kept going until another Polaroid dropped out. It landed on the rug face down and there was writing on the back: *Love was irrelevant and then I met you – Archie XXX.*

The words were straight from a greetings card, and were in a different handwriting this time. Evie wouldn't write such a sentence. It was signed from Archie, so this was her dandelion boy, and he was no poet. She turned it over, but the picture was overexposed and blurry. It had a small pinkish brown circle and she studied it until she realised it was a nipple. It was a clumsy photo of a torso of neither man nor boy but some gangly creature in between. It was Archie, but he was so different to the silverback of now. A lithe body and flat chest but the jaw was definitely his. The photograph ended where a dark mass of pubic hair began. Prue blushed and thought she really should stop looking. This boy, the one in the picture, the one who wrote sappy messages and gave his girlfriend naked photos. She knew this boy through Evie's words and the photographs way more than the man he was now. There were points where the two people merged, but other points were poles apart; he was open and vulnerable then. Maybe stupid and naïve. With renewed energy she kept searching through the books, moving flowers carefully, memorising the places to put them back. It took three whole shelves, the discovery of more money and she was about to call it a day when she found another piece of torn lined paper, but this one came alongside a small yellowing envelope.

Monday, 11th June 1973

My beautiful corruptor. The things you've done to me make the soles of my feet burn! Love drunk or drug stupid, I don't really know. OR CARE!!!!! I have to confess, I want you and I need you and I love you. I know you struggle with these things, so I'll do it first because I am the braver one. I love the way you agonise over every word; you stay quiet so often, but then I know when your face lights up you've had an idea and can't get it out fast enough! How you talk over me and interrupt me and then apologise and say if you don't get it out now it will be gone by the time it's your turn to speak. You remind me of my little brother! How you become enraged at inanimate objects and shout at them (they can't hear you). The way you appreciate the beauty in everything. I'm a gabbler. I wish I could only speak when I have something meaningful to say but it's the silences I can't stand. We have less than 86,000 seconds until I see you and try and make the arrogant laird man Anderson blush, again... Love, Evie.

It was the same as the ones before, but this one was dated earlier than the others. They were late August and the beginning of July, and this was early June. Prue opened the envelope; inside there was another Polaroid. This was of Evie, and she was posed naked. Prue remembered the wall in Archie's studio and all the little hairs on her body stood to attention. The pose she had been guided into by him only the day before was nearly identical to the one of Evie in the photograph. She had an arm draped over her head, her back arched and her head turned over her shoulder with her knees to the right corner, and the antlers – Evie wore them in the photo too. Mind out for those hunters, you'll find yourself the last pretty caribou on this deserted island. This was the clearest picture of Evie. She was slim with small breasts, similar to Prue, although Evie had long dark blonde hair and round apple cheeks. Evie was pretty, but more sweet-faced youth rather than the femme fatale Ronnie had described to her.

Prue was confused by the feelings that she had – shock, embarrassment, excitement – but the one that surprised her most was a tinge of jealousy. Evie looked so blissfully unaware of how ordinary she was. Prue didn't understand how she could display herself naked so easily. She put the letter and photos away. She needed to get out and think.

August was a month of tidying up loose ends, and hay making had started on Noost; it also meant the day of Prue's exam results wasn't far away. The cliffs once crowded with seabirds were fast deserted. It had been over a week since Archie had appeared to take her and James home when they had run into Charlie, and every day she'd been out driving with him and had completely neglected James. He wasn't the only one; she had also withdrawn from Ronnie.

When Prue eventually went to the hotel to find James he was emptying the ashtrays. He saw her and carried on tipping stale ash into the metal bucket with some venom. She was definitely in the doghouse.

'Oh, hello stranger. Did you get lost?' he said when she was within spitting distance.

'Come on, it's only been a few days. Been up to anything interesting?'

James huffed. 'Mum has been putting me to good use. Got some tourists from London in. Now I definitely know I don't want a career serving the public, especially in London, because they're all superior wankers – so that's progress. You?'

'Archie has been teaching me to drive.'

'Wow, look at you guys.' He emptied another ashtray with a clang.

'Come on.' Prue stood on the footrail and leaned over. 'Don't be like that. I came to see if you want to come out to play?' He shot her a filthy look and slammed another ashtray into the bucket. 'What's your problem with Archie? Apart from the obvious, which isn't true, but never let that get in the way of a good story.'

'I don't have a problem with Archie.'

'Then why are you acting weird?'

'Define weird.'

'Are you sulking?' Prue had to admit, there was a little twinge of pleasure in the power.

'I'm surprised how fickle you are – first you loudly profess to the bar you barely know the man and seem at great pains to clarify that you're only related by marriage. Now you're a fully subscribed member of the fan club.'

'Fan club?'

'Next, he'll be crying, telling you where he buried his girlfriend, saying how it wasn't his fault and it was an accident and she tripped and fell—'

'So, you think he did it?'

'I think the most boring and obvious answer is the most likely.'

'What's that then?'

'Evie leaves her house, the most likely route would see her walk past the hotel, down the hill and through the trees where she meets Archie. They argue, I dunno, maybe he dumped her or she dumped him. Either way, there's one almighty row and he ends up killing her, maybe by accident. He panics, gets rid of the body and runs away to the army once his dad pulls some strings.'

'Wow, you really do think he did it, don't you?'

'Yeah, I think I do,' nodded James. 'I think some people have the resources to get away with murder.'

'Whoever did it, surely it would be impossible to function?'

'You're acting like the murderer had a moral compass. Perhaps they carried on without a care in the world and never thought about it again,' James shrugged.

'I find that hard to believe.'

'Anyway, it doesn't matter what I think.'

Prue cupped her chin with her elbows on the bar and gazed up at James, trying her best cute face, like Evie with her round cheeks. James did a double take.

'What are you doing? You look strange. Besides, most people don't kill their girlfriends – even if they do feel like it on occasion,' he said.

Did he just call her his girlfriend?

'Look, I'm glad you can drive. All I'm saying is, whatever Archie has when it comes to women, I'd like some of it when I grow up. Literally, one minute he's your grumpy uncle, the next he's man of the year.'

'He's actually pretty cool once you get to know him.' James stopped what he was doing, looked at her and burst out laughing, head back, roaring.

'You sound like one of those women who marry serial killers on death row.'

'You know what? He smokes weed,' she whispered with hands either side of her mouth.

'With you? His sixteen-year-old niece?' He screwed up his face. 'What a guy.' James slammed the last ashtray and dropped the bucket on the floor. He leaned on the bar and they faced each other.

'Maybe we could get some. It might be fun,' Prue offered.

'All right, but there's only one person who sells weed on the island.'

'Who?'

James didn't answer before he leaned over and kissed her. All was forgiven; this had been easy.

James insisted Charlie O'Hara lived in a croft, but it looked like an abandoned farmhouse. It was a shit-tip, full of metal storage and bare uneven earth with oil-filled puddles. They walked a mile along a muddy track with wide open fields on either side. The landscape might have been beautiful, but the architecture wasn't. There was a wire fence so flimsy it wouldn't have kept anything out and the gate that led up to the house flapped around on one hinge. They stopped at the flappy gate.

'They say they deal in scrap metal, but I'm not sure if that's a real thing. I think they deliver stuff – dog food and stuff for livestock,' said James.

'Like a distribution centre?'

'Hmmm, that implies there's some kind of system. I think it's more that sometimes, some stuff ends up getting somewhere, somehow. Wait here.'

'Scream if you get scared.'

'Don't worry, I will,' said James.

He walked with his long loping strides, his head down, hands jammed in pockets. Prue turned her back and tried her best to act casual, but all around was pastureland so it wasn't as if she could pretend she was waiting for a bus. Archie had been clear she was to stay away from Charlie. She'd been told twice and now there she was loitering in plain sight. She hadn't told James about Charlie picking her up in the car and taking her home because it would induce more sulking, or irritating questions. Prue had to pin her hopes on Charlie not mentioning this to James in the next five minutes.

Charlie came to the door and spoke through the glass. He saw Prue, and she felt her stomach flutter. Everything about him was wrong. He clearly had no discernible skills and a criminal record. Case in point – they were there trying to buy drugs. He lived in a crumbling house on a dumping ground, and yet, she still felt bad for him driving around trying to track down his mum. Charlie let James in. Then an emaciated man with scabs on his arms and no shirt rode up on a child's BMX bike, screeched to a halt at the bottom of the path, dropped the bike and bowled up the path. Prue hopped out of the way, and he looked her over as he walked past and went inside without asking the strange girl why she was standing at the end of his path. She had to assume he lived there. Or maybe he was buying weed too.

After a few moments, James reappeared.

'Did you get it?'

'Nope.'

'Why not?'

'He wants you to ask for it.'

'Me?'

'Not sure what his rationale is. You're female, he's the most desirable man on the island... in his head.'

'Did he say anything else?'

'No, he was being his usual prick self.'

'Fine. I'll go.' Prue couldn't believe she was really going to buy drugs. This was not the girl she was familiar with. Mostly she was desperate to tell Subo. She walked past the child's bike that simply must have been stolen and rapped on the door. She could smell weed already.

'We're in here!' someone shouted. Prue stepped into a gloomy little hallway with three doors leading off, two of them open. The walls had patterned paper from the dark ages. The one to the right led to a kitchen which made Nana's look like a state-of-the-art science lab. There were drawers with no front, a cupboard with no door, one hanging off. None of it matched. Someone had made an attempt at homeliness with the addition of a red and white gingham tablecloth, decorated with burn holes. The seat of one of the chairs had been sat through. Prue peered round the next door as if she expected to be shot at. It was like a sweet little cottage had been abandoned and then defiled by the neglect and abuse of young men missing any purpose.

'We're in here, darlin',' said Charlie. The man who looked like he had rickets, riding the kid's bike, was on the arm of a sofa. Charlie was opposite.

The room was dark. The curtains drawn. Prue stepped in and saw Charlie had also taken his top off. She wasn't sure what this meant or what explained this urge to go shirtless, only that it was very distracting. Charlie sat back on his sofa, legs splayed, his hands behind his head, showing his armpit hair. A sleeping black and white staffie curled up beside him. A huge glass bong sat on the table.

'This is my cousin, Simon.' He pointed at the children's bike stealer. 'Your boyfriend said you want to buy weed?'

'He's not my boyfriend.' It embarrassed Prue how fast she clarified that misunderstanding. She didn't like how it sounded. It felt as if she were a possession, as if she had transferred the ownership of her mother's suffocating attention for James's. The dog woke up and fixed its square head on Prue. It hopped off the sofa, waddled over and sniffed her crotch.

'Don't mind him, he's friendly, aren't you, Umbro? Does he know that?'

'Does the dog know what?'

'Your boyfriend, does he know that?'

'I'm not sure why this is relevant,' said Prue, which was an awkward and dorky thing to say. The children's bike stealer was laughing along to anything Charlie said, with a noiseless chuckle. He was so thin that when he sat down, his body bent like a blown-out sail.

'Are you going to sell it to us or not?' she asked, trying to push the dog's nose away from her lady parts.

'Umbro, come here,' said Charlie. The dog padded back to the sofa. 'I know you're his niece, but how?'

'His wife is my mum's older sister.'

'Really? I'd never have guessed. You don't look like her.'

'I take after the other side.' She smiled at her own joke. 'Look, I know why you and him don't get on and I'm sorry, but in reality, it has nothing to do with me.'

Child bike snatcher gasped. Then started up with his little silent parrot chuckle.

'Why you asking me then?'

'I didn't. It was you who brought him up.' This little back and forth confused Charlie. There's always a hot boy in the class, the one that's good at skateboarding but holds a pen like someone has smashed every bone in their hand.

'How is your mum?' asked Prue.

Charlie's eyes flicked up as if he couldn't believe she'd asked. The other one looked between them, and Prue wondered what was so terrible about what she'd said. It was good manners to ask after people's mothers; people always asked after hers.

'Your English auntie, the Lady Archibald, she complained about my mother to the police. Said she'd been trespassing. She's gone over to the Mainland for a few days, waiting for things to quiet down. She's staying with her cousin.'

'I'm sorry, I had no idea.'

'How much do you want?' said Charlie. Why hadn't Ruth told her she'd called the police?

'An eighth?'

'Block?'

Prue tutted. 'I'm not from the seventies.' She'd heard Subo say that about block before. In reality Prue would have accepted anything, but she was starting to enjoy her role a little too much.

'Twenty-five.'

'OK,' and she gave him the money, not quite believing this was happening. Charlie leaned over the back of the sofa and rifled through what sounded like a plastic bag. He pulled out a little clear bag and threw it across the table.

'Thanks.' Prue picked it up.

'What you up to Saturday?' asked Charlie. She panicked

and tried to look noncommittal and shrugged. 'We might have a barbecue. You should drop by, we'll be on the beach doon fae the hotel.'

'Maybe...' she said, 'thank you,' and walked at speed to the door.

'See you Saturday,' called Charlie.

But she was already skipping down the path looking triumphant. She didn't mention anything about Saturday to James as she had no intention of making an appearance.

They spent the next few hours smoking weed and drinking the remnants of the warm limoncello at the gun tower, lying on the grass outside and laughing with dry eyes.

When Prue returned home, she had to endure dinner with the others and tried her very best to appear as normal as possible. She was still stoned and could only muster single word answers. Luckily, this passed for teenage moodiness so she ate a little and excused herself to slip back into the study. She locked her door and switched the main light off and armed herself with a torch. She had set herself a mission that night to thwart Ronnie's poisoning plans, but until it was safe to venture out, she would continue searching the books. There was only one whole row left to check, and inside a book on Celtic myths she found the fourth torn page from Evie's diary.

Saturday, 21st July 1973

I think I need glasses. Will you still love me if I have to wear glasses? How am I going to cope when you go?

I'll tell you one thing for nothing – there better be no girls! AT ALL. Not even in the canteen. Will they have a canteen? I'm guessing they do and if they have girls – they better be old and fat. I'm feeling needy. Help me!
PS: I think Ronnie suspects something. Maybe you should talk to her, she was asking questions.

Evie was anxious about Archie leaving to join the army, so Evie knew he was leaving. What if Archie wanted to dump her, but she turned into a crazy possessive girlfriend? But that didn't make sense: she could tell from the notes that Evie had too much pride and what would be the point of killing her? He would join the army and then dump her from a safe distance. What questions did Ronnie ask Evie? When Prue and she had spoken about Evie in the Morning Room, she hadn't mentioned that they'd talked at all, and made it seem as if Evie was a summer fling. Why would she play down the significance of their relationship unless it was to protect Archie?

At three in the morning, when everyone was in bed, Prue took the torch out to the garden and scoured the ground for the poisoned meatballs Ronnie had made. She'd scattered them in a trail starting at the metal gate and up to the pond of duckweed. Prue stuffed as many as she could find into a plastic bag and buried it in the kitchen bin under other rubbish and went to bed.

19

Prue tried to slip unseen into the house by entering through the front door. Everyone used the back door and in her stoned state she thought this was a mark of genius. For the last few days her brain capacity had been somewhat compromised by her and James disappearing to the gun tower to smoke the weed. Prue slipped out of her trainers, skated in her socks over the flagstones and was considering crawling up the stairs on her hands and knees when Ruth called out, 'Prue! Is that you!? Will you come in here for a moment?'

Prue wasn't in the right state to deal with conversation. She rubbed her squinty red eyes and walked into the Morning Room, where she found Ruth perched and upright; it was all a bit formal.

'I had a phone call from a solicitor today...' Ruth started before she'd sat down.

'A solicitor, what for?'

'I wanted to find out what I could do about the Gardner

case.' Ruth sat forward, her hands interlinked, her forearms on her knees, like a school counsellor.

'And?'

'It's a bit more developed than we thought. The campaigners you mentioned...'

'Hope—'

'Well, it isn't only one organisation that has been looking into her case. It looks as if various bodies have been gathering evidence for a while in order to press the review body, and after many delays they have made a decision and they are going to ask the appeal court to re-examine Joan Gardner's original conviction...'

Ruth carried on speaking but Prue's head was spinning. She could see Ruth and watch her mouth move but her voice was as meaningless as Nana's old kettle whistle. Ruth was picking her nails on her lap now and Prue wanted her to stop. If only she could stop doing that, then maybe Prue could concentrate on what she was saying. Ruth looked thin and the rash on her arms had spread to the backs of her hands. She would stop picking under her fingernails to scratch it every now and then and tiny flakes of skin would fall onto the rug like snowfall. A glass of white wine sat on the table in front of her with a half-empty packet of paracetamol.

'... The Criminal Cases Review Commission initially refused to send the case to the court of appeal but changed its decision after a legal challenge. The solicitor said this change was based on new evidence.'

'What new evidence?' Prue felt sick. But it could only be good, right?

'I don't know. She said it gave the impression that some

of the original statements may have been destroyed and the commission said this wasn't shown to the defence at the original trial.'

'I don't know what that means,' said Prue. 'Will they let her out?'

'I've no idea, Prue.'

Ruth talked on but Prue was trying to remember. The tables were covered in plant pots with thistles and purple flowers next to a tall white gladiolus. Bright green fern leaves splayed like fans as plants dangled from the beam above their heads. Now she could smell the wet earth, boggy mud, and Prue was seven again, and in woods near the cottage. Then she saw herself in the kitchen of the cottage as her mother stripped her naked. She tried to hug her mother's legs but she kept peeling her arms off her and then her mother slapped her, hard, around the face. The floor was wet. She was cold and shivering. Then she covered her head with her arms as her mother started to hit her.

'Am I going to have to talk to the police?' asked Prue. 'Because I can't remember. When I try and see her face it's blurry. I know her face because I've seen the picture in the paper and on the news but if they ask me now, what do I say?'

'Nothing. I... I don't know but we'll find out,' said Ruth. 'I'm going to speak to the solicitor again and meanwhile we need to think of all these questions, write everything down, and we'll find out.'

'It's so frustrating, why can't I remember?'

'No! Don't think about it. Prue, you don't need to. I'm only telling you because you wanted things to be different but there's nothing for you to worry about. Nothing at all.

None of this is your responsibility, that's the only thing you need to remember right now.' Ruth leaned over and put her hands over Prue's, which had clenched themselves into fists. 'We'll have your exam results in a week – exciting, isn't it?'

'A week? What date is it?' Prue wasn't keeping track of the days and thought it was mid-August.

'It's the twentieth today – not long now, that's what you should be focusing on.'

'Why did you call the police on Gladys O'Hara?' said Prue. 'You told me she was harmless.'

Ruth withdrew her hands. 'I wanted them to give her a warning, go and talk to her. Something. I do feel for the woman, Prue, but harassing us isn't going to bring her daughter back. It's time she moved on. I heard you met Evie's brother.'

Prue nodded. 'It's a small island.'

'Listen to me – Charlie O'Hara is a nasty piece of work. I would say Gladys O'Hara was cursed by both children: losing one and keeping the other. Please say you'll stay away from him, Prue?'

'Yes, of course.' But Prue knew she was lying.

Croydon, South London, 1983

Nana had been ten years old when the war started. She told Prue the war made her generation frugal and resilient. Prue wasn't so sure that was true, unless a pig-headed refusal to change an opinion based on evidence also passed as resilience, but she agreed on frugal. The right thing to do was to fix what was broken, even marriages, she had told her. They were obsessed with paying off their mortgage and saved to buy things. Things that Prue would never think of needing, like net curtains, head covers for sofa cushions, plastic runners for the hallway and fancy plastic trims around light switches. They were petrified of credit cards and loans, and store cards were up there with porn and gambling. In the end it was a good thing they were sensible with money because when Prue's grandfather died the mortgage was already paid off.

Nana's house was a time portal. The bathroom had a dark blue plastic bath suite with pink carpet on the floor. The kitchen was tiny. Her plates were orange with a brown floral trim and she didn't see the point in changing them. Toilet roll may be hidden under plastic dolls with knitted skirts out of decency but her false teeth would be found around the sink. There were doilies and frilly blinds and brass ornaments around a fireplace that wasn't real – it even had a brass poker. Prue asked what it was for.

'It's for nosy little girls who try and find where I hide the chocolate biscuits!' she'd teased. 'It's what you have around fireplaces. It's decoration.' It all seemed a bit pointless.

Nana refused to take the plastic off the sofa where the feet touched the floor then burned holes in the arms with her cigarettes. Ruth moved out when she started work in London and it was only the three of them: Prue, her mother and Nana – the way Prue thought it always would be.

When Nana was at the supermarket one afternoon doing the big shop, a white van pulled up outside the house and parked in the spot Nana always parked her yellow Allegro.

Her mother ran up to the net curtains and then over to Prue and grabbed both her knees – her eyes were wild.

'We're going on an adventure with my friend Billy. Come and meet him,' she said.

Prue was dragged down the hallway to put her coat and shoes on. Her mother ran to the bedroom and returned with huge bags stuffed with clothes and toys. The front door opened and a man cast a shadow down the hallway. When he stepped onto the plastic runner with his paint-covered boots, Prue cried. Minutes later she was sat in between them in the front of the van and Billy let her eat the sweets he had in the glove box. This was the time they ran away from Nana.

They moved miles away from Nana and Croydon and lived in the middle of the woods down a single-track road in a cottage with a thatched roof, like Hansel and Gretel, but it wasn't made of sweets. It had white walls and a low wooden fence around a garden covered in rabbit poo. Wild ponies roamed and blocked the road. It wasn't far to walk to the next cottage and every house was different. The gardens went all the way around the house, not in blocks in front and behind. Her mother would get up to sort the stove in the morning and they burned real wood in the fire. Billy left for work very early in the morning. Prue was told she had measles and stayed off from school for ages, but eventually she started to go to the village school. Billy bought her a pet rabbit, but a fox killed it one night and she was devastated, but Billy promised she could have a kitten once her baby brother or sister was born. That was how she learned her mother was pregnant for the second time.

'We'll have the baby first,' said Billy. 'We have to wait

until the baby can sit up on its own and then you can have a kitten.' Prue still regarded this as gospel when it came to deciding in what order to acquire a cat and a baby.

The cottage was surrounded by woods either side of the single-track road. During the day Prue was allowed to roam as long as she didn't stray too far from the house. She had freedom. Sometimes the ground would swell up with water as if someone had left the bath taps on because running through the woods was a narrow and very steep stream all the way from the river. The ground would flood and take a few days to drain away. Prue would pretend she lived in a swamp in the jungle. There was an old boardwalk covered with chicken wire weaving in among the trees that didn't seem to lead anywhere and sometimes the water came up higher than the boards. Her mother's belly blew up like a balloon, and one day, out popped Holly. Holly cried and kept everyone awake and her mother always gave her all the attention. When Billy came home, he was excited to see baby Holly. In the morning, before he went to work, she would hear him talking to baby Holly through the walls but he left the house without saying goodbye to Prue. She saw her mother kiss Holly and cuddle her. Holly would make silly baby gurgling noises and stamp her weak little Babygro feet on her mother's legs as she held her up. Her mother never touched or kissed Prue like that. Prue started to miss Nana and her stories and strange rules for decency and manners and was desperately willing Holly to hurry and sit up. Then she could have the kitten Billy had promised her and the kitten would be her friend and no one else's, certainly not Holly's.

A sensible girl, people would say. A quiet little thing.

Angel. Adults adored Prue. Other children not so much – they said she was a *fuddy duddy*. She didn't misbehave the way some children did. She didn't get bottles out of the kitchen and empty the contents on the carpet or draw on the walls or go through her mum's bag and destroy her cheque book. Often she would be left alone with Holly while her mother went on an errand, caught up on sleep, or did the housework. She was forever tired, and Holly took up all her time. Holly wasn't very good at playing yet, and she cried a lot. It was on one of these occasions that her mother came down and found Prue watching TV. Thunder cracked and it had started pouring down outside.

'Where's Holly?' she asked, and she looked frantically around the room with both hands on her face.

That's the last clear memory Prue has because when she tried to remember her brain became smothered in bubble wrap. It wrapped itself around her face until she couldn't breathe. Fear shut off part of her lungs and every nerve screamed like a kettle. What came next was indescribable. A shrieking heart-stopping terror. The world closed in on itself until it was nothing – a shrivelled-up vacuum-packed bag and Prue was nothing but some flesh and a pulse. The police came with angry barking dogs. Billy's van screeched down the track and almost hit one of the police vans. She saw him, sat on the ground with his head in his hands and he cried, and she never got over the shock of learning that boys could cry like that too.

She was put in the back of a police car and a policewoman gave her a McDonald's milkshake which she was never allowed, and her mother said those milkshakes were made of chicken fat. She still didn't know if that was true, but she still treated it with the same reverence as the cat theory. She drank it too fast and was too scared to tell the policewoman when she felt sick. The car stopped at traffic lights and Prue felt her cheeks fill with saliva as the indicators went *tick-tick-tick* and she threw up in her hands.

Joan Gardner loved babies. Her mother had bought dusters and cloths from Joan in the past. She would lean in their open window and shout and Prue didn't like it. Joan was a forty-six-year-old woman who went door to door selling cleaning products and lived with her seventy-year-old mother. Prue remembered being wary of her. Her mother told her she was only a child herself, but Prue didn't understand because she had a big fat body and was too big to play with children.

Joan would insist on squeezing Holly's feet when they crossed paths. She would squeeze her toes too hard, and Holly couldn't tell her to stop so Prue told her. She said Holly didn't like that. Joan laughed then turned her attention to Prue and she buried her face into her mother's legs as Joan tried to make her take sweets from her fat sweaty hands. Some of the mothers at the school had warned her mother about Joan. A couple of mummies had made complaints to the village school about her, and the locals had kicked back at the entitlement of village newcomers moving into the rural areas with their expectations of middle-class convenience and snobbery. She could be annoying and no doubt had made one or two children cry with her clumsy friendliness, but she was harmless and it was all innocent and well intended.

At the police station she told the police lady who she had seen at the window that day. The cleaning cloth lady.

Joan had a blue woollen coat and had left fibres behind on the mechanism of the window latch. The police said she must have come through the unlocked door when Prue was in another room and taken Holly. She stole her because she wanted her, like a toy, and then, scared of getting into trouble, left her on her blanket in the woods near the stream and when the water rose, a mere few inches, it was enough to take Holly into the water. No one told Prue any of that. She read it years later, in a newspaper when another child was abducted, and they mentioned Holly. They found her little body face down, tangled in branches. Ruth once told her Joan Gardner wasn't right in the head; she was *retarded*. Joan Gardner was to be detained in a secure hospital until it was no longer necessary, which was code for forever. They moved back to Nana's and Prue never saw Billy again. She never did get a kitten.

Maybe Joan Gardner's confession *was* obtained under duress, and maybe she did have special needs, but that didn't mean she *wasn't* guilty. The same way Archie's kinky paintings didn't mean he was guilty of murdering Evie – that's not how it works. It would be much simpler if it did.

Only a few days after moving back in with Nana, Prue got into trouble for stamping on the lip of a boy's skateboard. There was a patch of green in the shape of a big triangle outside Nana's house and the children from the street would play on it. Prue was outside with the other children and a boy from a house on the corner came down. He had a baseball cap and a flashy new skateboard. He flicked a piece of white dog poo at a girl with a moustache who lived in the road. Prue raised her foot and stamped on the lip of his skateboard. Prue and the girl with the moustache watched the boy hover in mid-air before he smashed his face into the kerb and split open his chin. There was blood everywhere and he needed stiches. The girl laughed as the boy scraped himself up, crying and bleeding, and ran back to his house on the corner.

When Prue brought her foot down, she had time to anticipate how bad a deed it was. And she still did it. She *wanted* to do it. She wanted to take a moment that was perfectly acceptable and ordinary and smash it to pieces.

After that, she wasn't allowed to play outside any more. She had to sit in the front room and look under those bloody net curtains and watch all the other children play on the green. This shrank the older she got until it became a tiny patch of grass with a couple of bollards to stop people dumping cars. Sometimes her mother would play with Prue, though; now it was only the two of them again she had the time. And they were back with Nana. In many ways it was better than it had been before. It was the three of them again – the way it would always be.

They would sit in the garden of Nana's house on the grass in the summer and pick flowers from the garden, daisies and buttercups and dandelions, and turn them upside down and pretend they were girls in ballgowns. There was a shed with a broken door where Nana kept her garden tools and chairs, and an old paddling pool with holes in it. Her mother took a thick lacy tablecloth and they sat underneath it, the ballroom between their knees and all the flowers dancing at this wonderful ball. The sun came through the holes in the tablecloth like spotlights on the ballroom floor.

'Do you remember the game, Prue?' her mother would say.

Perhaps she had asked her where Billy was now, or if Holly was coming back, or if another baby was going to come, or whatever happened to the kitten.

'It's magic, Prue. Close your eyes and think of a hallway full of open doors with lights on. You take that boy on the skateboard and put him inside a room. Now turn the light off and shut him inside and lock the door. That's what we do with bad things. We take them away and lock them up and forget them. This way, nothing bad ever happens.'

When you die they say your life flashes before your eyes and Prue had a clue what hers might look like and it wasn't so impressive. Spotlights on a ballroom of upturned flowers. Nana and her blown-out mouth. The uncooked prawn of her mother in a bath of strawberry-coloured water. The steak knife bouncing around the sink. Evie O'Hara's mother telling her to be quiet in the dark. Yellow skin. Blue skin. The look on her mother's face when she asked Prue where Holly was. Big fat raindrops and barking dogs. Crying boys. Feeling sick. Tick-tick-tick, and maybe even a winking cowboy tapping his spurs... *Cock-a-doodle-doodle-do.*

20

Prue was in James's bedroom with the door shut. Sharon had gone to the Mainland, and as soon as her car pulled away, James grabbed her and they ran upstairs leaving the new barmaid at the bar. When he closed the door, it was like a prison door slamming. Prue thought of naked Evie in the antlers and how at ease she had been and tried to play along. She imagined being Evie. Sweet, funny, articulate, personable, pretty and naked. Eager to please, and bang up for it.

He pushed her down on the bed, then he pulled up her top and tugged at her bra and kissed her above the belly button. Prue closed her eyes and tried to concentrate on the sensation as he covered her ribs with his mouth. He undid her jeans and she had to shift her hips so he could pull them down. Was this it? Was it really going to happen? When he kissed her over her knickers, she felt electric shocks, but when he pulled them down and uncovered her so she was as exposed as a newborn, she opened her eyes and it was Archie she saw between her legs, not James.

'No!' She pushed him off with a foot on his shoulder and scooted backwards, pulling up her underwear. Fuck! What just happened?

'I'm sorry,' she said. Shit.

James got up, humiliated and embarrassed, and worse – hurt. He stood with his back to her, looking out the window, and ruffled the back of his hair. Prue hated herself. What was wrong with her?

'I'm sorry,' she said again.

'Yeah, I heard you.' He still wouldn't look at her.

'I think we should try again. If you want.'

'Do you know what? I don't.' James picked up his T-shirt from the floor and pulled it over his head.

'This is really hard for me to say...' she started, and felt tingling in her cheeks, as if she couldn't really believe she was going to say it.

'I heard you the first time, you're sorry...'

'I am sorry, but... look, I haven't had sex before.'

He was in the middle of putting a jumper on and struggled to get his head through the hole. When he did, he had an expression of disbelief.

'What did you say?' He blinked like a malfunctioning robot. 'You said what?'

Prue found it hard to breathe and stared down at the duvet and pulled at a thread of unravelling stitched yellow flowers. She took a deep breath, exhaled and forced herself to look him in the face. 'I'm still a virgin – there you go.'

James, with his mouth open and his nose screwed up in a twist of confusion, still hadn't pulled his jumper down.

'Wait,' he started. 'What about the rock pool? You didn't seem much like a virgin then! Or... or... or the... hang on a minute, wait, is this why you ran off saying you were sick at the gun tower? Which I can tell you, when you have your cock out and think the other person is up for it because *they* made a flirty little game, and then they say they're going to be sick and run, like literally run, like they're escaping a rapist or a monster, isn't exactly a confidence boost!'

'I've said I'm sorry and I am. I realise I've perhaps given a few mixed messages, but I was trying... I don't know.' Prue covered her face with her hands. 'I get maybe, not maybe, I really was trying to flirt and—'

'What the fuck, Prue!' James had his hands on his head as Prue picked at the loose cotton. In hindsight, it might have been easier to mention all this to James nearer the beginning.

'This is why you avoid touching me, isn't it? You have no idea what you're doing, and you were trying to blag it the whole time.'

'Please! This is embarrassing enough, can we maybe move past this bit because—'

'What about your exes? Were they even real?'

'Sort of,' she said with a self-hating sigh. 'They were my friend's exes, not mine.'

'Oh God! I am so confused right now,' he said, and put his hands in his pockets and stared into the void like an old man inspecting his rose bushes and contemplating life.

'You did say you liked complicated,' offered Prue. God, he was right, she really did always try to manage the uncomfortable with a flippant comment. It wasn't appropriate, and this time, it didn't raise a smile. Even Prue wanted to punch herself.

'Look, I really should be downstairs, and you should get home. It'll be getting dark soon and you don't want to walk through the trees alone.'

'I don't mind,' shrugged Prue. Urgh, she was hopeless. She didn't mind anything. Didn't feel anything. Agreed with everything. An invertebrate.

'Well, I do. If we leave now, I can walk you and get back before my mum comes home.'

'Don't be daft, I'll walk myself.'

'I really don't think you should be walking through the trees on your own this late.'

'Then I'll go the long way, along the shoreline.'

'Good, call me when you get home?'

'Yes.'

'Don't forget.'

Prue took the long way home along the shoreline, as promised, deflated and hopeless. It was a fine evening, or braw as James would say. On the cusp of tears, she dawdled and took a detour past the croft with the Shetland ponies, knowing they would come to see her. She stroked the coarse thick fur of the squat little hippos, then once they'd tired of her and had figured no food was coming, they wandered off and she continued to dither along the shore.

When she saw the plume of smoke rising from the beach, she realised it was Saturday. That was the day Charlie had said he was having a barbecue on the beach and invited her. She had no intention of going, of course, but now she would have to walk past and the road was up from the beach so Charlie and his dubious friends would no doubt see her. She kept her head down and marched on and saw a group huddled around a fire down on the beach. Black clouds were rumbling towards them from far out at sea and torches of the last sunlight broke through gaps in the clouds and reflected off the water. A gannet flew past and an oystercatcher was screeching as Charlie looked up and waved. Great. Prue dragged herself down to say hello out of manners; the invite had seemed like an olive branch and she didn't want to be rude.

His cousin Simon was there, and the hard-faced barmaid who had slapped him around the face, but she didn't recognise the others. They were drinking cans and smoking, and as she got closer, she saw how much older they were – mid-twenties at least. A man in a green bomber jacket with a shaved head and acne-scarred cheeks looked even older, probably in his thirties.

'Hey,' said Charlie. He was the only one smiling; the rest had the same flat stare as the Polaroid girls on Archie's wall. There was a sense of anticipation, as if they were waiting to pounce, itching for her to say something to ridicule. It was like school.

'I'm on my way home so just thought I'd say hi,' she said.

'Who's the kid?' said the barmaid, who knew exactly who she was.

'Archie Anderson's niece,' said Simon. 'She's a proper London girl, *in it*,' affecting a terrible accent to mock her.

'OK, bye then,' said Prue, and walked off as they all burst out laughing.

She walked further along the beach and sat down on

the damp silken sand behind a large stack of rocks; the tide was going out. A streak of dark orange blazed across the sky along the line of the horizon. In a matter of days, Prue's exam results would be in, then a week after she would return to London to live with her mother in the same little flat, but this time there would be no Nana. Prue hugged her knees and stabbed a stick in the sand. She couldn't do it. She couldn't go home. Ruth was never going to tell her anything about her father. She would never be able to talk about her grandfather or what happened to Holly, and nothing would ever change until the next one of them died. It was purgatory. If she went back, it would be a matter of time before she fell into the old routine, but without Nana, she would have all of her mother's attention.

Before she knew it, she would be working at the same nursing home; maybe they could share shifts together and eat chips and beans every night and watch the soaps every Monday. Put dreamcatchers on a wall but never dream and keep the volume down so the ornaments stayed on top of the TV. Prue stabbed in the sand and disturbed a hermit crab. She picked it up and watched its purple legs try to crawl away on thin air.

'What are you doing?' Charlie appeared. Prue put the hermit crab down and he began making strides to get away – she should probably have followed his lead. Charlie sat on a low rock with his knees jutting upwards like a man on a child's chair.

'Your mates seem nice,' said Prue.

'Sorry, they're all right once you get to know them.'

'I should probably head home...' She stood up.

'No, don't. I wanted to say thank you.'

'For what?'

'You asked after my mam – nobody does, not even Simon. Everyone avoids it, guess they're bored of the subject.'

'It's OK, no worries,' she said, shrugging for what seemed like the fourteenth time that day. *Get an opinion, Prue, find some backbone.*

'Come back to mine,' he said, as if the urge forced the words out. She'd promised Ruth she'd keep her distance and Archie had told her to stay away in very clear terms.

When they got back to his house, the curtains were drawn, and the TV had been left on with the volume on a low mumble. Umbro was curled up on the sofa and jumped down; his tail worked overtime at the sight of Charlie who ordered him back on the sofa. The glass coffee table was full of dried spills, used matches, an ashtray that hadn't been emptied for months, torn cigarettes raped of their tobacco and damp skins stuck to the table. There were posters of Che Guevara and Kurt Cobain on the wall but no bongos or guitars that Prue could see.

'I'm sorry Ruth called the police on your mum. I think she was scared.'

Charlie snorted. 'Whatever – my mother brings it on herself.'

'Can I ask you a straight question?'

'Do what you like,' he said.

'Do you really think Archie killed your sister?'

Charlie leaned back, lit a cigarette, and draped an arm over the dog. He chewed on the inside of his cheek as he considered his answer.

'He was in the army. How many people did he kill there?'

'This was before the army, and anyway, that's different.'

'Is it?'

'I understand you need to hate someone but I really don't think he did it.'

'The Andersons have connections. Nothing ever sticks to Archie, he can do what he likes. If anyone could get away with murder – he could. You know how the weed gets onto the island?'

Prue shook her head. Charlie leaned forward with a look of incredulity and then his face broadened into a maniac's smirk.

'What's so funny?' she asked.

'I thought it was off when you came to me – it's Archie. You think I'd risk my arse? Comes from Denmark, that's all I ken. He goes on da fishing trips, right? Do yoos eat a lot of fish?'

'That can't be true,' she said. But Prue was already considering the complete absence of any fish since she'd been there.

'You sure about that? He only throws me the scraps because he has bigger things going on da Mainland, and that's all I know, God knows what else. You don't think he makes money from da painting, do yoos? Yeah, he throws us a line to keep me quiet – maybe it is out of pity, I dunna ken, and I dunna care. It benefits me and I won't grass – I may be a loser, but I'm no fucking snitch.'

'Does Ruth know?'

He laughed again. 'Your auntie makes me stand on da doorstep. She didna like me coming in the hoos, and she looks down on us. I seen the old lady knocking aboot so they all ken. Looks like yoos the one who dunna.'

'I don't get it. How can you work for Archie if you think there's even a remote chance he did something to your sister?'

'I used to fucking hate the man. Can you imagine having your mam going on for years after Evie went? I dunna ken when it happened, but I got tired of being angry at him and dat family. I realised not everyone's mam forgets to feed them and is pissed by lunchtime. She always hae wine in the fridge but there was no milk, no bread, no dinner. You get confused about who to be angry at. And I dunna work *for* him, I work *with* him. We have an understanding. Needs must, Prue, because he's the only one with money on this fucking island. I say I stay because of my mam but it's not that – it's all I ken. But one of these days – I'm going, and soon.'

'I didn't know any of that.'

'Yo ken, the day my mam saw yoos she went on a binge and put Evie's stuff in the bin.'

'Why?'

'She got upset and when she gets upset, she drinks and then the *why my Evie* starts. All da girls he brings to dat hoos and her peerie one never came home.'

'Surely that proves he can't be a murderer – he'd have done it again if he was.'

Charlie shrugged as if he didn't even care. 'She put a photo album in da bin but I took it out. I ken she'd regret throwing anything away about her favourite child.'

'I heard she was pretty.' Prue knew very well what Evie looked like, but she could hardly mention that to Charlie.

'Stay here.' He left her perched on the edge of the crusty armchair with Umbro. Moments later he came back with a leather-bound photo album. They sat side by side on the sofa and his weight brought them closer together, their legs touching. He put the album across their laps. The plastic of the pages stuck together as if they had to be wrenched apart for the first time in years. Inside were old photographs with chunky white borders, bleached out colours and blurry edges. Yellow streaky sun, single colour skies, skinny people with wavy hair and funky trousers.

'Have a look,' he said.

He pointed to a picture of Evie with the round cheeks and golden hair wearing a pink shirt and bell-bottomed jeans in a rowing boat on dry land. A little blond-haired boy sat between her knees, her arms wrapped around his shoulders.

'I know that boat, I've walked past it. Is that you?' she asked, nudging him with her knee. He looked embarrassed and nodded.

'You were cute,' she said.

'Still am,' he said, and nudged her back. Charlie flicked through the album of faded pictures, overexposed, sun hats, white dresses, picnics on beaches, Charlie being pushed by Evie on a swing.

Then he flicked over to pages of cut-out newspaper articles, brown and yellow. There was a picture of Evie at a much younger age, maybe eleven or twelve, holding a flower and wearing a thick knitted jumper. The headline said: *MISSING NOOST GIRL.* The sub headline: *Priest begs islanders for information on behalf of grief-stricken mother.*

It seemed odd to use a photo of a missing girl so much younger than the age she was at the time. The article spoke about a different girl to the one Prue thought she knew from the letters. This was insipid, the good old-fashioned reliable and sweet-natured girl, the shy and quiet girl who apparently wanted to be a nurse, only one rung below angel.

'What about the police?' she asked.

'Nothing. They interviewed da Andersons and no one saw Evie. She went into da trees, someone must have got to her there.'

'But no one saw her go into the trees, did they?'

Charlie shook his head.

'He's your uncle, what do yoos make of him?'

'He's been teaching me to drive, and then there's my mum – he paid for her to go to rehab.'

'I bet I earned dat for him.'

'You want to get off the island, right? Maybe you should try talking to him. Ask for advice, what have you got to lose exactly? He's a good person, once you get to know him – a bit like your mates, I guess.'

Charlie laughed again. 'Fair point.' He took the photo album away. 'You should go, it's dark already.'

At the door, Charlie shoved something in Prue's hand; when she looked it was a plastic bag with two little pills inside.

'What are these?'

'Ecstasy, for you and da boyfriend,' said Charlie. 'Consider it a freebie.'

'I thought you sold weed.'

'I'm branching out.'

'He's not my boyfriend,' she said, and walked out the door.

'Does he know that?' Charlie shouted after her.

'You said that last time.'

'And you didna answer then!'

Prue put the pills in the pocket of her jeans. Weed, everybody did it, but she wasn't so sure about Ecstasy. When she got back to the house, she peered through the gap in the door to the kitchen and saw Ruth talking to Archie and listened to their conversation.

'I was so desperate to get her here,' Ruth said. 'I thought I could help, but now it feels as if any moment it could all come out. To be honest, I'll be glad when she's gone so I can relax.' The words from her aunt stung like a slap in the face.

The phone rang. Prue skidded to the study to escape Ruth on her way to answer the phone in the hall, but carried on listening from the door.

'Hello, James. No, I don't think she's back yet. What time did she leave yours?'

Prue stepped out into the hall before her aunt panicked and called for the police helicopters.

'Here she is! Not to worry, James, she's here, safe and sound.' Ruth waved at Prue. 'I'll hand you over.'

Urgh. She didn't really want to speak to James. 'Hello? I'm back.'

'You forgot, didn't you?'

'Yes, sorry.'

'Look, I want to apologise for earlier.'

'Why? What do you have to apologise for?'

'I think I was a bit of a wanker. You don't need to apologise to me for not being... I dunno, up for it or nervous or whatever. Whatever you want to do, or not do, is fine by me. You're fine by me. OK?'

'OK.' She didn't know what to say. She was annoyed at him for being so impossibly sweet.

'But for the record, you should have told me the truth earlier...'

'I know, and I'm sorry, I...'

'Listen, I just need you to talk to me, Prue, be honest. There's no need to pretend or put up some front, it won't make me like you any less.'

'OK.'

'Good, I'll see you later then.'

She didn't know what tormented her more: being left exposed without a façade or him being so forgiving, or even *I'll be glad when she's gone*. She should feel better now James knew the truth, but she didn't. She wanted to push him away, and what was going to come out?

Back in the study Prue took the pills from her pocket and looked for a place to hide them. She could always put them in a book, she supposed, if it wasn't one stuffed with cash. There was only half a shelf left to search before she had opened the pages of every single book in that room and part of her didn't want to finish. Then it would be over and there would be no more Evie. Let there be one more, one more to savour and give her something to run on, like petrol. She put the pills back into her jeans, making a mental note to find somewhere to hide them after she'd finished looking through the books.

Halfway through her search she found the last note, and when she opened it inside there was one more photo and on the back was a message:

Ev, you are the only one who knows the real me. Love you forever – Archie. 30/04/73.

Evie was sat between Archie's legs and his arms, thin and stringy, were wrapped around her, and she was smiling, his nose in her ear. They looked sun drenched and happy. Prue turned to the torn page from the diary.

Monday, 28th May 1973

You are a conundrum. I think if anyone ever breaks your heart you will do one of two things: turn to stone or start crying and never stop!! So there... you HAVE to love me and you have to know I will never break your heart, so don't be a coward and love me back – it's the courageous thing to do... Evie

Prue searched the remaining books but there was nothing left to find. That was everything. It was over and she was bereft. How ridiculous to cry over no more torn pages from a missing girl to feed her petty obsession. Everything was ending. Ruth wanted her gone, James knew who she was, she didn't know any more about her father and she might have put an innocent woman in prison, and when she went home she would be going straight back to the start. No further forward at all. What she felt reading the diary pages was as real as anything else. What if she could still help Evie be found? Perhaps they could rescue each other. What if she was missing something glaringly obvious? Perhaps she wasn't seeing everything in the notes that was there to understand.

21

Prue laid all the torn pages and photos on the floor and put them in date order. The earliest letter turned out to be the last one she'd found, dated 28th May 1973. This one was fun and flirtatious, Evie seemed the stronger one, sticking the stake in the ground and telling Archie to love her back so she must have known he wanted her too, at least sexually. The next one was dated two weeks after, and in this one, Evie says they've done things that make her blush. This was puzzling to Prue, because if they were already having sex, what on earth was it they were doing? She talks of their mothers, or lack of; this gave them a connection and Prue could understand – she'd had the same feeling when Archie talked about his mother. The third note was around three weeks after the second and by this time Evie is having trouble functioning because of the intensity, but was it lust and not love? She did mention Ronnie and while Ronnie admitted to knowing Evie, she had downplayed the relationship to nothing more than a summer fling. That wasn't what Prue was picking up at all.

The fourth note was another three weeks later, but things seemed different. The earlier pages gave Prue a feeling that they were both besotted by each other but now there was a sense of angst. Evie was worrying she may need to wear glasses and if Archie would still find her attractive. Evie knew Archie was joining the army, but she had mentioned concerns about Ronnie asking questions. Questions about what? Ronnie hadn't mentioned that. The last letter was almost a whole month later, near the end of August. Evie says they are soul mates, and she is definitely under the impression that while Archie may be joining the army, it was only the beginning – they were going to *build an empire*. Evie even signed off as the future Mrs Anderson. Who else would have kept such notes other than Archie? It had to be. But had he kept them as the last mementoes of a tragically lost first love, or because they were mementoes of a murder he got away with?

'Prue! Are you in there?' Ronnie rattled the door.

'Hang on!' Prue scooped up the pages and photos and crawled over to the far corner and stuffed them on top of the books on the bottom shelf. She leapt up and opened the door, trying not to look flustered.

'Sorry, I was getting changed,' she said.

'Back into your jeans again?' Ronnie looked Prue up and down.

'You knocked so I pulled them back up.'

'You seem to be locking your door a lot lately.' Ronnie peered over her shoulder, but Prue was taller.

'For privacy.'

'Hmmm, I can't help but feel you've been keeping your distance from me.'

'No! Of course not.'

'I've been working on new cocktails; I was hoping you would try some for me.'

'Yes, I will, absolutely, but not tonight, I'm really tired.'

'Let's make a date for tomorrow.'

'All right, tomorrow,' but Ronnie lingered as Prue was smiling like an idiot and willing her to leave.

'Did you notice I put some flowers in there specially for you?'

'You did?' Prue looked around, her eyes searching furiously.

Ronnie pushed past and walked straight to the bookshelf. If she were to look down, she could see the letters, but she walked and pointed to a new vase of flowers.

'Ah, the tulips,' said Prue, sweating. 'You know, I forgot but I did notice, I love them, thank you.' She hadn't noticed at all.

'You said you liked tulips.' They both regarded the peach pink tulips with yellow tips. Prue was sure Ronnie was checking about the room, trying to find anything unusual, but she was standing too close to the shelves to see the letters.

'You are looking a bit pale,' she said, switching her attention back to Prue. 'Are you eating properly? I've made chicken soup – why don't I bring you some?'

'That sounds good.' Prue was happy to accept if it meant she would go.

'I'll warm some up, shan't be long,' she said, and finally left. As Prue closed the door, she pressed her back to it and exhaled with relief at how close that had been. Her nerves were jangled.

She recalled the other words Ruth had wounded her with, *it could all come out*. It had to be who her father was. She was still lying, after everything. But while whatever tryst had led to Prue's birth remained a mystery, she couldn't help but notice the distinct absence of love notes or photographs with silly teenage messages. Surely her mother would have kept them if they existed. She would have savoured them, or laughed at them, but at the very least shared them. Her father was a ghost and something to be forgotten, like the shadow in the painting of her at the aquarium. If her mother had loved her father the way Evie had loved Archie, she wouldn't have been able to keep it secret, even if Nana had forbidden her. She had found the strength to run away with Billy, after all.

When baby Holly had come along Prue had felt left out. Her mother had found it so easy to be affectionate to her baby sister, but never her and she had missed Nana terribly. After Holly died, Prue had been happy to go back to Nana. With Holly and Billy gone, it was the three of them again, and she hadn't felt left out then, but her mother had.

Ronnie returned with a bowl of chicken soup and a cloudy pink lemonade with a straw. 'Drink it through the straw, or you'll get bits in your mouth.'

'Bits of what?'

'Fermented bark, for restful dreams.'

She sipped it, feigning delight at the flavours although the overwhelming one was gin so no wonder it helped with sleeping. The soup was more herbs than chicken and she only managed part of it, but she finished the drink, returned the crockery to the kitchen, went back to the study and locked the door.

Back on her knees to retrieve the letters, she noticed a metal lever on the wall between two of the shelves. Old and rusty, it sat flat against the wall, and when she moved it there was a squeaking noise coming from somewhere. She looked but nothing moved in the room, and when she tried again she thought the noise might be coming from underneath the floor.

Peeling the rugs back, she knelt down and used the handle of the old wooden tennis racquet to move the lever, trying to get closer to where she thought the noise was coming from. It could have been a disused servicing hatch to a basement, or maybe even another priest hole. With the rugs back she became aware of a sharp, cold draught coming up between two floorboards over one particular spot. Then she noticed that three of the boards were loose and not sealed around the edges like the others. Grabbing one of the ice skates with the lethal blades, she was about to pry up one end when she saw a little nook carved out of one of the boards, like a groove for a finger. She hooked her finger in and lifted it up, a blast of stale air hitting her in the face as she did so.

She lifted the other boards and set them to one side; below were stone steps leading down into a dark hole. It was another priest hole, Prue reasoned, one Ronnie had forgotten to show her; she had said they were all over the house. On the wall was a mechanism, and when she tried the lever it moved; it must have been once attached to a kind of trapdoor. With the torch she looked around in the dark basement expecting it to be an empty hole, but things had been left down there: a rocking chair, a wooden table, some shelves on the wall with books and bottles and melted candles on the ground. Prue shifted down through the hole and onto the first step and hesitated. It was as if she was standing beside herself, watching this girl, a different one to the girl who had first arrived. She took a deep breath and shifted herself down each step until her head was below floor level. Sweeping the torch around, she could hear her own heavy breathing and see her breath in the cold stagnant air.

Along a wall at the end, someone had put up wooden shelves full of old web-covered glass bottles similar to the ones Ronnie kept upstairs, along with rotting and bloated books and various other unidentifiable items covered in cobwebs and ancient dust. The torch with its small beam illuminated only one spot, keeping the rest of the room blindingly black. She swung the torch to chase away anything that might be hiding, as ridiculous as she knew that was, but stopped the beam on the wooden rocking chair and saw that behind that was a door. Where did it lead to?

Prue lowered herself down until her bare feet were on the ground, then standing up and sweeping the torch around her, she walked to the door behind the rocking chair. With a trembling hand she tried the handle, and it opened, sending another blast of musty cold air towards her. Checking behind herself first, she peered into the doorway. It was a narrow corridor leading only left to somewhere, but the torch didn't light up far enough to see. It had to be an old escape route. Prue heard something scurry in the room behind her and swung the torch around searching but couldn't see anything. When she felt something run over her feet, she had to stop herself screaming and hopped from one foot to the other. She saw the rat run through the open door and down the narrow corridor. She nearly dropped the torch but managed to grab it with both hands and decided that was all she could stand. She flew up the stone steps, put the floorboards back, and then the rugs.

Something awful had happened in that room. It was as if the cloud of some terrible event had been waiting for a warm body to cling to, and it had found Prue. She shuddered. Ronnie had told her homes carry the energy of those who were there before, and the energy underneath the study was a desperate one.

Prue had set her alarm for early the next morning and slipped out of the house before she thought anyone else was around. Her plan was to work out where the narrow channel underground might lead to, by walking around the house. Outside she traced her location overground, and from what she could work out, the corridor had to lead to the cellarium.

The sound of flapping wings made her look up. The ravens had arrived to watch as one settled on the edge of the guttering, then a second, and then a third. There were only the four these days, but the other hadn't arrived yet. Prue had buried the fifth in the garden and hoped they didn't blame her for the death of their friend.

'You're up early,' said Archie. Prue spun around, adrenaline pumping straight to her chest. 'What are you up to, staring at the sky?'

'Erm… looking at the ravens.'

'Whatever floats your boat,' said Archie. 'I'm going to go to St Ninian's today, looks like it's going to be a clear day and might be one of the last if the weather turns. You want to come? I'll let you drive some of the way?'

'What, now?'

'Yeah, why not?'

'Can I... Before we go, can I see inside the cellarium?'

He shook his head, as if indulging her was an amusing inconvenience. 'Fine,' he said. 'Make it quick, I want to get going.'

He opened the door for her, and she stepped inside what really did look like a big vacant room with squat columns in two lines and arched windows that didn't let in much light. It was dark, gloomy and dusty – like a real church. Archie leaned in the doorway.

'It's a big larder really,' his voice echoed.

'Wasn't it a church?'

'Sort of, you'd have to ask Ronnie. The staircase leads up to the kitchen and the fuse boxes are at the top of the stairs, the electrics are pretty messed up here. One of the many problems...'

Prue walked along the wall lined with metal shelving units, the kind you'd find in any old garage. One of them must be blocking the door that led to the channel and would lead to the priest hole under the study.

'There's nothing here,' said Archie. 'It's just a creepy old room, come on.'

She made her way out and Archie shut the door behind them. They got into the pickup and he started the engine.

'What time are we going to be back?' she asked.

'No idea.'

'It won't be late, will it?'

'Nope. Look at it like an adventure,' he said.

They drove along the bumpy track watched by the ravens on the guttering and shadowed by the dark trees. Prue remembered what James had told her about ravens, how they knew where to find hidden bodies and how Evie's mother had asked her if the corbies, as she called them, still gathered at the house.

22

'You're leaving at a good time,' Archie said, as he drove. 'An island winter can be tough, and long. If you think the mould is bad now, wait until you can see your breath inside the house.'

'I'd rather take my chances with an island winter,' said Prue.

Her exam results were going to be here in a few days and Ruth's friend was going to collect them and phone with the results. Prue didn't even care; she was more worried about having to go back home. She brooded as she stared out of the window, wondering how the time had passed so fast and yet she had achieved nothing.

'How are you and James getting along?' asked Archie.

'Fine.'

'You sleeping with him?'

Prue tried not to react, willing the discomfort away.

'You can't ask me that,' she said.

'I'll take that as a yes then.'

'No.'

'No, what?'

'No, you can't ask me that,' she said, turning to him; he was smirking. 'Please, can we change the subject?'

He laughed. 'It's cute how you get so embarrassed.'

It wasn't cute, it was excruciating. She wasn't going to talk about her non-existent sex life with her uncle; even if he was comfortable with it, she wasn't. She crossed her legs and felt the two pills in the little plastic bag in her jeans pocket and thought she'd combust into flames; she had forgotten to hide them again. She pushed them further down into her pocket and hoped they wouldn't find a way to fly out like her knickers had in front of Ruth. Knickers were one thing, Class A drugs quite another.

They were on the ferry crossing the water when Prue started to notice a jitter as if she'd had too much coffee, except she hadn't drunk any. She kept checking the pills were still in her pocket to the point of neurosis and when they reached the other side and continued the drive south, her eyelids felt like lead weights were dragging them down and she struggled to focus; even things close up began to blur. Then her tongue cramped suddenly, and she retched, and then the urge disappeared.

'Are you OK?' asked Archie. When she looked, his face was smeared as if a hand had been dragged through a wet painting.

'I think I'm dehydrated,' she said. Archie said there was a bottle of water in his bag and she rifled through and found it, sipping at it the rest of the way.

He drove them to a beach, but it was in the form of a freakish slither of land where the waves broke on both sides and made a long sandy path to an isle at the end. They parked and walked down onto the strip of pure yellow sand. Prue ran ahead, took her shoes and socks off and paddled in the water. It could have been a tropical island, had it not been for the fact that the water was freezing. Archie lagged behind, walking with his thumbs in his pockets as he always did, with no intention of taking his socks off.

The isle had to be climbed up to and the rocks were covered with green sponge moss full of water with clusters of sea pink sprouting up in crevices. The underside of the isle was full of small watery caves and the sound of water leaking echoed everywhere. She put her trainers back on and climbed up where the thick wiry grass was littered with tufts of caught wool – *hentilagets*, James said they were called. She almost trod on the dried-out carcass of a dead rabbit. She was going to miss this strange place; although she'd panicked at the sparseness when she'd first arrived, she now knew the freedom in the absence of schedules and routines. She knew freedom from the feeling of never being able to do enough and of permanently running behind everyone else. She didn't want to pack herself onto a crowded bus with a million armpits in her face and sit in forced lines, cramped together, a repetitive existence at a soul-crushing pace. No time to think. No time to understand. No time to work out what her answer would be when the devil came and asked her what she wanted. At the last parents' evening, her Science teacher, Mrs Saldana, had been in the middle of telling Prue's mother how she had come top of the year in mocks.

'We are really proud of her progress, especially in Physics and Chemistry,' said Mrs Saldana.

'Oh, really? I've always thought Prue would be more the creative type.' Prue was not in any way creative and had no idea where her mother got this idea from, but that wasn't the end. 'We are an artistic family,' her mother added.

Except for Ruth and Archie, who else was creative?

Mrs Saldana persevered. 'It's really refreshing to have so many girls leaning towards the sciences these days and exploring their options. Recently we've been talking about careers in engineering—'

'Pah!' her mother said, and it had echoed around the room as Prue cringed. Who says that? It was so false... and loud. 'Greasy engines and oil? I don't think so.'

'Well,' Mrs Saldana gave a wry smile that barely masked her feelings, 'there are many different types of engineering and some of them have nothing to do with oil or grease. Anyway, I guess it doesn't matter what we think about it – it will be up to Prue to choose what she wants. One last thing I want to say that really impresses me is how she's a self-starter and so mature for her age, independent.' Well redirected, Prue thought, but her mother was still in combat mode.

'No,' she said, 'she's not independent. Prue is a very nervous and shy girl, and prefers being at home.'

It wasn't as if Prue had ever had a choice, though, was it? Not since what happened to Holly. She'd never been allowed to hang out with other children or play in groups in the park after that. She had to come straight home after school and her mother timed the journey so she knew exactly how long it would take for her to get home; she couldn't even dawdle or loiter on the corner with the others.

'Well,' Mrs Saldana said again (her mother would pick

up on that later), 'you should be really proud of her – she is turning into an intelligent young woman.'

'She's most certainly *not* a woman, she's just a child,' said her mother. Prue was mortified.

'Oh-kay…' said Mrs Saldana. 'Well…' There it was again. '… it was lovely to meet you, Mrs MacArthur. And Prue,' she said, addressing her, 'good luck.'

As soon as they got to the car her mother began ranting.

'The way that woman spoke to me was disgusting, condescending cow.'

'I don't think she meant to be rude, Mum,' said Prue. 'She's a Science teacher, it's not like she's going to push Drama, is it?'

'Do you like Science? I mean, really?'

'Yeah, I do, it's my best subject, that and Maths.'

'Maths?' She turned back to the steering wheel of her battered Fiesta and let out the biggest sigh. 'I remember you stripping your Barbies naked and ordering them into lines. Holding onto my legs and bringing me little gifts.'

'I'm sixteen. You can't expect me to play with Barbies any more, or cling to your leg – that would be weird.' The traffic lights turned green, but she didn't put the car into gear.

'I suppose.'

'You have to let me grow up at some point, you can't stop it. You can't keep me indoors forever.'

'Engineering, honestly? If you studied that, you realise you would probably be the only girl – you would hate it.'

'Would I? Isn't this the type of thing Nana used to tell you to stop you trying things?'

'Only because she loved me and wanted to keep me safe.'

'Statistically I read that most people are killed in their own homes by someone they know,' said Prue and her mother shot her a dirty look. 'Why didn't you correct Mrs Saldana when she called you *Mrs* MacArthur?' But the cars behind them beeped and her mother put the car into gear and pulled away before answering. She never did answer the question.

Archie climbed up to join her on the isle and together they sat on the edge of the grass overlooking the beach on one side.

'Why did we come here?' asked Prue.

'Sometimes I need to get out of the house. What's the point of being in a place like this if you don't get out and appreciate it?'

'I never realised it would be like this. I didn't think I'd like it at all and now I don't want to leave. Going home seemed ages away and now my results will be here in days. How did that happen? I'm dreading it,' said Prue.

'I'm sure you'll do fine, you're a bright girl.'

'It's not my exams I'm worried about.'

'Focus on what you can control, make a plan. You're going to change a lot over the next few years, trust me; you won't even recognise yourself.'

'I heard you and Ruth talking in the kitchen last night. I heard her say about it *all coming out*.'

'It's not what you think.'

'Ruth promised me we'd talk and I know she's lying. She knows who my father is, or at least his name, I know it.'

'I'm not lying to you.'

'You didn't deny *she* is, though, and you won't tell me either.'

'Prue, I've been told something in confidence, and if I told you, I'd be breaking that. You're going to have to sit down with Ruth.'

'You don't think I've tried?'

'Ask me about something I *can* tell you about.'

'All right then, tell me about Evie O'Hara. The islanders say you murdered her and buried her in the trees, and you told me that was horseshit the first time I was in your studio.'

At first he didn't react, and there was a horrible silence as he stared across the beach... Then Archie lay back with his hands behind his head, tufts of wool clumped in the grass and rabbit poo around them.

'Not many people say that name to me these days.'

'Why don't you tell me your version? I've heard everyone else's.'

'And then will you trust me?' He looked at her with those wicked lines around his eyes.

'I might.'

'I got kicked out of boarding school and came back home. My dad decided his new sport would be to break me, like a horse – that's when he wasn't bullying my mother. I'd known Evie for years; her family weren't islanders, which means they weren't born here. Ev and her brother were but not her mother or uncles, which meant she didn't have the same wariness the locals had about me being an Anderson. Actually, she didn't care that I was a landowner's son. When I told her that my family owned the island, I was trying to impress her.'

'And did it?' Remembering how Ronnie had cast Evie as the social climber.

'No! She called me an arrogant shit, laughed in my face in

front of her friends and walked away. I could have dropped to my knees with shame; instead I got the worst crush.'

'So, you chased her?'

'Are you kidding? Ev thought I was a grade A prick.' Archie leaned up towards Prue on an elbow and for a moment she saw the boy from the photos, the skinny lad with the glassy eyes dazzled by lust. 'After my disastrous introduction I tried to get her to notice me a second time and I blew a dandelion in her face but the seeds got in her eyes. She was blinded, staggering around and near crying and her friends all crowded around and told me to go away. I kept apologising and felt like a complete idiot and after that she called me *dandelion boy*. It wasn't exactly the most macho of nicknames. Whenever our paths crossed, she'd shout out, *Hey, dandelion boy, blind any girls lately?*'

This was the same as the letters, and now Prue understood the sappy nickname. It was as if the screw on the mystery of Evie was being slowly turned, and all the pieces might come together.

'Ev was one of a kind, she was honest and had a shit-load of integrity. She was fearless, but was also the sweetest person that ever walked the Earth, and she loved animals. She was funny and clever, and very good with words – unlike me. I could barely string a sentence together.

'You don't forget the day the love of your life disappears. On the twenty-sixth of August 1973 she was meant to meet me in Ronnie's greenhouse. Her mother said she left her house happy and had her canvas bag, a pale blue dress with yellow flowers with little buttons down the front that weren't real – I know because I'd tried to undo them once and she'd found it hilarious. I was late and stuck on the

Mainland because there was a problem with the ferry. She never made it to the greenhouse. She went into those trees and never came out the other side.'

'But from what I've heard no one can say anyone actually saw her go into the trees, is that right?'

'Yes, but her mother said she saw her leave the house, and witnesses said they saw her walking past the hotel. So, we have to assume she made it to them. The way I see it there are only two possibilities: either she ran into someone in those trees, or…'

'Or what?'

'What if she wasn't coming to meet me at all? What if she did leave her house, but went somewhere else?'

'What are you saying? You think she ran away?'

'I can't see how something wouldn't have turned up by now, after all these years. If someone did do something, either they'd have told someone, or she would have been found. I have to consider other possibilities.'

'Why would she run away? I thought you were in love?'

'So did I.' Archie sat up. 'We had a plan, or so I thought. I was going to join the army and she was worried about being left behind. Ronnie suggested she could have run away and at the time I wouldn't hear of it, but now? Ev was bright, funny, had everything going for her and I was leaving her with a lot to deal with, we were both so young.'

'What did she have to deal with?'

'Ev was pregnant,' said Archie.

That was the secret! Prue was shocked, and hadn't considered it; she was sure it was about running away and getting married. A baby wasn't the same as a plan. The shock must have shown on her face.

'Prue, I'm trusting you with this, this can't get out now and I've never told Ruth. I'm telling you because... I know you'll understand, like I understand how things are for you. We thought if we kept it a secret as long as possible, then it would be too far along and both our families would have to accept us being together. But what if it was Evie who changed her mind?'

'I had no idea...'

'No one does, or did, or can,' Archie laughed. 'I don't need any more oxygen on the fire, Prue. If Gladys finds out or Charlie – there'd be more trouble.'

'I won't say anything, I promise. I'll take it to my grave.'

'I'd never felt like that before, it was... an experience. I don't think I've ever really felt like that again. I've been looking for it ever since, but nothing quite beats your first love affair. We were both so innocent, you can't recapture that experience. It didn't matter that everyone thought I was a murderer because I couldn't have felt worse than I already did. I was a broken mess and I hope she ran away because the alternative is that someone murdered her and our baby, and where was I? Not there when it mattered. The things I have imagined that happened... But over the years, I have to admit maybe Ronnie had a point.'

'But why not dump you?'

'What if she ran away and had the baby? I have no idea if I have a son or daughter walking around thinking I didn't want them – like you. But I wouldn't have been a good dad anyway. You know the rest: I joined the army, left this place behind and it was the best thing I ever did.'

'Did anyone else know she was pregnant?'

'God no,' he said, and he was adamant. 'Ev thought we should tell Ronnie, but I didn't think it was a good idea. I'm not saying I don't trust Ronnie but... I don't trust her... not with everything. She was perfectly nice to Evie, but I knew she didn't really approve.'

'Why?'

'Ronnie comes from another era, one with bunting, toasts to the Royal Family, debutantes and servants, and handsome men in uniform.'

'She's eccentric, I'll give you that,' said Prue. 'She calls the plants her children, but she's been nice to me, and she adores Ruth.'

'She's mellowed a lot with age and she seems to like you too. Traditionally she's not got along with many females, shall we say. I had a few letters and photos – stupid teenage stuff – and Ronnie said I had to get rid of them because if the police found them, they would use them against me, so I gave them to her but asked her to hide them somewhere in case I needed to see them again, but I never have. I don't think I want to see them, it would hurt too much. Come on, enough heavy stuff, let's make a move.' Archie tugged on Prue's ponytail as he got to his feet and put out both his hands to yank her up.

He pulled her towards his chest and kissed her on the forehead. 'You're a sweet girl, Prue. Thank you for listening; sometimes you remind me a little of Ev.'

Prue instantly thought of the photo with Evie naked wearing the antlers, the ones he had made her wear. He was much bigger than her; even if she could have screamed, he could have squeezed the last breath from her and crushed her ribcage, and no one was around to hear anyway.

★ ★ ★

It was mid-afternoon by the time they made it to the car. On the way back to Lerwick Prue started to feel sick. She thought it was travel sickness and she stared straight ahead at the windscreen, concentrating on the road. Then her vision went streaky again and the cramp came back in her throat. When Archie parked, he suggested they go for a drink while they waited for the ferry. She didn't feel like it, but she didn't want to disappoint him so she trailed along. She was feeling odd and distant, as if she was watching everything happen from behind a thick glass porthole, like a fish-eye lens.

They went to a pub that stank of last night's booze and fags. It was small and claustrophobic and made Prue feel panicky and close even though there was hardly anyone inside. She asked for a Coke, but when Archie handed her a drink, she was sure there was vodka in it.

'Sorry. They must have poured it by mistake. You want me to change it?'

'No, it's fine. I'll drink it.'

The funny thing was the vodka made her feel better so when he asked if she wanted another, she said yes. She reminded him about the ferry but he said they had plenty of time. After the third drink, Prue felt herself getting drunk but the strange cramping in her throat had gone. When he asked if she wanted food, she said no because she was worried about feeling sick again. She thought they were about to leave, when three men came in who Archie knew. They were all similar to him, big and broad, rough, bearded or unshaven, beanie hats and jeans. They were friendly enough, so Prue didn't feel uncomfortable when they gathered around and bought more drinks, though she was sure they'd missed the ferry. She recognised one of them as the man who drove a van to pick up Archie's paintings on occasion, and she noted the display of back slapping, hand shaking and grabbing. They talked, but she wasn't in on the conversation. She wanted a cigarette and managed to bum one off a guy at a table as Archie was talking with his mates.

Prue staggered outside to smoke but the nicotine hit her and suddenly she felt very drunk. She went back inside and Archie was at the bar drinking shots and handed her one. A couple of his friends leaned over and dribbled lager in her ear as they asked her name, which she shouted repeatedly at them. She knocked back a tequila and they cheered and more followed. She remembered walking through the bar with the low ceiling almost scraping her head and the swirling carpet coming up dangerously close to her face, while people in conversation parted as she stumbled through them to find the toilet. Their mouths wide open like Nana's blown-out scream. Their eyes were large and round, staring at her as if everyone knew she'd done something terribly wrong. Prue found the toilets and sat on the loo with her head swirling and stretched out her tongue to check the cramps had gone.

Someone banged on the door and Prue was jolted awake and pulled up her jeans. She was careful to push down the pills in her pocket, giggling to herself, wishing James was there. He would take her home and tell her how she was a liability for getting in such a state. He would make sure she got undressed and brushed her teeth and drank water before putting her to bed. She washed her hands, checked in the mirror, and assessed with her questionable judgement that she looked fine. When she got back to the others, Archie asked if she wanted another drink.

'Can we go?' Prue shout-whispered. A band had set up and were playing loud music. People were talking over the top, many strands of noise fighting against each other; it was too much, and it was dark outside.

'After these, we go,' he said.

Prue hung on his arm, swaying. One of his friends offered to get her another drink, but all she could do was shake her head no, like a three-year-old refuses dinner.

Prue leaned up against Archie with her back to him, his arm around her waist, keeping her upright. When did it get dark? God knows what time it was. When they got to the pickup, Archie had to lift Prue into the passenger seat and she was laughing – really laughing. The next thing she remembered was bending over on the grass, her jeans and knickers around one ankle. The light was shining through her pee and it made a puddle and she was trying to stop it from hitting her feet. She was in socks. She didn't know where her shoes were. She pulled her knickers up and fell over onto her face. The grass was cold and wet. Prue found this hilarious.

When she next opened her eyes, she was on her side in a sleeping bag on a hard metal surface. She had no socks or jeans on and was just in her top and knickers. She put a hand out and touched metal a few inches from her face. It was the back of the pickup. Dim light came through the tinted windows. Her head banged and her mouth tasted like shit. Where the fuck were her jeans? Archie was behind her.

What the fuck. She panicked and tried to lean up on her elbows.

'What's the matter?' Archie stirred.

Why the fuck didn't they go home? All she could smell was sweat, alcohol and she wanted her toothbrush.

'What happened?' Prue felt around for her jeans. What if he'd found the pills? Where the fuck were her jeans? Did this mean he'd seen her in her knickers? Again.

'Where's my clothes?'

'You took your jeans off after you went for a piss and then you pissed on your socks so you took them off and threw them around. They're in the corner of the van. Don't worry, you haven't lost anything.' Archie was topless. Prue could see tattoos all over his chest. 'We missed the last ferry and I was too drunk to drive anyway. Chill out. Nothing bad has happened. Now, go back to sleep.'

Prue found her jeans and found the pills. They were still there. Undisturbed. How she'd got away with that was beyond her.

'What's the matter?' he asked.

'I can't remember anything.'

'Come on, it'll be all right in the morning,' he said, and he moved up behind her and put an arm over her. A naked arm. He rested his huge shovel-like hand on her naked shoulder. This was OK. He was being nice because she was upset. She should be grateful he'd been there to look after her. She must have passed out. The next thing, they were woken up by seagulls and being slowly baked alive in the metal pickup.

★ ★ ★

When they pulled up at the house the next morning Ruth came flying out and Prue thought she would kill them both.

'Where have you been?' Ruth screamed. 'You didn't call! How could you do this? What the fuck have you been up to?' Prue slipped out of the car, a dry-mouthed invertebrate.

'I went out, Prue tagged along… we bumped into friends, got drunk, slept in the pickup, happy?' answered Archie.

Ruth stared up at him with pure rage and then shot Prue a look that should have struck her dead.

'Well, I'm glad you had fun, Archie. While you were away, someone shot a bird and left it outside our front door last night. Did you hear me? Someone left a dead bird outside our house, but don't worry, you carry on doing whatever you want,' said Ruth.

Ronnie was at the door and flashed Prue a wide-eyed look that she took to mean she hadn't told Ruth about the first dead raven. Ruth shoved Archie with both hands, but he barely moved; he looked over her head and didn't react.

'I'll deal with it,' he said, and got his bag out of the car and walked to the house. Ruth followed, berating him along the way, while Prue slithered at a safe distance behind.

'Did you see who did it?' Prue whispered to Ronnie at the door.

'No. Ruth found it this morning,' she said. 'Another poor raven.'

23

As soon as Prue got back to the study, she took a book off the shelf to hide the pills inside but in her hungover state she knocked a flower onto the floor. Her heart stopped as she watched the vase fall and waited for the glass to shatter, but it bounced and rolled, spilling pollen onto the rug. In the rush to pick it up she got pollen on the back of her hand. She brushed it off and tried to rub away the stain from the rug, but it wouldn't budge. It was only small but bright yellow. She threw a pair of tracksuit bottoms over it and then a cardigan; this would have to buy her some time until she could find out how to get rid of it. Urgh, if only she could ask Nana. She was about to put the pills inside the book when Ronnie opened the door and she had to shove them back into her jeans yet again and ram the book under her pillow. Prue stood there with both hands jammed in her pockets as if she was about to start line dancing as Ronnie entered.

'Why are you standing there, smiling like that? You look retarded,' said Ronnie.

'You can't say retarded any more. I was thinking about going to bed for a bit.'

'Well, you should, you look a fright.' Ronnie came in and shut the door behind her. Prue's heart sank.

'Thanks, I don't feel great.'

'What happened? You missed our date last night, you agreed. I didn't know you'd run off with Archie. I thought something terrible might have happened to you both. I was very concerned, we both were.' Ronnie sat down on the bed.

'Nothing happened,' said Prue; she was so on edge, paranoid. 'I'm going to go to sleep for a few hours and see if I feel better later.' But Ronnie wasn't picking up the hint.

'Archie can drink, can't he? It worries me, he's not the best at controlling his impulses when he drinks. Did he...? Did he control himself?' asked Ronnie.

'He did – that's why we slept in the truck. He didn't drive drunk.'

Ronnie's eyes narrowed and she regarded Prue, who in turn felt the urge to fidget but did everything she could to stay absolutely still. 'That must have been charming, sleeping in the back of a pickup with your stinky old uncle. Hmmm, these things happen, I suppose. You must be dehydrated – I'll get you something.'

Prue gave her a double thumbs up, which appeared more sarcastic than she intended but it was only because she desperately wanted to go to bed. Ronnie returned with a pint of something she said included soaked grass and elderberries. Prue was so thirsty she'd have drunk anything and was soon dribbling on her pillow.

Hours later when she woke her throat was sore, her glands

were up and she had a monster of a headache and spent the next day laid up in bed, sweating with a temperature. She didn't take James's call or return Subo's. The hangover must have brought on her underlying exhaustion, said Ronnie. It was the culmination of months of stress and disruption, all of it, and it must have built up over weeks and her immune system had simply buckled under the strain. Ronnie checked on her periodically and Prue's muffled fever dreams were a thick blancmange of Ronnie wafting in and out of her room, administering fluids and pushing indigestible soup under her nose, and the return of vivid dreams. One had her swimming through the corridors as the house was flooded and chasing Ruth up the stairs while she carried her own eyes on a golden tray, like the painting of St Lucy, as she headed to the nursery where a baby was crying.

The morning after whatever virus or bug she'd had was gone, Prue was still weak and shaky but unwilling to let the last few days of precious freedom be wasted in bed. She had dragged herself up and dressed when she thought she heard raised voices. When she ventured out of the study, she could clearly hear men shouting and she ran into the hall. Charlie and Archie were fighting with the front door wide open; Ruth was pushing her way in between them trying to pull them apart, and everyone was shouting. Archie threw Charlie up against the wall with his toes scraping at the floor. Archie drew a fist back to punch him in the face as Ruth grabbed at Archie's arm trying to stop him.

'No!' shouted Prue and they all froze, and this took the momentum out of the scuffle.

Archie dropped Charlie and stepped away, pacing and pushing his hair back. Charlie slumped against the wall, pulling himself together. Both panted. Ruth flew at her with gritted teeth.

'What have you been saying!?' she screamed at her. Prue could smell her breath and she'd been drinking; she was sure it wasn't even midday yet.

'I thought I was clear!' shouted Archie, and Prue's knees rattled. She could only gormlessly shake her head, racking her brain. Her heart thumping and her head fuzzy, trying to unravel the wool between her ears and remember what she had done to cause this.

'I did what? What did I say?' Prue looked to Charlie, but he wouldn't return her gaze. 'Charlie?'

'That I give money away,' said Archie.

'No, no, I didn't. That's not what I said at all,' said Prue. 'Charlie? Tell them. I never said that. That's not true!' Charlie shifted from foot to foot, a shuffling weasel against the wall.

'I told you to stay away from him. I warned you, Prue, and you stabbed me in the back and did it anyway, hanging around with that beggar,' shouted Archie.

'Fuck off!' said Charlie.

'What's going on between you two?' said Archie, pointing at Charlie.

'Nothing's going on!' Prue shouted, mortified, but Charlie smirked. He *wanted* Archie to think something was going on between them and now she looked as if she was lying. A tease, a liar, what else could she be?

Ruth started on Charlie then. 'Was it you who left that bird on the doorstep? It was, wasn't it?'

'You daft bint, what would I do that for?' Charlie tutted.

'That's enough!' shouted Archie. 'Get the fuck out.'

It had to be the conversation at Charlie's house but that wasn't what she had said, had she? She had told him he'd paid for her mother's rehab and that Charlie might consider asking him for help. Was that it?

'I'm going, I'm going.' Charlie peeled himself off the wall.

'You came for a handout,' said Archie. 'Trading on guilt, but I'll tell you something – there is no guilt. If you're looking for someone to blame, try your mother.'

'Archie! Please!' Ruth tried to usher Charlie out but for some stupid reason Prue decided to interject.

'I don't understand. What did I do?'

'Prue!' said Ruth. 'Will you please go away? Go anywhere, actually.'

Charlie strode to the door with his ten-to-two strut, but before he could leave, he had to say one last thing.

'How much cock did you suck to get away with it?' Prue had seen Charlie revert to crudeness before when his words didn't permit him to dominate.

Ruth and Prue glanced at each other, expecting an explosion, but Archie laughed and his guttural roar bounced around the hall, then he put his thumbs in his pockets and tilted his head like a dog, and grinned.

'The question you should ask is – whose cock did your sister suck to get off the island?'

Charlie rushed at Archie as Prue ran forward and tried to stop him as he lunged towards Archie, but she was no match in her state or size and fell backwards and slid across the floor, knocking plants against the wall. Plants rolled around and a giant palm fell and smashed the glass uplighter above her head, shattering it. Ruth screamed as Prue shut her eyes and cowered as a million little splinters covered her like fine rain. Everything was silent and still until the faint strains of the radio in the kitchen drifted through the corridor. The song 'Gloria' by Laura Branigan cut through the tension, a hideously upbeat song. Prue stood up and shook the bits of glass out of her hair.

'Charlie, please will you leave,' said Prue.

'Fine by me,' he said, and he skipped down the steps as if this was simply another day, another confrontation. Nay bother. Ruth ran and slammed the door behind him.

'Thank fuck for that!' she said.

Standing in a circle of glass splinters with bare feet, Prue didn't move. Ruth walked up to her and cupped Prue's face in her hands and looked into her eyes. Archie stomped into the kitchen and tore the radio plug from the wall by the lead, swearing.

'Do you have any glass in your eyes?' Ruth asked, as hers bored into Prue's. She said she didn't think so. Ruth still cupped her face in both hands but Prue had the feeling she could as easily take a chunk out of her as kiss her.

'Very well.' Ruth let go and wrapped herself up in her shawl. 'I cannot have this. I *won't* have it. You are incapable of respecting boundaries, and these people... the O'Haras... have made our lives unbearable at times. To think you've been gossiping with them behind our backs—'

'But I haven't!' Prue shouted. But she had. Or had she? She hadn't said anything bad or divulged any secrets or... Prue racked her foggy brain.

'Archie, I would never....' Prue looked to him, but he kept his back to her.

'Shh! Please,' Ruth held up a hand. 'This... constant need for attention, it is exhausting.'

'Me!? Attention?' Prue looked to Archie again, but he was staring at the flagstones.

'The first few nights, the drama about the house, coming home with no knickers five minutes after meeting the nearest boy. Pestering and following Archie around like a puppy and then flirting with Charlie. It's never enough, is it? It's a form of self-sabotage.'

'Self-sabotage?' Prue had heard this before from her mother.

'Yes, sabotage, Prue. This constant need for attention; good or bad. It's as if you are bent on destroying something, even yourself. Quite frankly, you're scaring the shit out of me.'

'Are you kidding?'

'This is exactly the kind of behaviour your mother would indulge in… *You are becoming so like her*,' said Ruth.

Prue gasped; it felt as if she'd been stabbed in the stomach and the knife twisted and dragged up to the softest part.

'What about you?' Prue shouted back. 'You've done your best to avoid me and you promised! You said whatever you needed to say to get me up here and had no intention at all of telling me anything about my father.'

'I never promised anything.'

'You're a liar! You said to me on the phone, everything would be different. *We'll talk, Prue*. Nothing is different. You never had any intention of telling me anything! I know you are a liar and what hurts is I'm expected to be a good little girl and accept it.'

'How dare you! I wanted to look after you, to have you here with family, not strangers at some random house a million miles away.'

'Subo's family are not strangers! I've seen more of them in the last three years than I have of you – you're the stranger! And you lie to my face even when it's so fucking obvious—'

'All right! I'm done! You're angry with me and I'm the one who hasn't done anything! You really want to know, Prue? You want to be an adult and deal with reality, do you? Because if that's really what you want, let me unload this once and for all.'

'Ruth! Stop. Think. This isn't the way.' Archie tried to pull Ruth back, but both women were fuming, hell bent on releasing the pent-up rage only family can conjure.

'Yes! Yes, I fucking do! Just tell me!' screamed Prue.

'We all need to take a breath and calm down,' pleaded Archie, but no one was listening.

'Your father is my father!' shouted Ruth. 'There! Happy? It's the dirty MacArthur secret and I only ever wanted to protect you from it!'

'What? That doesn't make sense?'

'Caroline is your mother but your father was also your grandfather. I'm sorry,' said Ruth. Then she put her face in her hands and shouted, 'Fuck!'

'Wait, I always thought Grandad was a good person, it can't be,' said Prue. Not able to take in the brevity of the words, they hovered in front of her, a jumbled mess. Something you could grab at but not catch, like smoke rings.

'He was,' Ruth said, weary. 'But he was more than one man, it seems. Oh, Prue, I'm sorry...' Ruth reached out to Prue but she lunged out of her grasp.

'No, that can't be true. It's not fair,' said Prue, and she ran. She ran out the same way Charlie had, without any shoes, but it didn't matter. She ran round the side of the house, over the wall and into the trees. When she was sure she was far enough away she stopped running and threw up. She wiped her mouth with her hand and felt a tender spot. A tiny orange blister was on her hand where the pollen had been. Prue sat on the ground and burst into tears. Now she was grief stricken all over again. There would be no more dreams of someone coming to rescue her. No Christmases or new family to meet, no shared genetic quirks to laugh about. It made sense now – the shame, the depression, the physical inability to speak about something so disgusting. Prue had been a dirty secret, a hideous crime her own family cringed away from. And she'd let Archie down. Ruth was right, she was like her mother, and it seemed there was little she could do to change it – she couldn't even see it.

24

Slumped on the ground, Prue hadn't even bothered to move further away from where she'd thrown up. The argument with Ruth played over in her head. After everything she'd hoped for, it was *her grandfather*. This was as good as another death. How stupid and naïve she'd been. How they'd made her stupid and naïve. Ruth's paintings, the three women swung by their tongues – it *was* them, hobbled and silent. The portrait of the aquarium and the shadow man had been her grandfather, and all the other paintings – the hollowed-out woman, the blindfolded child – they were all about this awful secret. When Ruth had accused her of self-sabotage it had struck her because she'd heard this before.

In the final year of school Prue had shot up like a bean pole and the puppy fat disappeared at the same time as her mother discovered her first rogue chin hair. She started making comments about what Prue wore and then came the food battle. One Saturday morning she had barged into Prue's bedroom.

'I made lunch,' she said. She. Never. Made. Lunch.

'I'm not hungry, thanks,' said Prue, still in bed.

'You're getting skinny.'

'I'm not hungry. You eat it.'

'I want you to come into the lounge and eat your lunch, now.'

'But I'm not hungry.'

'Now!' she shouted. 'Come and eat what I've made for you.'

'No,' said Prue, sitting up in her teenage cesspit. 'You're being ridiculous. I'm going back to sleep, it's too early.'

That's how it started. Prue's weight became her mother's new focus and while war was never officially declared it was silently fought over the dinner table. A very cold war, played out with tins of beans and half-cindered chips, ultimately scraped into the bin by Prue because when she discovered this got a rise out of her mother, she started to push her food around her plate on purpose. The more weight Prue lost, the more people complimented her. Boys flirted. Grown men stared in the street. Older ones – ones who definitely knew better but didn't care.

'I think you have an eating disorder,' her mother had said after a few weeks of this dance. It was a fortnight before Nana had the heart attack.

'Don't be stupid, I don't have an eating disorder.' Prue retreated to her room but her mother followed.

'It's a form of *self-sabotage*,' she told her.

Prue burst out laughing. 'Self-sabotage?' And she looked at the raised scars on her mother's forearms hidden by her sleeves and nodded. 'I think that's your speciality, don't you?'

Her mother gasped and even Prue was shocked she'd said it. It wounded her mother but she doubled down.

'You don't look good, Prue. You look scrawny and ill.'

'Thanks, Mum, and you look like an old cuddly toy that's had the stuffing dragged out but I wasn't going to tell you because *I* didn't want to hurt your feelings.'

'Don't you dare talk to me like that, you little bitch!' Her mother had never called her a name before, and she raised a hand to slap Prue around the face. Like Nana the day she'd dared ask about the ceiling scar, except instead of being covered in wet cabbage, Prue caught her mother's wrist. She was shaking but could sense she was the stronger one; her mother could too.

'Please leave my room before this gets worse,' said Prue, and let go.

Her mother studied her as if she didn't recognise the vile little creature she had raised. Adrenaline ran wild and Prue had to take a walk around the block to calm down. The power between them had started to shift and she could feel it. Her mother had never looked so weak as when she'd tried to hit her.

Prue's feet had turned blue as she sat shivering at the base of a tree. She still had those stupid pills in her pocket. This was hopeless; she couldn't tell James because she'd have a lot of explaining to do about the state she was in, and she didn't want to tell him the awful secret. She hated the fact he knew she was a virgin and she'd lied to him like an idiot all this time. What about running away? It started as a little idea that popped its head around the corner to offer a helpful suggestion. It was the first time she'd thought of it, but why shouldn't she? If she wanted to leave, no one could technically stop her.

She heard a snort and looked up – there was the black dog, and he was still alive. Prue was so relieved she started to cry again. The dog settled on his stomach a little way in front of her and looked up at the trees, mesmerised by the leaves rippling like a mirror ball as dappled sunlight danced over them. They both stared upwards, and Prue closed her eyes and tried to remember who she wanted to be, what she wanted. Was the devil-dog asking her? What was the point of it all? She opened her eyes and stretched out her hand and the dog moved his bear-like head to sniff her, but a loud crack made the dog run away before she could touch him. Her heart sank.

'There you are,' said Archie, bulldozing his way through the brush. It was too late to run. He stopped over her, blocking out the sun.

'You frightened the dog,' she said.

'Probably best, it has a better chance of staying alive if it's wary of people.'

'Haven't we all.' Prue's feet were filthy and her eyes puffy.

'You OK?'

'Yeah, I'm having a great day.'

'You haven't any shoes,' he said, pointing at her feet.

'Really? I hadn't noticed.'

'Look,' he said, crouching down. 'None of us covered ourselves in glory back there. That was a bloody mess. We thought all the stuff to do with that family had died down. Gladys O'Hara coming into the house, then Charlie turning up – Ruth is struggling with your grandmother's death too, she's still grieving. Then there's the guilt over your mother and obviously Ruth's worried about you—'

'Because I'm *like my mother.*'

'You're nothing like your mother, Prue.'

'How do you know? You've met her, what, three times?'

'Because I know. Come on, I've got somewhere you can hide for a while, I think you both need a bit of space,' he said. Standing up, he held out his hand to pull her up. 'You want a piggyback?'

'No,' tutted Prue, then she walked over the ground in bare feet. 'Well... Maybe...'

'Come on, babe in the wood.' He bent down so she could jump on and he carried her off like a hunter carrying a deer on his back.

Archie weaved his way along a path until they came to the basin that gave the trees and plants shelter from the sea and wind. Almost hidden and overgrown was a small shack in the woods, something a bearded hermit might live in. Archie pushed the door open and let her down; inside was a room full of camping and fishing gear. There was a stove, enamel mugs, a tea towel that could have stood to attention by itself, but no electricity or heat, and Prue shivered with her feet a mud-tinged blue. Ladder-like steps led up to a sleeping level with a peaked roof where she could see a big skylight. Archie climbed halfway up, dragged down a jumper from upstairs and threw it at her.

'How long has this been here?' she asked.

'What, the jumper or the cabin?'

'The cabin,' and Prue cracked a smile. To be honest, she

didn't really want to know how long the jumper had been there as she put it on.

'Must be coming up to twenty years. You rest up and I'll be back in a bit.' As he closed the door, he stopped, and suddenly and only briefly, he resembled the boy again from the photos. 'You will be here when I get back – you're not going to do anything stupid, are you?'

'I'll be here.'

'Good, I don't need another girl disappearing on me.' He smiled but she saw genuine pain, and Prue felt a pang of sympathy for him. Thank God for Archie.

There was no obvious place to sit or even be comfortable downstairs. She climbed up the steps and there was a mattress on the floor, three battery operated lanterns and a telescope in the corner under the skylight. The mattress was covered in screwed-up blankets and by the side of the mattress there was an enamel mug with the dried remnants of something mysterious at the bottom, and a set of metal drawers. Without thinking Prue opened one of the drawers and inside she found socks, screwdrivers, a loose pack of playing cards, a bottle opener and a whole bunch of condoms. She slammed the drawer shut. For the love of God, when would she learn to stop poking around? It wasn't good. She wrapped herself up in one of the blankets and lay down on the mattress and she was soon asleep.

The ground had swollen with water until it was like a bog and everything was grown over with lichen and moss or tangled up in ivy from blue to neon green. Prue skipped over the boardwalk covered with chicken wire and each board she stepped on bowed so the cold water leaked through and made her socks wet. She saw the raven floating in the water and stepped in, no higher than her shins, and waded over to save the bird. When she touched the raven, two others swooped down and attacked her, pulling at her hair with their claws and snapping at her fingers with their beaks. Their wings beat her about the head, and she was scratched and bleeding. If she could pull the drowning raven free, they would know she wasn't trying to hurt it. She pulled with both hands as the ravens continued their assault. When she wrestled the raven free of the mossy water it wasn't a bird, but a crown made of raven wings and as she pulled more the head of Evie O'Hara emerged. A blue-veined face with eyes marble white. Prue screamed, dropping the head in the water, and fell backwards, slipping under.

'Prue, wake up,' said Archie gently, and she jolted awake. It was air in her lungs and not brown water. Archie was kneeling by the side of the mattress.

She was embarrassed to be found in his bed. She should have stayed on the bottom floor. 'I'm sorry, there was nowhere to sit.'

'Don't worry,' he said. 'Here, I brought these.' He threw down a couple of bananas. She ate both of them and left the peels on the floor. He took out a bottle of what looked like whisky from his inside coat pocket and held it up like a trophy. 'I brought this as well, thought you could do with some numbing,' he smiled. 'Hair of the dog and all that.'

'What time is it?'

'About eight, maybe a bit before.' That meant she'd been asleep for hours. Practically the whole day.

Whisky was the last thing she needed, even Prue knew

that. She should have gone back to the house and taken a bath, apologised to Ruth, and tried to read a book, even the weighty tome about Genoa being a trading port – anything – but given the promise of whisky making her numb and remembering what had happened earlier, she was willing to drink battery acid. Archie went downstairs and Prue moved to follow.

'No, stay up there,' he said. 'I'll come back up.'

He stuck his head up and put the whiskies on the floor and then disappeared, only to emerge with a lantern.

'What did Ruth say after I left?'

'That she regrets losing her temper, saying stupid things, and telling you like that, but then you had to find out some way. It's not like there was going to be a sugar-coated option, is there?'

'No.'

'So, now you know – what are you thinking?'

Prue shrugged. 'I don't know. Embarrassed maybe? I don't feel much of anything. I don't know what I think. I feel numb, I'm disappointed I guess.'

'What is it you were hoping for?'

'I really wanted my dad to be someone I could find one day. You know, find out how tall he was, does he have freckles, where are his parents from – that stuff. Stupid really.'

'It's not stupid. It's completely natural, but I still stand by the point I previously made – it doesn't mean anything. This doesn't have to define you. If you think about it, how we all came to be really isn't much of our business at all, but you're here now. Make your life your own. Drink this, you'll feel better.' He handed Prue a mug of whisky and she knocked it back. It burned, but immediately started to soften the harsh edges. As Ronnie would say, the angels were coming.

They smoked foul-tasting rolled-up cigarettes, followed by more shots of disgusting whisky. Archie took off his jumper and fiddled with the telescope, trying to show her constellations through the skylight.

'Haven't you ever looked at the moon through a telescope?'

'Nope,' said Prue, putting out her rollie in the enamel mug.

'Shocking.'

'Babes in the wood,' she said.

'What?'

'When you offered me the piggyback, you said *babe in the wood*. My grandmother's family came from Norfolk, and she used to tell me that story, the original, not the fluffy child-friendly version.'

'Yeah?' he said, still looking through the telescope.

'It was based on a true story. Two children were given to their uncle, but he paid men to take them into the forest and kill them.'

'And I thought my family were fucked up.'

'They don't kill them. They abandon them instead and the children end up getting lost and dying anyway. They die in the woods and the birds cover them over with leaves and they haunt the forest forever. The uncle comes to an end in a bad way, I can't remember how...'

'Sounds like a great story to tell a child,' he said. 'Your grandmother was certainly a character.'

'It's a morality tale – for adults. It's a warning to those

who take care of children not to mistreat them or they'll bring God's wrath on themselves.'

'God's wrath? Jesus, Prue, if you get any lower, you're going to start listening to Leonard Cohen.'

'I don't know who that is.'

'And you don't need to, not if you don't want to jump into a bath holding a toaster.'

'Ever since I've been here, Archie, I've been having the weirdest dreams. Unreal and real at the same time and I keep getting headaches and feeling dizzy and my eyes ache. I think it's eye strain. I really need to find my glasses. I keep dreaming about running in the woods, lost like the babes in the wood, but... it's wild and free and exciting and then... something awful happens. I know that it's awful and I can't take it back, but I don't know what it is. It's this heavy feeling in my stomach like a weight dragging me down. When you said I'd been saying things to Charlie, I thought it must be true without even thinking because I always think I've done something wrong, but I swear I didn't say anything. Ruth said I was like my mother, but I don't understand how because I've tried so hard to be different.' Prue began to cry.

Palpitations started, like a sparrow beating its wings inside her ribcage, and she felt woozy and hot. When she tried to remember the last thought she'd had – she couldn't hold onto it, it floated away and in front of her she thought she saw dandelion seeds, little white parachutes flying away on the air and she reached out a hand, but they disappeared.

'OK, no more whisky for you.' Archie came and sat next to her on the mattress and took her mug out of her grasp.

'What could you possibly feel guilty about?' he said, and

he brushed her hair behind her ear and wiped her tears away from her cheek with the back of his hand.

'What if it turns out I put an innocent woman in prison? Will I get into trouble?'

'You were a child, Prue. It's not possible for you to be guilty of anything – that's not opinion, it's the law.'

'Ronnie said that laws are for little people, or maybe it was tax?'

'Both, it doesn't matter – we are not little people.'

'Are we not?'

'No, we're better than that. You're going to be whoever you want to be, remember?' Archie put his arm around her.

'I don't know what I am, but I know I can't stop fucking everything up and making it worse.' She burst into tears again and buried her face in her hands because she didn't want Archie to see her ugly cry face.

He pulled her head up and her hands away from her face and then kissed her. With his tongue. As easy as putting the cup down or scratching a head. Something catastrophically huge and minor and irrelevant at the same time, depending on how you look at it. A series of movements that without the application of thoughts and opinions meant absolutely nothing. And that's how Prue would always think of it.

He kissed her again and this time his mouth stayed there, and his tongue went into her mouth. Prue did nothing but have palpitations. She thought of Ruth when his hand moved down to her nipple. He flicked off the strap of her vest and then he pulled her bra down. It really had gone too far now, and she knew she should have stopped it but she wasn't sure how or if she wanted to. She didn't care. Then he was on top of her, and still she did nothing. Not even when she felt his hands wander down to her flies and knew what he was going to do. Not even when he pulled her jeans off. He took off her knickers and then pulled off his own clothes and lay on top of Prue and she shut her eyes and wished she could disappear. He kept whispering to her and she thought of James and his cold hands and frail body. She could push him off and run away. But where would she go? She could never go back home now. Archie rolled over and opened the drawer in the metal unit and Prue knew what he was looking for. She was dizzy while she was lying down. She stared at the little yellow and white dots in the sky. Stupid boring stars. The skylight was open and the cold air filled the room but she was hot and giddy. Blame the whisky. Blame Ruth. Blame anything and everyone, anyone but herself... please.

'I'm sorry,' he said, his mouth all over her neck, 'I'm sorry, I'm sorry.'

'Don't worry,' she said. She didn't want to be rude.

25

The white and yellow stars stared down through the skylight. Prue was scared of moving and waking Archie and kept watch as his back rose and fell with each breath. His hair splayed across the pillow, and she brushed it away from where it touched her shoulder. She could smell him and taste him and feel him everywhere, all over her, and she hated herself.

It must have taken an hour for her to crawl out and slither across the floor. She slid down the stairs on her bottom carrying her clothes and put them on downstairs. Taking one of the lanterns, she set off for the house through the trees. The twigs under her bare feet hurt but the pain was irrelevant. She had left the jumper Archie had given her back in the cabin out of some delayed, self-appointed pride. Prue had followed her uncle around in his studio, got drunk, smoked drugs, and slept next to him in the back of his pickup truck. He had photos of her wearing barely anything. She had become another girl for the wall.

The lantern lit her up like a firefly to whatever might wish to hunt her down, so she turned it off and carried on in the pitch black. Her eyes were adjusting to the darkness but she wasn't scared at all. *Pick a direction and see it through.* Keep moving. When she made it to the metal gate, she hopped over the dog's trench and scurried like a rat up to the door. Grateful that the doors were never locked, she let herself in through the mud room and into the kitchen. The lights were out, and she was about to head for the study when the hall light was switched on and Ronnie was standing at the end of the corridor to the main hall. Prue squinted and held a hand up to shield her eyes as Ronnie approached.

'What have you been up to?' She looked a ghostly fright in her black silk dressing gown and no makeup. 'You let me down again, Prue. It hurts that I mean so little to you. You said we had a deal.' Ronnie looked down and saw Prue's freezing, blue-tinged dirty feet and then looked up at her face with pure disdain.

'I'm so sorry, Ronnie. I forgot. I'll make it up to you, I promise.'

'Don't you want to play any more, my dear?'

'What do you mean?'

'I had high hopes for you, Prue. I thought finally the universe has sent me someone I can nurture, the way Maud nurtured me, but you are weak. It breaks my heart.'

'I promise I'll make it right, Ronnie. I don't want to disappoint you. I can fix it.' Prue turned the handle to open the door, but Ronnie put her hand over Prue's and pulled it shut again. Then with a finger pointed at her face, she stared up at her.

'My dear girl, it can't be fixed now, and you should know

I will not tolerate being ignored.' Her translucent skin up close was like tracing paper.

'I'm sorry... I swear I'm not ignoring—'

'Shh! Do not whine! You sound like Dotty and look what happened to her. No one likes a victim. Now, let me see.' Ronnie grabbed her hand from the door handle and turned it over to study her palm, holding it with both hands. 'I thought as much: you have the mystic cross three times over. No healer's mark, though, such a shame.' Ronnie let go of her hand and turned to walk away. 'Good night, my dear Prudence.' Then she looked over her shoulder, adding, 'I hope you got what you wanted,' and turned off the light.

Ruth came bursting in the next morning and shook Prue awake. She sat up and braced herself to accept whatever would be thrown at her.

'Come on, let's get you up,' said Ruth, grinning like a maniac. 'Shower, dress, come on. You know what today is, don't you?'

'No? What is it?'

Ruth's smile collapsed into perplexed bemusement, and she searched Prue's face for a brain. 'It's results day!' she said, neck stretched like an anxious turkey, hands in the air.

'I thought I had a couple more days.'

'Gosh, no, it's September in a week, and you go home. Eek! Christ alive, Prue, I can't believe I'm more excited than you are! Anna could call any second with your results, now come on! Get dressed.'

Prue heaved her carcass out of bed, showered and stripped the sheets, dirty now from where her muddy feet had stained them. Intrusive flickers from the night before kept shooting at her like wasps. His mouth on her neck. The brittle leaves under her feet. Him undoing her flies. Her ridiculous need to be compliant. With each memory she felt a lurch in her stomach and a wave of nausea.

Downstairs Ruth was already swooshing about in an overtly chirpy mood as if the horrors from the day before had never happened. Prue plodded over to the fridge.

'What are you looking for?' asked Ruth, sweeping over as if floating on ice.

'Some water.'

'Water?' she repeated, the tendons in her neck straining. 'I'll get that, coffee too. You sit down, this is *your* day.' She guided Prue back to the table.

Prue took her seat and Ruth brought her water, and sat down and, head in both hands, stared as she sipped it.

'What are you hoping for?' she asked.

'Results?'

'Yes, you must have some instinct for how it went.'

'I think Maths went OK, and Science, but they're the easy ones.'

'Maths, easy?' she said, shaking her head. 'You don't know how lucky you are being a science person as opposed to an arts person. Honestly, you're better off. The arts are a hopeless pursuit and impossible to earn a living, unless you went to Eton, of course, then it seems you can make a living playing the spoons.'

The back door flew open, bounced off the wall and Ronnie flew in, ranting with her hands flapping around as if surrounded by flies.

'That bastard dog! It's still alive and it's been destroying the garden again.' She was on the verge of tears. 'It's really done it this time: dug up shrubs, dragged them all over and dug holes deep enough to… and it's taken another huge shit. Prue – you'll have to pick it up. I can't touch it. I poisoned the bastard, how is it still alive? That dog is the devil himself!'

The doorbell rang. Prue's heart flipped. Ruth and Ronnie jumped. Ruth ran to the front door and returned with James. He was wearing a cagoule over a wrinkled shirt with the buttons done up wrong. Prue felt awful as soon as she saw him.

'Hi, I thought I'd drop by to see if you got your results?' he said. He really was sickeningly sweet, like icing on a fairy cake. Whereas she was the human equivalent of bin juice.

'No, not yet.' James's face fell; he could tell something was wrong.

'Erm, have you spilled something?' he said, pointing to the table with his hand still inside the pocket of his jacket. She had knocked the water over.

'Oh shit,' said Prue. She picked up the glass and carried it to the sink.

'Why are you being weird?' James snuck up behind her and whispered.

'What do you mean?' she whispered back. Ruth was counselling Ronnie over the state of the garden on the other side of the kitchen.

'You look like someone died,' said James.

'It's nothing, I'll tell you later.'

'Where have you been the last few days?'

'Archie took me driving and then I was ill. Ruth said she told you.'

'You looking to be a taxi driver?'

'Ha-ha.'

Prue looked over her shoulder and saw Ruth turn away, pretending she hadn't been straining to hear what they were whispering about.

'Does anyone want a coffee? Ronnie, how about you?' Ruth asked.

'No, I'm getting myself a gin,' said Ronnie.

'It's ten o'clock in the morning,' James whispered to Prue.

'When are you off to university, James?' Ruth asked.

'I'm back home to Aberdeen in ten days and that gives me a couple of weeks to sort things out before term starts.'

'I should think your mum will miss you.'

'Maybe, but I doubt she'll miss the sloppy bartending and mess that comes with me.'

Everyone laughed too much, thankful for something inane to fill the void. Once it subsided, James gave an extra snort and the room fell flat and then the clunk of the front door groaned as if a tomb was being opened. It had to be Archie. Prue's stomach dropped through the floor. Past that. Down to the Earth's core and out the other side into hell. *Nothing happened. Nothing happened. Nothing happened.* She could hear his great booted feet as he walked across the hall. Heavy footsteps. Heart in her mouth. Her pulse throbbing double time to his footsteps.

'Archie! Good morning!' announced Ruth, as if his presence was a welcome surprise. His dark silhouette moved towards them until his face came into the light, and he smiled as if he was Jesus. Prue wanted to run but found herself welded to the floor.

Archie stepped into the kitchen and kissed Ruth who threw her arms around his neck, standing on tiptoes. He wrapped an arm around her waist and kissed her where her ear met her neck, and his eyes met Prue's, who looked away. Archie then shook James's hand with manly vigour, laying his hairy hand over James's skinny whitebait fingers.

'Morning, James, how are you?'

'Good, good, stopping to see if Prue got her exam results yet.'

'Ah, of course! It's results day.' He leaned over with a hand on the back of Prue's neck and kissed her on the cheek. She didn't look at him and didn't breathe. 'Nervous?' he asked. Prue dragged dead eyes up to meet his.

'No.'

The wrinkles around his eyes deepened as he cracked a broad smile. 'There's my girl,' he said. 'I'm going for a shower.'

Archie and Ruth had this unspoken little contract: she played house and stayed tethered to it by her complicit tongue like a maypole, and occasionally he would skip around her before going off to do what he wanted. She could pursue her art without financial struggle and reside in her bubble as long as she was careful not to pop it from the inside. Archie could hide in a cabin in the woods, keep condoms in a drawer, paint girls and smuggle weed onto the island, gaze at the stars and drink whisky from dirty mugs. It was a trade agreement with a large dose of unwillingness to see the whole. That is what families must be – otherwise no one would spend a single Christmas together. Ever. The phone rang. Prue jumped again and made James spill his coffee.

'This must be it!' Ruth squealed and sprinted to the phone. Archie came back.

'I thought you were going for a shower?' said Prue.

'And miss the big reveal?' He pulled out a chair and sat down.

Ruth had a garbled conversation and then hung up and floated back clutching a piece of paper. She held her other hand out as if to quiet the crowds, although the room was already silent.

'Should I turn the radio off?' James asked but no one answered.

'Prue, out of ten subjects, you have four As in Maths, Physics, Chemistry and RE, and six Bs.'

'You took RE?' asked James. 'Why would you do that?'

'It's interesting,' said Prue. 'I didn't get an A in Biology?'

'Are you kidding me?' said Ruth. 'You got a B! I don't think I got a B for anything other than Art. This is amazing! I had no idea you were a genius! You can do anything. You can be anything you want!'

'RE? I'm struggling to see what you planned to do with that,' James said.

Everyone was looking at Prue. Ruth seemed shocked and impressed in equal measure. Ronnie was on her way to getting tipsy but nodded as if she was also impressed. Archie beamed as if he was somehow responsible. The phone rang again.

'I'll get it,' said Ronnie.

'Good job, Prue,' said James, and they kind of patted each other on the back like sweaty cousins at a Bar Mitzvah. Archie stood up and took her by the shoulders.

'Prue, we'll look forward to you visiting at Christmas with your pretentious student stories.'

Everyone fake laughed again but Prue saw a flicker of fear on Ruth's face at the mention of her returning at Christmas. She could relax – that wasn't going to happen.

'Prue, it's your friend with the funny name again,' said Ronnie, returning from the hall.

Prue tutted. 'It's Su-bo. It's two syllables, it's hardly difficult.'

'Prue!' said Ruth.

Prue strutted past everyone to get to the phone.

'Hey! So, Johnny Five – what did you get?' asked Subo.

'As and Bs, all good, what about you?'

'I got a fucking A in Spanish; can you believe that? And a B in Maths? I have no idea how I scraped that. Worst was English Language, which was a C, so I'm good. Looks like we are off to college together! Whoop whoop. Let the good times roll...' Subo was excited, Prue should have been but couldn't muster the response.

'Yeah, it's great.'

'What's wrong?'

'Nothing.' Prue bit her lip as it threatened to tremble. She could keep up a pretence in front of these people but not in front of her best friend, even if it was on the phone.

'Bullshit, what's happened?'

'No, honestly, it's all good.'

'Have you popped your cherry yet?'

'No.'

'What about your dad, any closer?'

'No, and you know what? I'm not sure I even care any more.'

'What? Oh, OK. Hey, do you remember that last day of term with Mrs Fairy? I was thinking about it the other day and nearly pissed myself all over again. Do you remember how hard she tried to ignore us?'

Mrs Fairy was a scrub-faced, makeup-free teacher who had adored boys for being cheeky little rapscallions but thought girls scheming. Everyone hated her, even the boys because most children have an innate sense of justice. Mrs Fairy was at her most passionate when mindlessly walking through routine, because *that's how it's always been.* She wasn't even a proper teacher, she taught Home Economics and doubled up as a dance teacher if a PE teacher was off sick, and she couldn't dance. When she wasn't enforcing barn dancing, it was line dancing or Tudor court dancing – stuff that will really help you get a job or a mortgage. When she called Prue a killjoy, she'd answered back and told Mrs Fairy she would barn dance if she could explain the educational objective. The whole class fell silent, shocked at the standoff over barn dancing and the fact that Prudence MacArthur was playing Spartacus.

'Prue, you are being a real negative nelly,' said Mrs Fairy. 'I won't have you ruin the lesson, and if you carry on, the whole class will stay behind for detention. Be positive.' She was always saying *be positive*, it was like her own meaningless tagline.

No one wants to be responsible for keeping the whole class back, so Prue shut up and begrudgingly hopped around the hall feeling humiliated.

'Bet they don't do this at private school,' she muttered, but no one heard.

On the last day of term Mrs Fairy let a whole load of

balloons loose with *Be Positive!* on them. Most drifted into the nearest powerlines and popped. Prue and Subo had inched their way over to Mrs Fairy who was standing there, ignoring her own balloon massacre.

'Hey, Mrs Fairy,' said Subo, 'I guess your balloons should have had a more positive attitude.' Mrs Fairy refused to acknowledge either girl as they laughed and crossed their legs for fear of wetting themselves.

'Yeah, I remember, it was funny,' said Prue.

'Hey, come on, so what about your dad, who needs one anyway? My dad blocked the toilet the other morning and had to use a wire coat hanger to clear it, Mum was raging. And so what about being a virgin, it's not like it actually matters, Prue. It's like babies walking, it happens to everyone eventually. Maybe don't try and force it.'

'Maybe you're right.'

'Of course I am. When are you coming home?'

'In a week, I'll be back the weekend after this one.'

'Good, I miss you. Prue, are you really all right? I feel something is wrong.'

Prue's lip wobbled and her eyes started to fill with tears. What she would give to be back at Subo's house with everyone shouting.

'I'm good, I miss you, I've got to go,' said Prue and she hung up. When she got back to the kitchen, they were all standing up, waiting for her.

'I've an idea,' said Ruth, clapping like a seal. 'Why don't we have a celebratory dinner tonight? James, you're invited, of course.'

'Tonight? I can't, sorry, my mum's short-staffed and has a group staying, but thanks anyway.'

'Now, I'm going in the shower,' said Archie, and he got up and left the kitchen as Ruth followed him in her dressing gown, mumbling about getting to the Mainland and shopping, and Ronnie left to salvage her garden. That the dog was still alive and Prue had enabled that – well, at least there was something to feel good about.

'Wait here,' Prue said to James and she ran to the study, grabbed the pills from the book and shoved her feet into trainers. Then she ran back to the kitchen and grabbed James's hand, pulling him towards the door outside through the mud room.

'I'm going out!' she shouted to no one in particular.

'Where are we going?'

'Anywhere.'

James was hesitant at first, but Prue convinced him they should go to the gun tower and walked so fast he struggled to keep up.

'I don't understand, why are we rushing?'

'Is there any weed left?'

'We'll need to stop at mine to get it if you're that desperate. What's the matter?'

'Nothing,' and she changed direction for the hotel.

'Are you upset about your results?' he asked.

'No,' she said. 'I'm really happy…'

'Oh-kay… you don't seem very happy.'

'I told you, I'm fine.'

'Ha-ha! Even I know that when a female says she's fine it means the exact opposite. Tell me what's wrong,' he said, and he grabbed her arm and stopped her from marching ahead. Prue felt her lip wobble again and knew she would cry if he looked at her, so she hugged him and buried her face into his shirt with the wonky buttons.

'I don't want to go home,' she said. 'I'm dreading it and I don't know what to do.'

'I'm going to miss you as well, but it's going to be all right.' But that wasn't what she meant. James wrapped his skinny arms around her. What a vile creature she was.

They stopped at the hotel to retrieve the weed he'd bundled up in a pair of socks in a drawer, while Prue told his mother about her results. Sharon was made up on her behalf; she genuinely seemed happy for her, so obviously Prue despised herself a little more.

'Everyone here, a round of applause for Prue, our little summer helper – she passed all her exams! Isn't that wonderful!?' Sharon announced to the pub.

When she said *everyone*, she was referring to the same three people who always occupied the same seats; they nodded and lifted pints in congratulations as Prue blushed. Sharon was wearing another sparkly jumper, this one turquoise with gold sequins and congealed clumps of glue where she had stuck them on. Prue wondered if sticking sequins on jumpers would make her happy one day. They twinkled under the lights and made her sleepy.

'Let's go,' said James, breathless from running up and down the stairs.

He babbled on about a party of well-to-do English tourists at the hotel who had come to the island on a birdwatching trip with long lenses and Barbour jackets worth thousands, but wouldn't know a 'turnstone from a ringed plover', he said. His mother complained about a stain on the hallway rug, chipped crockery and an unusual number of missing teaspoons. They were loud, obnoxious and annoying the regulars.

'They have all the gear but it's more about being part of some cult. They're leaving tomorrow, thank God.'

'Hey, I want to show you something.' Prue reached inside her pocket and took out the two pills in the little plastic bag and dangled it in front of him.

'Please tell me they're paracetamol.'

'It's Ecstasy, I think, although I suppose we won't know until we try...'

'Where did you get those? Don't tell me – wonder-uncle gave them to you.'

'No, of course not.'

'Charlie?'

'No... I brought them with me – Subo gave them to me. I thought I'd save them as a surprise for us – for our celebration night, the one you said we would have before we both leave.' Prue impressed herself because she hadn't rehearsed the cover story before opening her mouth; she guessed it was a hereditary gift.

'You travelled with drugs? On the ferry!? Are you mad? What if they had dogs on board? They could be anything, Prue. For the love of God, don't take them. Besides, I get the feeling I'd be the one to get the bad pill and die,' he said.

'You won't take them with me?'

'Absolutely not, no. It's a dumb idea, and skanky.'

She thought he'd be pleased. Prue only wanted to have some last-minute mind-bending escape that would relieve the itch of being trapped in the person she had been issued.

She stuck the pills back in her jeans. It emerged that in the hurry to get to the gun tower James had forgotten to bring the flipping keys, not that it would have taken much to kick the door in.

'Lift me up,' she said and stood on James's shoulders. The wood on the window frame crumbled in her hands and she easily stuck her fingers under the gap and flicked the handle up and opened it. She looked down at James and saw him gormlessly gazing up, her knees on his shoulders and a hand over his eyes. Crawling in sideways, she jumped down and unlocked the door from the inside.

'Who are you?' he said, as she opened it. 'There was a time you were scared of sheep.'

'Oh yeah, I forgot about that.'

They smoked the last of the weed and engaged in polite sex. Prue liked James, but she didn't get butterflies when she saw him. She didn't have wicked thoughts about him and throughout the whole experience her heart didn't thump, although his did, she could feel it. She shut her eyes, but Archie crept in and she felt disgusted and confused. James kept asking her if she was all right and she wanted him to stop asking the question over and over because she had answered several times. She wanted him to hurry up and get it over with and get off.

Afterwards, they lay upstairs on one of the old army bunks with the springs digging in her back as he kept trying to reassure her, although she hadn't asked for reassurance.

'Will you come back at Christmas?' he asked. 'I will if you will?'

'I don't think my mum will let me.' That was only part of the issue, of course. Let's face it, she wasn't coming back.

'Prue, can I say something? Although I know you're going to find it annoying.'

'Don't say it then.'

'Do you think, perhaps, it's only an idea – you might be a bit depressed?' She turned to look at him, wondering where this had come from.

'What makes you say that?'

'Well, you don't really talk about stuff. Except Evie O'Hara, who your dad might be, and Archie, and how much you don't want to go home, and I know you're worried about that.'

'I don't think *worried* is the right word.'

'Look,' he said, sitting up on his elbows. 'You do everything your mother wants, right?'

'It's the way it's always been.'

'Don't you think you need to stand up to her, not in a rude or rebellious way, but in an assertive way?'

'Do we have to talk about this right now?'

'Not if you don't want to.' They fell back into silence. Prue had no idea what kind of silence it was for James, but hers was an empty, bereft one.

'I sound unbearable,' she said after a while.

'No, you're beautiful and intriguing, and complex – I'll give you that. If you were unbearable, I wouldn't feel like I do and I wouldn't be here with you now.'

Please, please God, do not tell me you love me.

If he knew who she really was, he wouldn't be there either. She was a liar. Now she was a depressed liar. She really was turning into her mother. James fell asleep like a contented baby as she lay there, staring at the ceiling, which absolutely had asbestos in it. Prue wanted the illusion of her father back to cling to. It was better before when she thought he might come and rescue her one day and offer her something different. How she dreamed he would have had mumps and couldn't have any more children and was desperate to find her after all these years. Or he'd divorced his wife and his three children were living with his ex and he wanted one to live with him. He was going to be reliable and wise and full of amazing stories from his time in the Armed Forces, or Amnesty International, or a doctor at a refugee camp. Something honourable and at great risk to himself, and now he wanted to save her and teach her how to live and how to be what she wanted.

She extracted herself from the tangle with James, pulling her hair out from underneath him, but woke him up. He had to get back for his shift at the hotel and Prue had her celebratory dinner. When they parted ways, she had every intention of going straight home.

But she didn't. She went straight to Charlie's house and walked through the broken gate and thumped on the door. His cousin Simon opened it.

'Charlie! Da jail bait's here!'

'I'm sixteen.'

'Good, is it rag week?'

'Why, you need a jumbo tampon?'

Simon tutted and stood aside as she walked in. Charlie came out, bleary-eyed and confused.

'Relax, I'm here to buy more weed, that's all.'

'Fair enough,' he shrugged. 'Come on through.'

Simon stood in the kitchen watching with hollow eyes. He didn't have a top on, yet again, only jeans, and could have played the glockenspiel on his own ribs. Charlie ushered her into his room, which stank of old socks and stale smoke. He started banging on about how his mate, Big Sean, was coming round. Umbro had picked up on his agitation and jumped on and off the sofa, knocking over piles of crap with his tail until Charlie shouted at him, which made his excitement worse.

Apparently, Big Sean (a name he'd clearly come up with himself, as most would have called him Fat Sean by virtue of honesty) had over forty convictions. Prue wanted to point out that perhaps having forty convictions wasn't the most stellar record but couldn't be bothered. Charlie seemed to think time served increased his friend's credibility whereas Prue thought it made him a shitty criminal. Big Sean had been scoping for a job, he said. Prue looked at Umbro, white and tan, floppy ears and rounded head; an irrepressibly friendly bear, by far the most redeemable character in the room, including herself.

Charlie fired up the bong, thick with yellow water and the glass scorched black. Bubbles and smoke filled the room.

'I'd rather skin up,' she said.

'I've got no baccy.'

'Fine, I'll do the bong.'

'Shit, you dunna have to—'

'Give it here,' she said and took it from him. She leaned back and exhaled and let the bong rest against her stomach, slumping back on his sofa. Charlie leaned over and stuck his tongue in her mouth. It tasted of bong smoke and tea. Prue pulled away and stood up.

'I better go,' she said and rushed out, but at the door, she stopped. 'What did you tell Archie I told you?'

'That wasn't my fault.'

'I never said he would give you money.'

'You said help. What is help if it isna money? I said I'd move to the Mainland and work selling for him over there. It was a business proposal. Expansion. Business stuff.' He shrugged as he said it; even he didn't think it was a convincing proposition. 'It dusna matter anyway,' he carried on. 'I'm leaving, fuck it. I'm done. At some point, a man has to strike out on his own.'

'What about the ravens? Was that you? Did you do that? I won't say anything. I just need to know.'

'What aboot da ravens?'

'Did you shoot them?'

'What would I do dat for? I love animals,' he tutted. Prue looked at Umbro, still wagging his tail.

'Sorry, stupid question.'

Prue was nearly back home and congratulating herself for escaping without causing more damage, when she remembered she'd paid a tenner for a bag of weed and left it at Charlie's.

26

Prue sat in the study waiting for eight o'clock to come. She had showered and dressed in jeans and a black baggy jumper that hung past her knees. She didn't care what she looked like and would rather blend into the walls. She thought of the similarities between her and her mother and how upsetting that realisation was. History had come within a hair's breadth of repeating itself. She was in no mood for celebrating, grieving the loss of a father – not her grandfather, but the man she had hoped he might be. It had been a childish fantasy of a paternal messiah, someone who would offer hope and would show her the way, but he wasn't coming. She'd been warned about strange men lurking in bushes in the dark but not of the monsters in the same house. Perhaps if her own mother had told her the truth of what shape monsters can take, she might have seen it coming. Even Vegas Mary lamp looked to be judging.

'What?' Prue said. 'You may as well offer an opinion,' but she didn't answer, though it would have been good if she had. Prue's eyes followed Mary's outstretched hand and it looked as if she was gesturing towards the loose floorboards. 'Absolutely not, I've done enough damage,' she said to the lamp.

It was twenty minutes until dinner. If Archie was telling her the truth about Evie being pregnant, and she wasn't sure what to believe, could that have been the reason he killed her? What if the story of love was to draw Prue in? He would pretend to be a good person, as he had to Evie, and, being an idiot, she had fallen for it – could Evie have fallen for it too? Prue got the pages out and laid them down in date order and studied them again, examining every word, trying to understand with jaded eyes.

Evie was in love and had set down many words to prove her feelings while Archie had all but scrawled a few unimaginative words on the back of photos. There were other hints that he might not have felt as strongly as Evie.

In the beginning she had been the brave one openly declaring her feelings and that meant he was the guarded one, holding back or maybe he didn't really have them. Evie called Archie arrogant. What if it wasn't only Ronnie who thought Evie wasn't good enough, what if deep down really Archie thought it too and wasn't prepared to be tied down by a local girl and a baby? It would have been embarrassing for the Andersons given their social standing, and how they regarded themselves. Ronnie had asked questions, but the letters ended with Evie talking about their big adventure, which could have been the baby. Prue remembered the cabin in the trees and when she'd asked how long it had been there, Archie had answered, *twenty years*. What if Evie's body had never been found because the Andersons had built a cabin on top of where she was buried? But she still felt as if there was something about the hole underground. She looked up at Mary again; now it seemed as if she was really pointing at the floorboards.

'Fine, have it your way,' said Prue, and she pulled back the rugs and lifted up the boards.

She still had the lantern from the night before and when she put it on the floor it lit up the entire room. The hole seemed much smaller now and less frightening as she could see all of it. It was a dank little hole, eerie and damp, but no rats in sight. Prue started to sift through the dusty, web-covered shelves holding glass bottles, like the bottles Ronnie used. There were bloated stinky old books alongside a small pewter box. Prue opened it and inside was a clump of curly blonde hair; she shut the box and put it back. She took one of the books down and tried to open it but the pages were stiff and puffy and the writing inside illegible and smeared. The faded marks had disappeared over the years, but on the hard inside cover a list had been written with some words in capitals, still legible:

THE GOD, the HUMAN IDENTIFICATION and the ANIMAL.
ADMISSION ceremonies, RENUNCIATION and VOWS, the COVENANT, BAPTISM
THE MARKS of the MYSTIC CROSS and HEALERS.
THE ASSEMBLIES, the SITE, the HOUR. The ESBAT.
RITES & HOMAGE, the FEASTS and the SACRAMENT

They meant nothing to Prue, just nonsensical ramblings. She bumped into the rocking chair and it started to rock;

she waited for it to stop, petrified that it might keep going by itself. She returned the book and was about to leave when something caught her eye.

'What the fuck?' Prue said aloud. There, plain as day, as if waiting for her to find them, were her missing glasses.

She put them on and they were definitely hers, but what were they doing down here? That meant someone had been down here very recently. It could only be Ruth or Ronnie, since they had been the ones at dinner that first night she lost her glasses, but they both seemed upset when she moved into the study. Ruth had form in lying but Ronnie adored Archie and would do anything for him. Why would either of them put her glasses down here? She couldn't trust any of them. She slid her glasses in the pocket in her baggy jumper and was about to go when she saw a green canvas bag. She felt all the blood rush to the soles of her feet; her nerves screamed out for her to get out, but she couldn't leave now.

That day at the beach Archie had told her Evie left the house with a canvas bag. Prue opened it and inside she found a purse with coins, a door key, some lidless pens, a letter in an envelope that had nearly fallen apart and a lip salve. And there was a faded blue diary with a peeling daisy pattern on the cover; it wasn't as damaged as the other books as it had been protected by the bag. She had to hurry. She had only a couple of minutes before she would have to go to dinner and no doubt one of them would come rattling at the door.

As she rushed through the stiff pages, she felt ecstatic when she saw Evie's familiar handwriting. Evie leapt off the page and Prue's heart started to rapid fire. In the top right-hand corner were the same printed dates in the same font as the notes she had found in the books. When she checked the dates of the letters, the pages had been torn out and on the inside cover, in Evie's handwriting, was the name: *Evelyn Mary O'Hara, 1973.* Prue ran her fingers over the handwriting, to bring herself closer to Evie. That horrible damp room had something to do with Evie and, despite how mad it sounded, it was as if she was trying to speak to Prue. She had goosebumps as she turned to the last entry:

24th August 1973

I can't believe it! I'm too young! It's OK. It will be fine. We will be OK. I am a pioneer. If Mum finds out, she'll go mad and tell me my life is over but I refuse to accept that. This is not the end, but the beginning of one more! My baby. My family. A new beginning!

12 weeks – mid-October. Due date mid-April 1974. Aries. Help! Archie is an Aries!

Headstrong. Stubborn. Always has to be right. Help!

Archie *was* telling the truth. Evie was pregnant and whoever killed her also killed their baby. Evie used her diary mostly to make shopping lists, appointments, birthday reminders, doodles and some god-awful poetry. One word Evie used bothered Prue – *pioneer.* She had heard Ronnie use it before; had Evie picked it up from her? It wasn't an ordinary word for a teenage girl to use. Prue had to hurry. She placed the book back inside the bag, and put the bag back on the shelf behind the bottles and left.

* * *

Ruth gave Prue a good once over as soon as she entered the kitchen and let her know she was disappointed. Ronnie was wearing a dark green, crushed-velvet dress with heels and Ruth was wearing a caramel-coloured silk dress with a kimono. She had fine-tuned her hair into a sculpture and wore heavy earrings that looked as if they might tear her earlobes with one energetic swing of her head. Prue had come to the party dressed as her mother.

'Are you not dressing up?' Ruth asked.

'What's wrong with this?' Prue looked down at herself.

'Nothing, I suppose. Although you may want to wear shoes as we are eating in the dining room and the floor is absolutely freezing.'

'How come the dining room? We never eat in there.'

'It's a special occasion. We're celebrating! Go on, go see!' Prue tried to control her lack of enthusiasm and spun on her heels and dutifully went to inspect whatever awaited her. The only time she'd been in the dining room the entire time was the day Ronnie showed her the house.

The dining room, with its pretend marble walls and swirls painted by a kidnapped Frenchman, was cold and dark. The wall lights were covered in dust and only mustered a dark amber. The pistachio green walls appeared a faded grey and the drapes were closed. The table, big enough for eight floated in the middle of the room, although someone had made a valiant attempt to decorate it with fairy lights. A gobo machine whirred on the mantelpiece above the redundant fire, throwing snowflakes and star shapes across the wall opposite. The fairy lights blinked on and off in a slow clap. In the centre of the table were clusters of tea lights that flickered, making the little gold cupids under the wall lights look as if they were giggling. A record player played an LP from Ronnie's eclectic collection of vinyl. They'd gone to such effort, and almost because it looked like a Christmas party at a particularly run-down school, Prue felt guilty and had to remind herself that she was the one who had been toyed with all along.

The ever-present plants seemed to be creeping, forever moving in the corner of her eye. The dancing candlelight made them appear alive and the giant shadows of ferns splayed across the walls made for a disorienting experience.

Prue offered to help but Ruth insisted she sit at the table, and this made her feel even more awkward. The gobo machine whirred away like a hamster on a wheel on the cusp of collapse and the stars and snowflakes migrated across the wall in a painful and jagged path. The record playing was 'Sh-Boom' by an old band, The Chords. The song seemed adamant life could be a dream, but Prue felt stupid sitting alone as they all scuttled around playing along with the farce. Ronnie wheeled in the drinks trolley from the Morning Room on which was an ice bucket and Ruth entered carrying serving dishes and platters as Frank Sinatra started singing next.

'You must have spent all day cooking. You didn't have to do all this, thank you,' said Prue, feeling like a burden.

'Thank Ronnie – she's the wonder woman and as much as possible is from her garden. I was merely the sous chef, wasn't I, Ronnie?' said Ruth.

'That's right, my dear. It's wonderful to have an occasion

to cook for and I can't remember the last time I had a reason to put these shoes on.'

'Is Archie coming?' asked Prue.

The door's hinges screamed and on cue he pushed the door open and strode in as if he should be wearing spurs, as the brass band took hold of an energetic instrumental, grating on Prue's adrenaline-strained nerves. He wore boots and jeans covered in paint. It would appear he hadn't got the brief about dressing up either and they'd both decided to come as their worst selves.

'Aren't you going to get changed?' said Ruth. Prue had never seen her in dark lipstick and it made her mouth look mean.

'What for?' he asked, oblivious.

'Prue's dinner,' said Ruth, fixing him with a stare.

'Prue doesn't care what I'm wearing,' he said and flashed a dismissive smile.

They made their way through the starter with endless questions: what A levels did Prue want to take? What degree would she choose? What did she want to be? Did she want to travel? Did she want to work in an office? Did she like working with people? They all came from Ruth. She asked a million of them and didn't wait for a response, which was helpful since Prue didn't have much in the way of answers.

'I'll open another bottle of wine,' said Ronnie.

'Have we really finished three already?' said Ruth. Everyone was knocking back alcohol at breakneck speed – except for Prue who'd decided to abstain. All the effort and the pretence towards making this perfect dinner and she felt a growing urge to smash it. To take this celebratory ritual and destroy it, like the time with the boy and the skateboard – if she drank, she wouldn't be able to trust herself.

'Archie, have you seen that demon dog?' asked Ronnie.

'No,' he said, without looking up, shovelling in smoked salmon.

'I have,' said Prue. Ronnie's face was a picture; she was sitting opposite Prue and put the bottle she was holding down on the table with a thud. Ruth and Archie were at each end – the king and queen of their mouldy kingdom.

'Poor thing,' said Ruth. 'I wonder what it's eating, it must be starving.'

'Archie, it's in those trees,' said Ronnie, near hysterical. 'You have to find it!'

The record stopped and the needle hissed and dropped into Chubby Checker's 'Let's Twist Again' as Prue ignored the small talk and considered each one of them around the table.

Ruth, she had been dismissive of Evie and was happily chatting away, her glass always full, always in hand. Could she be happy to go about blindly believing what she needed to keep her bubble intact? It was Ruth who had said she feared whatever it was would *come out*. If it wasn't her father, then it had to be about Evie. Archie hunched over his food, finding the demands on his presence a strain. Ruth could be fierce – she had confronted Prue's mother and Prue herself, but Ronnie was the one who had showed her the priest holes, and had painted Evie as the peasant trollop. Ronnie was on edge this evening and was drinking very fast and watching everyone from behind her glass, but then so was Ruth. It was beginning to feel as if the ravens were the only honest creatures in the vicinity and two of them had been killed. Prue reached into her pocket as Frank Sinatra started singing 'That's Life'.

'Look what I found,' she said, and put her glasses on the table to see who reacted.

'What a stroke of luck, Prue! Where were they?' said Ruth, sounding genuinely pleased. Archie didn't look and Ronnie's face remained unmoved – it was impossible to tell.

'They'd... fallen down a gap. I was tidying up and found them.'

'Where?' said Ruth.

'Under my bed, they must have fallen down the gap by the wall.'

Ruth screwed her face up. 'That's odd. You lost them as soon as you got here and you were still upstairs in the nursery then.' Shit. Ruth was right, she was.

'Yes, I found them again at the bottom of my rucksack and then lost them again, I'm terrible.' Oops, that sounded weak.

'At least you have them now,' said Ruth, who held up her glass in a theatrical flourish and it took everyone a few seconds to understand before they joined her.

Prue raised hers. Ronnie thrust hers up in annoyance, spilling its contents, and Archie just about picked his up off the table, his face resting on his hand as Ruth cleared her throat.

'I want us to make a promise from this day forward. We need to make conscious efforts to celebrate success for the positive moments in life. We are far too good at paying attention only when things go wrong.'

'Can we put our arms down now?' said Ronnie. Archie had already. Ruth ignored her.

'Let us break that habit, now, tonight, and celebrate Prue's success. Congratulations, Prue!' said Ruth and everyone mumbled the same. Prue smiled as if her soul had been stolen by a particularly traumatic school photo.

The record had stopped, and they continued to eat under the scrapes of cutlery and people chewing. Then Ronnie attempted to put another record on but couldn't see well enough to set the needle and asked Archie to help. When he got up, he tripped over one of the plants and knocked it down. Ronnie squealed as if her only child had been pushed over in the playground.

'Fuck me!' said Archie. 'It's like the Day of the Triffids in here.' He set the needle down gently and Bobby Darin started singing 'Beyond the Sea' and Prue wished she could join him.

Ruth had blue teeth from the red wine and grew more animated. She dipped the sleeve of her kimono into her food and, when she stood up, dragged half the fairy lights with her.

'Ruth! Sit down! For fuck's sake!' Archie shouted and everyone jumped, his reaction far too severe. Prue pushed her food around her plate, finding it difficult to eat; she could feel something brewing, a jangle in her belly. Then Ruth started blathering on about self-esteem.

'Sometimes it feels as if the universe has us by the coattails and it can seem that every door is closed.'

'What are you talking about, Ruth?' said Archie. 'Prue doesn't have any doors shut, she's sixteen.'

'You know what I mean, *Archibald*,' said Ruth. She'd never called him that. It *was* a stupid name. 'The universe can make us uncomfortable when it wants us to divert to a new path. Nothing will work and everything will fail. You have to keep faith in yourself, in God, whatever works…'

Ruth paused and drew breath to start explaining further since no one was picking up the end of the rope she was dangling. Archie huffed and puffed, and they all did their best to ignore him.

'I hope you spend the time really getting to know yourself. It's the hardest thing, it really is. You don't realise until you're ancient, like me, that what you thought was the right way of living is only the pattern you find familiar enough to repeat…' She drifted off again. 'I hope you've enjoyed your summer with us – although I know I've not been the most present and we've had our moments.'

'I have something I'd like to share,' Archie piped up, and everyone turned to rest their eyes on him with a mix of shock and bemusement since he'd made it obvious he wasn't interested in being there but now demanded centre stage.

'Who's dead?' said Ronnie, slurring and full of drunken looks, running her tongue over her teeth.

'I haven't made any decisions yet, but I think the time is right to tell you all that for the last few months I have been meeting with my cousin.'

'What?!' said Ronnie, standing up. 'You've been meeting with the Tullochs and didn't tell me? I know what they want – they want my house and my part of this island.'

Prue knew that the island was tied up in terms of land ownership and how much keeping it meant to Ronnie, but she'd never heard Archie talk about selling.

Archie carried on. 'Technically, Ronnie, it's mine and… but that is what I've been discussing.' He addressed the table. 'I've been to see my cousin, Christopher, and it was good to catch up. We've had several constructive meetings and some promising conversations.'

'About what?' asked Ruth. Her mouth a dark spot floating in the middle of a colourless face.

'He does want the house, and the land. Everything – he's made me an offer and it's a good one and I'd be stupid not to consider it. It could change our lives – Ruth, we could live anywhere, literally – anywhere.' The family CEO had given his update to the board.

Ruth loved this house. Ronnie was devoted to it and would rather die than let it be sold. That was the whole point of passing it on to Archie while she was alive – *to keep it from falling into speculators' hands.*

'*You* haven't made a decision?' said Ruth. 'You haven't discussed it with *me* at all.'

'We're discussing it now,' he said.

'How could you!' growled Ronnie. It was as if a demon had entered straight from hell. 'You cannot sell this house. My house! My garden! My land! You selfish little shit!' She slammed her tiny fists on the table and some tea lights went out with the venom. Then, much to everyone's surprise, she hurled a wine glass at Archie's head, who ducked just in time as it smashed into the wall above the whirring hamster machine, which carried on; the fairy lights also continued their tactless blinking. Everyone shrank, except Archie.

'Ronnie, this house is too much – it needs work and investment. It needs serious money and Christopher wants to take that on. Why not let him! They have big ideas about restoring it, making it a hotel, leveraging the wildlife aspect

– weekenders looking for a quick escape from the Mainland or even Scotland. It's not like we'd leave you destitute.'

'Weekenders?' she said, as if the word choked her. 'So this is how you show loyalty! Do you have any idea what you are doing? No, of course you don't – you're an ignorant pig!' It looked as if Ronnie might leap over the table like a mad chimpanzee, rip his arm off and beat him with it.

'Ronnie, nothing has happened yet. It's a discussion, isn't it, Archie?' Ruth spat through gritted teeth, blue ones.

'Fresh news can sting a little, I'll let it sink in,' said Archie. That really didn't help.

There was a stomach-churning moment of silence and then Ronnie stood. 'I'm going to get the main course now.' She dragged herself to the door.

'I'll come and help,' said Ruth, but Ronnie stopped her with a hand.

'My dear, I think I'm going to need a few moments alone if you don't mind. Besides, I have a little preparation to do – I'll be a few minutes.' Ronnie left and Ruth looked back at the table.

'Actually, I think I'll go to the bathroom. I won't be a moment,' she said.

This left Prue and Archie alone together for the first time since the cabin. She had assumed, somewhat naïvely, that he would be as uncomfortable as herself. When they'd sat down to eat, she'd made a point of trying to meet his eye, not for him, but for herself. To prove that her body would obey what her brain commanded but Archie appeared to barely notice. It hurt. She felt rejected. How pathetic is that? She despised him and yet wanted his approval at the same time. She still wanted him to like her. What did that make her?

The record player dropped and burst into a cheerful American folk song, all guitars, harmonicas and banjos, but something about it seemed familiar.

> All around the kitchen.
> Cock-a-doodle-doodle-do.
> All around the kitchen.
> Cock-a-doodle-doodle-do.
> Now stop right there,
> Cock-a-doodle-doodle do…

It was the song the winking cowboy with the spurs had played on the ferry. How odd. Prue burst out laughing.

'What *is* this music?' said Archie.

'No, leave it, please, I like it.'

'You know this song?'

'Sort of.'

The electrics buckled and the lights went out but the insensitive fairy lights and a few tea lights clung on, much like the rest of them. Archie walked to the record player and scratched the record.

'Fuck's sake,' he said. Then the lights came back on again.

Ruth returned with a fresh application of the dark lipstick but it didn't hide the fact she appeared to be dragging her crushed soul behind her. She took her seat and together they sat in uncomfortable silence. Prue stared down at the table waiting for a suitable topic of conversation to spring to mind, but all she could think of were entirely inappropriate moments from the last few days and each one made her cringe to the point of her stomach contracting into a tornado-shaped knot. Ruth cleared her throat several times, anything to fill the void. Archie huffed and Prue could hear a very slight whistle from his nose as he breathed and it made her want to pick something up, preferably hard and flat, like a stainless-steel tray, and smash it into his face.

'Prue, I don't suppose you want to go and check on Ronnie, do you?' said Ruth. 'She's taking a rather long time, perhaps she needs some help?'

'Oh, yes, of course,' said Prue, scraping her chair across the floor which echoed around the room. Lift or scrape, her Nana had said, that told you a lot about a person – whether they lifted a chair or scraped it across the floor. Prue had failed her own grandmother's test.

Prue went to look for Ronnie in the kitchen, assuming she was struggling with the preparation of the main course, but she wasn't there. It was strange, but maybe she was too upset and she thought to check in the Morning Room, thinking she might have escaped there for a moment of peace to collect herself. But Ronnie wasn't in the Morning Room either. She went back to the kitchen where, through the window, she saw her heading back from the garden. What on earth was she doing outside? Ronnie entered from the back door and stopped as soon as she saw Prue.

'Ruth sent me,' said Prue. Ronnie looked cross and she thought it best to offer up quickly why she was checking on her.

'What on earth for?'

'She thought you might need help.'

'Well, I don't. Why don't you go back to the dining room and tell them I'll be back in a moment, and, while you're at it, that patience is a virtue.'

'I think Ruth thought you might be a little upset.'

Ronnie stopped at the counter, sighed and placed what looked like a bundle of freshly cut parsley on a wooden chopping board. She shot Prue a look and for a moment her eyes seemed to be carrying tears that hadn't yet quite spilled. Ronnie sniffed hard through her nose and pulled her shoulders back and thrust her chin in the air.

'I'll be all right, thank you. You tell your aunt I'm very well. I'm preparing something very special and I shan't be much longer – would you do that for me? Buy me a little time to pull myself together, my dear?'

'Of course.'

'Thank you.' Prue went back to the dining room.

After what seemed like an ordeal of tension, Ronnie finally appeared with the main course on a trolley already plated and dumped the plates on the table with the manners of a bad-tempered waitress. Ruth looked crushed. Archie had his head on one hand and both elbows on the table, which would have enraged Nana, who would have hit him with a wooden spoon. God, when would it be over? Prue stared down at her sliced beef and then Ronnie circled them all again, administering a sauce which she poured without asking over her beef, and proceeded to do the same to Archie's, but when Ronnie went to do the same to Ruth's she covered her plate with a hand.

'I'll have mine plain, thank you.'

'Oh, but Ruth, I've worked on this for hours, especially for tonight. You have to try some,' said Ronnie.

'I can't, Ronnie. If I do, I'll be up all night. You know I've been having problems.'

'Try a little bit—'

'I said no! For fuck's sake,' snapped Ruth, slamming a palm down on the table and rattling the crockery. Ronnie plonked the sauce jug down with a thud through gritted teeth, sat back at her seat and made a ballet out of placing her napkin across her lap.

'Are you not having any?' Prue asked.

'For some reason I cannot fathom I'm not that hungry,' said Ronnie.

Prue's stomach turned at the creamy and lumpy sauce oozing all over her beef. She wasn't feeling particularly hungry herself but she picked up a fork and nibbled on some broccoli. Having perfected the irritating art of pushing food around from her food wars with her mother, she did the same here.

'What was that weird music?' said Archie. The record had shifted from the winking cowboy's song to more of Ronnie's music.

'It's my music, Archie. I like it, it makes me happy, not that you would be remotely interested in something as irrelevant as my happiness,' said Ronnie.

Archie groaned. 'May I put something different on?'

'Why ask – you'll only do what you want anyway,' she said.

Archie shovelled in his food like a lion, the kill brought to him by the females of the herd as he lounged in the sun. Ronnie stared daggers as he ate, and Prue caught Ruth wiping a tear away. Prue drew breath and stared down at her cut-up dinner; she couldn't eat a bite.

'Do you know what we used to call each other?' Ronnie asked no one in particular. She put her cutlery down and filled her wine glass again as she carried on talking. 'When Archibald was little, he was such a runt, such a crying, little bitch of a boy that I had to coddle him, wipe his arse, dry his tears and tie his shoelaces because his own mother would be laughing at the walls all day. He was Socrates and I, Diotima – those were our names for each other. You see, the high priestess Diotima taught Socrates about love, and I taught Archibald, only it turns out I didn't teach him very well,' she said as she held her swaying wine glass.

This was excruciating. The lights flickered on and off again; even they were trying to call it a night.

'I'll miss having you here, Prue.' Ruth had transcended suddenly to a melancholic state.

Then Ronnie started gently sobbing as Archie chewed away his meat dinner. It was such a disastrous evening that Prue didn't think it could possibly get any worse.

'I heard you, Ruth,' said Prue. 'I heard you in the kitchen talking to Archie the other night. I heard you say you were scared of it *all coming out* and how you wanted me to go home and at the time I thought you were talking about my father but... now I think it might be about something else.'

Ruth closed her eyes; she couldn't deny having said the words. 'You are taking it out of context—'

'Seriously, Prue?' Archie chimed in. 'We're still entertaining the idea of me murdering my girlfriend? At seventeen. So dramatic.' When Prue looked at him his face was dark on a wobbling head; she hadn't noticed him get so drunk.

'Here's a crazy idea. If it wasn't about my father, which we can all agree has come out, then what could it be about?' asked Prue. No one said a word. 'There we go, silence. What else could it be?'

'What is it?' said Ruth, her features pointed. 'What is this bizarre preoccupation with something that has nothing to do with you? That actually has very little to do with any of us?'

'And what about the secrets and lies that *do* have something to do with me, Ruth? Not allowed to talk about those either, am I? Although you're allowed to paint about them. What else do you paint about, I wonder?'

'For the love of God, can we not have a simple fucking dinner!' said Ruth, and Prue struggled not to leap across the table.

'Ruth, tell her,' said Archie. 'Be done with it. Tell her. Get this over and done with.'

Ruth's eyes went wild. 'Are you insane? Stay out of this, Archie, it has nothing to do with you. This is *my* family. Prue, we weren't talking about what you think.'

'Then tell me what you were talking about.'

It couldn't be about her grandfather hanging himself and it couldn't be about her father, so it had to be about Evie, surely.

The lights gave up and now all that was left was a single tea light, the stupid fairy lights and the shadows of the plants closing in.

'I'll go,' said Archie, but as he stood up the lights came back on and he sat down again. 'Ruth, please. Tell her – she has to find out some time or this is never going to end.'

The record stopped and the room filled with the sound of the needle trying to find something else to play.

'I see,' said Ruth eventually. 'All right,' she put her napkin down, 'the evening is ruined anyway. Let's get it over with.'

27

No one said a word. Ruth pulled at an earring. Ronnie's eyes darted between them. Archie spun his knife around by the point on the table. Everyone was waiting for someone else to say something and the record player still searched for something to play. Prue got up, lifted the needle, turned the record player off and sat back down, and Ruth started to speak.

'When you were born we agreed never to tell you who your father was. It was your grandmother's wish that you would never learn the truth. That was the first real lie, but it set a precedent, Prue, and in many ways we've been lying ever since.'

'Lying about what?' asked Prue.

Ruth turned to Ronnie. 'Would you mind leaving us, Ronnie? I'm afraid this conversation must remain private.'

'What about him?' Prue nodded at Archie.

'Archie knows,' said Ruth. 'We don't keep secrets from each other.' Wouldn't be so sure of that, thought Prue.

'Fine by me, I've had enough honesty for one night.' Ronnie stood up, swaying, grabbed the bottle of wine by her, tottered to the door and switched the main lights off.

'Ronnie! We are still here,' Ruth called out.

'Oops-a-daisy! If anyone needs me, I'll be in my bedroom drinking myself to death.' Ronnie flicked the lights back on and slammed the door.

'I feel sick,' said Ruth, one hand on her heart, the other clutching her glass.

'I'll get some water,' said Archie. He tried to stand but wobbled. 'Maybe not,' he said, sitting back down.

'When we found out your mother was pregnant and what had been happening, it was very difficult,' said Ruth. 'We adored Dad. I know it doesn't make sense. It didn't then and it doesn't now. I know the truth should be logical and make sense, but here is where I must disappoint you.' She paused and drew breath. 'We thought the best thing to do was to keep it a secret – to protect his memory and also so you wouldn't have to grow up under the shadow of *that*. He was an amazing dad and I loved him very much. I can't *not* love him, Prue.'

'What about Mum? This has to be why she's had all the... problems.'

'It was a terrible shock and we didn't find out until your mother was nearly six months pregnant with you. She was hiding it, in denial, for as long as possible and who could blame her?'

'I always thought the reason we weren't allowed to talk about Grandad was because Nana missed him. But it wasn't, was it? It was because she couldn't bear to face up to what he was. What does Mum think?' .

'I don't know because I've never asked. I was too scared, so we swept it under the rug and willed it away and your Nana was adamant that if we acted as if nothing ever happened, it was as good as. That sounds mad but families are mad. That and we didn't know how else to cope,' said Ruth.

'You make it sound like an accident.'

'The earth had been ripped out from beneath us, Prue, and we didn't know what to do. There wasn't an instruction manual.'

'You shouldn't need one. Mum was forgotten about, and it wasn't her fault.'

Archie chimed in, 'Look, this isn't as unusual as you might think. These things happen. I'm not defending it, it's fucked up, but it is what it is.'

'Why not make something up?' Prue ignored Archie, although she'd heard every word. 'How could you tell me you did this for *my* benefit and then let me live with a mystery?'

'Your Nana wouldn't let us. If we made something up, it was as good as a clean slate for your mother, but by leaving it a mystery it was always there to remember, if even by omission. I think she blamed her in some way, but Nana didn't mean it to haunt you. She kept telling us how lots of people grew up without fathers after the war and they just bloody well got on with it.'

'How could Nana blame her!? My own mother must hate me. Having to look after me and being reminded of that, every single day. It makes sense now.'

'What makes sense?' asked Ruth.

'When we ran away from Nana, and we lived in the forest

353

with Holly and Billy. I felt like the odd one out because Mum was always so affectionate to Holly, but never me. I thought it was because I was older and put it down to big sister jealousy, but she did love her more than me, and why wouldn't she?'

'Look, Caroline and I have never got on, that's true, but I assure you, she loves you and would give her right arm to protect you. She would do anything, and I mean anything for you. She knows it's not your fault.'

The air stopped moving. Archie and Ruth locked eyes as if they were connected by string.

'Don't back out now – tell her, everything,' he said.

'Tell me what?'

Ruth started to cry. 'This was meant to be a celebration.'

Archie leaned across the table. 'Then make this a purge, Ruth. It's fucking her up, big time. Trust me.' He pointed to his temple as if Prue wasn't even in the room. He heaved himself up and staggered over to sit by Ruth.

'You need to listen, Prue,' slurred Archie. 'Once you've heard what Ruth has to say, more will fall into place.'

'Will someone please tell me what's going on?'

'Just listen,' he said, and he kissed the back of Ruth's hand. Prue had to turn away because she could feel his lips against her neck. *I'm sorry. I'm sorry.*

'The day we cleared out Nana's house,' said Ruth, wiping tears away. 'That evening your mum called me. She said you were over at Subo's and I thought she was calling to build bridges. We both apologised and then she started to talk about you. She said she was worried, frightened, that she was petrified that the Joan Gardner case would be reviewed by the police again and that there might be a new investigation. She said how you'd been fighting and that you wanted more independence, and she was scared. I need to ask you – what exactly can you remember about the day Holly died?'

Prue pushed her plate with the gloopy sauce as far away as she could. Her eyeballs thumped with a tense headache, so she poured herself a glass of water.

'I was in the front room. Joan Gardner was at the window. She always came to the window. We spoke briefly then she left. Later when Mum came downstairs, she asked me where Holly was and that's when we saw she was missing from her basket. The police came, it was horrible. There were cars and sirens and dogs barking. Billy came back, and he cried. At the station I told the police I saw her at the window that morning. Then they found fibres from her coat on the window latch... and she confessed.'

'Forget what you know, Prue. What do you *remember*?'

What were memories really? A series of images, cut and spliced, like flicking through a photo album from photograph to photograph with no clear path. Prue wasn't sure what was a real memory, or something stuck in her head from dreams, opinions or nightmares.

'I remember Holly in her Moses basket. I remember Joan Gardner but not her face. I know I didn't like her. She came back to take Holly when I left the room.'

Something stirred in Prue's gut, something that had been left to rot was rising up – an oil slick crawling up her insides. Her head started to spin, and she heard heavy rain, dogs barking and the sound of water and wheels screeching.

'Prue,' said Archie, 'you told me you had dreams about woods, trees, guilt, that deep down you'd done something terrible that couldn't be taken back. What if that guilt has a cause, one that you can't remember?'

The last tea light extinguished itself. They all watched it expire and were left with the dull wall lights, burning with dust, the laughing cupids and fairy lights. On and off. On and off. *Tick, tick, tick. Cock-a-doodle-doodle-do.* Prue saw her winking cowboy and his spurs tapping. It had started to rain outside, hard, and the wind threw the rain against the windows as if pellets were being fired at them.

'I remember being scared and trying to hug Mum's legs, but she was crying and kept pushing me away, and hitting me. Not hard. But she was hitting me, and her skirt was wet. I was wet too and I was cold. I wanted her to hug me back, but she wouldn't. She stripped me naked and took her skirt off and we put dry clothes on.'

'How did you both get wet?' asked Archie.

Her heart thumped and when Prue looked down at her legs, they were swinging off the end of a plastic chair in those white socks. She was at the police station. Then she heard her mother wailing like an animal and she wanted to make it stop. Make her happy and fix it. When she looked up there was the sympathetic face of a policewoman leaning over from the front seat.

'How we doing in the back, sweetheart?' she said and moments later, when the indicators started, Prue would be sick in her own hands.

'Your mother told me what really happened to Holly – the truth,' said Ruth. 'It was a tragic accident, but it wasn't your fault – you were only a child.'

'And a child can't be guilty in the eyes of the law,' said Archie. 'Remember? I told you that.'

'Guilty of what? What did Mum tell you?'

'You took Holly,' said Ruth. 'You were the one who took her out to the woods while Caroline was asleep. You were allowed to carry her into the garden and you had asked her already if you could take Holly to the stream to play, but she'd said no – only the garden. It was July and there had been thunderstorms, the river was always bursting its banks and that stream was too narrow and the ground would flood. She said you carried her out there and set her down. Then you left her, on the blanket by the stream, and came back to the house as it started raining. What a bizarre thing to do, Prue, and so very unlike you...'

'That can't be true, I wouldn't do that.'

'You were such a good little girl. You *are* a good girl. It was an accident. It was such an unfortunate unlucky horrible accident. Holly was starting to roll over and trying to sit up. Your mum thought she must have tried to sit up and accidentally rolled into the water when you left her and she takes full responsibility, she should never have left you alone. No one should ever leave a child watching over a baby,' said Ruth. 'When she realised Holly was gone, you both ran and she found the blanket still where you'd left it but Holly wasn't there. She saw her floating in the water face down, it was her white Babygro she spotted, her little legs had become tangled in some branches only a few feet away.'

'No, no,' said Prue. 'What about Joan Gardner? I saw her.'

'I'm so sorry, Prue. It wasn't her,' said Ruth, through her tears. 'Caroline said she waded through the water but Holly was dead. You jumped in behind her. She said she hated you in that moment, she hated you and she hit you and you were begging her to stop and you told her you were sorry over and over and tried to cling at her legs and that's when she knew she couldn't hate you. You'd done nothing wrong. How you came to exist, what happened to Holly, none of it was your fault. She was frightened if the truth came out, about who your father was and what had happened, that she would lose you as well. She had to leave Holly in the water and take you back to the house. She changed you both and called the police.' Ruth sobbed and Archie comforted her, a hand on her shoulder.

'She remembered how Joan Gardner would come to the window. How she loved babies and could be a pest. She told you it was Joan who had taken her. You were so desperate to believe her, you went along with it, then you really thought it was true. You must have been so frightened, Prue, and in shock, and if your mother tells you something at that age you believe it, don't you? When your mother told me during that phone call the night of the argument, I was in shock too, then when you arrived I didn't know how to act. It's why I didn't tell you about Evie O'Hara. It's why I didn't want you to see my paintings and it's why I've kept my distance, scared it might leak out of me. I was in shock myself.'

'But I saw her. I swear I saw *someone*.'

'Caroline wanted her own life and I don't blame her. Nana could be so controlling, rigid, it was her way or the highway, and after what happened with Dad. There was only one person who needed punishing and he'd killed himself, so Nana punished your mum with a million cuts every day – putting her down, criticising, making her incapable of making a decision, eroding any sense of self-worth she had... and I wasn't much help. When I found out about Dad, I couldn't help it. Whenever I looked at Caroline, I felt disgusted – by my own baby sister.'

'Why are you doing this to me?' asked Prue.

'Because this is the truth! All of it!'

'But wait! There were fibres... from Joan Gardner's coat.'

'Joan Gardner sold cleaning products, she'd been to your house and had a blue coat. Your mum was petrified you'd give it away but the truth was easy to blur because you wanted to believe it. The real shock was when Joan Gardner bloody confessed! The police railroaded that poor woman.'

'Who else knows?'

'Me and Archie. Your mother. Nana knew, and now you. We're rather good at keeping secrets, aren't we? Not even secrets, at altering history altogether.'

'I need to get out.' Prue stood, knocking her chair over.

'No!' said Ruth. 'You can't. It's dark. There's no way you're leaving this house, you're not in the right state, I know *I'm* not.'

'I'm going to see James,' she said. He would know what to say to make this bearable.

'Impossible. Not going to happen,' said Ruth.

Archie blurted, 'Everyone stays here tonight. This house is in lockdown.' The family CEO stood as if to assert some authority but staggered, tripped over his own chair and fell to the floor. Ruth rushed to him, but he was laughing and rolling about the floor on his back.

The lights finally gave up and left only the fairy lights. A second of blackness, then a moment of Ruth trying to pull

Archie up from the floor. Then more blackness. This was her chance.

'The lights, Archie, please get up,' said Ruth.

Prue ran and pushed open the French doors and ran outside into the rain. Ruth screamed her name, but she kept running, wishing she might disappear into the darkness too.

28

Prue didn't know what to do. They'd all lied so many times it was difficult to know who or what to believe any more. The track had turned into a mud-slide under such heavy rain, and she slipped and fell. Not now. One day she would crumble, but not now, and for the time being she was still numb. It was as if a brick wall had appeared to block anything trying to reach her, and she was encased within its thick walls, and felt nothing. The thing she had to do now was to keep those walls high, and watertight. But she could never go back home now.

By the time she knocked on Charlie's door it had stopped raining, but she stood on the doorstep wet through. She'd gone there under the pretence of picking up the weed she'd left earlier. She wasn't looking for comfort and she certainly wasn't looking for sympathy. He had said he was leaving the island that night and she wanted to go too. Simon opened the door.

'I left my weed here,' she said, before he had a chance to insult her.

'Be quick – we've got plans and yoos not invited.'

She followed him to the kitchen where she recognised Big Sean from the beach, the older man in the green jacket. Charlie and a younger boy she'd never seen before were at the table. They stopped talking as soon as they saw her. The young boy looked nervous. He had an Adam's apple too big for his neck and it moved up and down like a stopcock. Charlie's knees bounced as if he was on something. Sean leaned back in his chair, and it groaned under his weight. He was a fat man who carried himself like a body builder and had an unevenly shaped, shaved head like a pear. He smoked cigarettes like little London boys do when they want to be the Krays, pinching it between thumb and forefinger. This was the man with the forty convictions Charlie was so impressed by, which was a bit like being proud of failing your driving test forty times.

Charlie leapt up and tried to block Prue from entering.

'I left my weed here.'

'Whar's your money?'

'I gave it to you already.'

'No, you didna.'

'I definitely did, remember? I left it here when you made a move and it got really awkward and I left in a rush.'

The others sniggered and Charlie, his jaw jutting out, rolled his eyes and tutted.

'Fine, come on then.' Whatever crush or infatuation she'd ever had for him had truly expired.

The bag of weed and the money were still on the windowsill and Prue snatched it up.

'Why are you all acting weird?' she asked.

'What? I dunna ken what you mean,' he said, bouncing on his heels as if he was getting ready to make a run for it.

'Oh God, Charlie, I don't care but it's as if you are plotting to blow up the Houses of Parliament.'

'OK, look, I didna want to say anything, but...' Charlie spilled his guts as he was clearly desperate to. '... it's top secret – we're going on a job.'

'What job?'

He leapt into overexcitedly explaining the long version, but the only part Prue was interested in was how they were getting off the island.

'What about Umbro?' asked Prue, but looking around she realised he wasn't there.

'He's with my mam.'

'Does she know what you're up to?'

'No, I asked her to have the dog for da night, nobody kens.'

They were going to smash their way into a place with cash in a safe. This place, he said, banked it on a Friday when the van came over from the Mainland and it was Thursday night. They were driving a car with dodgy plates Sean had procured and were going to smash their way in, grab the safe and run. In and out in minutes.

'We drive down to the water, dump the car and row a boat to the Mainland. That's why we're going tonight, it's still calm. Sean has a mate who's gonna pick wis up the other side, then we make wir way doon to Scotland.'

'How are you getting to Scotland?'

It turned out Sean's mate worked on the ferry to Aberdeen. They were going to get picked up on the

Mainland, hide out at his house until the ferry the evening after. He would get them on, no problem. Once they were in Aberdeen they would be home free. The more he talked, the more flaws sprung to mind. It's an island, surely once someone had done a head count in the morning, they'd work out who was missing. Wouldn't they put alerts on the ferry? But Prue didn't want to ask questions. Maybe she was overthinking; she was always doing that and to be honest she admired the recklessness of it. The thought of even seeing James after her initial impulse to run to him seemed stupid now. She could never tell him anything. She only wanted to be somewhere where no one knew anything about her.

'We ken the layout – Sean wis banging a lass there for a spell.'

'Aren't you worried about getting caught?'

'There's no security. We grab the safe and go. They'll be insured, so actually everyone wins.'

Prue had several questions: what if the money was contained in those bags that had that explosive ink, like in movies? What if someone saw them? More were coming but nervous boy flew into the hallway, only stopping to look at Charlie, one hand on the door, his Adam's apple working overtime.

'Not for me.' And like that, nervous boy was gone. Prue recognised his expression, as if he'd found himself somewhere he should never have been and hated himself for it.

'What happened?' asked Charlie, walking back into the kitchen with Prue.

'He bottled it,' said Sean.

'He was driving da fucking car!' said Charlie, who had already gone to catastrophic, his hands at his hairline.

'I'll drive the car?' said Simon.

'No, we need you inside wi wis, for da manpower.'

Prue sniggered. 'Manpower? Did Bambi phone in sick?' Simon shot her a look. 'Sorry,' she said.

'Aye, thanks for stopping by then,' said Simon. 'You sure she can keep her trap shut?' he said to Charlie.

'I'll drive,' said Prue.

'Fuck off, you're a bairn. You haven't even got a licence,' said Simon.

'Are you telling me that you don't mind robbing a place but draw the line at having an unlicensed driver? I can drive. I'm not robbing anyone, but I'll drive if you take me to the Mainland and get me on that ferry to Aberdeen. Give me some money and I'll go my own way. I want off the island too.'

'No way! She'll stall it,' said Simon.

'I'll do it,' she said. This wasn't her. She had no idea who this person was.

Sean eyeballed her. Charlie still had his hands glued to his head. Simon kept looking between them, gauging which way the wind was blowing. When Sean gave it the nod it was settled. This was really happening.

The unregistered car turned out to be a 1987 Citroën AX with a leaky sunroof and a gear stick that never felt as if it was in any gear at all.

Prue did stall it, twice; her knee kept shaking.

'See, I told you she couldna do it,' said Simon.

'I can do it.'

'It has got a high bite point, to be fair,' said Sean.

'See? It's got a high bite point, Simon.'

Sean told her to drive back in the direction of the village, but on the way she was told to take a turn and ended up being told to pull over about fifty metres from the hotel. The trees were past the hotel at the bottom of the hill and, beyond them, the house. It was a bit close for comfort. Prue turned the lights out, as instructed. There was nothing else around except the hotel. Sean pulled out balaclavas and threw one at each of them.

'Where do you even buy these from?' she asked.

'Don't ask, or you wouldn't put it on.' Hers stank of fags and someone else's breath.

Prue left the engine running. This was stupid. Yet, she was still there, knowing it was stupid.

'We look like a shit version of the IRA,' she said, but actually it was worse than that. Sean looked like Sean with a balaclava on, still with his shiny green bomber jacket. Charlie had his white boy dreads sticking out from under the balaclava, and Simon looked like a cuttlefish bone that would snap with one peck of a canary. It was obvious who they were to anyone that had seen them even once.

'Why are we stopping here?' Prue asked.

'This is da job,' said Charlie.

'You've got to be kidding.'

'We're doing the hotel over,' said Sean.

'You can't! That's crazy! I'm sure the doors are alarmed. What if someone comes downstairs? You said a place, you didn't say the hotel. What about James and Sharon? You *know* them. They'll be scared shitless.'

'It's better that they're scared,' said Sean.

'This is fucked up,' said Prue. 'Listen to me, Charlie, you

need cash, right? I know where there's money. The weed money. I know where they keep it.' Prue leaned over in between the seats. 'It's stashed in all the books in the study. The downstairs study, near the kitchen. You don't have to do this. I could sneak back in the house. I'll bring it to you. There must be hundreds, thousands. Let's do that, yeah?'

'Shut the fuck up! We're doing this,' he said.

'I can walk in. I can get it.' Prue was begging.

'Look, if you want wis to come, shut up and drive the car.'

Sean took out an axe from a holdall, and Prue thought her stomach would fall out.

'What are you going to do with that?' she asked.

'It's for intimidation,' said Sean.

'I'll hae da hammer,' said Simon. What. The. Fuck. But it got worse when Charlie took out a shotgun.

'Oh my God! What are you doing? You said no one would get hurt!' shrieked Prue. Charlie grabbed the back of her balaclava and a handful of hair and yanked Prue towards him through the gap in the front seats. It hurt.

'For fuck's sake, shut up! No one will get hurt if they leave us alone,' said Charlie. He let go of Prue and she pulled away, a hand to the back of her neck where he'd pulled the delicate strands.

She watched them get out of the car, slam the doors one by one. Each slam sent a thousand volts through her hands on the steering wheel like a defibrillator trying to start her heart. Her head told her now would be a good time to run. James and his mother had only ever been kind and generous to her. She could dump the car, walk away, go to bed, and hide under the duvet. She could leave the keys in the ignition; she wouldn't be a complete arsehole. She was hardly adding value anyway. But she stayed welded to the spot, through fear and a misguided feeling that she would be letting people down. Some innate trained docility to do whatever she was told. To always do as she was told, whatever that was.

She knew now it was Charlie who shot the ravens. She had been such a gullible idiot feeling sorry for him. He only wanted to get near her to get at Archie. She was nothing but a plaything between them, a soft toy to be tossed between dogs. Ruth was right about one thing: she had been desperate for attention.

Prue watched their silhouettes shrink as they ran to the hotel. There were lights on upstairs. They were nuts – worse, imbeciles. If this was her crossroads, she would very much like the devil to appear and ask her what she wanted and she would accept the consequences of getting out of this. Until he turned up, was she really going to sit there and accept her fate with the three buffoons?

No. This was it. She had to do something. Even though every nerve and fibre shook to the point where her brain cells screamed, she left the keys in the ignition and got out the car. She strode in their path towards the hotel. She could sabotage. She was good at that. She would stand in front of the hotel and scream her head off. They would hear, James and Sharon would hear, it would cause a scene, and they would have to abandon the robbery. Fuck it. She didn't owe any of them anything. This was the right thing to do, and she had to find the guts to do it or she would hate herself forever. Prue ran and stood under the windows, but as she inhaled to scream someone bowled into her, tackled her to the ground and then pulled her up by her arm and dragged her back to the car. It was Simon. He pushed her into the driving seat and ran to the passenger side and jumped in, still clutching the hammer and screamed, 'Fucking drive!'

'What about the others?'

'Go!'

'I'm trying!' Prue's hand struggled to turn the key in the ignition; it was as if her wrist was made of jelly. There was a loud pop and they both looked back towards the hotel.

'What was that?'

'That was a shotgun,' said Simon.

'No.'

'Fucking drive!'

The car started and they lurched back the way they came. Adrenaline screamed along with the engine. Simon clutched onto the dashboard; an old air freshener with a smiley face swung between them. He spoke in frantic breaths as Prue tried to handle the car.

'They couldn't get da back doors open. Charlie lost his shit and picked up a paving slab and smashed it. Sean was hacking away with the axe. Charlie cut his leg kicking at da door and was pissing blood everywhere. We couldn't get da safe out. They were trying to tear it out of da wall, but people upstairs were shouting. That was it for me. I legged it.'

Two headlights came flying towards them in the opposite direction. The road was not wide enough for two cars. This was not passing traffic.

'Fuck, we're gonna have to ditch da car,' said Simon. 'Drive towards the trees!' Prue turned the car back in a horseshoe down the hill and drove towards the woods.

They lurched and bumped about so hard Simon's head hit the ceiling. Prue thought the car would roll but they managed to get within thirty metres of the trees. She looked behind to see two blinding headlights chasing them. The car hadn't even stopped, and Simon had the door open and was running. He left the hammer on the seat; Prue picked it up and ran. Simon was ahead but tired and Prue overtook him. She thought about losing the hammer but was scared she would need it. Simon was behind but then she heard shouting.

'I've got one! I got him!' They had to mean Simon.

She forced her way through sharp leaves and branches in the dark as the balaclava slipped over her eyes. A thud square in her back sent her flying straight onto her front. She scraped her chin on the ground, lost the hammer and the air from her lungs. It was like falling on a pin cushion and her face burned. She tried to crawl, but they jumped on her back and grabbed her arms, yanking them behind her so hard she screamed. They held her bony wrists with one hand and, with the other, ripped off the balaclava.

'What the fuck?' he said and expelled a sound as if he had been punched. He let go of her wrists, got off and Prue flipped over onto her back.

James's face was silver in the moonlight. Prue held up her scraped hands in surrender. Her lungs were on fire. She couldn't speak and neither could he. She couldn't name the expression on his face, but she couldn't forgive him for it. It was all the things Prue couldn't bear – hurt, betrayal, disgust, confusion – the feeling that she didn't matter.

'James! James!' Sharon screamed for her son as he backed away.

'I'm coming,' he shouted, then to Prue, 'You bitch. I don't want to see you ever again. Run. Go on – run.'

She scrabbled to her feet and ran further into the trees. Around her lights flashed and men shouted. Prue had to get to the centre of the wood, where their torchlight couldn't find her. She found the path to the low ground where she knew Archie's cabin was and let herself in. She crawled upstairs to the filthy mattress, wrapped herself in a blanket and looked up at the yellow stars that had seen her there before. After the performance tonight, they would have no better impression. She reached into the pocket of her jumper to check her glasses were there along with the weed and then remembered she still had the pills in her jeans. She took out the little plastic bag and looked at them, took one out and swallowed it without hesitation and waited to feel something different.

That night Prue saw the most amazing skies. Unreal. Insane. It came in crazy colours; purple, pink, blue with bright white stars and a strange green streak, like oil across concrete. Pin pricks of pink and yellow. Pulsating. One day she would be gone. Life may be an insurmountable nightmare to the people who crowned themselves kings and queens, but to the universe they were rats in a frenzy, racing around with their all-important pigeonholes, tribes and labels, boxing themselves in, desperate to be understood but never bothering to understand. It felt as if something was reaching out to her, showing her its existence, and that was the moment Prue realised she might possibly be a little high.

29

A crack rang out, like something had been snapped in two, and it ricocheted over the sky, but this time Prue knew what it was – gunshot. She remembered how Charlie had grabbed her in the car when she'd begged him to steal the money in the books instead, and despite the waves of beautiful tingling rippling through her body, he only knew where to find the money because of her and that meant she had to go back. What if he'd gone straight to the house? What if Big Sean was with him, with the axe? *Please, don't let anyone be hurt.*

Prue had no idea what time it was as she navigated her way back through the trees, her giant eyes absorbing as much of the moonlight as possible, but it was hard not to be slowed down by her senses, even deep breaths creating waves of elation all the way to her teeth and fingernails. Her body too blissed out with euphoric sensations to fully comprehend everything that was going on. The black dog appeared and skipped ahead of her; she could hear him panting in the dark as he led the way back to the metal gate and wriggled underneath, rubbing his belly in the trench he had dug again, and Prue followed behind. She made her way through the garden as the dog ran around her, leaping in and out from the bushes, sniffing and digging, spinning around in circles with excitement at his new night-time playmate.

At the back door to the mud room Prue pressed her face to the glass but it was all dark inside. Maybe it hadn't been a gunshot, maybe it was something else or she had imagined it. Prue put a hand up to open the door, but the dog ran up to her and dropped something at her feet which landed with a clatter. He backed away, tail wagging, desperate for her to throw whatever it was. Prue bent down to pick up what looked like a long, white curved stick. It wasn't really a stick; it wasn't even made of wood. It was hard and solid, and covered in wet mud from wherever he had dug it up. She brushed it clean, trying to figure out what it was. The texture was pitted and rough, but smooth in places and there was a curve to it, and rounded edges, one end larger than the other, and lumpy. Prue was struggling to focus as her eyes blurred but thought the stick could be an animal bone. The back door opened and long white arms pulled her inside. Prue gripped the bone to her chest and stumbled into the dark mud room, fingers digging into the flesh of her arm. The door slammed shut, and she heard the latch go in the lock; the door was locked from the inside.

'How did you get outside?' hissed a low voice. It was Ronnie, still wearing her makeup from dinner. Prue clenched her jaw as her eyes juddered in the inky blue and silver moonlight through the window.

'I went for a walk,' she whispered.

'What?'

Prue started to laugh; it seemed like a natural reaction, then she remembered the gunshot and stopped. 'Where are Ruth and Archie? Are they OK?'

Ronnie leaned forward and her skin shone like a pearl, her black eyebrows dark flicks. 'Why? What did you do?'

'Nothing,' said Prue. 'I... I thought I heard something. I'm not sure what I heard but—'

'Terrible things have happened, Prue, terrible things,' said Ronnie. 'Come with me, you have to see.'

Ronnie led her through the mud room into the kitchen, lights out, mess everywhere from dinner, crockery piled up. There was a strong draught blowing as they entered the main hall and the front door was wide open. Ronnie let go of Prue and left her standing, clutching the bone, as she shut the door and turned the latch so that the front door was locked too.

'Why was the door open? Where's Ruth?' asked Prue.

'Follow me,' said Ronnie, and she took her by the arm again and led her along the corridor to the study where the main light was on. Prue had a foreboding that things were very wrong, but her head wasn't working; her body, her lungs all felt wonderful, but her jaw and eyes ached. When they reached the study, she peered around the door and couldn't help stumbling into the carnage.

The study had been ripped apart. Plants had been thrown with abandon, books ripped off shelves, petals and leaves everywhere. The little vases and mason jars were smashed, and glass was all over the floor. The bright red book of *Fifty Favourite Songs Everybody Loves to Hear!* lay by the ice skates. The boat with the yellow sails was now splinters. Even the redundant clock had been hurled across the room. But there was also blood. Prue tiptoed over the debris and saw blood in spots, trails and puddles, and as she turned back to face Ronnie in the doorway, there were spots of blood trailing up the wall behind the door and below them a bloody handprint.

'We've been violated, yet again. They came straight to this room; someone must have told them. How else would they know there was money to find in the books?' said Ronnie, still wearing the serpent green dress from dinner.

'There's blood, look, all over the rug. What about Ruth and Archie? Where are they?'

'Upstairs,' said Ronnie, her deathly pallor stark against her dress. When she stepped back into the corridor, Prue passed her and headed upstairs.

Ronnie followed at a distance, watching Prue, as she climbed the stairs through the plants holding the bone to her chest. On the landing Prue saw the door to Ruth and Archie's bedroom was ajar and there was a light on inside. Something wasn't right but she forced herself to walk on as the landing seemed to get longer and the bedroom move further away with each step. At the door, she pushed it and there was Archie lying in bed, but no Ruth.

At first, she thought he was sleeping, and was angry how he could have slept through all the commotion but then she saw his eyes were wide open fixed to the ceiling and his mouth gaped. She crept over to his side of the bed. He was frozen with a tortured expression on his face, his brow screwed together and his palms facing the sky. Archie was dead. The blanket covered him from the hips down and his naked ribcage wasn't moving. There was no blood, no sign of violence or disturbance in the room. It was as if he had taken to his bed and turned to stone, his cooling body a grey marble sculpture on the crypt of a young king.

'I knew things would change when you came here, but I didn't know how,' said Ronnie, who had appeared at the door.

Prue looked at her and back at Archie; she couldn't comprehend what was happening.

'What happened to him? Have you called for an ambulance?'

'It's too late for him. Poor Archie, it must be the family flaw – weak hearts, all the men have it, I had hoped it had skipped Archie. My poor, sweet boy, Archie.' Prue stared at her; this wasn't right, it was as if she was talking about one of the ravens. Prue stepped back from the bedside and out to the landing. Ronnie closed the bedroom door behind her, and Prue went to turn the light on.

'No! Don't do that!' said Ronnie. 'What if the burglar is still out there? He might come back.'

'What? How do we know he's not still here? The front door was open.'

'I saw him,' said Ronnie. 'I saw him leave through the front door. I heard the gunshot and when I opened the door I saw him, running away. I came straight upstairs to wake them and found Archie like that.'

'But where's Ruth? That blood could be hers. We need to call for help – I'll go and do it.' Prue put a foot on the stairs, but Ronnie grabbed her arm.

'We can't, the phone is dead – whoever it was must have

cut it. We have no choice but to wait for Ruth to return. She must have gone for help, it's the only explanation.'

'But what if she's somewhere bleeding to death?'

'There's blood on the hall floor, it must be from the burglar. Ruth has gone for help. We must stay and wait.'

'I suppose...'

Ronnie stepped beside Prue on the stairs and led her down. 'You don't look well, my girl, your eyes are huge and you're hot to the touch. Terrible things have happened here again, the most awful things. We'll wait in the kitchen. I've locked the doors so no one can get in. I'll take care of you, but first things first, we should have a drink to steady the nerves.'

They retreated to the kitchen to sit in the dark, save for some candles, and wait for Ruth to come back, which didn't feel right at all. Prue had had her fair share of emergencies in her young life and the answer had never involved sitting around doing nothing, waiting for the cavalry to arrive to rescue her. How could they sit there with Archie dead upstairs? The thought made her shudder. How could he have been living and breathing, strong as an ox – the great silverback – only a few hours before and now... Something was horribly wrong.

'I could take one of the cars,' offered Prue. Something was telling her to get out of the house. 'I can drive. I just need to find the keys.' She moved to stand up.

'No,' came the abrupt reply. 'I'll get the brandy,' said Ronnie. 'Sometimes the most intelligent thing one can do is wait and that's what we must do.'

The exhilaration Prue had felt running through every nerve was waning. The waves of euphoria each breath had given her now were jittery twitches. Her eyes still throbbed and jerked about, her jaw ached, but she was beginning to feel bleak, like an overcast sky. Her brain thick as cotton wool. Opaque blobs of all that she had been told at dinner and now all this had happened, and Archie was dead. She couldn't take it in. How could he possibly be gone? Gone. Never to get up. It couldn't be real. It was too much. She put the old bone down on the table, her head in her hands and tried to cry, but the tears wouldn't come.

'Oh, Prue,' said Ronnie, setting down a brandy in front of her. 'Not to worry, it won't last forever.' Ronnie took a seat opposite her at the table. 'Are you going to give that to me?'

Prue still held her head in her hands as she looked up to see what Ronnie was referring to. It was the bone she wanted. Prue looked down at what she had absentmindedly brought in from the garden. The world shrank until all that existed was the room with her and Ronnie and this dirty bone in it. Then the memory of Ronnie screaming at her when the dog had dug up the dead raven burst into her head. *It's not an animal bone, you idiot, it's a human femur. And that's why you didn't get an A in Biology, you fool.*

'I found the second raven dead the morning you came back from the Mainland with Archie,' said Ronnie. 'The outside bin was full so the lid wouldn't shut, and the ravens had been picking at the bin liner. A few of the meatballs were on the ground where they'd torn open the bag. You picked them up, didn't you?'

'I couldn't let you kill the dog.'

'And yet you killed a raven.'

'I didn't mean to, I only wanted to save the dog.'

'What did you ask the devil for, Prue? Is the price worth paying?'

Prue stared down at her brandy. What if the reason no one found Evie in the trees was because she wasn't there? What if she *did* make it to the house? No, it couldn't be that. Prue was the bad one. Prue was always responsible for everything that went wrong. Somehow, it was always her. She was the guilty one who had caused all this, but what if... Prue reached out and touched the bone again, almost asking it through touch to confirm this wild leap that had come to her only now, wild and outrageous but at the same time... No, it couldn't be possible. Ronnie was just a little old lady, and old ladies are harmless.

'It's most impolite to make someone drink alone, you know,' said Ronnie, forcing Prue to look up from under her eyelids.

'Thank you, but I don't like brandy.'

'No one drinks brandy because they like it, my dear. Now, are you going to pass that to me?'

Oh God, she knows what it is. Of course she does. Ronnie was sitting with her hand outstretched towards her, reaching out, but all Prue saw were insidious tentacles trying to take away the proof that would tell everyone that Evie had made it to the house, and somehow, what was left of her was in Ronnie's precious garden. It was so screamingly obvious that Prue didn't want it to be true. Her stomach felt sick and oily. Her mouth filled with saliva. The rashes, the dreams, the dizziness, the sudden vomiting, and

Ruth as well. She had been losing weight the whole summer. Ronnie had given them creams and lotions, crushed herbs and flowers and fed them to them. The special homemade cocktails. The warnings about touching the plants and the long mysterious absence at dinner under the pretence of preparing *something special* after Archie had told them he wanted to sell the estate. Well, it had been special all right. Ronnie was poisoning them all along but that night she had killed her own grandson, and attempted to poison all of them at dinner.

'Where did you go?' asked Ronnie. Her tone had changed, she wasn't pretending to be the affectionate grandmother any more. When Prue looked at her she saw those eyes from the picture of Ronnie as a young woman, the haughty penetrating stare.

'What?'

'Archie went upstairs to bed but Ruth stayed up waiting for you. Where did you go?'

'I needed time to think.'

'Rather a funny coincidence, don't you think? You not being here when the O'Hara boy strolls into my house. I had to listen to him tearing that room apart. Breaking all those things. Throwing the books around, the flowers, the glass, and I thought to myself, I wonder how he knows where to find the money?'

'What have you done to my aunt?' Prue couldn't help it. The bewilderment had turned to rage – how dare this woman play God with them all! 'Where's Ruth? What have you done to her?'

'Nothing, I told you – she must have gone to get help.'

'But there's blood on the rug.'

'I wouldn't be so worried about her if I were you. What did you ask the devil for, I wonder?'

'I only ever asked for the truth.'

'And the devil delivered, I take it?'

'I may have argued with Ruth but that certainly doesn't make her the devil.'

'Stupid girl! The devil isn't a person. When Robert Johnson asked to become the greatest blues guitarist in the world, it wasn't talent he needed – he had that, but what's the point unless people know? He wanted fame! To be adored! The man died of syphilis, so we have to assume he got a lot of what he wanted.'

'Ruth is missing, and Archie is dead and you're talking in riddles.'

'Of course, you don't understand – you're young and stupid. What I'm saying, my dear girl, is that when you convince yourself you must have something so desperately, it can only ever end in one's own destruction. It becomes a weakness. Allow me to put it into context. Archie, now his weaknesses, he was partial to the young fillies and he was forever distracted by the next exciting thing. How do you think he got himself involved in smuggling drugs in the first place?'

'You knew about the drugs?'

'I know everything, Prue. Archie thought he could keep the O'Hara boy in line, but unfortunately he judged him by his own principles – materialism and vanity. Charlie O'Hara never was grateful because he thought the world owed him, and his sister was the same. Ruth's weakness was that hobby of hers she called Art.' Ronnie rolled her eyes and sipped her brandy. 'She neglected herself, her husband

and her own fragile niece because she wanted to be a success again.'

'Are you working your way around to me?'

'Are you sure you don't want a nip of brandy?' Prue shook her head as Ronnie poured herself another drink. 'Dry mouth? Foggy head? Your pupils are very large, Prue. You've been very away with the fairies, haven't you? You can't have long left.'

Ronnie had mistaken Prue's physical symptoms from the Ecstasy for poison she had tried to kill her with at dinner. It was the sauce, it had to be. Ruth had refused and Prue had been unable to stomach it, but Archie had eaten it. Oh, what had she done! The rumours she'd been told about missing people, this must have been going on for years. The plants – they were everywhere. The whole time they had been consuming them, inhaling them, eating them. Ronnie was a psychopath – she had to be. They had *all* been her children to play with. This was her kingdom and she could sign any death warrant she wished and now Prue was trapped in the house with her, alone.

Ronnie was smiling and nodding at her brandy glass.

'You might want that drink now,' she suggested.

'There are no weak hearts, are there?'

'Not in the medical sense,' she said. 'Archie betrayed me. I gave everything to that boy, and he was going to sell my home from underneath me. I had no choice. Ruth was meant to go with him but… it's better this way. I was angry before and this will arouse less suspicion. Ruth and I will get along, for a while. Truth is, I've been experimenting with you ever since you got here.' She smirked like a naughty schoolgirl.

'Why?' All the times Prue had felt odd or queasy and the

decisions she'd made, or the thoughts she'd had – had they even been hers?

'For fun,' shrugged Ronnie. 'It's a source of joy to find I can move people and change how they are; they're like my little puppets – it's fun to watch. Years ago, I used to play with the help. Maud would let me practise on them, never the locals she'd say, only the foreigners because no one ever comes looking for them. I made mistakes once or twice but no one seemed to care.'

'I think I will have that brandy now,' said Prue. 'As long as it *is* brandy.'

'It is – I promise.' With that Prue stared into the drink hoping she could trust what it was and forced it back in one.

'Salut!' said Ronnie, lifting her own glass as she put her other hand out for Prue to slide her glass back so she could refill both of them.

'You never said what my weakness is,' Prue reminded her.

'Ah! You, my dear, you believe the truth will unlock the world to you, starting with yourself, but the truth will only be the messy beginning, and I'm guessing whatever it was Ruth told you after I was rudely exiled from my own dining room will tie you down, lock you up and bury you deeper inside more than ever before. Am I right?'

'What about you? Do you come with weaknesses too?'

'Hmmm, I think you can work that out for yourself, my girl. Now, are you going to give me that?' She pointed at the bone on the table in front of her.

'Seeing as I've not got long – indulge me? I think I know who this belongs to.'

Ronnie looked wistfully towards the windows. 'What can

I say? I'm a magician, Evie disappeared.' Ronnie snapped her fingers. 'Like that.'

'What did you do to her?'

'I magicked her away.' Ronnie smiled, proud of what she'd done.

'Tell me what you did – I have to know before I die.'

'There was a problem with the ferry that day and Archie was late coming home. Evelyn waltzed into the garden, as if she had every right to be there. As soon as I saw her, I could tell – she was radiant, and her breasts were larger. It only took a little teasing and the girl told me she was pregnant. I was devastated, but she babbled on about their grand plan. It was hardly a meeting of minds; she had this fantasy of becoming a doctor and living the life of an army wife! How ridiculous!'

'Why was it ridiculous?'

'Girls like her do not become doctors, and they certainly do not make good wives. I smiled along but I thought not on my watch, you manipulative little whore, worming her way into my home. There was no way I was going to let that happen.' Ronnie knocked back another brandy, refilled her glass and offered Prue more, but she refused.

'You're soon going to feel worse. You must have eaten a lot less, but never mind, it's still fatal.'

'Maybe I will have that drink after all, you best hurry up,' said Prue, and slid her glass back across the table for another shot.

'I played the excited fool and went to fix pink lemonades since we couldn't celebrate with champagne. We talked about how they were going to get married and have the baby and everything would be wonderful! Like a fairy tale!

There's a tropical shrub native to the West Indies called the peacock flower and it has beautiful bright orange flowers – hummingbirds love them and the seeds can *bring down the flowers*, as the Dutch in the colonies used to say. Slave women used to take the seeds to end their pregnancies – now, when I say pregnancies, I mean the babies they carried after being raped by their masters. They didn't want their babies born into slavery, so as an act of defiance, they got rid of them. I thought about giving her those, to bring down the flowers, so to speak. But when she started to talk about moving into the house and what room would be best for her and the baby. That… that was too much. In many ways I did her a favour because I stopped time when she was happy and she'll never know the disappointment a child can bring its parents, or grandparents. Everything that has a soul has an energy; she's still here. Evie and her baby are frozen together forever, that's the best way to think of it; not that I think of it much, or didn't until you arrived. I couldn't help myself. She had to understand she would always lose.'

'Lose what?'

'What she wanted – what we have. Evie O'Hara didn't belong at our table and never would. Her kind don't understand what it takes to be a success. The dedication and sacrifice, the difficult decisions. You can't always be good if you want to win, Prue, life is about winners and losers. That's what poor people don't understand, there are no rules! This is why rich people succeed. They legislate and create rules for other people to follow and then stand back in bemusement as the sheep blindly follow. I gave Evie a huge dose of hemlock in that pink lemonade, and she was dead within hours.'

'Then you hid her in the hole under the study, didn't you? The one you missed out showing me on purpose and where you hid my glasses.'

'I was hopping mad at Archie when he let you sleep in there, but he had no idea about the priest hole. I knew you'd find it; you are very sensitive to the things people often miss, an empath – you had such potential, but never mind. Ruth was under the delusion you were an angel and wouldn't be nosy and Archie was probably already thinking how he would break you in – it's his thing.' She leaned forward to drive her point home. 'It'd be amusing if it weren't so predictable.'

'What about the letters? I found them in the books. Why did you hide them there?'

'The islanders were out for him from the start, and I told Archie that anything the police found could be used against him to conjure up a motive, so he handed me those pages, torn from a diary she'd scribbled all over, and the photographs. I was going to burn them, but he begged me not to. I did what he asked because I loved him, but I did not love his weakness. I hid them in the books, same with the money he gave me; no one had ever found either. I didn't want you to stay in there. I was worried about the plants, but I knew you'd be careful. You're a little cavalier at times but no rebel. You want to be but you're too cautious. You regret things as soon as you've done them; it's as if you're trying to be something else. I wonder what could have made you hate yourself so much.'

'Why take my glasses?'

'It seemed funny at the time,' Ronnie shrugged. 'It helps with the spells to have something to focus the spells on.

I took Dotty's hair from her hairbrush and kept Evie's journal.'

'I can't believe you poisoned your own grandson – you said you loved him?'

'I do! But one must keep going. One must skip over life, like a rock skimming over water.'

'But these are people, your own family.'

'Those too.' Ronnie was a different species; she really seemed to regard people as energy and spirits, fluid with life and death and interchangeable with her plants.

'Back to Evie. You poisoned her – what happened then?'

'This is where it all got rather messy. As she was dying, I had Dotty help me move her into the priest hole. She died before Archie got back. I had time to cover her in quicklime. People think quicklime disposes of corpses – it doesn't but it will cover up a stench. Poor Archie slept that night in that study, unaware his beloved was dead underneath him.'

Prue brought the brandy up to her lips and tried to sip but couldn't bring herself to swallow and spat it back into the glass.

'Dotty struggled with it too. I had her help me get Evie out to my greenhouse. I had to cut her up so I could boil her in lime – that wasn't easy, but it makes the flesh easier to strip away from the bones. You should have heard Dotty squeal, a twittering gerbil. I buried her, piece by piece, in the garden. Evelyn O'Hara and her baby are human bonemeal. But Dotty wasn't coping so I had to dose her up with morning glory. I was scared she would say something so I made her appear more unstable than usual, but the seeds contain lysergic acid amide and, in all honesty, I wasn't aware of the violent hallucinations that come with such a dosage. She was shouting about cat people when she jumped out of the window.'

'What about when the police searched the house?'

'They never found the priest hole and never searched the books. Incompetent idiots and back then they had respect for our station.'

'That's why you wanted to kill the dog; you were scared of him digging Evie up.' Prue was feeling more normal, if not the lowest she had ever felt before in her life. It was all creeping up towards her and any synthetic elation had deserted her. Her eyes throbbed and her jaw ached from clenching, but the grip had gone. She leaned forward, letting her head roll on her neck and resting a cheek on the table, trying to feign feeling worse. From that angle she looked through the gap in the curtain. The sky was growing pinker and there was a hazy yellow on the horizon – the sun was coming up. It wasn't all lost yet. There was always a little hope.

'How will you get rid of me?'

'You can go the same way as Evie – you'll disappear – like magic.' Ronnie snapped her fingers again.

'But there's no Dotty to help you this time and you're twenty years older. How are you going to get me into the priest hole when you can barely lift a shovel?'

Ronnie took out the old handgun she had hidden in the folds of her velvet gown and pointed it at Prue.

'I'm going to give you the proper motivation to get into the hole yourself,' said Ronnie.

'Are you serious?' Prue sat back up, leaning forward over the table, palms down. 'Isn't that from the war?'

Archie had assured her the only gun in the house was his grandfather's old Enfield .38 and didn't have any bullets. Ronnie was bluffing. Nothing about her could be trusted. It might have worked at one time when social class meant everything, and she was wealthy and those around her had no choice but to suck it up, but times had moved on.

'At least that's a historic reference you've heard of. I will give you a choice: you can walk to the study and get into the hole yourself and I'll give you a tonic to make you pass out so you don't suffer, or I shoot you in the stomach and you bleed out, in agony.'

'It'll never work – it's 1993, Ronnie, times have changed. The world has moved on. Just because you want the world to stay frozen in time doesn't mean the rest of us do, it won't work. The police won't respect your station, Ruth won't accept me missing, or her husband suddenly dead, Archie will have a post-mortem or whatever it is... How can you be this deluded? Actually, I know the answer: because you're like Nana. She had the same approach, stick to the same beliefs because you can't be bothered to change. It's tragic really, you live a life of fantasy with rose-tinted memories and all the bad bits filtered out, but they're still there!'

'Get up and start moving or I will shoot you. Don't think I won't.'

'I didn't even eat your disgusting sauce.' Prue stood up.

'Of course you did, you've been lolling about, your eyes...' A look of panic crossed over Ronnie's face; the woman couldn't comprehend such a thing was possible.

'I'm leaving.' Prue turned and walked to the door to the mud room.

'Don't you dare turn your back on me!' There was the demon growl again. 'I will shoot! I will not suffer such disrespect!'

As Prue opened the door inward and stepped out to the mud room a shot rang out from Ronnie's archaic gun and flew past Prue's nose and shattered a glass pane in the door. Prue gasped and stopped; the bullet had flown within inches of her face. She turned to see Ronnie struggling to get the next bullet in the chamber. Prue ran into the mud room, shutting the door behind her. She fumbled with the latch, and ripped open the door to the garden. Prue sprinted over the patio and behind the first bush as Ronnie fired again, the bullet flying wildly overhead. Prue kept running, heading towards the cover of the trees.

30

The sky was lilac with fuchsia clouds rolling overhead. She made a promise that if she were to get through this, she would try her best to live a good life. A fearless one. It wasn't justice but it would have to be enough. Now, if only the devil would accept her offer.

As she ran past the studio, she remembered the photos Archie had taken of her – what if someone found them? The police would search the house. They would ask questions and she couldn't tell anyone what had happened. She had to find the photos. Just one more secret. Just this little one, and then no more.

She tore open the door to the studio and there on the sofa curled up in the foetal position was an injured Ruth.

'Ruth! I thought you were dead!' Prue ran to shake her awake. 'Wake up! What happened? Come on, we've got to go. Now!'

Ruth was barely conscious and with one of Prue's blood-soaked jumpers pressed to the side of her head like a pillow.

She pulled Ruth's struggling hands away from her head. It was still bleeding, and she was worried about Ruth's ear, but she couldn't see for the blood and didn't know what to do.

'He shot me, Charlie,' whispered Ruth. 'He didn't mean to, but I saw him in the study, he was stealing the money. He said it was his money. I tried to stop him. I shouldn't have done that. I should have let him. So stupid, I thought it was you.'

'Stay there, I... I just need... Wait,' said Prue, looking around the studio at all the canvases, wondering how on earth she was going to locate those photographs.

She rifled through the studio, pulling canvases in stacks up against the wall until they fell like dominoes on the floor. There were so many, but she knew Archie had pinned the photos of her to the top right-hand side.

'What's going on?' asked Ruth.

'Nothing, don't worry. Hang on a minute.'

She was fighting against herself: should she save her dignity or her aunt? Then she saw a canvas with a stack of photos pinned to it sticking out at one corner. She'd found them! Prue ripped them off the canvas and stuffed them into the pockets of her jeans.

'Ruth, we need to go! Now!'

'Wait, what about Ronnie? Is she all right? Where's Archie? Are they both all right?!'

'They're fine,' she lied, but it was the most she could do to get her out of the studio door.

Still with the jumper pressed to Ruth's bleeding ear, Prue and Ruth staggered and stumbled up the garden and through the trees. At the stile at the other end, Prue looked ahead at the big hill up to the village and knew it would be too much for Ruth.

'You have to wait for me here. I'm going to run and get help – please promise me you will stay here,' Prue told her aunt. Ruth obligingly nodded; it was obvious she was in a lot of pain and Prue left her sitting on the ground by the stile.

Prue leapt over and ran up the hill, breathless and much slower than usual – the Ecstasy had left her so much weaker – but she kept pushing, having to stop every few metres to muster the strength to keep going, scared she would hear another gunshot. When she made it to the top and stumbled into the village shop, covered in her aunt's blood, she begged the girl with the crispy fringe to call for help.

The crispy-fringed girl tried to hold onto Prue and wouldn't let her go back to her aunt, kept trying to keep her there until the police and the ambulance arrived. Prue broke free and ran back; there was no way she was going to leave her aunt alone. She found Ruth in exactly the same spot, but the black dog had also found her and was lying on his belly by her side. Ruth had got closer to the dog in one sitting than she had the entire summer. She helped Ruth up and they moved out to wait for help on the road. The black dog disappeared back into the trees.

They were taken over to the hospital on the Mainland and quickly separated. At the hospital the medics assumed Prue had been attacked, but there wasn't much wrong with her except for the scab on her chin, scratches from running through the trees, a particularly awful comedown and a large amount of emotional damage that hadn't fully hit her yet. That would circle and hit her many, many years later, but for now, she was protected by the numbness of youth.

The first real lucid thought she had was that her mother must hate her, and she didn't blame her, she hated herself. She was taken to a ward and sat on the bed waiting to be seen by the doctors with a police officer.

'I need to go to the toilet,' said Prue, and hopped off the bed.

The policewoman followed her until she found a toilet in the corridor.

'What? Are you going to come in and watch me pee?' she said to the policewoman, who really didn't look that much older than herself.

'I'll wait out here,' she said, and Prue stepped in and locked the door.

Sitting on the toilet she took out the photographs in her pocket and started to tear them up, worried by the noise she was making. She flushed the toilet and ran the tap on the sink so she could rip them up into little bits, as small as possible. There it was in her hands, hard evidence of her shame, her humiliation, her naïvety, but now it was torn into pieces, never to be put back together, erased from history. She put the bits into the bin for hazardous waste and covered it in tissue and then opened the door.

'You took your time,' said the policewoman.

'I thought it was a number one, but you know how it goes,' said Prue, and the policewoman cracked her first smile and rolled her eyes.

★ ★ ★

Over the following days and weeks, the full extent of Ronnie's talents were revealed to the world. She had poisoned Archie with *Conium maculatum*, or hemlock, and he had died of respiratory failure – not a weak heart. Ruth and Prue would have gone the same way had they eaten the special sauce that was left congealing on the dining table when the police entered the property. In Prue's blood they found traces of *Atropa belladonna*, or deadly nightshade as it was more commonly known, among the other substances she'd already confessed to taking and various traces of further substances and hallucinogens they couldn't fully identify. Deadly nightshade can cause hallucinations, confusion, dilated pupils, loss of balance, dry mouth, among other symptoms.

Ronnie was found on the bed alongside Archie's body. She had laid herself out beside him on top of the covers but had first taken the time to change into a long-beaded silver and white dress and thrown petals of every colour around them both. There was no doubt in Prue's mind that it would have been a death scene worthy of a painting; she imagined the famous painting of Ophelia in the stream covered with flowers; purple loosestrife, forget-me-nots, poppies. But instead of the Pre-Raphaelite muse she could see Ronnie. Only because of this woman Prue knew that those flowers didn't bloom at the same time and she could name them on sight. It would have been a beautiful and elegant scene, worthy of Diotima and Socrates. Ronnie had committed suicide by drinking a concoction of the same poison with which she had so deftly executed her beloved grandson: hemlock, which incidentally is the same poison Socrates was executed with supposedly for corrupting the youth of Athens. Evie O'Hara's femur was left sitting on the kitchen table.

Prue would often see Ronnie in her dreams. But it was always her as a young woman, the misleadingly beautiful face from the black and white photograph. Fine-featured with haughty black brows. Those grey cat's eyes and Byzantine profile, the perfectly round mouth with a cupid bow you could measure by spirit level. Those exquisite features, bewitching, all that is feminine, were nothing more than ice frosting on a leaden cake and underneath there was a bitter will to control at any cost. Unafraid of death, Ronnie was simply open to avoiding it as long as she could continue to reign on her terms. Now she could possess Archie forever.

The house was a collection of poisons and dangerous plants – a botanical horror-show for the police to unpick, discover and catalogue. How perfectly British, another ghoulish house of horrors to add to the national list. *Venom Island, The Toxic Gardener, Lady Death, The Wicked Alchemist, Nanny Noxious* – there were headlines flying about for an audience that demanded digestible slogans to comprehend the horrors that had been permitted to go on for so many years without anyone asking questions. Ronnie was infamous; she would have appreciated that.

The authorities had already found over a thousand species. Several in the heated greenhouse were illegal. During her police interview, Prue attempted to recollect all the strange teas made with brewed bark and leaves. The beans that came from plants with the fat red blossoms they ate at dinner, descriptions of the cocktails, the lotions, creams and oils. She was told there were leaves and flowers in plain sight in the garden that could stop a heart within minutes or make someone lose control of their bowels, cause vomiting and induce comas. Some could make people believe creatures were crawling over the walls, and give those who had ingested them wild dreams, along with the odd bout of blurred vision and dilated pupils.

Then there were the plants *inside* the house. Ones that caused skin rashes, burning of the mouth, trouble swallowing and sickness. Delirium, blisters and abdominal cramps. Prue had lived among the collection of immobile assassins without a clue that a simple miscalculation or mishap by Ronnie could have killed her at any moment.

Among the flowers they found Evie's remains, but the diggers and shovels obliterated years of beauty, nurture and craftsmanship. When they found what was left of her skull, they identified her by dental records.

The once very beautiful and beguiling Veronique Charlotte Lewthwaite MacNair Anderson had become a toxic matriarch who demanded blind loyalty in exchange for the keys to an extremely dilapidated kingdom, and she died twenty years to the day Evie had – there's no such thing as coincidence, right?

Simon was arrested the night of the break-in, but despite hating Prue's guts he never squealed. James didn't say a word either and she'll never understand what she did to earn such loyalty. Sean managed to get all the way to Aberdeen, where he was arrested for burglary one month later and now has forty-one convictions. Charlie O'Hara didn't get nearly as far. His body was found in a rowing boat near the Mainland the next morning. He was poisoned with *Aconitum*, or wolfsbane, sometimes called monkshood. They said he must have grabbed one of the plants in front of the books with his whole palm or it went into his bloodstream from the open wound on his arm, because he absorbed enough to give himself multiple organ failure.

Ruth let her little sister Caroline have their mother's house in Thornton Heath, and sold Dynrost House to Archie's cousins, the Tullochs. This allowed her to set herself up in a large house in Cornwall, minus her left earlobe which she rather enjoyed telling people was shot off. She still paints, but her recent work features a lot of plants and landscapes, and she loves talking about them. Prue and Ruth have grown close again, somehow, and Prue moved in with Ruth in her new house for a few weeks while she decided what to do with her life.

Prue was adamant that there was one left behind to save from those cursed trees and it turned out *he* was a *she* and she really didn't like having a lead on at first. They had planned to hand her into a shelter, but Ruth adopted Prue's woodland chaperone – the black demon-dog, as Ronnie had called her. Ruth calls her Demon and not one person in Noost had a clue where she could have come from. Prue knew more than anyone that the origins of something are only as important as the beholder decides to believe, and that monsters do not have horns or roar as they introduce themselves.

A year later, in the autumn of 1994, Joan Gardner was released quietly and without fuss. No one knows if the case of Holly's drowning is going to be reopened, but it doesn't seem like much is going on. All they hear is that resources are under pressure, and there are cuts.

That was all the neatly tied-up loose ends that were in

the public domain and printed in the newspapers. They were the details that needed to be defined, the questions that demanded an answer to enable the collective consciousness to move on. Then they could rationalise it would never happen to them and to dismiss it as evidence of how odd other people's families are, but it wasn't where such things ended. They never end, of course; they continue to be passed down like batons in a relay, from generation to generation, until someone fearless comes along to break the curse.

Epilogue

When the police came to the village shop on Noost, Prue and Ruth were initially taken to the hospital in Lerwick. Later they were moved to a bigger hospital in Glasgow, because of the complexity of the emerging case and the growing press interest.

Prue was given her own room as extensive blood tests were carried out and the endless questioning began. Finally free from being progressively dosed, she started to feel quite different; alert, clear, and a feeling she had known before until it was taken from her – hopeful. Strangely enough, it was the best she'd felt in a long time, maybe ever.

It was the noise that woke her. A cry that bounced off the sterile walls outside her room. It made it seem as if the noise was very far away and everywhere all at once.

When Prue looked through the reinforced glass of the door she saw a young woman with brown hair, skinny, her jeans sagging on her bottom and hair scraped back in a messy bun jiggling an unhappy baby. She looked stressed and embarrassed, but the baby continued to grizzle. The woman saw Prue and gave an apologetic smile. Prue smiled back. Holly had cried a lot – all babies did. Tearless wailing and red-faced screaming, babies were innately selfish creatures.

The hospital room was a typical soulless setting. The temperature too hot. Prue couldn't help but think of how a thousand people must have shed skin, hair and potentially died in her lumpen bed. There was a pathetic attempt to cheer up the sickly yellow walls with some bland artwork. Prue had got back into bed and lain down on her side when her eyes fell on the picture opposite: it was a pencil sketch of three dandelions floating in the air, nothing to hold them together – simply there. It was a terrible piece of art, she thought, and the baby still screamed outside. *Dandelion boy.* The day James had asked her if she wanted to blow. *No, I don't. Dandelions.* Prue shut her eyes to try to push the intrusions away but saw herself again all those years ago in those horrible white socks with the holes in; she leaned forward to her mind's eye and blew a dandelion, and all the white fluffy parachutes flew everywhere. And still the baby cried. Prue sat up, feeling sick, her heart racing. She put a hand on her chest and could feel it thump. She couldn't help but look at that terrible picture on the wall again, and the dandelion seeds were everywhere and the baby cried and cried and cried. *Shut up! Make it stop!* Prue squeezed her eyes as tight as they would shut and put her hands over her ears. Her cheeks filled with saliva…

Her mother was upstairs and Prue had been dumped with Holly, again. It wasn't fair. She never had time alone with her mother any more, Holly did. All the time, and Prue missed her Nana, Nana loved her. Billy was nice but he didn't *love* her – but he adored Holly.

The little cottage by the woods with the stream in Fordingbridge was a jigsaw of badly fitting parts. It didn't matter what combination was tried, the only way things fitted was if one piece sat outside and watched – that piece was Prue.

There was no point trying to play with a baby, they were boring and couldn't do anything interesting. Prue had wanted to take her outside to the trees where she could play in the jungle. She could pretend she was the mother and Holly was her baby, but her mother had said no and she wasn't allowed outside when Mummy was upstairs. Earlier, her mother had shouted at her for pushing Holly over when she sat up and grabbed at the bald-headed Barbie Prue played with. Prue had a habit of cutting their hair and then being disappointed when it didn't grow back but Nana would buy her a new one each time, but her mother said no and she would have to lump it. Holly had grabbed at it and Prue had snatched it away and pushed her over. Holly could almost sit up now, but she had fallen on her face and cried and her mummy had rushed to scoop her off the floor and cuddled her. Prue never got cuddles.

Prue picked Holly up from her basket and wrapped her in her blanket. Holly gurgled and her legs went stiff, but she didn't struggle. Prue carried her outside, but Holly began to get heavy and when she reached the side of the stream it was already spitting with rain and the sky was growing dark and thunderous. The stream was high, and the boards would bow as she walked across them and made her socks wet. It was the most she could do to get to the spot and she put Holly down on the blanket on her back. Prue's arms hurt from carrying her. She sat on the ground and felt the rain start. She wouldn't be long and her mother would never know. Holly thrust her legs and arms out, trying to roll over on her blanket and Prue helped her sit up. She wobbled but watched Prue with wide eyes – Holly's were brown, like their mother's, and that wasn't fair either. Prue played out her game, talking about how she would have to roast a pig on the fire for Holly, who watched her intently and dribbled. Holly lost her balance and fell on her back again and was soon making warning cries of frustration as she kicked out her legs and tried to roll. Prue pulled Holly up by her arm and Holly started to grizzle. It wasn't a real cry, only the engine trying to start type of cry that Billy's van made in the cold.

Prue picked a dandelion and blew it in Holly's face to make her laugh, but the fluffy white bits went in Holly's eyes and now she cried for real and let out the loudest wail. Prue was scared her mother would hear, so she tried another dandelion but Holly cried harder, leaned forward over her legs, was red in the face with spit dribbling from her mouth. Prue wanted very much to squeeze her. Holly had ruined everything and she couldn't even let her play. She had tried to make her laugh but it wasn't Prue she wanted. No one wanted Prue. They only ever wanted Holly. She wanted to squeeze Holly until she stopped crying. Holly's mouth hung open, her gummy mouth exposed, and now real tears fell. Prue pushed her. That really was all it was. She pushed her. Holly fell over and rolled and splashed into the water. As easy as that. Child's play. Holly stopped crying and then it was quiet. With her face down in the water like that she looked like a doll her Nana had bought her that cried real tears. Her wispy head facing the sky. Her white Babygro soaking up water. Prue stood up. That wasn't meant to happen. She couldn't take Holly back wet. Maybe she would float away? They might forget her. Prue still had hold of the bare dandelion stalk in her hand. She dropped it and ran back to the cottage and switched on the TV.

Prue made it to the bin where she threw up. When she had finished and opened her eyes again the crying had stopped and the woman with the baby was gone. But the picture of the dandelions was still there. She took it off the wall and started to cry. *I'm so sorry, Holly. I'm so sorry. I didn't mean to. God, I'm sorry.* She sobbed and sobbed until her guts hurt. Then when she couldn't cry anymore she threw the picture across the room and watched it smash against the wall.

Prue was still in hospital when her mother came. She took one look at Prue and saw she knew. She seemed frightened by what her daughter might say but Prue was turning herself inside out with what might happen to her.

To this day they have never discussed anything, it's as if nothing ever happened. Like magic. Prue will never talk about it. She'll take her turn fostering the guilty secrets until the cross disappears into dust. She accepts the burden, keeps her mouth shut and rewards herself with the occasional bout of guilt and self-loathing. This was Prue's crossroads, and she made her deal with the devil. She wanted the truth and now... she's cursed to keep it.

Acknowledgements

I will be forever grateful to the people who have nudged me along the way with encouragement, useful criticism and inspiration. To the lecturers at the University of Winchester; Judith Hennegan, Susmita Bhattacharya and Stephen S. Thompson – all talented writers, as well as teachers. I am especially grateful for the confidence I gained from their feedback.

To all the team at DHH Literary Agency, especially David and Emily, who took a chance on me; although I used to like champagne I'm not sure I can drink it ever again. The team at Head of Zeus who are an incredible bunch of people to work with and fun to be with. Thank you Maddy for spotting my story and showing me the ropes, and to Charlie for picking those ropes up and continuing to push me. Yes, I think I am an editorial masochist.

To Duncan and Caitlin, who always believed that I could write and get a book published and were the biggest supporters from the beginning, despite the fact that neither of them enjoy reading and think me an awful geek. I have often forced both of them to read my words and work on ideas with me against their will. And to my best friends of old; Jodie, Ruth, Katie, Anna and Ewan. I have no idea how you have put up with me all these years and continue to do so.

Lastly, thank you to all the booksellers, big and small, indie or otherwise. They are the real reason any new writing gets a chance to reach the hands of readers. Not all heroes wear capes but they are likely to have a couple of books in their bag.

About the Author

CLARE WHITFIELD was born in 1978 in Morden (at the bottom of the Northern line) in Greater London. After university she worked at a publishing company before going on to hold various positions in buying and marketing. She now lives in Hampshire with her family. Her debut novel, *People of Abandoned Character*, won the Goldsboro Glass Bell Award and is also published by Head of Zeus.